THE
LOST TESTAMENT

A HOLY WAR

'Ready?' screamed Berg, and his followers let out a mighty roar and began to lay into the defenceless monks with their batons and clubs. Careful not to hit skulls, which could lead to deaths, they attacked the bodies of the defenders of the church, pummelling rib cages, arms and legs.

The brawl turned into a melee as the centre of one of the holiest shrines of Christianity became a battleground between Jew and Christian. Men shouted in anger, women screamed and protected their children, dragging them into inconspicuous corners behind columns and iron railings, and even lying on top of them. Men screamed, 'Stop', 'Halt', 'No' in a dozen different languages. Nobody really understood what was happening or why.

The priests had one mission—to save their heritage.

Books by Alan Gold

The Jericho Files
The Lost Testament

Published by HarperPaperbacks

THE LOST TESTAMENT

ALAN GOLD

HarperPaperbacks
A Division of HarperCollinsPublishers

HarperPaperbacks   *A Division of* HarperCollins*Publishers*
                    10 East 53rd Street, New York, N.Y. 10022

Copyright © 1994 by Alan Gold
All rights reserved. No part of this book may be used or
reproduced in any manner whatsoever without written
permission of the publisher, except in the case of brief
quotations embodied in critical articles and reviews. For
information address HarperCollins*Publishers,*
10 East 53rd Street, New York, N.Y. 10022.

A paperback edition of this book was published in 1994 in
Australia by HarperCollins*Publishers.*

Cover illustration by Jeff Walker

First HarperPaperbacks printing: April 1996

Printed in the United States of America

HarperPaperbacks and colophon are trademarks of
HarperCollins*Publishers*

10 9 8 7 6 5 4 3 2 1

THE DEAD SEA SCROLLS CONTROVERSY

The first biblical and non-biblical scrolls from the Dead Sea were found accidentally by an Arab shepherd and smuggler in the spring of 1947. From 1949 onwards archaeologists explored the caves in the entire Qumran area of the Negev wilderness in Israel. Between February 1952 and January 1956, ten further caves were found, some of them containing a treasury of biblical fragments.

The members of the International Team who have been translating and publishing the Dead Sea Scrolls since they were first discovered have recently been the centre of an international controversy. Scholars throughout the world believe that much material has been deliberately withheld, and are eagerly awaiting the International Team's future announcements.

In the beginning, God created the Heavens and the Earth. And He created Man in His own image.

But man has turned away from the sight of God, and has become evil, corrupt, and proud.

And proudest of all are the men of Rome, the Legions of the Damned.

He looked down again, far below, at the hideous sight. In his mind's eye, he saw maggots begin their slow ascent from the dark nether regions of the earth into the still-warm body deep in the valley. He saw vultures landing and tearing strips of bleeding flesh. He shuddered with the horror. He picked up his stylus, and continued writing:

I, Jesus, son of Joseph, of the generations of David and Aaron, born of Beit Lehem and who grew to manhood among the Desert People of the Book, have looked with sadness through the eyes of my Father, Yahweh, into the land of the world to come, and I have seen and understood many things.

The boy was petrified. He clung to the precipice of crumbling yellow rock, and painfully inched his way higher. His jet black hair was matted with dirt, his olive skin streaked with sweat.

Far below him, the roar of British jeeps echoed through the wadi, exhaust sullying the pure desert air. He flattened himself into a crevice, praying to the Almighty One that they wouldn't see him. He had been told that these men loved picking off Bedou, firing at them for sport.

He heard the jeeps slide to a halt deep in the valley, skidding on the loose stones and debris. Never had he felt so exposed. He cursed his stupidity for wearing black robes. He had broken the rule of the smuggler, to be as one with his surroundings. Now he was paying the price. He mumbled a prayer.

The commander of the troops bellowed orders to his men. The boy was too scared to turn his head and look down, but in his mind he felt them fanning out into the wadi, guns cocked in anticipation of the sport, eager for him to show himself. He glanced upwards—the top of the cliff was just a few tantalising feet away.

His pocket bulged with the treasure from the cave. If he got out of this alive, he would go to Bethlehem and demand the best possible price. The trader must compensate him for the dangers retrieving the scroll.

There was a shout from the valley floor far below. They were running towards the cliff face below him. In desperation, he looked down. At the base of the cliff, soldiers were congregating, pointing upwards towards him. He saw the officer, stiff and formal, walking over to the throng. He gasped in fear and scrambled upwards, fighting his panic. He heard a shout and struggled up the vertical face, rivulets of powdery rock cascading downwards into his eyes. He began to recite what he could remember of the *Koran*.

There was another shout from below, then a fusillade of bullets suddenly exploded around him, chipping off rock fragments, spraying him with debris. Desperation made him move even faster. He no longer noticed the cuts and injuries to his hands and feet, was no longer concerned with the security of foot and handholds.

Another barrage. One bullet punctured his burnous, another grazed his thigh, stinging him. More volleys. He was now so close to the top of the cliff that his eyes could see the expanse of the desert before him. He found a new reserve of strength, and with one final huge effort, his arms straining against the weight of his body, he hauled himself over the top. He was safe. Exhausted, sweating, panting for breath, he lay flat on the ground as the bullets whistled and whined ineffectually high into the air. He mumbled a prayer to Allah.

He lay still for a minute, then pivoted on his stomach, and cautiously peered over the edge of the protective cliff to see what the soldiers were doing.

Eventually, he saw them disperse back to their jeeps, then disappear, plunging the wadi back into its primordial silence. At last he felt safe to examine his contraband. In one pocket of his burnous he carried the object he had been sent to trade in Bethlehem. A jewelled dagger, encrusted with lapis lazuli and leaves of gold, and set with small rubies and azure sapphires. His father had acquired the heirloom from an impoverished Saudi. It should fetch good money.

He sat down crosslegged on the top of the cliff, looking towards the distant shore of the Dead Sea, at the

Mountains of Moab. He reached into his other pocket and took out the scroll which he had just taken from the cave. It was old. Very old. The parchment crumbled in his fingers. He tried to read some of the symbols, but they were written in a language other than his own.

1948

'Of course I realise their value, brother. Do you think I'm a complete ignoramus?'

The Frenchman ignored the barb. 'Then why does your excellency persist in refusing my request to remove the scrolls to a safer place? To Rome. They will be safe in the Vatican.' He paused a moment, considering, then continued. 'I must warn you that if you don't accede to my demands, the pressure I will bring against you will be irresistible.'

Barely able to control his anger, the Syrian stood up and walked from behind his desk to stare out of the window. A British troop patrol was passing by.

Mar Athanasius Yeshue Samuel, Metropolitan of the Monastery of Saint Mark in Old Jerusalem, stroked his glistening black beard and toyed with the heavy gold cross and the ikon of the Virgin that hung on large chains around his neck. Normally he was a well-tempered man, a godly man. Not one given to extremes of emotions. He was even-handed in his treatment of both Jews and Arabs in the hope that he and his monks could be spared the traumas of the approaching war. In the coming months, when the British removed their troops from Palestine, only diplomatic skill on his part would enable him and his fellow monks to survive.

Mar Samuel was liked by most people for his generous disposition. As well as being thought of kindly by the rulers of the land, he was adored by the Bedouin who asked exorbitant prices for the manuscripts they were continuously discovering somewhere near the shores of the Dead Sea. He was also respected by those who demanded access to the scrolls, the Christian scholars from the École Biblique, the academics from the Department of Antiquities in Transjordan and Jewish scholars from Hebrew University. But the awful young monk sitting opposite him, the diminutive Father Romain de la Tour, pompous and arrogant, had just succeeded in driving away all of Mar Samuel's good nature. He was furious.

'How dare you threaten me, brother. How dare you come into my monastery as though you were a member of the police force, issuing orders to my monks, and —'

'Mar Samuel, the streets are full of snipers, Jew and Arab. And shooting at the snipers are the Transjordanian army and the British. Any day the godless communists from Moscow may descend upon this place. Syria, Iraq, Egypt and a host of other nations are set to plunge this land into an apocalypse. I haven't time to pay a courtesy call, sip coffee and negotiate. I have one task, and that is to rescue the Dead Sea Scrolls before they're destroyed, or worse, before they fall into the hands of the Jews.'

Mar Samuel raised an eyebrow at the priest's wanton turn of phrase. Biblical archaeology in Palestine seemed an odd calling for someone of his background, someone who hated the people of the Book. For all the little priest's arrogance, though, Mar Samuel was seriously worried about the safety of the scrolls. The Monastery of Saint Mark was situated in the middle of what might, in a matter of weeks, be Armageddon. But the arrogant Frenchman was so obnoxious, so callous and indifferent to the Metropolitan's status, that he could not bring himself to listen any further.

'No! I am the guardian of the scrolls. They were purchased by me. They are mine to do with as I see fit. Now get out, brother, before I have you escorted from this holy place.'

Père Romain de la Tour looked coldly at the Syrian priest, barely controlling his anger. 'Excellency, understand clearly what I am about to say. It is my intention to retrieve the scrolls for posterity and to take them to a place of safety. After the war, and when the Jews are driven into the sea, I will return with them to Jerusalem, where I will set up around me a team of scholars to examine them. Nothing, not you, not the British, will stand in my way. If I have to use money, or force, or invoke the wrath of the Vatican, then I shall.'

With that, de la Tour turned and walked out of the room, leaving the Metropolitan standing by the window fuming. He watched as Père de la Tour walked out of the monastery and back up the crater-strewn road towards the École, reflecting angrily that only a man as young as Father de la Tour could be so confident in his righteousness, so arrogant and vindictive. He shook his head, and stroked his beard.

The high-pitched 'ping' of a rifle shot rang out. A single sniper's bullet. There was a distant scream of pain. Mar Samuel looked in horror as Père de la Tour collapsed on the sidewalk, clutching his leg, bellowing in rage. Some monks from the monastery cautiously ran towards him, crouching, concerned for their own safety. Eventually, de la Tour was helped to his feet and supported by two of the monks as he hopped towards safety.

Mar Athanasius Yeshue Samuel realised he was smiling at the Frenchman's agony. He felt ashamed of himself, and began to mutter a silent prayer.

THE
LOST TESTAMENT

CHAPTER 1

It had been dark for a thousand years. And a thousand years before that. It had been shrouded in blackness for a hundred generations. Since the time that the Romans had trampled the world underfoot. Since the fall of the Second Temple, the Temple rebuilt as the glory of the ancient world by a paranoid King Herod in order to pacify the Jews.

It was in darkness when wild men with lice in their matted hair and destruction in their eyes razed the city of Rome and burned its seven hills.

It was dark when sun-beaten men with leather skin, riding foaming white horses, galloped across the desert and inspired half the world with the word of the Prophet.

It was dark when tall men and short men, wearing blinding armour, with red crosses emblazoned on their breasts, hacked a path from Europe through defenceless villages, killing Turks and Jews and Arabs, to liberate a squalid city called Jerusalem. And it was still dark when a priest nailed his anger to the wooden doors of Wittenberg and protested against the avarice of Rome.

The light shone after two thousand violent years when a Bedouin goatherd wandered among the sandstone cliffs above the fetid Dead Sea. He saw a cave. Bored and tired, the Bedou, Muhammad the Wolf, threw a stone. He heard the hollow, incriminating sound of breaking pottery. He climbed high up the cliff face into the cave. There were dozens of tall dun-coloured clay jars. Muhammad prised open the bitumen sealing the lid of one of them, disturbing the dust of aeons.

He let in the light.

Fifty years later, the arc-lights of a dozen television cameras flooded the lecture hall. People in the front rows cast elongated shadows over the green baize table-cloth. Their shadows climbed the back wall and danced a jig as the cameramen positioned and repositioned their cameras for an uninterrupted view of the proceedings. Sound recordists crouched in front of the table:

Newspaper and magazine reporters sat back in their chairs, viewing the antics of their electronic cousins in fascination and disdain. And interspersed between the reporters sat academy and religion. Five hundred philologists, archaeologists, biblical scholars and theologians, sat beside Rabbis, Monsignors, Reverends, Fathers and Pastors. All heads turned towards Jerusalem. All eyes on the podium.

As the first of the twelve men trooped single-file into the room, the murmur lapsed and there was silence. Everyone watched the scholars walk nervously towards their places. After a few moments, a priest in the fourth row began, self-consciously, to applaud. Others joined in. Then the room rose to its feet in appreciation of the deed. Eleven of the twelve scholars raised their eyes cautiously as they walked to their seats and surveyed the audience, smiling back in thankfulness.

The twelfth continued towards his place, indifferent to his reception. Shorter than the rest, more hunched, he walked painfully, a gold-handled stick supporting his weight as he took his place. He was wearing the simple habit of a Dominican monk. He and his PR consultant had debated whether he should walk into the assembly using his stick. The PR man thought it might be construed as a visible cliché; Père de la Tour insisted that it was part of his identity. For fifty years, it had supported him as he trudged the Judean wilderness in search of the truth. *'Thy rod and thy staff, they comfort me. Thou preparest a table before me in the presence of mine enemies.*' He turned to stare at his audience. The room fell into a respectful silence. He had the look of the austere, drawn searcher, the tired countenance and emaciated bearing of the bookish cleric.

The twelve men arranged themselves in a row behind the table.

The priest walked over towards the lectern clearing his throat. He stood blinking in the light, a heavy crucifix theatrically hanging from his neck, its golden Christ genuflecting before the microphones. Another symbol of identity. He leaned the handle of the cane against the lectern.

His head was obscured by the bunch of microphones, the head of an electronic gorgon. The technicians leapt forward to lower the microphones so that his face would be seen by the cameras and his audience. As he waited, an historian in the front row called out, 'Wasn't this announcement supposed to have given you greater stature, Romain?'

The priest grinned and, given their cue, the audience burst out laughing. The tension began to ease.

When the technicians had finished their fiddling, Père Romain again cleared his throat. He surveyed the audience. Silence fell.

'Ladies and gentlemen,' Père Romain said in English. By agreement. He would have preferred Latin or French. They were more fitting languages. One of his colleagues had even suggested that Hebrew or Aramaic should be used. Père de la Tour was comfortable in any. And all.

'Since the 1947 discovery of the Dead Sea Scrolls in the caves above the Essene community at Qumran, there has been much controversy surrounding the silence of the team appointed to translate and identify them.'

Straight to the point. That was his style. The consensus view in the audience was that he would gloss over

3

the half-century in which many of the details of the scrolls had been hidden from the public; that he would cite research or caution as the explanation for so little having been published. Maybe, at last, the world would find out the reason.

'We have been placed under great pressure by the world scientific community, biblical scholars, and especially by the Israeli government—everybody wanted us to rush into publication of the most important documents ever to have been discovered. We were even made the subjects of a ludicrous conspiracy theory.' He giggled self-consciously. A nervous habit.

A wave of irritation rippled through the audience. One American palaeographer whispered to a colleague sitting nearby: 'In case you hadn't noticed, we're being insulted.' A German philosopher sitting in the row ahead of the two men leaned back, and whispered: 'Listen to him! As if we were a class of his students.'

Father de la Tour continued, 'Many of you will have wondered why so little of the discovery has been published. Perhaps for the world-wide congregation of viewers, I can offer a short synopsis to put things into perspective.

'The Dead Sea Scrolls are the oldest biblical writings ever discovered. They pre-date the Christian era by several hundred years. They are the writings of the Essenes, a monastic community of Jews who withdrew from the body politic and the various military occupations of their country to live a simple, peaceful, worshipful life in the Judean desert, waiting for the End Times to come, and their delivery by a Messiah.'

The audience began to shift uncomfortably in their seats. Each of them was intimately familiar with the history of the scrolls. All they wanted to know were the details of the most recent discoveries. That was what they had come to Jerusalem to be told.

'When they were first discovered, and the initial scrolls translated, a tenuous link was established between the Essenes and Jesus Christ. Many of His philosophies have been identified in the scrolls, which were written long before His birth. Because this link was disturbing to many devout Christians, we, the International Team, became very circumspect about allowing unauthorised publication and speculation.'

A dozen reporters began to write. Sound recordists noted the position on their tapes. They needed controversy for instant replay when the press conference was over.

'And as it turned out, our decision to withhold publication and outside examination was absolutely correct.' He banged the table to emphasise his point. The microphones jumped in response. The technicians reacted instantly.

'The initial publications of the Isaiah Scroll, the Habakkuk Commentary, the Jeremiah fragments and others were greeted with sensationalism and unauthorised commentary. Much nonsense was published, especially by uninformed populist writers, eager to profit from book sales.

'Our silence was justified on the grounds that research and investigation take time, and can only be accomplished in the absence of external pressures.' He cleared his throat once again. 'So today, for the first time, we are pleased to publish the complete translations and explanations of the Dead Sea Scroll material not previously made public.

'For the benefit of the media, always keen for a headline, let me draw your attention to a particular item which, I am sure, will capture your interest and imagination. Something which you've been waiting for these past fifty years. In the caves close to Masada, where later material dating to the Roman occupation was discovered ten years ago, a most interesting fragment has been unearthed.

'It is a list of treasures which were hidden two thousand years ago. Treasures from the Temple, the Essene community, and of the Pharisees. Treasures, we believe, which were collected by unknown people of the first century of our Lord, in order to hide them from the rapacious Romans.'

Frowns appeared on foreheads. Journalists wrote hastily, thinking in headlines: 'BURIED TREASURE', 'TEMPLE RICHES'. Academics smiled sceptically. There had been talk a dozen times before about the Temple treasures. Earlier manuscripts had made reference to them. Most were apocryphal but it hadn't stopped the bounty hunters.

'Other treasure lists found in the past have been rightly dismissed. Clever ruses to foil the Romans or genuine lists which were deciphered by scavengers in the time of the post-Roman occupiers. But, ladies and gentlemen, this document containing a list of hidden treasures cannot be discounted.' He paused for effect. 'For the list makes no mention of vast hordes of gold or silver. Merely documents and a few relatively unimportant trinkets.'

At this, a great many sat up and began to pay serious attention. Here was something new, something surprising. Representatives of Judaism and Christianity listened with interest.

'We have, of course, deciphered the list. It talks of documents giving the Order of Service of the Great Temple, the Order of Precedence in the Hierarchy of the Temple, and details of sacred texts used by the High Priest on the High Holy Days of the Jewish calendar.

'But there is more. The list also deals with other documents which these first-century historians, these

men or women who were desirous of preserving artefacts of importance to their community, thought were
too valuable to risk remaining unrecorded or falling into
the hands of the conquerors.

'They also collected together the civil documents of
their community leaders. These documents have been
secreted somewhere. We have not yet traced their hiding
place. When we do, they will make fascinating reading.'

He paused again and took a sip of water. His public
relations director had taught him how to use a short
pause to build up tension and drama. Père Romain
scanned the audience and felt the tension in the room.
They were hanging on his every word. They had been
primed. They were ready. He reached down to his side
and grasped the golden handle of his walking stick.

'As a matter of interest, there is an unmistakable
reference to a certain Testament of a man who was a
member of the Essene community. A man who
remained with the Essenes for many years in the
community of Qumran, until he left and preached His
doctrine throughout the length and breadth of Palestine.
Someone called Jeshua the Nazarene.'

The academics froze in their chairs, instantly realising
the meaning of the bombshell. The journalists didn't
understand immediately but could feel the shock of the
revelation amongst the scholars. The most perceptive of
the Christian clerics began to cross himself.

Père Romain smiled as he explained, 'You may
understand it more easily when I tell you that we have
found evidence of the Testament of Jesus Christ.'

Michael Farber felt his knees crack as he levered his tired
body off the kneeler and joined the handful of early
morning congregants. The desultory line shuffled down

7

the aisle to celebrate Communion. Two hours of squash the previous night had played havoc with his muscles.

He cast his eyes towards the cold stone floor of the church, the morning light drowning the aisle in hues of reds, golds and blues. He was sure that only the few remaining churches which still professed the Tridentine Mass were suffused by the light of God.

They lined up in single file, like spectators before a game, eagerly awaiting their chance to kneel before the priest at the altar rail to accept the wafer of life.

Michael knelt between an elderly, wheezing man and a young woman conservatively dressed in a black business suit, and bowed his head in anticipation of the priest. But as so often happened when he was about to celebrate the most spiritual of all the rites of the Catholic Church, his mind vaulted from thought to thought, the past invading the tranquillity which should, by right, have been his.

He closed his eyes tightly to squeeze out the images, but inexorably, they returned; ghosts of a younger life, haunting the crux of his adult existence. The more tightly he shut his eyes, the more insistent the images became. His old Jewish father, *yarmulka* on his grey hair, sitting behind the mahogany desk in his study, shaking in rage, clenching and unclenching his fist as if to pump venom into his muscles before he attacked Michael. Yet the attack never came. He wouldn't even look at Michael. Instead, the old man, his moist, bloodshot eyes strained from decades of studying holy books in half-light, stared at his wife, shaking his head in disbelief. Rose, his forgiving mother, her own eyes hollow and red-rimmed, sobbed as she begged her husband.

'But, Shmuel, he's your son. You can't do this to him. For God's sake, listen to him.'

'I hear no one. There's just you and me in this room.'

His mother wiped her nose with a linen handkerchief. 'Shmuel, please, I'm begging you. Don't do this thing. Once it's done, it's done forever. Forever! Do you understand me?'

'I'm going to stand up now, Rosele. I'm going to get my *tallis* and go to the *shul* and say *kaddish* for my dead son. I have no son any more, Rosele. He's dead. Finished. End.'

'Please, Shmuel. Please don't.'

His father adjusted the *yarmulka* on his head. Michael heard himself saying quietly, 'Please, father. Don't do this to me. I'm your son. I love you.'

The old man spoke only to his wife. 'Rosele, I'm going to *shul* now to say *kaddish*. To say the memorial prayer for my son. As it must be. A rabbi must say *kaddish* when his son dies!'

The old man raised his head towards the ceiling and shouted the opening cadences of the holy prayer of mourning. *'Yisgaddal V'Yiskaddash Sh'mai Rabboh.'*

Michael knew from that moment onwards he was dead. He heard himself crying, 'Father please . . .'

'Father, please.'

'Are you here for Holy Communion, my son?' asked the priest, looking quizzically at the taut man, head bent, kneeling before him.

Michael opened his eyes and whispered an apology as he accepted the wafer placed in his mouth by the priest. *'Corpus Domini Nostrum Jesu Christi,'* recited the priest before moving on to the next communicant. His acolyte, carrying a silver salver, followed close behind.

It was a week since he had last confessed, a long and difficult week. Anger and tension at the university over his decision concerning Dr Meg Thornton, and her damnable book on the marriage of Christ. Contemptible, stupid, arrogant woman! With all the titanic problems besetting the department, the last thing he needed was a tidal wave of indignation and emotion from the Christian hierarchy of Sydney.

Then to top it all, his son, Christopher, had begun to go from bad to worse. Deirdre had phoned him in the middle of a faculty review and begged him to come to the hospital. His colleagues had been unctuously understanding, as only God-fearing people knew how.

Michael looked around the beautiful and harmonious church of Saint Clare, an island of stillness in the frenetic heart of Sydney, and fought to retrieve the passion and security he had once known in the bosom of the church of Christ. Why was it so very different now compared to when he was a young convert, full of urgency, luxuriating in the potency of his Messiah?

Again childhood invaded his present. He was a boy, sitting at the foot of his father's seat in synagogue, watching the venerated rabbi *daven* the evening prayers, smelling his acrid cigarette-laden breath. Or being forced to follow his father's angular finger chart the alien letters in the prayer book as it traced every syllable intoned by the cantor. He was the rabbi's son, and it was ordained that he would be good at Hebrew and knowledgeable of the Bible. If his eyes wandered, or his attention was distracted by other boys, his father would 'tut' disapprovingly. He wore the shame of his father's condemnation as he wore his prayer shawl, a visible rebuke which stung him bitterly. His weekends comprised hours of agony, sitting in boredom as the men of the community prayed in a foreign language to a God whom he tried desperately to envisage. He was the *rebbe*'s son, yet he felt no pride. Just alienation from the other boys in *shul*. When they played, he prayed. When they talked and ate sweets, he followed his father's lips.

Later, as he approached his coming of age, his bar mitzvah, he was called upon to participate more frequently in the service and his worst fears were realised. He cringed in embarrassment at being called to the reader's desk before the entire congregation, to participate in the reading of the Law; he was studied by all the men and women of the community and judged for his performance, every word. As the rabbi's son, his conduct and delivery were expected to be flawless. It exerted a relentless pressure upon his boyish head, one which he could share with nobody. He was desperate to belong, to be like the others his age, having fun in the House of the Lord, being a part of the synagogue. But every Friday night and all throughout Saturday, his father imposed upon his shoulders the duty of worship, building an impenetrable barrier between Michael and his immersion in the faith. *Shul* became a place of apprehension, a hostile environment where he felt exposed to scrutiny and open to judgement.

But his embarrassment within the synagogue was as nothing compared to the mortification he felt descending the steps into the outside world. There his blue suit and skull cap identified him, unmasking his secret. When he set foot on the busy main road after the service he bowed his head, praying that no one would see him. His father, wearing a rabbi's long frock coat and a homburg hat, looked foreign and out of place in the hot Australian sun. Michael did his best to become invisible, but every passing car, every pedestrian, every schoolchild playing Saturday morning games would look at him as he walked the tortured path from the *shul* to his home. He felt their ridicule, he sensed them staring at him, whispering about him; he saw people spying at him from behind curtained windows.

It was a month before his bar mitzvah. He could not bear the confusion any longer. In despair, he approached the dark study door behind which his father was ensconced, writing his sermon. He knocked cautiously. He discussed his fears with his father. The rabbi, by then grey and stooped, looked at him with questioning eyes. 'You are ashamed of your heritage?' Close to tears, Michael told him he was not ashamed, simply embarrassed at being different. 'When I was your age,' his father continued, 'I was interned in Bergen Belsen by the Nazis.' The old man rolled up his sleeve, and showed Michael the faded blue tattoo on his arm, the brand of the Jew. 'I was forbidden to be a Jew by those monsters. So am I ashamed to be a Jew today? No! I'm proud to be Jewish. To continue the obligations of my father, and my father's father. As you, Michael, will carry on after me.'

Chastened, he performed his bar mitzvah perfectly, winning the admiration of his family and the community. As time passed, he started to feel more at ease within his society, relaxing in himself, and in his heritage. But his fears were savagely reawakened when he was fourteen and a car full of teenagers pulled over screaming 'Fucking yids' out of the window. Shamed, and furious beyond control, he screamed back 'Fucking goys' but earned a slap in the back of the head from his father. 'Never grovel in the gutter with people like that. You incite them to more obscenities, and demean yourself.'

Michael saw Father Driscoll walk towards the confessional. He went forward, heading off an elderly parishioner. It was time to share some of his burdens with the priest. Not that he would confess his indignation at being excluded from the Dead Sea Scrolls announcement taking place in the Holy Land. Nor would he participate in similar soul-searching about the running of his department.

He walked into the confessional. While he waited, he tried to define which of his sins he would admit to Father Driscoll. His yearning for an end to his desert of a marriage? His daily prayer for his son to die?

How he wished he could have been in Israel. He looked at his watch, and realised that the announcement would already have been made. Damn the Israeli government. Despite intervention from colleagues in America and England, an invitation had not been forthcoming. He wondered whether Judith had been invited.

He knelt in the confessional room. Father Driscoll slid open the door between them and Michael looked at his variegated profile, chequered by the grille in the confessional partition.

'Bless me, father, for I have sinned. It is a week since my last confession and since then I have committed the sins of pride, intolerance and lustful thoughts. I have also been guilty of wishing harm upon my wife and son.'

Father Driscoll 'tutted'. 'God sees into your heart, and knows what resides in there. Did you do what I told you, and read the Book of Job?'

'Yes I did, father. It's not unfamiliar to me. But every man has to come to terms with his own problems.'

'True. But it was God who helped Job to come to terms with his, because Job displayed great faith in the Almighty.'

Michael looked up and frowned. 'Do you think I've lost faith?'

The old priest hesitated before answering. 'I think that if your faith was stronger, you would not feel such a crushing weight on your shoulders. Have you done what I advised and seen a marriage counsellor?'

'No,' said Michael. 'Deirdre doesn't accept the need.'

Father Driscoll remained silent. After reflection, he asked, 'What other sins do you wish to confess, my son?'

Michael went through the motions of unburdening his conscience. In the beginning, shortly after his conversion, confession was one of his most blissful experiences; the ability to square the books, to relieve the weight of guilt. But in the ten years since Christopher's flaccid and useless body had been delivered into the world, during the time that he and Deirdre had become strangers, Michael had been plagued with such a diverse range of emotions, from anger and frustration to grief and wallowing self-pity, that confession had become an extra burden, a regular and mandatory rubbing of salt into his raw wounds.

He rushed through what he had to say, accepted the priest's blessing, and left the room. As he walked back down the aisle, his mobile phone began to ring, a thin electronic bleat in the vast Gothic expanse of the church. An old parishioner looked up in surprise as Michael hurried away looking for an empty part of the church.

'Hello,' he whispered.

'Michael,' boomed the enormous voice of Ari Wallenstein, his old teacher and close friend. 'How are you?'

'Ari,' Michael breathed. 'You've caught me in the middle of something. Tell me quickly what happened at the announcement and I'll phone you back in an hour or two.'

'*In flagrante delicto?*'

'Don't be ridiculous. In church, rather than *in flagrante*. Tell me, what was the announcement?'

Ari told him quickly of the findings announced by de la Tour. By the time he had finished, Michael was sitting down, the shock making him feel suddenly weak. 'I don't believe you.'

'It's only a list, Michael. There's nothing more than a list,' Ari stressed.

'But—'

'A list, Michael, not the document.'

'To you it's a list, Ari. To me, it's proof.'

'Anyway, you old bastard . . . Sorry, I shouldn't have said that if you're in church. Phone me in a couple of hours and we'll talk more. This time you can pay for the call. Shalom.'

'Shalom, my friend, and thanks for phoning.'

Professor Wallenstein grunted and rang off.

Michael closed the car door and rested his body momentarily against it before entering the house. If ever a day in his life could be called traumatic, this was the day. By the time he had got to the university that morning the extraordinary announcement of the International Team was already known. The first to bear down on him, shrieking like an ageing harlot, was Meg Thornton.

'Michael! I want to talk to you. I've just heard the news. This is a vindication of everything I've been saying.'

'Meg, it's a vindication of nothing. I've also heard what was announced. They've found a list.'

'It goes to prove—'

'It goes to prove nothing. It indicates the existence of a will written by Jesus. It's historical proof of His existence. But not proof that He was married. And certainly not that He spent the rest of his life after His trial disguised as St Paul, dying by crucifixion in Rome.'

'I'll be proved right. You'll see. And then I'll have your head on a plate for the insults you've meted out to me.'

'Meg, you're no Salome, and I'm certainly not John the Baptist. But one thing I will promise you. When the day arrives that your scandalous hypothesis is proved right, I'll happily step aside, because then I'll have no further interest in Christianity.'

He'd stalked off, slammed his door shut and become a prisoner of the telephone. Everybody had wanted to speak to him: the Catholic Archbishop of Sydney; the religious correspondents for the *Sydney Morning Herald*, the *Age*, the *Australian* and the Brisbane *Courier-Mail*; the current affairs producers for the ABC and Channel 9 . . . everyone wanting instant opinions on a subject of which he knew as yet next to nothing. And no sooner had he finished with the local media than producers from American networks NBC, CBC and CNN were vying with the BBC and Channel 4 in England begging him to go into television studios so they could get his opinions by satellite.

One of the reasons he had left Oxford to come back to Australia was so he could get out of the limelight, away from controversy, a Christian fending off the lions of the broadcast media. But his reputation as one of the world's most original and audacious biblical scholars had followed him and at least once a year he was dragged into a television studio to participate in a televised biblical debate somewhere in the world. His fame and reputation brought renown to his department, but created petty jealousies amongst his colleagues, enmity which had recently bubbled over as once-reputable scholars paraded fantasy for fact in order to share the limelight.

After fending off the media he'd had a large tutorial group on biblical archaeology and there was no way he could avoid discussing the implications of a Testament having been left by Jesus Christ. He'd allowed his students to speculate while his mind wandered, considering the possibilities—the end of religious uncertainty, the ultimate fusion of Judaism and Catholicism, the end to the heresy of England and the Protestant experiment.

All these things could now happen if Christ's Testament were found. It would be the beginning of the beginning, and not, as Ari Wallenstein had predicted on the phone, the beginning of the end.

It was clear to Michael. God had given the Old Testament to Jews, and the New to Christians. He saw a clear lineal integrity, the Old joined to the New through the Apocrypha and the Dead Sea Scrolls. Since that day on the Via Dolorosa, Michael's burning ambition was to fuse Judaism and Catholicism, and bring Protestantism back into the fold; to meld emotions, intellects and faith of the peoples of the Book. To end the divisions and the petty bureaucratic rules and regulations which were barriers to the flowering of belief. To create a unified loving family under God. One day . . . maybe today?

As he walked into his neat, comfortable home, Michael smelt the affluent aromas of the kitchen, as well as the antiseptic cleanliness of the laundry and bathroom. So normal, so placid in appearance. So sterile. Even the empty wheelchair in the hall no longer looked threatening.

'Michael?' Deirdre called from the kitchen.

How changed she was from the woman he first knew. Once a wonderful intellect, bold and imaginative in her field of mathematics. Now a cook, cleaner and nursemaid. He couldn't even remember the last time they had gone out socially, or said words of softness, tenderness to each other.

'How's Christopher?' he called.

'Much better. They think they've stabilised the temperature. He could possibly come home in a couple of days.'

Michael's shoulders shrugged in disappointment. He was thankful that there was nobody to witness his reaction. He picked up the mail from the telephone table. American Express bills, council rates, and a couple of flyers offering aluminium siding and discount window cleaning. Deirdre always opened the interesting ones—letters from overseas, invitations to a charity or church do, or cards from her peripatetic family. Someone was always travelling by four-wheel drive somewhere in Australia, or bussing around the Top End or to Ayers Rock. Michael was left to open the bills.

He walked into the kitchen. Deirdre didn't look up. She was spreading a thick paste of mashed potatoes over mincemeat to make a shepherd's pie. Christopher's favourite. *In absentia.* Once he would have kissed her on the cheek and they would have discussed the day's events in enthusiastic detail.

'I've been teaching or doing bloody media interviews about the Testament all day. It's been bedlam. Ari phoned me early this morning. I was in confession,' he said, wanting to talk.

'Any progress in the faculty?' she asked. But he knew she was merely being polite.

He turned away. 'I'm bogged down in the bloody stuff all day, every day. I really don't want to talk about the place.'

Deirdre was stung. He did not mean it to sound harsh, but she felt rebuked. 'I'm concerned.'

'I know. I'm sorry. Yes, there's been some progress. Kevin's crossed the floor, and seems to be onside. And a couple of the PhD candidates have written to say they're supporting me. Some signs too that Meg and Terry and the others are feeling isolated. Once they lose a couple more, I'll march into the vice-chancellor's office and demand—'

'Careful, Michael. You know that the VC's wife and Meg have been thick as thieves since their time together as deaconesses. Meg isn't a good person to have as an enemy, no matter how important you are. Most people think of her as an amiable eccentric. It doesn't do to underestimate her.'

'I can't help it. She's split everyone. She's wrecking the place with her holier-than-thou moralising. It's a secular department of religious studies, Deirdre. Not a meeting place for disaffected mystics or some theological seminary for strange beliefs. She can join the Hare Krishna or the Zen Buddhists if she wants to, but while ever I'm in charge, the department will be run my way!'

He opened the refrigerator and took out a beer. For Michael, a bottle of beer was a catalyst for music. Suddenly he needed to listen to Bach or Liszt, or better still, lose himself in the intellectual purity of a symphony by Mahler. Just sinking back into his armchair as the opening chords immersed him in their beauty nullified all the tensions and traumas of his life. He retreated and set himself up in his study.

After Mahler and dinner, he broke the news to his wife. 'I'm going to have to go to Israel. I got the approval of the vice-chancellor. We both agree that the discovery of the team is sufficiently important for me to be there.' Deirdre continued to sip her coffee. Her reaction told him her feelings. 'I know you'll be angry, but it's necessary.'

She looked at him coldly. 'And Christopher?' He remained silent. 'I see! So, you and the VC have discussed it, have you? Didn't you think about discussing it with me first?'

Michael readied himself for an argument. It was the last thing he wanted. Dealing with tension at the university was one thing. There, he was an empowered bureaucrat. Everyone was answerable to him in one form or another despite the current ruckus. At home, his powers evaporated and he became a single unit of a family in crisis.

'Deirdre, please, don't make this difficult. You know I can't help you with Chris. I've done all I can.'

The phone rang. She walked into the hall. He listened to the muffled conversation, trying to figure out who it was. Deirdre walked back into the room. 'It's Israel. Judith.'

He felt himself flush. He felt exposed. 'Judith?'

He walked out and closed the door. He stared at the phone resting by the side of its cradle. His heart was pounding. He wanted to pick it up and hear her voice. He held back. The telephone felt alien to his hand.

'Judith?' he asked softly.

'Hello, Michael.'

Her voice sounded as though she were present in the room. Strong. Confident. He wondered how he sounded to her. She broke the pause. 'It's good to talk to you.'

He felt exultant. 'Do you know how often I've wanted to pick up the phone and call you?' he asked. He wondered whether she was smiling.

'How are you keeping?' she asked.

'Where do I start?'

He laughed. In the echo he heard his laughter. It was thin and hollow.

'Me too,' she said.

'I'm glad you phoned. Really glad. I think it's been long enough.'

Another long pause. He prayed she agreed.

'Michael, I know it's strange after all these years, but when the news came through about the Jesus list, I wanted to call you.'

'You didn't need an excuse, Judith.'

'Neither did you. I thought you should know the news behind the news.'

'Ari's already rung me.'

'The whole department is in an absolute uproar. I've

never seen anything like it. Elderly biblical scholars running up and down corridors like kids. It's quite a scream.'

'Same here,' he told her. 'I suppose you've been reading about Meg Thornton.' He bit his lip in anger. Why talk about Meg? For twenty years he had been yearning to talk to Judith about a thousand different things, not about stupid university politics.

Judith replied, 'She doesn't have much credibility any more, does she?'

'She's going around telling everybody that she's been utterly vindicated.' He stopped. 'Judith, I'm rambling. You've caught me by surprise. Never mind about Meg. Let's talk about you. Ari's told me about your career, but he refuses to talk about your personal life. Are you well? Have you changed much? Are you happy?'

She allowed another long pause. 'Are you coming over to Israel, Michael?'

'Yes. Tomorrow.'

'Good, we'll talk then.'

He smiled and said goodbye.

When he had hung up, he walked back into the loungeroom. Deirdre was curled up reading a book. He sat down in a chair and picked up a copy of the newspaper.

By the following morning, it was apparent that international reaction was explosive. In churches everywhere, hymns were sung and prayers raised in thanks that a new and positive link had been established to Jesus. Here was a Testament which would cement the connective tissue between themselves and their Messiah previously only found in the observations of Matthew, Mark, Luke and John.

Newspaper editors from Japan to America, Africa to Finland, scrapped front pages of all other news to carry the story. They played it according to the nature of their audience. Papers like *The Times*, the *Washington Post*, the *Wall Street Journal* and the *Australian* carried it on their front pages. Inside, they published reflective articles by theologians, historians and atheists about the impact the Testament might have on Christianity and speculated on what it might possibly say. Alongside their articles were maps of the Dead Sea area, library pictures of the cliffs of Qumran, and even more articles by scholars.

But it was not only the better papers which carried the detail. The world's popular press gave the story a sensational coverage, with blown-up pictures of the twelve scholars accompanying headlines that would have done credit to a Hollywood movie. Artists' representations of Jesus, from cartoons to the works of Renaissance painters, greeted readers as they started their day. In one cartoon, a biblical figure pondered with stylus in hand. In another he was dictating to a female secretary. In others, he had rejected a laptop computer in favour of a papyrus scroll. The New York *Daily News* offered its readers a chance to win a fourteen day, thirteen night all-expenses trip to the Holy Land. *Berliner Zeitung* offered a fortune in Deutschmarks for any reader finding the Testament and returning it to the newspaper.

Television stations went wild, running footage from the press conference repeatedly along with thirty second grabs from their archives of anyone who had speculated on Jesus in the past. Religious departments, which were rarely involved in the rush and bustle of daily news, were raided by the famous faces of prime-time TV, demanding the names of contacts or good talking heads who could be co-opted onto the news and current affairs programs.

Men and women who had previously led reclusive and contemplative lives in the timeless atmosphere of biblical research were dragged by clock-watching harpies into the glare of television lights, to be bombarded with artless questions and naive speculation from presenters who mispronounced their names or misrepresented their positions.

As the new day dawned, the clamour grew louder. Père Romain de la Tour read a large selection of newspapers and was horrified by all the uninformed speculation. He'd known that the story would be enormous but had never expected that what would be written would be so speculative, such guesswork. He read paper after paper, from all over Europe and America, and grew increasingly despondent. He issued an edict to the other members of the International Team. Not one further word was to be announced without his consent. For nearly half a century he had managed to keep prying eyes out. Now, because of a damned stiff-necked Israeli, he had been forced into a position which he could not control. He picked up the phone in his Jerusalem hotel room and dialled Rome to discuss the situation with his friend, Kitzinger.

Members of the Israeli government were also concerned and dismayed, but for different reasons. In the twelve hours since the announcement, their phone lines had been overloaded. The Ministry of Tourism had already begun to receive the first of hundreds of requests from travel agencies around the world for permission to put together archaeological-site visits and discount packages. The Ministry of Religious Affairs had been inundated with requests from church groups seeking permission to visit the Qumran caves and the site of the Essene monastery. Schools, universities, seminaries, common-interest groups and dozens of others called

Israel to request further information about the latest Dead Sea Scrolls find for projects and research data.

The Religious Departments at both Hebrew and Tel Aviv universities were contacted by universities in America, Canada, Britain, France, Germany and Japan and asked to send out experts on the Dead Sea Scrolls for a series of all-expenses-paid lecture tours.

The switchboard of the Holy See was swamped with calls from the faithful asking about the significance of the latest discovery. The Prefect of the Congregation for Divine Worship and the Discipline of the Sacraments, Cardinal Achille Pio Pirondini, instructed his under-secretary to employ the services of three multilingual priests to explain to the faithful that the Vatican had not yet considered the matter, and would make an announce-ment in churches around the world through its bishops.

In response to the furore, there was a hastily convened meeting in Room 4D of the Knesset building in Jerusalem. It was a small gathering of the kitchen Cabinet and its military adviser. Only the Ashkenazic Chief Rabbi of Israel, the Prime Minister, the Minister for Religious Affairs and the head of Israel's internal security, General Dov Baer, were present. The Prime Minister outlined the world reaction, and then de-manded to know why the Minister for Religious Affairs had not informed him of the announcement ahead of time so he could prepare the government.

'Moishe,' said the minister, 'I didn't know. Sure, I knew they were going to announce something about the scrolls but I thought it would be more of the same. Nobody told me they'd found this list and the connection to Jesus. Those Papist bastards on the International Team have made fools of us.'

Moishe Rabbinowitz, whose tenure as Prime Minister during the past three years had been strained as he lurched from one factional crisis to another, banged the table in anger and said, 'But that's why we put what's-his-name on the team. So he would let us know what was going on. Do I have to remind you that these scrolls belong to us?'

'*Rosh ha Memshalah,*' the Chief Rabbi intervened, looking through hooded eyes at the Prime Minister. 'Do I have to remind you that both the International Team and the Vatican do not agree about ownership? The scrolls were discovered in Jordan and it's only since the Six Day War that the new material has been under our control. Putting an Israeli on the International Team, even one as distinguished as Amos Arachi, hasn't really helped us, I'm afraid. He's a scholar, not a fighter.'

The Prime Minister reacted angrily. 'What the hell are we going to do? Why can't we just fire the International Team, send them packing and have our own scholars do the work? For God's sake, we've got a thousand biblical scholars who are capable of translating the Dead Sea Scrolls, and five times that number in Jewish communities and universities throughout the world. Why should we let a team of Catholics dominate the research?'

'You're absolutely right. We should've moved against these Papal pricks a decade ago,' the Minister for Religious Affairs said. 'But more to the point, what are we going to do about the announcement of Jesus' Testament? This could spell serious trouble between us and the *goyim*.'

'It's only a list that's been discovered,' the Chief Rabbi reminded them. 'The Testament has not yet been unearthed.'

'Well, I don't want millions of fanatical Christians traipsing all over Qumran,' said the minister. 'We have to control this. The area's a tourist gold-mine. It's worth hundreds of millions of dollars a year to us. And even more, I don't want anybody clambering over the cliffs in Masada. All we need is a couple of *alter kacker* elderly tourists falling to their deaths and we can kiss goodbye to half our income.'

The Prime Minister nodded in agreement and turned to General Dov Baer. 'Well, general, what do you think? Any suggestions?'

'Have we got a problem?' the general asked.

The others looked at him. He was blasé about nearly everything.

'You think we don't have a problem?' asked the Prime Minister.

'Look, maybe we do, maybe we don't. They've discovered a list. Christ's Testament may be buried in the desert. This land's been pillaged from the time of St Helena to the Victorian romantics. We're organised. If there's trouble, we'll deal with it.'

The Minister for Religious Affairs groaned. 'But, Dov, this is more important than just some archaeological find. There's a billion Christians who could descend on the Holy Land looking for it. That's enough to stretch the resources of El Al to its limits.'

Dov smiled. The Minister for Tourism continued, 'Well, you're all aware of the plans my department's currently working on, in spite of General Baer's confidence. But I think we've got to restrict visa applications to bona fide researchers and university groups. Anybody who wants to explore the desert must get a permit. And we've got to vet all incoming tourists.'

'Doesn't that mean setting up road blocks on the entrance to the Negev Desert and Masada? It'll make us look like a police state,' said the Prime Minister.

'A bit like Judea in the time of Christ?' said the Chief Rabbi, smiling wryly.

Dov Baer looked at the rabbi and shrugged, '*Plus ça change, plus c'est la même chose.*'

CHAPTER 2

Michael Farber had forgotten how impressive an Israeli cappuccino was. The waitress brought him a Tower of Babel, a steeple of whipped cream and sugar which masked the sweet black heart lurking clandestinely in the bottom of the cup.

He looked at his companion, waves of endearment inundating his exhausted body. Neither jet lag nor lack of sleep could dilute the joy Michael felt at being in Ari's company again. It was as though the pressures of his life were lifted, as though the sudden clarity of mind which he had enjoyed shortly after he converted to Christianity had returned to him. The intervening years melted away, and he remembered the sweetness of living, the pleasure of being.

Ari had picked him up from the airport the previous night. It took thirty hours of travel from Sydney to Jerusalem via Rome; hours spent huddled in economy class, trying to fend off enquiries from backpacking students or Sicilian mamas returning home. Although he had slept well during the afternoon, he still felt as though his head was a balloon filled with water, slowly oscillating inside his skull. It would take another long sleep for him to recover fully. But the news he had come to discuss with Ari was more important than bodily gratification.

Ari smiled wryly and sipped his cup of coffee. He had not seen Michael Farber for over a year. Their relationship during the last twelve months had been conducted through correspondence, exchange students, and the occasional telephone call.

Rabbi Professor Ari Wallenstein had taught Michael the wonders of the Old Testament when Michael was a student at the Hebrew University. When Michael was a

Jew. And Ari was one of the first people to whom Michael had turned when he made the decision to convert to Catholicism. Typically Ari had not been censorious, but the following day wrote him a long impassioned letter setting out the benefits of both religions to its adherents. In the end, he told Michael that he must do whatever his conscience dictated.

Ari had been shocked when he saw Michael emerge through customs. He had aged visibly in the year since they had last seen each other. His care-worn face carried even more scars. The two vertical worry lines which dissected his eyebrows seemed deeper, like a barrier which separated one side of his emotions from the other. Ari ached for his friend, but there was nothing he could do. Christopher was Michael and Deirdre's problem. Deirdre had come to terms with it years ago. Michael still agonised. And their marriage, once so joyous, so vibrant, was now arid and unfulfilled.

Ari sipped his coffee, remembering Michael as a student. When he'd first arrived, full of hope and expectation, he'd strode manfully off the path which his father had laid down, left the *yeshiva* and entered Ari's Department of Jewish History at the Hebrew University; the lanky youth, full of experiment and daring who talked with passion and verve about the tortured path of the Jewish experience. Michael had impressed Ari and his colleagues, and even in the early days was talked about as a potential candidate for a first. Teaching him had been a challenge. Instead of soaking up the facts like the others, Michael persistently tried to see events from different points of view. It was as though leaving the rabbinic school had opened his mind, and he was no longer a sponge for the *yeshiva*'s mandate on faith.

Ari had known plenty of brilliant students in his time as a teacher. But Michael had a glittering essence which surprised, delighted and sometimes worried him. It was as though there was a box of gems locked up in his heart, a box whose key was just beyond Michael's grasp. Sometimes his innate goodness would shine through, giving Ari a glimpse of the young man's potential.

Of all those who knew him, Ari had been the least surprised when Michael made the decision to convert. Michael was a seeker, and would never be satisfied until he held the answer in his hands, even if he came to realise ultimately that the answer didn't exist.

His friends were ill at ease with his constant seeking of answers to unanswerable questions. They said that he was the type of person who created the troubles in his own life by refusing to flow with the tides of fortune. One of his fellow students remarked to Ari that Michael was like a solitary pier on a beach, opposing the onrush of the deluge. Michael was surprised by their reaction. He saw his questioning of established values, his doubting of received wisdom, as nothing more than a search for expansion and enlightenment.

When, shortly after his conversion, Michael had gone to Rome, he had considered joining the priesthood. But despite the pressure of the Roman establishment, he decided not to, realising that while he was intellectually and emotionally a convert, he was not the type to preach or to accept the enormous responsibility which was part and parcel of life in pastoral care.

In the twenty years since then Michael had become an academic, first as a lay teacher in a theological seminary in Rome where he took his doctorate, and subsequently as a visiting professor at Harvard and Oxford universities. His stature as an international authority had grown year by year, as he continued to astound—and often annoy—fellow academics with his perception, insights and audacious discoveries.

It was when he'd returned to receive an honorary degree from Phillip University in his old home town, Sydney, that he had met Deirdre. They had fallen in love at the same time as the Chair of Bible Studies at Phillip University fell vacant. Michael was the natural candidate. Many were surprised that a scholar of his stature had left the mainstream for such a remote university but in the dozen years since his appointment as professor, he had built the department to international standing.

The orthodox Jewish community of Sydney ostracised him. His only connection with his past life as a Jew was on his regular visits to Israel, when he contacted old friends who respected the man rather than his faith. Despite the difficulty of travelling with Christopher, he had brought his family to Israel on some of his visits to show them the wonders of the land which was the origin of their faith. Deirdre, a fervent Catholic, had grown to understand Michael's love for the country although Christopher could neither see nor hear his parents' rapture as they extolled their pleasure.

Ari ached for Michael. He wanted to reach out and touch him. To take the problems off his shoulders. But there was no way anybody could solve them. When he had first met her, Ari had wondered whether Deirdre was right for Michael. She was reserved, introspective and carried the inner tensions of the religious fanatic. But Michael was attracted to her fervent love of Christ, her certainty of the absoluteness of Christianity. For Michael, Deirdre embodied the rock-solid truth of everything in which he then believed.

When Chris had been born, their paths diverged. Deirdre draped her body around the crucified figure of Jesus in order to fulfil her understanding. Michael reached out for her to help him cope, but found her wanting. The marriage was doomed as each failed to fulfil the other's needs and expectations. Any love which had once been between them departed.

Michael had talked about the unhappiness of his marriage to Ari and Shulamit before. Shuli, always the pragmatist, had suggested he should bring the relationship to a halt while he was still young. But Michael's religious convictions were affronted by the idea. And so, for the past decade, Michael had lived a life in limbo. Married but not married. Together but apart. His visits to Israel were a profound relief from the stresses of living in a house devoid of love.

Both Michael and Ari were still stunned by the International Team's announcement. For years the conspiracy theorists had trumpeted links between the monastic Essene community, who had lived for two centuries on the shores of the Dead Sea, and Jesus Christ. From the 1960s, scholars throughout the world had become increasingly contemptuous of the way in which the international translators had taken the scrolls into their custody. Recently the criticism had been led by Michael and Ari. Sceptics still wondered how much material would be published, and how much would be held back. And if material was being censored, at whose direction? The theorists and hysterics even suggested that the team was working at the behest of the Catholic Church.

None of the scholars, journalists or ministers of religion had expected such a momentous disclosure.

Ari stirred his coffee. His huge hands dwarfed the spoon. Every time the spoon completed a circle of the cup, the gold chain on his wrist hit the handle, sounding like a record with a crack. 'Don't you think it was unbelievably lucky, remarkable even, that they found this list?'

Michael leaned closer to hear. He had chosen this cafe because it was one of the few in Jerusalem that played live jazz in the evenings. It reminded him of his early days as a student. It reminded him of Judith.

'I think it was even luckier that they decided to publish it. Heaven only knows what else they've still got up their sleeves,' said Michael.

'Then why do you suppose they decided to release the document now?' asked Ari. Michael didn't know, and shrugged. 'I can't bear them,' Ari continued, 'the way they act as though they were on the committee of a gentlemen's club in Mayfair.'

Michael laughed but he knew Ari was right. 'They'll only allow in people that they can control.'

'Hence you and I are on the outside. Especially you! You're the last person they'd ever let into their cosy little fraternity.'

'Meaning?'

'Meaning as a scholar you're okay, but you go off on wild flights of fancy,' said Ari. 'Like that article you wrote claiming the Essenes were the original Wise Men from the East in the story of Christ's birth, and had come from Northern India. Michael!'

Michael grinned. It had been one of those moments of deduction and insight resulting from his interpretation of a hidden code which he had discovered in one of the Dead Sea Scroll fragments. But his interpretation had been questioned by other scholars, and caused him considerable embarrassment in the letters columns of biblical review magazines, much of the criticism led by Meg Thornton.

'Ari, you of all people should realise the role that deduction and inspiration plays in our work. Would Troy have been discovered, or Masada, without people having an idea, and sticking their necks out?'

'People who stick their necks out get them chopped off. That's why I'm so surprised that the International

Team released the fragment. I would have thought they'd have sat on it from now until Doomsday,' said Ari. 'Mind you,' he continued, sipping another mouthful of coffee, 'since the Israeli government took control, access has eased up a bit.'

Michael burst out laughing. 'Ari, don't be so bloody naive. The only concession the International Team's made to the Israeli government is the appointment of Amos Arachi. We both know him. A brilliant scholar but about as worldly as a virgin on his wedding night.'

The cafe became noisier as a group of American visitors walked in. Michael looked at Ari. Ari always looked young and fit. Now he was looking more and more like a man rapidly approaching the end of his middle years. His large face was growing jowls, his hands acquiring liver spots, his hairline receding.

And Ari had put on even more weight than Michael remembered from his previous visit. His stomach now protruded so that his black cotton shirt rode up to expose a strip of white skin, in the middle of which was his navel. The Hebrew University meeting had been a formal occasion, requiring jackets and ties, but that didn't concern Ari. His uniform of black tops and black jeans was his signature throughout the academic world, as instantly recognisable as Père de la Tour's walking stick. Yet Ari's emblem was worn unaffected. The gentle Goliath looked like a German Fascist, but the image went no further because Ari, huge as he was, was incapable of a vicious thought.

Ari put down his cup. 'Well, the material's been published now. What do you think of its contents?'

'Most of the material other than the Testament is of enormous interest but it pales into insignificance, doesn't it. Let's face it, Ari, the other translations can't exactly be called crucial to our understanding of the early church. But the fragment referring to the Christ's Testament! Unbelievable!'

'There speaks a *goy*. What about the scroll called "Stars to Light the Early Days of the Messiahs"? As a scholar, you must be excited by that,' said Ari.

Michael winced when Ari said 'Messiahs'. He had been studying the Dead Sea Scrolls for most of his adult life and still could not get used to hearing the word Messiah spoken of as a plural. The ancient Essenes believed that there were two Messiahs or 'anointed people' who had come from the lines of King David and Aaron. They ascribed no unique spiritual significance to the title, but looked on the chosen ones as leading the Elect of God in the End Times.

'Oh certainly. I've often wondered about the use of the "star" imagery by the Essenes. Bar Kozeba was called "Bar Kochba" or "Son of the Star" by Rabbi Akiva. There's the Star of Bethlehem, and lots of other allusions. I'm sure if anything was going to clear it up definitively, it would be this scroll, if only we could find it.'

'But what about the other material they've translated?' Ari took out his notes and read. "The Commentary on Esther", "The Son of Moses", "The Prayers of Samuel", "The Order of Precedents of the Temple" . . . I could go on and on. Surely these excite you just as much as the last will and Testament of Jeshua of Nazareth?'

'What are you talking about? This find is more than a matter of scholarship and archaeology. This proves that Christianity has a basis in more then faith alone. It goes to the very heart of all I believe in.'

Ari shrugged his shoulders again. 'What chance that they're wrong?' he asked.

Michael shook his head. 'I don't think there's any chance of them being wrong. But that doesn't mean there's much chance of finding the Testament itself.'

'So you'll go off on another intellectual wild goose chase again, will you? Another search. But what if?' Ari let the question hang in the air.

'What if it's found?' said Michael. 'What will be the effect on the devout? What will happen if Jesus' Testament is something less than rapturous? Do you think I haven't been thinking about that?'

Ari nodded. 'Maybe it doesn't talk about the hereafter. Maybe it talks about leaving His shoes and cloak to the community.' They both laughed. 'But seriously, maybe it denies the speculation that He was the Son of God. What if it talks of Him being born of woman and directly contradicts the claims made by the Gospels?'

Michael ate the last of the whipped cream with his spoon, scraping the sides and bottom of his cup. 'Do you think there's any value in speculation? Apart from the fact that now we know that Jesus left a Testament, presumably in His own hand, we've still only got the accounts of Matthew, Mark, Luke and John.'

'That's just not right, Michael,' Ari said, shaking his head in disagreement. 'The mere fact of finding the reference to Christ's Testament takes Christianity a quantum leap forward. With the exception of brief mentions in Flavius Josephus and Pliny, up till now there's been no direct contemporary evidence of the existence of Jesus. John Allegro even suggested He might be a sacred mushroom, a drug and fertility cult. Now, suddenly, you have direct evidence, proof for your religion.'

Many years had passed since he had forsworn Judaism for Christianity, but Michael still felt a tinge of discomfort when Ari referred to Christianity as 'his religion'. Intellectually, emotionally, he was Catholic, but by birth and heritage he was still a Jew, no matter what layers of Christianity were gathered around him.

His friends at the university joked that he had the best of all worlds. He did not share in the humour.

When Christopher was born, Michael had opened his eyes to reality and perceived the difference between being a Jew, and being a convert to Catholicism. Those friends whom he had gathered around him since his marriage to Deirdre were solicitous but proper, and maintained a dignified reserve. Not even his priest had been able to break through the barriers. Although he was often present in their home following Christopher's birth, Father Driscoll played the part of the pastor, looking after their welfare, but offering them no insights into how to deal with the burden.

It was so different from when this kind of tragedy happened in the Jewish culture. Then it was the community which rallied, which looked after itself, enfolding its members in a protective cloak, shielding those whose emotions were raw from the coldness of the outside world. It was only when Christopher was born that Michael realised how badly he needed the cosseting for which Jews were so renowned. And, for him, it was too late. He often thought of himself as a traveller standing on a railway platform, surrounded by hundreds of people, yet alone. Waiting, always waiting.

More people came into the cafe for dinner. Ari finished his coffee and touched Michael on the arm. 'Shuli asked if you would like to come tonight for a meal.'

Michael smiled. 'Ari, would Shuli mind if I was alone tonight? I don't want to sound cold, but I really would like to go back to my hotel and think. And I'm still suffering from jet lag. I used to be able to take these journeys in my stride. The older I get, the harder they become.'

Of all the people with whom he was in contact in Israel, Michael loved Ari and Shulamit the most.

Shulamit, the eternal Jewish mother, was one of those tireless women who managed to accomplish everything and still end up smiling at the end of the day. Their home was always full of family, visitors and friends, and whoever happened to be there was guaranteed a delicious meal made without fuss and clamour. Her energy was boundless. And Ari, the bearded giant, was devoted to her, as well as loving his many children. He still enjoyed playing an occasional game of soccer, though now, in his late fifties, with a stomach taking control of his body and his knees giving out, he preferred to coach the kids' team rather than play.

'Michael, there's something I have to tell you.' Michael looked at him quizzically. 'I know Judith phoned you in Sydney.'

The mention of her name was like an electric shock. 'How?'

Ari didn't answer for a moment. 'I told her to.'

'You?'

Ari nodded. 'Me! I felt it was time you two saw each other again. Made up the quarrel.'

Michael was dumbfounded. 'Why?'

'Michael, I love her as much as I love you. Remember that.'

'I'm married. Judith's married.'

Ari stood. He took out his wallet to pay for the drinks but Michael shook his head. Before Ari left he paused for a moment. 'Michael, about this list. Only time will tell whether it's a good or a bad thing. Nobody can see into their future. But I can't help remembering the words of St Mark: "What shall it profit a man, if he shall gain the whole world, and lose his own soul". I just pray that this revelation will benefit mankind and that it isn't the beginning of insuperable problems.' He turned to walk out of the cafe, but stopped, as if thinking.

Reflectively, he turned back and looked sadly at Michael. 'Remember the story of Ahasuerus? I love telling apocryphal stories. It's the rabbi in me. Ahasuerus is said to return to earth every millennium as a precursor of momentous change. Every thousand years! Michael, let's not forget that we're coming up to the end of the second millennium.'

'Ari, Ahasuerus is the Wandering Jew. Cursed for denying the majesty of Christ and for ridiculing Him on His way to His crucifixion. Like Cain, he was cast into the wilderness for his sins.'

The two men looked at each other. The older man walked out of the restaurant. Michael was left alone. But he wasn't thinking about the scrolls anymore. He was thinking about Judith.

He had not been back in his hotel room for more than ten minutes when the phone rang. Michael sighed in exhaustion.

He picked up the phone and barked, 'Yes?'

'Professor Farber? I'm Kay Casubin. I'm calling you from LA. I work for CNN here. I'm wondering if you can give me some quotes on the implications of this incredible find announced a couple of days ago?'

'How did you get through, Miss Casubin? I've left clear instructions with the hotel that I'm not taking media calls!'

'I said I was your daughter.' She laughed.

Michael smiled, disarmed by her honesty. 'Why do you want to talk to me? Surely you want to talk to a member of the International Team.'

'I spoke to Father de la Tour yesterday, and he was . . . well let's just say he was not exactly forthcoming. I managed to catch Professor Wallenstein a couple of minutes ago, and he suggested I phone you.' Michael smiled. Ari had landed him in it yet again.

'What do you want me to say? It's the most exciting find . . . It's the greatest development since . . . Miss Casubin, all that's been found is a list. It's indicative that there may have been something more but nothing concrete at this stage.'

'But professor, surely you must be excited.'

'Certainly I'm excited. It's an extraordinary piece of archaeological detective work, but little more. The question must now be asked, "Where is the Testament?" or more to the point, "Does it still exist?" These are questions which will be debated in academic circles following the team's announcement.'

'And do you think there's much chance of the Testament being discovered?'

'I pray that it will be, but I have no idea, no concrete idea whether it will or not. Now we know for certain that Jesus was an Essene in His earlier life, I need to think more about the life and times of the Qumran community, and make a decision as to where our Lord could have hidden His words.'

'Professor, I know this might sound dumb to you. I'm no Bible scholar. But why is this list so important? So it mentions Jesus! Why is it better than the Gospels?'

Michael was so steeped in the Bible, it was so integral to his daily professional and personal existence, that he sometimes forgot that for most people it was a marginalised, superfluous document, irrelevant to their needs and aspirations.

'Kay, Christians for two thousand years have been searching for proof of a Christ who lived. That's why, in the old days, so much significance was placed on fragments of blood or bone or wood from the Cross. It was a link to the living Jesus.'

'The Shroud of Turin!'

'Exactly! Now we have a list which says not only that He lived but that He left a Testament. If we find it, we'll know for sure that His appearance on earth really happened. We'll know His thoughts first-person. Not third-person from the Gospels. The Testament may give us a clue to His mind just before His death. It may even magnify the glory of the Gospels.'

'And how will it affect Judaism?'

He smiled. 'Good question. But that's something which you should ask a Jewish theologian.'

'That's fine, sir. Thank you very much. Before I go, is there anybody else that I should talk to?'

'I think you're going to get the same story from other academics as you've got from me. Why don't you approach the churches for a theologian's point of view?'

'I've already spoken to the Catholic and Protestant churches. All they're doing is making no comment at this stage.'

'How about an American evangelist? They're always good for a bit of sensation.'

'Great idea,' she said. 'We've got more than enough holy rollers this side of town. I'll call Jimmy Wilson. He's the latest noise in the Pentecostal movement.'

'Good luck,' said Michael. He put the phone down and decided to go straight to bed.

He lay back on the bed and worked out the time difference between Jerusalem and Sydney. If he phoned straight away, he'd catch Deirdre while Christopher was still asleep. Even after all these years, sometimes when he thought of Chris's spindly legs and drooling mouth, lolling in the wheelchair as Deirdre pushed him for his daily walk, he came to the verge of tears. He thought back, as he often did, to his son's birth. When Christopher had been born so prematurely, hardly bigger than the size of Michael's hand, he believed that God was inflicting some cruel, personal punishment upon him.

They had stuck needles into Christopher's arms and legs, put him on artificial respiration machines, flushed his tiny body with antibiotics, fed him watery milk through a tiny dropper, and splayed him under the arc-lights of the humidicrib as though he was some piece of meat in a butcher's window. Every time Michael visited the humidicrib, the nurses encouraged him to touch and stroke the baby—bonding they called it—but he was repelled by the dry, plastic skin and the fragile hold which the tiny baby held on life.

It was in the early hours of the third morning after Christopher's birth, hours following an evening of prayer for his life, that the neo-natologist told them that he had taken a turn for the worse . . . massive amounts of oxygen must be given . . . sticky lungs . . . blood transfusion . . . probably blind, dumb, deaf, spastic . . . never be like a normal child . . . never walk talk feel speak smile . . . strongly recommend withdraw food and medication . . . pray for peaceful ending . . . best thing for him, and the two of you. Michael had said yes. Deirdre had said no. Vehemently No!

Deirdre had given up her university post to look after Christopher. Every morning, noon, and night. Every day of the year.

He sometimes felt he had failed her. He had allowed his academic work to become everything, while his wife's burden continued to grow. But what could he do about that now? It was all too late. And he no longer cared. As compensation Deirdre had become even more fanatical and was now spending every spare minute she had attending to church affairs. Not his affairs.

He stabbed the numbers on the telephone, which was answered almost immediately. 'Hello,' he said.

'Hello Michael!' replied his wife. His body sank back into the bed, weighed down by the guilt of where he was and what he was doing. There was no anger or insinuation in his wife's voice as she asked him about the trip and whether he had seen the Wallensteins. Her understanding made him feel even more guilty.

'Any news about Chris?' he asked.

'He's fine. They got the temperature under control with antibiotics, and he's back home now.'

'Christ! What a stuff-up.' He wanted to apologise, but it would have sounded false. He told her about meeting Ari, and recounted their conversation. Avoiding any mention of Judith. He wanted sympathy. But she was half a world away, and more concerned about breakfast and dealing with Chris than with his crises. They said goodbye.

He looked out of the window at the darkening Israeli sky. He felt greater comfort looking at the clear crisp stars over high Jerusalem, the stars of the Bible, than he felt at home, looking up at the pallid and muted stars over humid and alien Sydney. Exhaustion dulled his thinking but his body was washed with such a depth of tiredness and deflation that he felt like sobbing. Within minutes he was asleep, fully dressed, on top of the bed.

He awoke in anger. His mind had been mulling over the little priest's rejection of his request to be at the announcement. Who in hell did Romain de la Tour think he was dealing with? Some neophyte, a supplicant with a begging bowl waiting for crumbs from the table? Michael sent a letter to Father de la Tour which one of the hotel staff delivered. A scrawled message came back within an hour. Michael gritted his teeth as he re-read the letter. He was damned if he was going to allow some diminutive, ascetic, arrogant, anti-Semitic scholar to treat him as though he were a schoolboy requesting the headmaster's permission. For decades, the team which Romain now headed up had acted with the divine right of kings, or, more aptly, like the Sadducees in the Temple—protectors of God-endowed knowledge. And for the past twenty years Romain had been the leader of the team, taking over from another priest who people said owed his allegiance to the Holy See, rather than the altar of scholarship. More than his predecessor, it was Romain de la Tour who had decided that only those endowed with the priestly garb could enter the Holy of Holies. Only those who knew the Name of God had the right to commune with the hermetic secrets.

Romain, and the other members of the International Team acted like fundamentalist Hasids and orthodox rabbis, the very people who had caused Michael to re-think his ties to Judaism. It was the rigidity of rabbinic thinking that had caused his greatest disillusion. Till then, Judaism had been the life he had been born to. He was predestined to become a rabbi. But when he studied his religion in depth, he discovered that the *rabbonim* had encased the Torah in a fence—originally a fence of protection, but ultimately, it had become like the walls of a ghetto. And the godhead worship of the fundamental Hasids, modern-day versions of the messianic sects of the eighteenth century in Eastern Europe had further alienated him. He cringed in embarrassment when he saw Hasidic Jews fawning or supplicating before the feet of the Lubavitcher Rebbe in New York, fighting each other for the crumbs left over from his plate. At his rabbinic school, Michael was interested in the revolution of liberal Judaism, which had breathed new life into the Jewish faith, but when he discussed their rites with his rabbis and teachers, they became furious, forbidding him to talk about them. Michael reacted badly at being told what to do. As a result of their strictures, he began to investigate other creeds, and found much in the teachings of Christ that accorded with his thinking.

The memory of all the old anger against his rabbis flooded back as he tore open the letter from Romain de la Tour which had been delivered to his hotel room that morning.

Dear Professor Farber

I am extremely busy at the moment, and cannot take time for a private interview with you. Further, I must deny you special access to the new Dead Sea Scroll material.

Time has been made available to bona fide scholars. Your time allocation is available from my secretary.

The new texts and their translations will be available to you in printed form when released by the International Team's official publisher.

The Israeli government will probably put the deciphered and translated documents on public exhibition in the fullness of time. You must ask them.

Yours truly,

R. de la Tour

Director

This man wrote as if to one of his students, not a leading scholar. Michael picked up the phone and dialled the number of the International Team's headquarters. He spoke to Romain's secretary, to whom he had spoken on a number of previous occasions. Despite her entreaties, Michael said he was coming round straight away. 'And don't bother offering me a cup of coffee. This won't be a social visit.' Half an hour later, he was sitting in the small, spartan reception vestibule, lino-floored and utilitarian. Romain's portrait shaking hands with Pope Paul VI was the only decoration on the walls.

'Please, Professor Farber, Father de la Tour simply cannot see you,' said the secretary, despair in her voice. Michael felt sorry for her. Adopting a more gentle and kindly tone, Michael again said, 'Tell Romain that I'm not leaving until I've seen him. Tell him I'm prepared to sleep here all night.'

She retreated into the inner sanctum, the door beyond which no one but the International Team could enter. Five minutes later, she emerged. Michael looked up expectantly. She avoided his eyes.

'Well?'

'Father de la Tour suggests you go and buy yourself a toothbrush and pair of pyjamas.'

There was hardly a week went by that Michael didn't think, even fleetingly, about Judith. When he saw her picture in *The Biblical Review* or read extracts from her lectures, he heard the gentleness in her voice. He felt again the comforting way in which she would reach out and touch him. He saw afresh the gleam in her eyes as they discussed some matter of esoteric biblical interest. How often had he wanted to pick up the phone and hear her voice. How often had he slammed it down before she answered it. On the flight from Australia, he had pondered their phone call. What circumstances might have led him to pick up the phone and say, 'Hello Judith, it's Michael.'

Yesterday, when he had phoned her she'd been strangely courteous, noncommittal. He felt a coldness that had not been there when he spoke to her from Australia. She had told him to meet her in the Valley of Jehoshaphat, at the foothills which led up to ancient

Jerusalem. The valley was reputed to be the place where momentous battles would take place in the End Times between the Elect of God and the Unbelievers.

They were to meet near the Tomb of Zechariah, the man stoned to death for accusing the Hebrew nation of forsaking God. Also the place where Christians believed St James hid himself at the time of the arrest of Jesus. Zechariah was the prophet who first mentioned payment of thirty pieces of silver, who predicted the Messiah's arrival into Jerusalem riding on the foal of an ass, creating the Kingdom of Peace on earth. His visions had inspired the Gospel writers in reference to Jesus. Michael arrived early, reflecting nervously as he looked at the dry, dusty ground and fleshy trees, baking in the heat of the midsummer morning. He realised how carefully chosen the location was. Despite rehearsing the meeting in his mind a dozen times over breakfast, he did not know what to expect, what she would look like after all these years.

When they'd been students together she'd been a magnet for his attention. Her presence within a room was more than the physical beauty. There was an aura which drew him to her whenever she walked into a lecture hall. His heart would leap when she looked his way, and when she smiled at him, his mind reeled, and fantasised about marching up to her, introducing himself, and asking her to go out to a movie, or for a cup of coffee.

In meal breaks, he conspired to sit close to her in the refectory. In the library, he would hang around the entrance for hours until she appeared; then wait for her to sit and contrive to find a table close by. He would choose books from a bookshelf near to where she sat. She must have wondered about his changing interests, his sudden passions for chemistry or handicrafts.

The time came when she began to acknowledge his presence, and eventually she breached the divide by coming over and talking to him. That first time, his throat dried up and he must have sounded like a timorous eunuch. The second time, two days later, he stammered while telling her about his home in Sydney and the beauty of its harbour. He hated himself for his lack of resolve, for the waste of opportunity.

But Judith found it appealing, a contrast to the swaggering Sabra boys, flaunting their good looks and manhood, thrusting their personalities at her through their bodies. She was surprised at his shyness. She asked if he would like to take her out. They went to a movie. They had supper. They went back to her apartment for coffee. They talked until the early hours. It was too late for him to catch the Egged bus home. He stayed the night. They did not make love. He lay awake on the couch, watching her sleep. He remembered getting up and going over to the bed, smelling her hair. Its fragrance was the still summer air in a mountain garden. He yearned to touch it, to run its sheer glossy blackness through his fingers, to kiss it gently with his lips. But he returned to his couch.

The following morning, they went to the university together. Then, that night, he took her to a cellar in New Jerusalem which had been converted into a jazz club. At first, she was bemused. It was noisy, atonal, smoky. But during the evening he explained—or over-explained in his anxious way—the musical complexities of jazz and she began to hear harmony within the discord. They went back to her apartment. They drank too much. They made love, badly. Judith had been entranced by his lingering timidity and the doubts he felt. She realised with a shock that he had been a virgin. She looked him tenderly in the eyes, smoothed his creased brow, and told him that it would be all right. She blew warm breath on his forehead, on his eyebrows, on his eyelids. She kissed him gently, and let him suckle at her breasts. She told him how virile he was.

During the rest of the night and into the following morning things improved. And as time passed she expanded the depth and range of his experiences. He felt more able to give her what she wanted. His range of sexual performances expanded. Slowly, he began to participate rather than be a recipient of her largesse, her experience.

After that, they were never separate. He knew he was the envy of the entire university. He didn't have a clue why she had selected him. When they walked into cafes, women would turn to admire them; men would wonder what an Israeli beauty saw in this emaciated Anglo. Friends whispered about their relationship. It was an odd match—he ascetic, scholastic; she outgoing, ebullient. But it seemed it would outlast the scepticism of the multitudes.

Their relationship was total. She was hungry for his gentleness and ardour, and drew on his inner strength and convictions. He revelled in her unabashed, unself-conscious love of being a woman and buried himself in her intellect and contentment. She enfolded and enclosed him as wife, lover, mother. He was different from the war-hardened, superficial, indifferent Israeli boys, just as she was different from young pampered Australian Jewesses of his youth who scorned him as a dork for his bookishness and introversion. Judith moved her possessions into Michael's apartment. His huge jazz collection was moved out of his bedroom into the living area to make room for her.

As their relationship blossomed during the arid summer, he matured from a timorous boy to a confident young man. Judith also revelled in their love. It was assumed they would marry when both had finished their studies in Biblical Archaeology.

His decision to convert to Christianity was made on the Via Dolorosa, walking up the steep, narrow cobbled path where Jesus had carried His cross and had been taunted by Ahasuerus. He had spent most of the evening in the company of his Jesuit instructor and friend, and at midnight wandered the streets of Jerusalem. There was only one road for him to take. His path was ordained. His mind was already there, his body waiting to follow.

In the early hours of the morning, he fell into bed beside Judith. She was fast asleep. He looked at her soft, beautiful profile in the ambient light from the street. The rain-washed window dispersed the coloured hues, causing the white light from the street lamp to refract into swathes of blue and yellow. Her black hair was bathed by the coloured glow from outdoors. He kissed her forehead, hoping she would wake up. She didn't. Michael fell asleep in the curve of her body.

She was quietly passive next morning when he told her. She did little more than nod. She didn't even ask him if he was sure. Not that it was a surprise. He had been talking to her about it for months. At first, she tried to persuade him against it, begging him not to do it, invoking the help of religious friends, and counsellors. He went against the combined weight of advice.

'It shouldn't make a difference to us!' he beseeched her.

'If you had any understanding of what you were doing, you wouldn't say that. Of course it makes a difference.'

'But I love you. I want to marry you.'

'Don't be ridiculous.' She was furious. Her impassive granite-like face was flushed. She shook her head.

Then she was suddenly weary and sad. She sighed, all the words having been spoken. She stood, cleared her plates, and went into the bedroom. She emerged fifteen minutes later, dressed, and packed. Without looking at him, she walked through the door.

She avoided him completely. Even during lectures she looked the other way. Only his new faith prevented him from falling apart.

And now it was twenty years, seven months and four days since that cold bleak morning.

'Hello, Michael.'

Her voice was slightly deeper than it had been on the phone, but her beauty was hardly diminished. She was maturer, fuller in the face, yet still fresh and vital. He held his breath, frightened to speak. She was wearing the uniform of an Israeli army colonel. Crisp, efficient.

Her hair was cropped shorter than before, but with its shortness it had lost none of its sheen, its vitality. Her face was still as strong as he remembered.

He was staring at her. He felt exposed. He wondered how he looked to her.

'Hello, Judith.'

They stood and looked at each other. Neither moved. Should they shake hands? Should they kiss? Hesitation! The quicksand of the past.

They both started to talk at once, then broke off and smiled, acknowledging the tension between them.

'Why so suddenly? There have been other reasons to contact me before this,' Michael said.

She shrugged her shoulders. They walked deeper into the garden. 'You know,' she said quietly, 'in the early days, after you left Israel and went to Rome, I fantasised about keeping a large knife carefully honed and sharpened for the moment when I saw you again.'

He stopped walking and stared at her in horror. 'I see

you've lost your sense of humour,' she quipped, and continued to walk. He was forced to catch up with her.

'I see you're still angry,' he said.

'Oh, I'm not angry any more, Michael. You're no longer important in my life. You were once, but I have other priorities now. I just felt that twenty years was long enough for a hurt to last. So! How are things working out for you?'

'My work keeps me busy,' Michael told her. 'And you?'

'Same. I'm working part-time at the university and part-time as an army officer. Both feel like full-time jobs.'

'What regiment?'

'First Golan. I'm a colonel. How about that?'

Michael was shocked. The Golan regiment was a fighting unit which was always first into the heart of a battle. Casualties were often high. Hers was no sinecure.

'Is it dangerous?'

'Only if I get killed.' She laughed.

'How's Uri?' She turned in surprise. 'Ari told me. He won't go into detail about you or what you've been up to but I know you're married. Your husband was a paratrooper. He's now an electronics specialist. You don't have children.'

'Mossad's missed out.'

'If you knew the number of times—'

She stopped him. 'How's Deirdre?' she asked.

He laughed. 'Mossad?'

'Ari!' she said. 'He's kept me informed.'

Michael sighed. 'It seems Ari's been a lot more frank with you than he's been with me.'

She reached over and threaded her arm through his. He felt a *frisson* of excitement shudder through his body.

'You and your husband?'

She ignored his question and they walked passed the Pillar of Absalom in silence. Then she said: 'Remember what was written about Absalom, Michael? "For he said 'I have no son to keep my name in remembrance' and he called the Pillar after his own name, and it is called Absalom's monument unto this day."'

They walked down the dusty path through the olive groves, eyes fixed on a distant point. Cicadas chirped in the trees—summer's orchestra. 'You know, legend has it that in the Middle Ages, passers-by would hurl stones at the monument,' Judith continued. 'They were incensed that Absalom had rebelled against his father David. To them, it was inconceivable that children could be so uncaring. The residents of Jerusalem would bring their sons by the scruffs of their necks to the monument and say: "Look, this is what a rebellious son comes to".'

'Judith, please.'

They walked on in the increasing heat of the morning into the Valley of Jehoshaphat. On the opposite hillside, the Mount of Olives, was the world's oldest, largest, and most sacred Jewish cemetery. They were walking close to the bed of the Kidron, almost dry in the summer heat.

High above them, on top of the white rocks, blinding in the sun, sat the City of Jerusalem, poised between the valley floor and the rich blue sky. Its synagogues, mosques and churches symbols of man's attempts to reach upwards. To be closer to God. Light scintillating from windows and golden roofs. The air was still, but busy with insects and the cries of birds wheeling in the sky above their heads. Goats bleating in the distance. A camel, invisible from where they walked, belching and growling in stubbornness against the will of its Bedouin master.

Judith sat down on a rock. Michael sat beside her. 'There's another legend. One about this valley. Do you know it?' The anger was seeping from her, like the bile which floated to the surface of the Dead Sea.

'No, tell me about it,' he said, quietly.

'Come Resurrection day, all men, women and children will gather on the Mount of Olives.' She nodded towards the hillside opposite. 'God will place the Judgement Seat on Mount Moriah, over there. In the air above the Valley of Jehoshaphat, two bridges will appear, linking the two mountains. Everyone who has been resurrected after death will have to cross one of the two bridges for judgement. One bridge will be made of iron, and legend has it that it will be massive, strong and formidable. The other bridge will be made from paper. It will be light, frail, and temporary. All the heathens will choose the iron bridge. But their combined weight will make the bridge collapse. They'll fall into the eternal abyss. None will be saved. But the Jews will pass over the bridge of paper in safety and peace, and they will all be saved and live an eternal life.'

She turned to him. 'Do you know why? Because there are so very few of us. Each of us is precious.'

Michael remained silent. Judith stood and continued to walk down the path at the base of the Valley of Jehoshaphat.

'Why don't we go up to Jerusalem and have a cup of coffee?' he asked eventually.

Judith agreed. The valley had served its purpose.

CHAPTER 3

When Daniel Francis Xavier, Cardinal Rhymer, the Vatican's Secretary of State, was a boy of twelve, he sat rock-rigid and terrified on one of the hard leather chairs in the second reception room of his parents' Connecticut home. He watched as the clock on the mantelpiece ticked away slowly and inexorably under his tearful gaze. The longer he waited for his father to come home, the more distraught he became.

Every now and again, one of his eight brothers or sisters would poke their mocking head into the room—contrary to their mother's explicit instructions—and gleefully inform him of what was to come.

'You're in for it now, Danny boy.'

'It's the cellar, you lustful wanker. Good luck, Danny, 'cause you're going to need it.'

'God's looking into your black and evil heart at this very minute, Danny.' Their taunting brought on more tears, and deepened his despair. His mother had said not to move and he had hardly moved a muscle.

As the clock struck 6.30, the bell sounded at the distant front door. His ears heard every sound, the maid scurried to open the door for his father, polite muffled conversation about the weather, and what was for dinner, his mother asking his father if she could have a word with him before he went upstairs to wash and change. Then the marching of feet, the warden walking with finality to the condemned man's cell.

His lower lip began to quiver. Try as he might, he could no longer hold back the flood of tears. He had wanted to greet his father dry-eyed and manly, but fear made him weep. He moved. He put his hand in his pocket to take out a handkerchief. He fondled himself for comfort. The action aroused his penis. Oh God! No! That had been the start of it all.

The door opened slowly. His father stood framed by the entry, his body silhouetted by the light from the hallway. He looked like one of the horsemen of the Apocalypse. Daniel's terror was unbounded. 'Your mother tells me you have committed the sin of exposing your body to another child and doing unspeakable things.' Daniel opened his mouth to say something but no words came out.

His throat was dry, his dread too palpable. His father walked into the room, staring sternly at him. 'I was hoping that you of all people, you of all my children would be free of the sin of lust. But you're not. I look upon you in great disappointment, Daniel. You have the power to follow two paths in life. One is the path of goodness which leads to everlasting salvation and one-ness with God, and the other is the path that you have just started to follow. You've put your feet on the first brick of this awful and terrible path. A path which leads to damnation and destruction. Daniel, I'm going to have to punish you for what you've done so that you will know with absolute certainty what will happen to you in future unless you curb these bodily weaknesses,' he said with the finality of a prophet.

Daniel's tears began to fall from his tightly clenched eyelids. In a trembling voice, he said, 'Please, Father. Please don't. I swear I'll never do it again. I swear.'

'Daniel, don't make this more difficult for me than it is already. As it is, I'm ashamed of you.'

He held out his hand and Daniel clutched it timorously. Together, man and boy walked through the door, down the hallway. Beneath the stairs was a short narrow entryway which led down to the basement beneath the house to the furnace room. Daniel's knees weakened. He could hardly walk.

His father reached for the door handle. A blast of warm air from the furnace came up to engulf them. Daniel looked at the black mouth and the top rung of the stairs. He felt his father's hand behind his shoulder, gently pushing him. He could see mysterious objects behind recesses. He could hear the gushing noise from the furnace, could smell its coke-laden breath. He turned to his father. 'Please, Daddy. Please don't. I'm so scared.'

Daniel felt like a little boy again. Had it not been for the severe gazes of the Swiss Guard, he would probably have skipped along the broad road in front of the Belvedere Palace. But Cardinals didn't behave like that, not even American cardinals. The news had been extraordinary, carried on Italian television all night. He and the Pope had spent the time since reassuring heads of state. The Vatican switchboard had nearly blown a fuse with the number of calls from journalists and priests wanting to talk to people in authority for comments or for further information.

But there was no further information. Like the hapless president of America receiving his latest information not from the CIA, but from CNN, he and Pope Innocent were forced to rely on television news coverage to tell them the details of the discovery—the miracle which had happened in Israel.

Initially ecstatic, Daniel had now had time to consider the implications of the find, and caution had begun to mute his reaction. A nagging voice deep within him told him to stop and consider the implications.

Daniel walked across the darkened square, away from the Renaissance splendour of Vatican City, towards his home. A tightness constricted his throat as he moved from the well-lit area into the darkness of narrower lanes in the more ancient part of Rome. He looked behind him when he was halfway down one of the laneways. Even now he still had a fear of dark places.

Finally he reached his house and stepped into the illuminated entryway. He tapped gently on his front door. There was no point in bringing out a key because the nuns were always there in advance of his every requirement. Sister Domenica opened the door and bowed low. 'Good evening, eminence.'

'Good evening, sister.'

'Will you be wanting supper, or have you eaten in the Papal Palace?'

'We've been too excited to eat, dear sister,' he said. 'I don't know whether you've heard the news?'

'Yes, we've been listening in joy. Let's pray that they find Our Lord's Testament.'

He ate some linguini with a small bottle of red Chianti, then apple pie with cream. When he had finished, he said, 'Sister, why don't you join me in my private rooms and we'll pray for guidance from the Lord for the recovery of Christ's Testament.'

Sister Domenica beamed a smile. Rarely did he ask her to join him in private worship. She wasn't one of the clever nuns and had accepted her life of service to God's representatives on earth with equanimity. She walked one pace behind him into his study and they stood before the crucifix hanging on the wall.

Daniel turned on the side lights beside the little altar. They knelt and began in prayer. 'Heavenly Father, we thank you for your blessing in revealing to us the reality which makes our faith absolute. We pray that in the coming weeks or months You will make known to us what is Your plan and what we should do to fulfil it. We thank You Lord for this marvellous revelation and we remember with love and reverence those Christian martyrs from the early days who gave their lives to the sanctification of Your holy name. We thank all those early Christians who suffered the torments of the body in order to fulfil Your commandments through Your son, Jesus Christ Our Lord.'

Abram lay back and looked up at the sky, listening to the gentle bleating melodies of his sheep. It was the time of the day he enjoyed best, a time of peace and quiet when he could think about Jesus Christ, the Messiah, and His forthcoming return to earth. He studied the clouds skudding across the broad sweep of the sky, and was able to envisage Christ sitting on one of them, looking down on the earth, and smiling in pleasure at those who had chosen to follow His way.

He closed his eyes and saw the shining face of Jesus.

The silence of the meadow was rent by the urgency of a panic-stricken voice. 'Abram! Abram!' the voice screamed. Shocked at the disturbance, the young shepherd opened his eyes, sat upright, and looked around to see where the shouting was coming from. His friend Reuben was running so quickly towards him that his feet hardly touched the ground. He looked like he was flying over the hillocks and tall tufts of grass. Reaching Abram, the young man threw himself on the ground, clawing the air for breath.

'What in the name of God is going on? What's happened?' asked Abram, alarmed.

Between gasps and pants, Reuben said, 'You've got to come. Now. Come and see.'

'Come where? What's going on? I can't leave my sheep. You know that.'

'You must come now. I need you. It's urgent.'

'Tell me what's happened. Is it bad news? Is it the Romans? What?'

'Just come,' said Reuben, still panting, sweat running down his ruddy cheeks. He got up and began to run back in the direction from which he had come. 'Never mind about your stupid sheep. This is more important than all the sheep in Judea together. We're going to attack the Romans.'

'*What*?' But then he thought beyond the words. 'The revolt?'

Reuben stopped. 'No. You and me. We're going to attack the Romans. You know Bar Kochba won't be ready for months.'

The look on Reuben's face was so innocent, so ingenuous, that Abram burst out laughing. 'Please, Abram. It's vital. And we haven't got any time,' said Reuben.

'I'm not moving until you tell me what's going on.'

'Some boys were taken from my village an hour ago. We have to save them.'

Abram dropped his crook on the ground and began to jog after his friend. The two of them—Abram tall, thin, powerfully muscular but still youthful; Reuben ruddy, shorter, stouter, showing budding confidence and strength—ran quickly over the hill of Abram's valley and down into the valley where Reuben's village nestled beside its stream. They skirted the north of the village, hardly exchanging words until they came to a pass in between the hills where the river joined with other streams and flowed into one of the tributaries of the Jordan. They forded the tributary over smooth rocks which they had placed there last season and climbed up a grassy hill. As they came to the top, Reuben turned to Abram and said quietly, 'Get down.'

Both young men had grown up as vassals to the might of the Roman Empire. Since the time of the cursed King Herod, there had been Romans in the land of Judea and the two young men knew how to negotiate the Judean countryside without being spotted. They reduced their body size by crouching, and crawled the last twenty paces to the crest of the hill.

'There,' said Reuben. In the distance, Abram could see a legionnaire riding imperiously in front of a dozen or so horsemen and a bullock cart. As they moved closer, Abram saw that there were two young boys, hands tied behind their backs, lying terrified on the floor of the cart, surrounded by sacks of provisions.

'See? I told you,' Reuben hissed. 'We have to save them. The word's spread. The Emperor Hadrian is coming to Judea. He'll be here to ensure that Bar Kochba and Rabbi Akiva don't cause trouble. Some chance! They say he's bringing legions from Syria to ensure that we see his army's strength and understand what will happen to us if we attack.'

'Then we're doomed,' said Abram.

'No,' whispered Reuben angrily. 'No matter how many they send against us, we'll defeat them. This is our land, our home. Bar Kochba has raised enough militia to destroy the garrisons in Jerusalem, Caesarea and Joppa. By the time Hadrian arrives, we'll have killed all the Romans. We'll send Hadrian packing in Joppa and Akko or wherever he lands.'

Abram knew Reuben badly underestimated the power of the conquerors. The Roman armies owned the entire world. Hadrian had been emperor now for fourteen years and had strengthened and fortified all of Rome's conquered territories.

'What do you expect us to do here, Reuben? What makes you think we're any match for them?' By now, the troop of men was so close they could hear the creaking of the bullock cart. Reuben whispered, 'Those boys are the sons of one of my mother's cousins.'

'Why did they take them?' asked Abram.

'Don't you know about Hadrian's love of young boys?'

Abram recoiled in horror. Judaism condemned the bestial practice, as did the small secret sect of Christians to which Abram's family belonged. 'But what can we do? March down there and just grab them away from the Romans?'

'No,' said Reuben angrily. 'Follow them. See where they camp. Then at night release them.'

'Don't be stupid. It's certain death. If we're captured, which we almost certainly will be, they'll crucify us!'

Reuben angrily tore a fistful of grass. 'Go back, then. Go back to your mother and father if you won't help me. Go back to your sheep if you're scared of the Romans. I'll do it myself.'

'But it's certain death.'

'It's certain death if we march in with a troop of Zealots behind us and free them. The army would come after us and decimate our villages in reprisal. So we must release them in such a way that the Romans think they've managed to get away themselves and won't seek reprisals. It's the only way.'

Abram breathed deeply and reluctantly agreed. He prayed that his father wouldn't punish him too severely for leaving the sheep unattended.

Four hours later the Romans stopped near the bend of the river. A small fire was made in the middle of the camp. The smell of food soon wafted up, reminding Abram that he hadn't eaten since morning.

Occasionally there was a muffled exchange between the commander and his men. Abram spoke a small amount of Latin but hardly enough to understand what was being said. They waited and watched hungrily as the men ate and then gradually dispersed.

A guard was placed on the perimeter of the camp. An hour later, the rest of the camp was asleep, and the two young men began to crawl down on their stomachs. The fire under the cauldron had already burned low. Thirty paces away, the guard sat, hunched, holding his spear, a cloak over his head. They waited for a while longer and saw his head start to nod. Then he slipped sideways, asleep. It was what they'd prayed for.

Reuben tapped Abram on the shoulder and they started towards the cart. The noise of their crawling over the grassy approaches was covered by the loud snoring of the men. They carefully timed their movements to the rise and fall of the guard's breathing.

Arriving at the cart, Abram prised himself up until he could see inside. The two boys lay like trussed rabbits on the filthy floor, their heads supported by sacks of corn. He indicated to Reuben to put his hand over one boy's mouth while he put his hand over the other's. They roused the boys, who looked at them in shock and incomprehension. Abram carefully untied the ropes binding their hands and feet in order to look as though they had escaped. Then he spent precious minutes rubbing and massaging the boys' limbs to get the circulation back.

Cautiously, with an eye on the guard, they crept away from the camp and walked as quickly as possible to the river so as to mask their footsteps. They waded into the shallow river and followed its path for several leagues. Eventually, they left the river bed and climbed a hill to begin the long journey back into the villages.

Many hours later, the four sat on the ground and felt free to talk. Abram looked at the two boys and felt an overwhelming hatred towards the Romans. They had wanted to defile such perfect works of God. When Christ returned to earth, He would put a stop to all of this. But only Abram knew that. In the meanwhile, it was a secret he must keep to himself, while his friends relied upon their hopes of the coming revolution to keep them going.

'*Where* is Hell?'

The chorus answered in one voice, fifty children indifferently intoning a litany they barely understood, 'Hell is everywhere outside of the sight of God, Dr Wilson.'

The preacher smiled benignly. He nodded. 'Very good, children. I'm proud of you all. Now, how many of you know the answer to this one, and this is a real humdinger, because if you know the answer to this, then sure as God's in His Heaven, you'll know the enemy when he confronts you, and you'll be aware of evil for the rest of your lives. *What* is Hell?'

As before, they answered as a body, a group possessed of collective knowledge, devoid of individual thought, 'Hell is the punishment of those who have rejected the Christ, our True Redeemer.' Jimmy Wilson clapped his hands, and shouted out, 'Wonderful. I love you all. Every single one of you.' The children looked at each other and beamed, basking in the glory.

Jimmy Wilson surveyed the dozens of sunrise faces in the large room, and was content. For years, he had conducted the Earlybird Sunday school service prior to the main ceremonies of the day, despite the pleas of his associates that the extra hour on a Sunday morning placed too great a strain on him.

'Children, I'm shortly goin' to go into the great cathedral yonder, to preach the word of the Lord to your mammies and pappies. But before I go and let you kids free to run riot in the playground, or cause mayhem in the gymnasium'—the children squealed in delight—'I want to tell you the real story of Hell. Now some of you may be shocked, frightened even. But that's okay. That's fine. Because when you're out there playin' in the sunshine, under the eternal and blessed watchful gaze of Almighty God, it's important to remember that beneath your feet there dwell souls who are forever and perpetually tormented, souls writhin' in pain and misery in the blackest pits of the hottest and most violent inferno you can imagine.'

Most of the children sat agape, listening in awe, trying to absorb the dimensions of horror of the place beneath their playground.

'The Devil himself is waitin' out there like a hyena, lookin' for the weak ones among you to pull down into the stinking pit.' He pointed to the playground outside the classroom window. The children looked out, eyes wide. 'Out there right now. Standin' there, with his cold slimy skin, pitchfork and horns, just waitin' for one of you to commit a sin. Waitin' for you, or you, or you to swear or cuss, or do something immoral or deliberately hurt your friends. He's waitin' there to trap you, tryin' to cause you to do wrong.'

The children peered intently out the window, searching for their nemesis. Most wore a look of consternation on their faces. It pleased Jimmy. For when they were concerned, they listened.

'Or maybe the Devil is in this very classroom, standin' invisible by the door, smilin' his sickly smile, lickin' his cold wet lips. Maybe right now, he's gettin' out his computer notebook and typin' your names down, wonderin' which one of you will sin, and be cast into the foul and pestilential pits of burning sulphur and flames forever.'

Dr Wilson stopped, then smiled. 'But children, I'll tell you a secret. I'm goin' to whisper somethin' that the Devil can't hear. Only you can hear it, because you've got God in your hearts, and the Devil is deaf and blind to the word of God.'

The children strained forward to listen. Jimmy Wilson whispered, 'If you say your prayers every night, and read eight passages from the scriptures every mornin' before you go to school, then the Devil won't be able to get his hands on you. That's all you got to do. Simple. Now, get out of here, go on, off you go. And remember, don't tell the Devil what I just told you.'

The children laughed and shouted in relief, then rushed out. Dr Wilson watched them leave. When the room was empty he stood up, and walked pensively back to his apartments, greeting church officials on the way.

Annabelle was waiting for him. 'How was Sunday school?' she asked, pouring him a cup of coffee as he entered their apartment. As she listened to his answer, she tried to judge his mood. She decided that he needed to be left alone. He was feeling introspective. Maybe it was the news from Israel about Christ's Testament. Maybe it was something one of the children had said. She walked back into the kitchen, and piled a dinner plate high with crispy bacon, eggs, and blueberry muffins. She took it out to him. He hadn't even touched his coffee.

She started to feel apprehensive. Jimmy picked up his fork, toyed with his food, and said, 'Honey, forgive me, but I'm not all that hungry this morning. I get the feelin' that today is the first proper day of my ministry. That all the work I've been doin' up till now has been a preparation for what's about to come. I feel like the Prophet Isaiah, Annabelle, a voice that crieth in the wilderness, "Prepare ye the way of the Lord". Annabelle, honey,' he said, standing and kissing her tenderly on the cheek, 'I gotta go and prepare my flock for the coming of the Lord.'

He walked out of the room. She stared at his retreating body, picked up a napkin, and scraped the feeling of his kiss off her cheek.

The Reverend Dr Jimmy Wilson felt good. Damn, but he felt good. He felt strong and powerful. This morning he was imbued with the spirit of Jesus. The son of God was by his side as he sat in a comfortable cushioned leatherette armchair forty-three feet above the stage, hidden from the massive audience by purple satin drapes. The auditorium was already full, bursting at the seams. People milling around aisles, waiting for the action to begin. The big nigger soprano had been doing her handclapping routine for ten minutes and they were all primed up, hot and ready to trot. He looked at the back of the auditorium to see who was late coming in. He noticed a niggerwoman and her kid in the stroller, walking with a marshal down the left-hand aisle. Towards the front of the stage. She was coming to be touched by Jimmy. They all came to be touched. To get the magic of Jesus flowing into their sick and ailing bodies. Praying for Jimmy to restore them, like Jesus cured the lepers and the blind and the sick.

As she walked towards the front of the auditorium, Loretta looked upwards to where the preacherman would be preaching the word of God to the poor souls in the audience. Please God, please Jesus, that He could help her baby, LaVern.

LaVern had been born frail. Downy, wet and dishevelled, she had slipped effortlessly out of Loretta's body. A victim of the modern age, the hollow age, she appeared, not with a cry, but a whimper. The doctor waited until the following day when Loretta was stronger before telling her that LaVern was blind, dumb and that her spasticity would confine her to a bed until the day she died. Because of the dangers of lawsuits and the cost of liability insurance, they cocooned the tot with wires, catheters and monitors and talked to Loretta of the miracles of medicine. They told her of the advancements in their understanding of cerebral processes and the way in which genetic engineering may one day transform her pliant child into a playful kitten. Loretta didn't understand what they were talking about and she didn't believe them. No one had been censorious or judgemental. No one condemned her, or said that the coke she'd been sniffing all the way through her pregnancy had passed through the delicate tissues of her placenta causing strokes in LaVern's developing brain. But Loretta wailed for her sins, holding her tiny baby's useless ear to her lips and whispering prayers, kissing her sightless eye sockets and promising before God that she would atone if only He would make her baby well.

Loretta made good her promise. She went on a detox program, off welfare and got a job selling athletic shoes. One of the customers to whom she sold shoes was a good-looking man called Jonas. Jonas was interested in her. After he bought his kidskin shoes he came back the following day to thank her. He said they were the most comfortable shoes he'd ever worn. Jonas was an assistant preacher in a church. He told her about Jesus and what the Lord could do for LaVern. After she and Jonas spent a few lunchtimes together, she visited the church and straight away admitted Jesus into her heart. Sweet Jesus. Loving Jesus. Jesus her Lord. Jesus was now controlling Loretta's every movement and thought. Everything she did, praise the Lord, was in the name of Jesus himself.

All the shoes she sold, praise the Lord, earned her a commission, part of which she gave back to the Lord and used for LaVern's medical treatment.

Every Sunday morning at 9.30, come rain, or shine, Loretta and baby LaVern were among the faithful in the congregation of the Lord at the Chrome Cathedral in Peppermint Grove, Southern California. She was the staunchest, the most dedicated member of the First Evangeline Church of the Witnesses of the Lord.

From his Pulpit in the Sky, the Reverend Dr Jimmy Wilson checked that everyone was in position. Only when there was complete order, when the marshals had done their job, would he press the button on the arm of his chair and start the choir singing. He looked directly down to the front of the stage and saw that the woman had completed the journey from the vast doors at the back of the hall down to the front.

The marshals closed the doors. What was the tally? 5000? Maybe 5500. At an average $50 a donation, that was a cool quarter of a mill. And there were another four sessions. Though none as big as the 9.30. Come sundown, he could be looking at the better part of half a mill. Money for the service of the Lord of Hosts.

His Pulpit in the Sky was trussed high above the proscenium arch of the stage. The wires holding it were a combination of high-tensile polycarbonate and plastic, designed to be invisible to the audience. When the Heavenly Choir had finished their medley of hymns, Jimmy would be lowered and a cloud of frozen carbon dioxide would rise to meet him. It was a powerful entrance, choreographed by one of those fancy LA types. All cologne and earrings, probably HIV-infested; but the best.

Jimmy Wilson closed his blue eyes and said a silent prayer to the Lord Jesus before making his entrance. He looked at his Rolex. 9.35. He would have words with the chief marshal after the service.

The Heavenly Choir began their hymn. It was a series of 'hums', without organ, guitar or accordion. Jimmy had insisted upon the hums. They reminded him of his favourite marching song—'hum, hum, hum, hum, When Johnnie comes marchin' home again, hurrah, hurrah.' And they allowed the congregation to join in. The organ started, swelling the volume of worship, escorting the words of the Heavenly Choir upwards. The congregation came to attention and the first row of the choir, fat black women, stepped forward looking like inflated sausage balloons in their purple silk robes.

Jimmy scanned the notes of his sermon to refresh his memory. He would deliver the introduction after a full one-minute silence, which he used to concentrate the minds of his flock. He'd read about Adolf Hitler doing it at the Nuremberg rallies. He'd stand there, hands clasped behind his back, rocking on his toes, waiting for inspiration. God! But Adolf had been a powerful speaker.

Jimmy too would start softly, modestly, so that all the congregation would strain to hear. He would whisper, low and slow:

I have seen Lord Jesus this week. With my own eyes, brothers and sisters. He came to me in a vision as I was watching a group of little children play. Black, white, Hispanic. Playing together in a rundown neighbourhood near to Watts; they knew only love, these children. They knew not hatred. Jesus was there.

And as passion and the Good Lord took over from him, the audio-visual people would switch on his lapel microphone and he would leave his pulpit, walk to the front of the stage and, with stentorian resonances, declare the ministry of Jesus. When he felt the congregation was getting passionate, he would go down amongst them and touch them. Show them he loved them. Stroke their cheeks. Hold their hands. Hope that they didn't mob him. Two weeks ago, some niggerwoman had thrown her arms around him. Damn near suffocated him. Took two monitors to pull her off. He wouldn't let that happen again.

Then he would go back to the podium. It was the part he loved the best. He would say the words that he had written himself about the work of the ministry in bringing the Bible and the Word of the Lord Jesus to the non-believers who weren't witnesses—the atheists and the Communist fellow-travellers and the godless ones in Washington. He never allowed anyone else to write that stuff. That was the reason for his success, why his ministry had succeeded when the others had failed. God, but he was good at it. By the time he'd finished, he'd have the audience begging to give him money. But he wouldn't let them. Not yet awhile, anyway!

Then the sick and weak would come unto him. As they struggled towards the stage, he would make a grand gesture and come down to their level yet again. And as he stood among them, he would perform the laying on of hands when the Lord Jesus entered his body and enabled him to be the vessel through which he was able to heal the sick and dispirited, to lift them up and make them whole, give them hope and let them see the shining light of the Lord. Who had been chosen this week? There was the black woman with her dumb kid, an old man with Parkinson's, a kid with leukemia and a dozen others.

Jimmy took skin-tight surgical gloves out from his purple cassock, snapped them on and pulled smooth the wrinkles. He took out the three gold rings, two for the left hand and one for the right, and slipped them over the latex gloves. He took out a comb and carefully manoeuvred the fair hair over his balding crown. The choir was halfway through the second hymn. Jimmy undid the wrapper of a throat sweet and prepared to descend.

The hall was empty. The choir had left to have an early lunch and prepare for the later services. Jimmy and his entourage had retreated back into their private suites and offices. The electricians were checking that the lighting systems were in order for the next service, the audio-visual technicians were adjusting and rebalancing the sound and video systems, teams of cleaners were vacuuming the alleyways, aisles and floors, and janitors were straightening chairs to look like row upon row of grave headstones.

Duane Clarke adjusted his crimson tie, starched white collar and surplice in the antechamber and walked into the body of the hall to check that all the drones employed by the church were busily tidying the hive so that it would be perfect when the next onslaught of parishioners started to line up. He walked up onto the stage where, twenty minutes earlier, Jimmy had roused his congregation to tears in a final crescendo of love and hope and faith. Duane caught sight of himself in the mirror hidden behind Jimmy's lectern. His image pleased him. Young, trim, and getting richer every day. God bless Jimmy. Duane had everything he wanted. It was four years now since Jimmy had picked him up, off his skull with crack and speed and heroin, a bum on the streets of Los Angeles. He was now the fourth most senior person in the church.

He might not have Harlin's legal training, smoothness or wisdom, nor Luke's ease with the media and talent as a fund raiser, and he certainly didn't have Jimmy's way with an audience—the man could make a stone cry warm tears—but he was getting there. His mother was so proud of him. From heroin to heaven in four years.

He smoothed back the soft brown hair falling down his forehead. He must get the ceiling air-conditioning vent turned down above Jimmy's head. It was mussing up Jimmy's hair, as well as dispersing the cloud of frozen carbon dioxide gas too quickly at the beginning of the session. As he walked away from the lectern and descended the stairs, he saw in the fourth row from the back a black woman with a kid in a pram. Damn, what was she still doing here? The hall was supposed to have been cleared by the monitors. He would kick ass for this.

'Scuse me, ma'am, 'fraid you have to leave now. Service is over.' As he walked closer towards her, he saw she was crying. Red eyes. And salty tears streaked the powder on her face. 'Ma'am?'

'I'm going soon, sir,' she mumbled.

'That's fine, ma'am. I'm sorry to hurry you but we've got another service starting and we've got to get things ready. Is everything all right? Are you feeling okay?'

The black woman's eyes were caked with wet mascara. She looked at him as though he was transparent. 'I been touch by the Lord. He touch my LaVern. I praying to God He make my LaVern better. God bless you, sir.'

Duane was suffused with warmth. This was Christian ministry at its best. This was what it was all about. He walked over and sat beside her. He put his hand on hers and grasped her fingers. 'What's your name, honey?'

'Loretta.'

'And LaVern is your baby?'

'My only child. She was born real bad and it was my fault 'cause I'm a sinner.'

'Loretta, we're all sinners in the eyes of the Lord and only through God can we be saved.'

'That's why I come. Reverend Jimmy, he so good. He got the Lord in him. He look at my LaVern and he reach down and he touched her on the forehead.' She moved back the blanket covering her child. 'Right there on the forehead, and he said "Dear God, make this child whole and well again. Imbue her with your loving kindness and your spirit. And if you can't make her well then make the child happy, Lord. You are the resurrection and the life."'

Tears cascaded down her cheeks. 'She may never be whole like proper kids but now I know she happy 'cause the Lord's going to make her happy. I'm just so grateful to Reverend Wilson and I swear I'm going to spend my life atoning for my sins.'

Duane reached over and kissed the black woman on her forehead. 'Amen to that, Loretta.'

'I want it!'

The three men in the spacious air-conditioned office looked at each other. Then at Jimmy. Their expressions were blank. None wanted their faces to reveal their thoughts. They were silent.

'I said, I want it!'

One of the men picked up a glass of Pepsi. 'Jimmy, whether we can get it is another matter. We'd all love it, but finding it ain't gonna to be that easy.'

Jimmy Wilson sat back in his armchair and put his Nubuck leather shoes onto the low coffee table. The three-inch heels and built-up soles made him look like a cripple. The glasses rattled. He put his hands behind the back of his neck. He didn't say a word. Another of the men gathered around the coffee table, emboldened by his colleague's words, said, 'Ain't like it's lying there waiting for someone to go pick it up. Shit, this thing's been hidden two thousand years. Who in hell knows where it is now? If'n it's still around. Jimmy, it could have been lost, destroyed.'

The cabal had been debating the news item backwards and forwards for the past hour. They had another fifteen minutes before Jimmy had to leave. Jimmy was about to explode. His group had exhibited the usual aura of negativity. One hundred reasons why things couldn't be. He restrained his anger. Restraint gave him greater control. These weren't congregants.

'Boys, when I say I want it, I don't mean "I'd like it". I don't mean "Gee, it'd be kind of cute to have it". I mean, I want it!' He pitched forward in his chair and banged the table hard. Bottles, glasses, plates, cutlery, jumped to attention. The paper sprang open and the headline stared at them. 'WHERE IS JESUS' TESTAMENT? HIDDEN IN DUST OF AGES? EXPERTS PREDICT'.

'This, gentlemen,' Jimmy said, thudding the headline, 'is fifty million, one hun'red million, maybe even one billion dollars a year. This is the future for my church. Puttin' together an expedition's going to raise us ten million. If we find the goddamn thing, we'll make five hun'red million out of it in the first year alone. We'll have to fight them away from the doors. This church'll be a "whites only, come and see the Testament and pay a thousand a look" church—the kind of place Jesus him- self would have been proud of. You think Jesus would have brought His divine message to blacks? Christ, he went and sought out the Gentiles. People like us! He said to the Jew boys, "This ain't good enough for you. I'm startin' my own religion. I don't want you Jews, I don't want you blacks or yellows." He brought religion to us. To white folk.'

The older man in the royal blue vicuña suit eyed him coldly. 'Jimmy, can I suggest that you keep that sort of language to yourself. You've got fifteen thousand people coming to see you every Sunday. More than half are black. The rest are Hispanic. Know what I mean?'

Jimmy shook his head. 'I'm sorry, Gerald. Sometimes I get carried away. 'Course we're preachin' His word to everybody, regardless of race and colour.'

The Reverend Dr Jimmy Wilson drank some Pepsi, cleared his throat and said in a less aggressive voice, 'What I'm sayin' to you boys is that this is our chance to strike gold. The jackpot! This is the big opportunity. Luke, I want you to prepare a marketin' approach to this thing. I want us to be the ones to go out there and get it. Draw me up some plans by Thursday so that we can launch the appeal Sunday. Harlin, you write some of your golden words for me to use from the pulpit. Get on to network channels and local TV, and get me prime time. I'm goin' to start an appeal. We're goin' to put together an expedition out of the First Evangeline Church of the Witnesses of the Lord—$5000 to be an expedition sponsor, $50000 a gold sponsor, $100000 a platinum sponsor and $250000 to join the expedition. In return for sponsorship, people can have first access to lookin', or touchin' or doin' somethin' with the Lord's Testament. Maximum of ten people on the expedition. How much does that work out to?' he asked Harlin.

'Let's say you've got fifty sponsors, ten gold and five platinum. That's less than four million dollars,' Harlin answered him.

Jimmy shook his head. 'Not enough. Double the figures. Treble them, if you have to. Now move it.'

The two men left the room, leaving Jimmy alone with Gerald Curtis. When the room was quiet and the doors were closed Gerald looked at Jimmy Wilson.

'James, I thought we had an agreement that you'd keep all that racist shit to yourself. That shit gets out and we're all finished.'

The Reverend Dr Jimmy Wilson threw his head back and laughed. 'Come on, Gerald. The boys are like my sons. They wouldn't say a thing.'

'They're as close to you as their next pay check. If some reporter paid them enough, they'd spill their guts,' Gerald said, massaging the small of his back. His arthritis didn't allow him to sit in any one position for too long. He walked to the window. He felt its reflected heat. It was comfortingly warm, much warmer than the room. Beyond the cool room, beyond the warm window, was the blisteringly hot southern Californian desert.

Jimmy had come to Gerald's bank five years earlier to borrow money for expansion and Gerald had hated him the moment he walked into his office. All bonhomie and backslapping and 'Hey, how you doin'?' But he had a charisma, a magnetism. And Gerald was looking for something to do in his retirement. The seed money Gerald had given him had been repaid a hundred times over. He was a money-making machine—provided Gerald and the other backers could control him.

The idea of mounting an expedition to search for Jesus' last Testament was good, he had to hand it to him. Handled properly, it would raise ten million dollars. 'Jimmy, my fellow directors and I have a lot of confidence in you and where our church will be going. But you can bring it all down around our heads if the niggers and the Jews and the spics ever get to hear you're a racist.'

Jimmy walked back towards his office. Halfway there he met his secretary. 'Dr Wilson, I have CNN on the line.'

Jimmy shrugged. 'Put them on to the press boys.'

'Sir, they want to talk to you particularly.'

He sighed. Everybody wanted to speak to him. He reached his office, picked up the phone and hit the flashing light.

'Dr Wilson, I'm Kay Casubin of CNN. I'm doing a world whip-round of reaction now there's been some time to digest the news out of Jerusalem. I was wondering if you could provide me with some quotes for West Coast news?'

Jimmy had heard it all before. 'Well, Kay, I'd be proud to help you but who else have you spoken to?'

'I've spoken to a number of world authorities on the Bible and early Christian history, Professor Ari Wallenstein, Father de la Tour, Professor Michael Farber.'

'Kay, why are you callin' me? I don't profess to be an expert on archaeology.'

'Correct, Dr Wilson. But I've also got the views of the Orthodox and Catholic Churches and the Jews. I'd like the view of the Pentecostalist movement and you're probably its best known spokesman.'

Jimmy felt puffed up with pride. 'Well, my dear, you can quote me as sayin' that this is the greatest discovery since the birth of Christ and I have some news which you might like to hear. This comin' Sunday, you should send a camera crew to the church because I think you'll have some pretty interestin' footage.'

'Sir?'

'I'm not prepared to say more than that because the news has only just come to hand but I think this will make pretty good copy for you.'

'Are you planning something to do with the Testament, sir?'

Jimmy smiled. 'Kay, you're not goin' to catch me out. I've been around too long for that. You just be there Sunday and I promise you a good story.'

'Exclusive?'

'If you can guarantee me nationwide coverage, then I'll guarantee you exclusive for television media.'

'I'll get back to you.'

'You do that.' Jimmy put the phone down and laughed.

Annabelle Wilson listened to the metallic rasp of her husband's voice, then took the earphones off her head and primped her hair back to revitalise her dyed blonde curls. Annabelle took pleasure in unplugging the jack of the earphones from the wall socket. It felt good to disconnect her husband. She carefully folded the cord around the earmuffs in exactly the way Jimmy left them. Just as carefully she lifted the lid of Jimmy's trunk and replaced the phones in the same position she'd found them. She locked the trunk and replaced the key in the secret inner pocket of Jimmy's black suit, then checked the bedroom to ensure that even the most rigorous inspection by Jimmy or one of his devotees would give no evidence of her spying. Or that she had any knowledge that the study downstairs was bugged.

Annabelle sat at the dressing table in their pink and gold bedroom. She picked up a comb and used its pointed end to finish plumping her curls. It had become a nervous habit, one she couldn't break. Whenever she and Jimmy were together she would spend endless minutes looking at herself and her curls, preening herself, anything but be with Jimmy.

She felt the vibration of the study door closing downstairs. There were muffled sounds of conversation. She braced herself. Jimmy would be coming upstairs to wash his hands and face and change his shirt before the twelve o'clock prayer meeting. She would be expected to attend. He demanded her presence at all of the four prayer meetings on Sundays.

She would sit on the stage looking ornate and beautiful, all pink and gold. She would look lovingly, devotedly, passionately at her husband. Thank the sweet Lord Jesus that the congregation of decent, wonderful, God-fearing Christians could not see into her heart.

The door opened and Jimmy bounded in. His energy knew no limits. Every triumph, every audience, seemed to reinvigorate him.

'Darlin'. You look beautiful,' he said, without looking at her. 'Are you ready for the twelve o'clock? Got less than three-quarters of an hour. I gotta good feelin' about this. I know the Lord is with me. Did you feel His presence this mornin'?'

'I did,' she said, nodding enthusiastically, mechanically.

'First reports say we made close to three hundred thou' this mornin'. That's up on last week. Heavily up. It's 'cause of this amazing news that come out of the Holy Land.'

'Lord be praised,' she said.

'Next week I'm gonna do somethin' about it, Annabelle, honey.'

'What's that Jimmy? What's happenin' next week?'

Jimmy told her about the expedition. Her eyes and face lit up in excitement, wonder and admiration for her husband. It was what he liked. She stood and walked over to him as he foraged through the closet to find a clean shirt. She had forgotten to lay one out on the bed. She hoped he wouldn't be angry.

'Why Jimmy, I think that's the most marvellous idea. I'll look after things here while you're gone. I'll—'

He turned around and smiled. 'Oh no, honey, you're comin' with me. You think Jimmy and Tammie Bakker would've gone separate ways? I want you there.'

'But Jimmy—'

He looked at her and laid his finger to her lips. 'I said I want you there. You know, whenever you get that expression, that hang-dog, little girl lost look, it sends shivers down my spine.'

Her eyes widened in apprehension of what she knew was coming. 'Jimmy,' she said, turning busily and walking to the other end of the bedroom, 'I gotta get ready for the midday service.'

He walked over to her and grabbed her tenderly around the waist. 'C'mon now, sweets, you and me got time for a bit of messin'.'

He turned her around, bent her over and rolled down her panties. She bit her lip until it hurt. It was preferable to the pain she felt as he entered her, the nausea she knew she must endure. She blotted his actions out of her mind. She felt his thighs thump against her buttocks. She felt his hands groping underneath her blouse, straining forwards like hideous caterpillars searching for her breasts. His fingers felt the outside of her brassiere, grasped the fringes of the silky material and pulled it down. As her soft flesh fell out of the cups, it impelled him to greater heights of ecstasy. She felt his warm flesh become clammy, his breath become shorter, his muscles tense as his fingers closed over her plump nipples.

When they closed and squeezed, she cried out in pain. Jimmy burst inside her, yelling until he was hoarse, clasping her breasts as if they were handles, consuming every inch of her privacy, pulling her closer and closer until they were one body, until she was his slave and he dominated her every movement.

Flaccid, spent, rapidly losing his hardness, he withdrew. She stopped biting her lips, musing on her ultimate victory over him. No matter what strength he had, or how much he might command her actions, in the end it was she who won. It must be, or she would lose her mind.

Three hours later, Jimmy lay in his spa bath. They had collected a record amount in donations from his midday service. There were two more services to go, one at 5 p.m. and one at 8 p.m. Then it would be all over for another week. The rest of his week was much easier. There would be the usual TV, radio and personal appearances, but nothing as enervating as preaching to fifteen or twenty thousand people in a day. In half an hour, Jimmy's masseuse would be working on him, so Annabelle was free for two hours.

She got into her car and drove down the long driveway, away from the Chrome Cathedral. As she neared the gates, the building seemed to follow her, its image, dominating the horizon, still clearly visible in her rearview mirror. Wherever she went, it was there, like a conscience. As she drove towards the gates, locked after the last of the midday congregants had driven out of the vast carpark, the gate man, Oscar, smiled, saluted and pressed the electronic eye. The gates slowly opened outwards. He liked Miss Annabelle. She was a real lady. She always waved to him.

Annabelle drove down the main road until she came to the turnoff south to San Diego. She drove on side roads until she reached houses belonging to the millionaire community who relished the proximity of nature, living in their air-conditioned mansions on the fringes of the wilderness. Beyond the verdant gardens and the imported trees, beyond the manicured lawns and the sprinkler systems, was nothing. Mile after mile of dusty, rocky desert. The road became a four lane track with orange groves on either side. She drove inland for another five miles. She checked in her mirror. She slowed the car and looked around. She was alone. As she approached Dumaresque Road she turned left. The road petered out into a dusty track. She stopped the car in a skid of spitting stones and dirt.

Annabelle walked away from her damnable car, away from the thing bought for her by her husband's ministry. She sauntered promiscuously towards the shed, hips rolling, bag slung over her shoulder, feeling like Marilyn Monroe. As she approached the door, the entryway was lit by a shaft of brilliant sunshine. Sitting on a bare wooden chair beside the dusty table was Jonas. He smiled at her. She walked into the shed and smiled back. He stood to greet her: 'Hello, Annabelle.'

'Hello, Jonas,' she said, her voice deep and sensuous.

She walked over and he enclosed her in his arms. She buried her head in his muscular chest, smelt his masculine smell, sweat, strength. She lifted her head and he kissed her tenderly at first, then passionately. They didn't say a word to each other. This was not a time for words, it was a time for love, passion, sex. Gentle sex. Loving sex. Real, proper, honest sex. Jonas was kind to Annabelle. Annabelle loved him. Just as she had loved Abraham before Jonas, and Simon before Abraham. Just so long as they were big and beautiful and gentle and did it to her properly.

CHAPTER 4

In the thirteenth year of the reign of the Emperor Tiberius

The spare, olive-skinned man sat on top of a huge crumbling rock at the very edge of the sandstone cliff. A kestrel, its feathers a sheen of burnished bronze, hovered motionless in the air. It was preparing to swoop down the cliff face to the distant valley floor.

The midday sun shone on the man's bleached brown hair. His leathery skin was tight as parchment over his cheekbones, stretched by the fierceness of the summer sun. It was too late, he reflected, too late to visit Mount Nebo and pay homage at the final resting place of Moses, the lawgiver, the man who knew God. Too late to become one with his brothers. Too late for peace and tranquillity.

His body had become numb to the hard rock. It no longer bothered him. He had been staring into the distance at the misted Mountains of Moab for an age, veiled angelic brides in the vapours which rose above the Sea of Salt. From where he was sitting, he was invisible to his brethren in Ain Fashkha and neither could he be seen from the road snaking around the foot of the sandstone cliffs.

He wore a simple white robe. The colour of the robe defined the man and his mission, its whiteness branding him as an apostate by the priests in Jerusalem. On his blistered feet were sandals made from reeds and bark. Like the other Essenes at Ain Fashkha, he refused to wear the hide of animals.

The man's eyes were fixed on a far-off image, a point beyond the horizon. Even the occasional screaming of ravens failed to distract him. His head became heavy, half buried in the robe's cowl. He lowered his head onto his chest and breathed deeply, each breath lightening his spirit, clearing his mind.

He took up his stylus, but before he could write a noise from below caught his attention. He blinked to clear his eyes of sweat and focused on the road. Through the heat haze, he saw an elderly shepherd and a solitary goat wander into sight. The old man walked with the pain of age and the weight of labour, the goat clopped over the rocks, the bell around its neck tinkling like the bells on the breastplate of the holy Torah, the Law of God given to Moses on Mount Sinai. The man smiled at the ancient scene. For a thousand years, and for a thousand years before that, since the Holy One, blessed be He, created the world, elderly shepherds had wandered these tracks with their herds, searching for scraps of sedge and grasses in the sulphurous heat. The shepherds came from the Wilderness of Judea, beyond En-gedi, and travelled north to the Wadi Kidron or the Wadi Qumran then on further to the Jordan River and the fertile regions of the Sea of Galilee. Always searching for pasture.

The man continued to muse, watching the shepherd absently. Suddenly the noise of metal and straining leather and creaking wood jolted him out of his reverie. It was the noise of angry feet, marching to a forced beat. It grew louder. His fears were confirmed as eighty legionaries emerged into the clearing below him, on the track of the shepherd. He watched as the shepherd turned and scurried off the road to hide himself in a rock crevice. The man above could feel his fear. The goat followed its master, bleating, its bell tinkling to a more frantic rhythm.

The centurion sat erect on his horse, impassive and imposing, a man of authority, leading his troops as they marched along the road. As confident as a conqueror. As vain as an idol. Proudly wearing his badges of office, greaves on his legs, and the head of a lion on an amulet emblazoned on his chest and studded belt.

Sweat poured from their faces, their skin glistened in the brilliant sun, their arms strained under the weight of their heavy oblong wooden shields bonded with iron over stretched leather.

Soon, the old shepherd was spotted. The centurion held up his gloved hand, and the troop came to a halt. The centurion turned in his saddle and said something to his men. The man on the rock was too high to hear; nor did he understand the Roman tongue. He spoke only Aramaic and Koine. Not the language of the conquerors, the legions of the evil emperor, the child defiler, the abomination in the eyes of the Lord.

The legionaries laughed. Three came forward, and put down the satchels they were carrying and braced their pilums. They took off their heavy iron plumed helmets to give them better vision to throw their spears. The man above continued to watch, horrified. The shepherd stumbled on frantically, his back to the Romans.

The soldiers drew their arms back, and three pilums flew through the air, seeking out the old man's back. One, then another, and finally the third hit boulders. Bits of rock spat into the air. The shepherd stopped running and turned to see what the noise was behind him. He saw the spears and let out a cry of fear. The goat bounded away over the rocks, leaving its owner alone to meet his fate. The man above clenched his fists in rage, feeling the agony of human limitations.

The centurion growled angrily at the three spearmen, who retreated, shamed, back into the squad. The centurion barked another command. Three more men stepped out from the ranks. These were archers. They drew bows from their backs, and each leisurely selected an arrow from his quiver. The old shepherd clawed his way over boulders and rocks, trying to reach the sheer rock walls. The man high above stood up from his seat on the rock. Gaunt-eyed, sharing the old man's pain, he viewed the scene far below him with horror. The archers unleashed their arrows, which whistled through the air. Two missed, flying past the old man's retreating body. The third hit him deep in the back and buried itself silently up to its shank. He fell to the ground. The other men in the troop let out a cheer. The archers laughed and slapped each other, each claiming his was the victorious arrow. The centurion ordered the first three to retrieve their spears. When they reassembled, they marshalled themselves into a long thin line and awaited their orders. He lifted his gloved hand and commanded them forward.

They marched out of sight, and the wadi returned to solitude. The only noises were the clopping of the goat's hooves over the rocky ground, the hollow, lonely tinkling of its bell, its bleating and the occasional screaming of birds.

The man on the high rock wiped the sweat from his eyes. He sat again, shaking his head in anguish. Firmly, he gripped the stylus and wrote. He re-read his words to see whether they accorded with his feelings:

I, Jesus, son of Joseph, of the generations of David and Aaron, born of Beit Lehem and who grew to manhood among the Desert People of the Book, have looked with sadness through the eyes of my Father, Yahweh, into the land of the world to come, and I have seen and understood many things.

The pain of the old goatherd lying dead in the wadi had reached up and gripped Jeshua's heart. The callous indifference of the Roman soldiers outraged and saddened him. Every time his mind applied itself to the task of writing his Testament to the End Days, the calm which should have descended was overcome by feelings of anger and hopelessness. But he had finished his Testament to the Afterlife, and now he was left wondering what was the point of writing a Testament when there was so much evil abroad; when clearly the Kingdom of Infamy reigned on earth and men and women of goodness were hounded by the minions of Satan. His brethren were preparing for the fight of good against evil, but their confidence was foolish. To use weapons against the host of Rome would bring untold misery and devastation. No! There was a better way. A new way.

Jeshua wiped the tears from his cheek, and looked up into the sky. A kestrel, fleet and arrow-like, soared and plummeted between the peaks and the valleys, its body made for the gentle currents which floated upwards between the cliffs. It was a joy to behold. It flew lower looking for a place to land, then wheeled in decreasing circles, its wings beating noisily, slapping against each other and against nearby rocks. When its legs touched the rocky ground, it overbalanced and fell on its chest with an indignant squawk. The bird hopped around the rock, looking defiantly at Jeshua.

Jeshua was exhausted from the writing, the thinking. His hand hurt from the difficulty of scratching ink onto vellum. His eyes stung from the dryness in the air, from the dust and the intensity of his day's work. His neck and back ached from the strain of sitting hunched over his knees on a hard rock. He had been pondering infinities, defining feelings, coming to terms with monumental decisions—decisions which would alter his life and the lives of those around him.

He wanted to say prayers over the dead man's body. But to do so would entail an arduous walk down into the valley. And for what? The man was dead. His soul had already flown to Heaven, released from the burden of life under the Romans. In a way, Jeshua envied the old man. Death never affected the mortal body, only those left behind to mourn what was, or what could have been. But what if death held no dominion over life? What if life on earth was merely an interlude of time away from the hosts of Heaven. He recalled the words of the Teacher of Righteousness and the sages who had gone before and wondered when the battle would take place between the Sons of Light and the Sons of Darkness. In the community, they said that only then would the ungodly of the Covenant be forced to flee Jerusalem so that the righteous could cleanse the Temple and establish the new age.

The Teacher said that there would be war for nine years against the Sons of Shem, then for ten years against the Sons of Ham and for another ten years against the Sons of Japheth. He spoke aloud the words of the Teacher:

> O Zion, rejoice greatly!
> Rejoice all you cities of Judah!
> Keep your gates ever open
> that the host of the nations may be brought in!
> Their kings shall serve you
> and all your oppressors shall bow down before you;
> they shall lick the dust of your feet.

Was it right? All his brothers were convinced that there would be a war and that the Righteous would win. But was war the way? With its death and destruction, its blood and anger? Surely not. Look at the Greeks and their once mighty empires. And before them, the omnipotent Persians. They had all gone to war. They had all won their battles. They had all swelled their chests and talked of their empires lasting a thousand years. They had left grieving parents, bereft widows in their wake. And they had all crumbled to dust. As would the Romans. Today they were rulers of the world, but in a hundred years time or a hundred years after that, who would remember the men whose names were carved for eternity on the plinths of their stone statues? Surely not the pathetic old man lying dead amid swarming flies, his flesh already being stripped from his bones by vultures and barking hyenas. Not Jeshua and his brothers. Not the people of Israel. Nor even the Romans themselves. Only the Father in Heaven.

He had heard rumours of what was happening in Jerusalem, in Joppa, in Akko. War would bring a swift resolution to the hideous life that the children of Israel were living. Life under Roman tyranny was a living misery.

But war was not the way. Even a righteous war. His brothers and his teachers were wrong! The way was through love, and peace and understanding, through showing your enemy that you were not his enemy. Through proving to him that he had nothing to fear from you. By turning the cheek if he slapped it, and presenting him with the other. By helping him understand that what he was doing was wrong.

Jeshua of Nazareth looked again at the roll of vellum on which he had written and felt a sudden peace. His Testament to the end days was complete. Whatever happened to him now would not matter. His thoughts would last forever. He would deposit his Testament in the *geniza* along with the Testaments of the other brethren. Then he would tell his friends in the community that he was leaving them. Leaving to travel north into unknown lands. He must leave the rigidity of life in the community in the desert.

They would despise him. They would forbid him. They would excommunicate him. But he had communed with his Father in Heaven and his Father had told him what to do. As his Father had said to Abraham so long ago: 'Be a Father to a Nation,' and as his Father had said to Moses: 'Deliver my people from bondage', so his Father had said to him: 'Take my Word and deliver it unto the strangers.'

Jeshua looked at the kestrel. It eyed him suspiciously, making no noise. He carefully rolled the scroll and tied it with a leather thong. Placing it into his pocket, he bade the bird goodbye and walked down from the rock to regain the path which would lead him back to his community. He turned to see what the bird was doing but it was no longer there. He looked up and saw the black outline of the kestrel wheeling freely, ever upwards. He smiled to himself.

'To soar like the birds, to leave this earth and to rise into the pure welcoming sky. To rise heavenwards. To sit at the right hand of the Father.'

It was the stuff of visions dreamed by the sleeping. Or given to the Prophets. It was what he had written while sitting on the cliff overlooking the Salt Sea.

By late afternoon he was within sight of his community. Ir-hammelah, the City of Salt, had been his home since he was a boy. It was his life, his family, his security. It was his memory. He was a respected member of the community.

He looked with pleasure as he walked down the valley and saw again the comforting stone walls, so secure, so strong. To the left of the buildings was the cave which he and twelve other young men occupied, where they slept and talked and prayed. Closer to the edge of the city as it approached the Salt Sea was the huge scriptorium where he had spent years reading, studying scriptures. The entire city, his city, was devoted to staying alive in order to study the Books of the Ancients, to copy them and distribute them to other communities of Essenes, so that when the End Times came, all would be in readiness.

He and the other members of his community were despised by the teachers and priests of the Temple in Jerusalem. But the Temple was filled with men who had lost their way. Men who were leading the children of Israel along the road to destruction. These men had taken the books of Moses, Isaiah, Daniel, Samuel and the others and had debased them. They had substituted greed for faith. Their thoughts and actions were not dedicated to God through Moses, but to their own need for power and prestige. Grand houses in place of spirituality. Fine clothes instead of prayer. The Law of God corrupted by a few and used against the many.

In his community the Law was the fulcrum of existence. It was studied night and day. When they worked in the fields, when they ate, before going to bed, and when rising, they recited the Law. The community Rule said: 'In the place where ten are, let there not lack a man who studies the Law night and day, continually concerning the duties of each towards the other. And let the congregation watch in common for a third of all the nights of the year to read the Book and study the Law and pray together.'

Before Jeshua trod the remaining few hundred paces into the community he stopped beneath a date palm growing close to one of the irrigation beds. A date was lying on the ground. It had just fallen. He could not eat it. The Law forbade eating fruit that had already dropped. It was corrupted by the earth. He was tempted, for soon he would live by a new set of rules. But while he was still with the community, he would abide by the strictures they imposed. Instead, he picked up the large stick leaning against the tree and hooked its curved end around a clump. Moving it towards him, he picked three or four of the black plump fruits off the bunch. He let go, reciting a blessing, and the branch sprang back. He ate the juicy dates, their sweetness filling his mouth with pleasure, then walked onwards towards the fields where men were growing the roots and tubers for the community's food. Grazing on the littoral grasses were the scraggly herds of goats, sheep and camels.

Jeshua walked past the community dining room with its rough-hewn wooden tables and its hard-packed dirt floor, past the scriptorium with its bronzed inkwells and scrolls of holy books, past the House of the Elders where the righteous ones lived, until he arrived at the *geniza*. Within these walls were held sacred texts, scrolls so precious that they could not be entrusted into the hands of any but the leader of the community. Within the small room were shelf after shelf, row after row, of tightly rolled scrolls, like bricks of clay, building a solid wall of history, the thoughts of the community, the Testaments of the righteous ones. Collections of hundreds of years of the ideas and philosophies of brethren and members. Jeshua would now deposit his scroll with the rest, another brick.

Each community member was given one day of his life which was free from work and prayer in which he took himself into the desert. Among the solitude and purity of the rocks, he wrote his thoughts to the afterlife.

It was a time of exposition. A time of completion. A time in which the mind of the brother rose towards the dominion of God. These were among the most sacred of scrolls and to be entrusted to none other than the repositorian. They were identified only by the name on the outside of the scroll. They were sealed with the great seal of the community.

Jeshua entered the *geniza*. The elder in custody, Nahum bar Noah, was seated behind his desk, barely visible in the dark light of the room. A shaft of brilliant sunlight filtered through the window, illuminating a table on which a hundred scrolls were haphazardly cast. It looked like disorder, yet Nahum knew the purpose of every scroll, and each had its place. Jeshua's eyes adjusted to the half-light.

'Blessed are you, Jeshua, who is numbered among the righteous of the brotherhood to have communed with the Holy One, blessed be He, and to have opened your heart for everlasting peace.'

Jeshua nodded.

'And are these your own thoughts, or are they the thoughts of others?'

'They're the thoughts of my Father. And they are my poor interpretation of what He willed of me.'

Nahum nodded, like one of the sages of old, like Abraham, Isaac or Jacob. 'And do these thoughts accord with the *Rule of the Community*, with what you have been taught, and what you have professed to believe?'

'Nahum, my Testament is between myself and my Father. As God peers into my soul He sees the pure heart of one who has written words in which he believes.'

Nahum looked thoughtfully at the young man. He had known Jeshua since he had come to the community as a boy. Something had changed him in the desert. It often happened.

'Nahum, tomorrow I will see the Teacher of Righteousness.' The librarian said nothing. Jeshua continued: 'I intend to leave our community.'

'Leave? Where will you go?' said Nahum, taken aback.

For Nahum and for the two hundred other members of the community, this was the world. Outside was hostility, bitterness, envy, greed, impurity. To set foot outside the boundary of the community, to leave the confines of the pure desert, was to invite destruction. If one left, one would be tainted with the pestilence of the outside world. Was it not written in the War Rule that the Righteous Ones, the exiles in the desert, shall battle against the sons of Levi, Judah, and Benjamin? Did it not talk of the unleashing of the attack of the Sons of Light against the company of the Sons of Darkness, the Army of Satan? Against the band of Edom, Moab, the Sons of Ammon and against the army of the Sons of the East, and the Philistines? And their allies, the ungodly of the Covenant? How could Jeshua contemplate leaving the safety and purity of the Righteous Ones?

'But you invite death!' whispered Nahum.

'Not if I take the word of my Father and tell those outside what it is in which we believe. Not if I open the minds of those who dwell throughout Israel to the words of the Teacher of Righteousness. Not if I go up to Jerusalem, and purify my Father's holy Temple, so that it is again in the hands of the righteous.'

'Are you mad?' the old man gasped. 'Has Satan invaded your mind? You cannot take our Law, our Rules and talk to those outside. They are impure. You and our Law will be defiled,' he said, fidgeting with an inkwell in his distress.

'Nahum, old friend, you have been my teacher for most of my life, but the mantle has passed to me. In the desert there is no life. It is a barren wilderness. The light which we have created in our corner of darkness can ignite those in Jerusalem, in Beit Lehem, in Gaza, in Tyre, and throughout the world.' He gazed distantly through the window. 'Even to Rome itself. Understand me. My Father has told me to leave this holy congregation and to take its thoughts to the outside. I intend to do as my Father demands.'

There was silence. Nahum picked up Jeshua's Testament and handed it back. 'There is no room for this in the library of the pure.'

Jeshua refused to accept it. 'Nahum, these are the words of my Father. To refuse them is to refuse Him.' There was a quality in Jeshua's eyes, in his bearing, that had not been there when he had left the community this morning, to walk alone into the desert. 'Take them and keep them safe for me. For one day I will return and lead a host, a multitude into the wilderness and they will read my words. I leave the community with no possessions. All I need to sustain me is already in my mind. Do not betray me, Nahum. Be faithful to me.'

Jeshua turned and left the old man sitting behind the desk holding the Testament.

When he had disappeared from the room, Nahum could still feel Jeshua's presence. He placed the scroll in front of him and looked at the other scrolls around the room. They were the writings of the great ones of the past. Dear God Almighty in Heaven, he thought. What should he do? Should he reject the Testament? Should he raise the matter at the next meeting of the elders? He sighed deeply, feeling the unaccustomed weight of responsibility on his shoulders. Then he did something that was normally only done once a Testament had been in the repository for fifty years. He sealed Jeshua's Testament with a leather thong, and pressed the ends of the thong into the mouth of a small disk of lead, imprinting on the lid the great seal of the community. He put it in a jar and, with his metal stylus, scratched Jeshua's name on the outside. He stood and placed it amongst the other jars which would, this year or next, be taken down to the caves. He thought silent thoughts of anger and incomprehension and returned to his desk. He spent another hour writing and thinking then he stood and repositioned the jar containing Jeshua's scroll on another shelf, one which it shared with the sacred writings of the ancients.

Abram prayed fervently, silently to Jesus as he felt the heavy feet marching ever closer. Reverberations through the downtrodden earth of the floor, compacted by generations of worshippers, where a colourful and delicate mosaic had once graced the building.

The fifty men sat in a fear-induced silence. They crouched lower, making themselves less visible. No one looked through the windows. No one spoke. People hardly breathed. The fear grew within the room. Lips moved silently, mumbling homilies and silent prayers. Children were gathered firmly to quell the sounds of their fear.

The feet kept marching. It was a long column. More than a hundred. Perhaps even a thousand. The vibrations told the story. Slowly, after an eternity of waiting, the tramping diminished. The vibrations lessened. Bodies unfurled. The restrictions on the children became less oppressive. People looked at each other and nodded. There was even a smile or two.

But there was a residual danger. Other communities had been lulled into security and suffered the anger of the Roman conquerors. They would not make the same mistake. As if to give authority to everyone's thoughts, the rabbi looked up from the front of the building and theatrically tapped his finger against his lips.

Five minutes they waited. And another five just to make certain.

Finally Rabbi Johanan leaned over and whispered something to a boy. Gingerly, the boy got up, walked carefully over to a window, picking his way through the congregation, and looked out over the sill. The congregation watched the boy's reaction avidly. When he turned around to smile at the rabbi, a feeling of relief swept through the men.

The rabbi, sensitive to the needs of his community, said a few prayers to thank God for delivering them from evil, and ushered his flock, a few at a time, away from the devastated remains of the synagogue. All that was left were four walls, and the ribs of a roof. And where once the magnificent sandalwood ark had stood, there was little more than a niche in the wall pointing towards Jerusalem where the scroll of the Five Books of Moses could be rested.

The congregants of the synagogue disappeared into the day, scattering over the countryside back to their homes. However strong and mighty the Romans, they were no match for the local knowledge of the Judean hills possessed by these men.

Raphael ben Eliezer and his son Abram ben Raphael assisted each other over the rocky ground. Their synagogue had been razed to the ground by the Romans. Within an hour of the Romans' arrival on some pretext, the village had been decimated and the synagogue destroyed. Ten men were killed, speared while strapped to stakes like carcasses of meat, their wives and children forced to look on, eyelids held open by Roman guards.

The villagers had rebuilt their homes but were forced to travel in danger and in secret across to the valley of the River Jordan, then down as far as Beit Hanun before reaching another synagogue. And even this one, the last remaining in the area where there was still a practising congregation, was little more than a ruin. They knew they were breaking a law to travel on the Sabbath, but the local rabbi gave them his permission, terrified that the religion would die under the Roman yoke if Jews were stopped from assembling.

The man and his son rested when they reached the top of the hill. Now they had said their *Shabbat* prayers, they could eat the bread, meat, corn, olives, oil, and wine that Sarah had packed for them. Raphael tore a hunk of lamb for his son. They ate hungrily. The boy seemed pensive. He was normally garrulous. In his eighteen years, he had grown into a fine lad, one of whom his father was proud. He was the eldest of six, his firstborn.

'Abram. You were praying very hard in synagogue today.'

Abram chewed the lamb and nodded. Despite his size, he was still growing. In the past year, he had grown a head taller than his father.

'Are you drifting away from the Nazarene?' asked Raphael.

The boy stopped chewing and shook his head vigorously. 'How can you say such a thing, Father?'

'If you are, then you must speak with a disciple of Jeshua. He died for our everlasting souls. He is the way and the light.'

Abram took a draught of wine to help swallow what was in his mouth. 'Father, my faith is in God and His Son Jeshua. How can you doubt that?'

'The way you were praying. It was like you used to pray before we became Nazarenes.'

Abram was silent for a while, contemplating. 'Why do we still attend the synagogue? If we're no longer children of Abraham and disciples of Moses, why keep up the pretence?'

Raphael smacked his son playfully across the back of

the head. 'Idiot! How many times do I have to tell you? The Sanhedrin in Jabneh has banned—'

'I know that, Father, but why must we go to synagogue? Why pretend to be something we're not?'

His father delayed a while before answering, 'At times, Abram, there's more danger from our neighbours than from our enemies. If our village believed that we had become Nazarenes, we would be cursed and expelled. Then where would we go?'

'To the community of Nazarenes,' said his son, his eyes brightening. 'There's talk that a leader will be visiting Jerusalem soon. He's coming from Smyrna to convert the Jews.'

Raphael burst out laughing. 'He has as much chance of doing that as a man from our village becoming rich. They're set in their ways, those Jerusalemites. And what about the Romans? What chance that they'll allow a Nazarene into the city? Especially now that there's talk of it being rebuilt.'

Abram wanted to continue talking, but Raphael stood. Staying in one place too long could leave them open to a surprise attack. The two continued walking into the hills towards their village.

They moved quickly in a half crouch. They went nowhere near the crests of ridges or the tops of the hills. They knew they would be endangered if their silhouettes were spotted against the bright sky.

As the air began to cool in the late afternoon, the father and son rounded an arête and saw their village. They descended the hill, crossed the stream, and climbed up to their house.

Raphael felt a sense of foreboding. He opened the door and his wife Sarah greeted him. Normally open and hearty, today she was surly, wearing a frown. Sitting in the corner of the room was an elderly man. Even in the dim half-light of the small chamber, Raphael could see that he wore the torn garb of a traveller. He looked as though he had hardly eaten in days. His eyes were haunted by fatigue, his hair and beard matted with grasses from where he had last slept, his cheeks emaciated from lack of food.

Sarah whispered, 'He's been here since you left early this morning. He won't say who he is, or what he wants. All he does is eat and sleep.'

The old man stood to greet the father and son. He was sunbeaten and travelworn, his sparse white hair long and unkempt, his few remaining teeth stained and yellow.

'Raphael ben Eliezar. In the name of Jesus of Nazareth, Son of God, greetings.'

Raphael reacted in shock. The name of the Messiah was never spoken out loud in his house.

'Who are you?' he whispered.

'John of Syracuse. Disciple of Our Lord Jesus. Carrier of the Good Name.'

Within the burgeoning hierarchy of the Nazarene Church, he was one of the most important figures! According to recent travellers who had met secretly with devotees, John of Syracuse had recently been appointed apostle and elder.

Raphael fell to his knees and grasped John's hand. Abram, too, knelt. Only Sarah remained standing, her scepticism overwhelming the atmosphere in the room.

'Master, in the name of the Christ, greetings. What can I do for you?' asked Raphael.

John looked at the woman and the younger people in the room. Raphael's other children were attending to the animals or resting on the *Shabbat*.

'May I speak in front of your family?'

'My family follows the Anointed One.'

The old man nodded. 'Good,' he said, and resumed his seat.

'Raphael ben Eliezar, I have come to you to request of your son a mission. It is a mission which I cannot carry out myself. The danger of my discovery is too great. The distances are too far for me to travel. We need a young man, a fervent man, a man of strength, both of body and spirit. A man of faith.'

Raphael frowned. Sarah bit her lip. Abram listened attentively.

'One hundred years ago, when Our Lord Jesus was preaching His blessed ministry, He wrote a Testament which he left with the desert people for safekeeping.'

'The desert people?' Abram interrupted.

Raphael turned and explained. 'At the time when the Romans destroyed Herod's holy Temple, there was a people called the Essenes who lived in communities in the desert.'

'Our Lord was once a member,' John interrupted.

'What?' replied Raphael, stunned.

'Oh yes!' said the old man. 'Jesus of Nazareth lived for many years with the Essenes. He left their community to preach His ministry in Galilee. The Essenes were a rigid group, incapable of bending to the needs of their people, Israel, who were crying out for new ways, the ways of the Messiah. Just as the Jews in this village, and in the towns and cities beyond, are unwilling even today to tread the path of Our Lord and accept His Word.'

The father, son and mother all remained silent.

'What is this dangerous mission you want my son to perform?' Sarah asked.

John of Syracuse was shocked that she had spoken without the permission of her husband. It was years since he had last been in Judea. He had forgotten that women of the Hebrew nation were different from women of other nations. The Jews revered their great women. Women like Rebecca, Leah, Deborah, Ruth, and this woman's namesake, Sarah. His own people, the Greeks, enjoyed women, but allowed them to play no part in governance.

'It is a mission to retrieve the Testament of Our Lord Jesus, and to take it to a safer place. A place recommended by Timothy of Brindisi, whose father, Nicodemus of Alexandria, was the son of one of the desert people. Before he died, Nicodemus told Timothy of a secret repository of sacred objects from the Temple of King Solomon.'

'Solomon! In the blessed age of the Kings of Israel.' Raphael was impressed. 'When King David ruled with a mighty hand and an outstretched arm.'

The old man had spoken to many Jews in his long life, and still found difficulty with their way of introducing liturgy into everyday speech.

'It appears that the legendary Queen Sheba and King Solomon created a race called the Agau. Their home is close to the Kingdom of Nubia where Meroe is the capital. A six-day trek inland from a city called Asmera, which is on the coast of the Sea of Reeds.' He looked at the terrified faces of Raphael and his wife. For there was worse news to come. 'But where precisely he will go will be known only to the boy. God forbid that our mission becomes known to the Romans and a body of men is sent to capture the word of Our Lord. I will whisper the location of the people of the Agau into the boy's ear.'

'Then we will not know where our son is going,' said Sarah in panic.

'Woman, were I able, I would go myself. But the Romans know me. If they arrest and crucify me here, my death will be of no importance. My soul will fly to join my Messiah's. But were I to be carrying treasures, my Lord's Testament and the other sacred relics of Solomon's Temple, it would be a grievous loss to Christians everywhere. That is why an unknown boy must find the secret place where the Testament is buried, retrieve it, and take it to a safe place.'

'Are you mad?' said Sarah, shaking her head vigorously. 'Do you know the danger of travelling in Judea? The Romans stop and search everyone. If you're more than a dozen leagues from your village, they arrest you, flay you and take you to Caesarea for questioning and crucifixion.'

'Woman, understand,' said Raphael, trying to quieten his wife, 'this is the work of the Lord.'

'And you understand, husband, that my son is precious to me,' she said angrily.

'Just like the Son of God was precious to Him, Sarah,' John of Syracuse reminded her. 'Yet He bequeathed His only Son to us to be crucified for our sins.'

Her husband said 'Amen'. Sarah remained quiet. She had not the burning faith of Raphael. She had accepted his conversion to the creed of the Nazarenes since he had come under the spell of the travelling preacher eight years before. And she'd accepted her children being raised as Nazarenes. But she found it difficult to overthrow the heritage of the rabbis that she had learned from her mother. And she was not willing to see her son's precious life wasted for the glory of a long-dead Messiah.

There was a strained silence. Sarah turned towards John, and told him, 'Sir, you are not a Jew. You are a Greek. We Jews live through our children. My son Abram is called ben Raphael after his father. Raphael is called ben Eliezar after his father before him. Through our children we continue to live in the afterworld when we have died. To sacrifice one of our children needlessly is a crime against God.'

'Woman, you are no longer only a Jew. You are also a Nazarene. You have been baptised and have accepted Christ into your heart. You have made a commitment to the teachings of Jesus. Do you seek to abandon Him now when He needs you?'

'But why take the precious objects if they are safe in a cave? They have rested there for a hundred years, why take them now, when Roman legions patrol every road and stop every traveller? Leave them and let my children's children remove them when the Romans have left our soil,' she said, fighting to keep the emotion and fear out of her voice.

John supported himself on his wooden staff and shuffled forward. He craved sleep but until he had agreement he could not rest.

'Sarah, every day Our Lord's Testament remains in Judea, the danger grows of its discovery. The Emperor Hadrian plans to rebuild the city. There will be architects, stone-cutters, masons, carpenters. They will search for sources of material and make quarries in the desert. For years Judea has been held down by the Roman boot. While the soldiers were keeping control, the danger of Our Lord's Testament being discovered were slight. But now Hadrian is planning this building he will undoubtedly uncover hidden treasures beneath Jerusalem. Treasures like the Ark of the Covenant of the blessed Moses. Then he will ravage all Judea for more. It will not take him long to search the Essene monasteries and caves for treasure. Either he, or a rogue soldier and fortune-hunter. And what will they care for a scroll of leather, hidden in a clay jar? The Testament must be removed to a safer place.'

'But it's not gold, it's only a document,' said Sarah.

Raphael looked at his wife in anger, then turned to John, 'Master, what is it you wish of my son?'

John turned to Raphael. 'He is to travel from here to the land of the desert. In your tongue it is the Negev. There he is to journey beside the Salt Sea until he reaches the ruins of a city called Ir-hammelah, at Qumran. He must travel beyond Qumran until he reaches an oasis in the desert called En-gedi. And beyond that place to the Winter Palace of your King Herod, a place called by the Jews, Masada. In the hills south of the fortress he will see caves. I will explain to him exactly where the cave is as it was told to me by Timothy of Brindisi.

'In this cave he will find many jars containing scrolls. One contains the Testament of Our Lord as well as other sacred scrolls once used by the priests of the Temple. He will take them all from the cave south to the port of Eilath. From there, only the boy and I will know. Have faith in the Lord.'

'He will surely die,' Sarah said, beginning to sob. 'I will never see him again.'

Raphael comforted her then said to John, 'Master, what you ask is for our boy to undertake a treacherous journey, but the holy martyrs sit in eternity on the right hand of God. For this, I know that I must risk sacrificing my oldest son. But why do we also save the sacred writings of the old Temple? What is this to us? These scrolls are of the Jews. Not of the Nazarenes.'

John nodded. 'It is on the advice of Timothy of Brindisi. Timothy says that to know where one is going, one must also know whence one has come. Although Jesus Our Lord is the New Way, Timothy says that our converts will be from the Old Way. Your own family, before your baptism, followed the Old Way. In synagogue, you still read and venerate the Testament of

Moses. Those Jews who see the light and come across to us will find comfort in the ancient books of the Temple.'

John of Syracuse could see a look of doubt on Raphael ben Eliezar's face. 'But there is also another reason. Tell me, brother, why is it you think we are called Nazarenes?'

Raphael answered simply. 'After Nazareth, the village where Our Lord lived.'

The old man smiled. 'So said my brother Saul of Tarsus, the one known as Paul, of blessed memory. But why not Beit Lehemites, after the place where Our Lord was born? Or Essenes, where Our Lord grew to manhood? Or latter-day Jerusalemites, where Our Lord was crucified? Truth is different from the story invented to protect the followers of the faith.'

Raphael frowned, as did Sarah and Abram. The old man continued. 'For we are also known in your tongue, the tongue of the Hebrews, as the *Nozrei Habb'rit*, or keepers of the Covenant. The Covenant referred to is that of the Ossim, or Essenes as they are now called. The *Nozrei Habb'rit* were known as the *Nozreem*, or "keepers". The Covenant we kept was the Covenant of the Essenes, of which Our Lord Jesus was a follower, until He left the desert community, and wandered throughout the land of the Jews, converting them to the true way. But it was dangerous for us to be known as the *Nozreem*, for the Pharisees, the doctors of the Jewish law, sought our destruction. So we became the Nazarenes.'

Raphael smiled. 'I have often wondered why the Son of God should have lived in the small and inconsequential village of Nazareth.'

'Lord, all of this danger points to the death of my son if he goes on this mission,' said Sarah, ignoring him. 'Let Raphael go. He is used to the ways of the Romans. He has travelled further than Abram. He is more experienced. What if wild animals attack him at night, or Jews from an unfriendly village report him to the Romans?' She started to whimper.

For the first time, Abram spoke. 'Mother, I swear this to you by the sacred name of my Messiah, Jesus of Nazareth. I will undertake this mission and I will return.'

Sarah looked at her son and shook her head. 'Would that it was so. Abram. I will pray to the God of the Jews *Adonai* and to the God of the Christians, Jesus. Between them, they may save you, for you are beyond my help when you leave this home.'

'*Why* won't you tell me where you're going?'

Abram looked at his lifelong friend and for the fifth time shook his head. 'I just can't, Reuben. Please, let's just embrace, say goodbye and pray for each other.'

'You're going to join Bar Kochba, aren't you? You're going to the rebellion. Let me join you. Let me go with you. Please.'

'I'm not going to Bar Kochba. I'm leaving Judea. I'm going far away. You must believe me and you mustn't tell anybody. On your honour.'

'Not even my parents?'

'Not even your parents.'

'When will you be back?'

'I don't know.' A silence descended between the two young men. They had played together as children, stolen bread together from the bakers of Caesarea. And recently they had risked death together in saving the lives of two young boys. They had shared every thought and emotion and now there was a void between them. 'Reuben, if I tell you something, do you swear to me on the books of Moses that you will tell no one. No one at all. If you do, it will endanger my family. And our village.' Reuben looked at the young man questioningly. He nodded. 'Five years ago a man came to our village. He was old and starving. My parents took him in, comforted him. In the time that he stayed with us he told us that he was a follower of Jesus of Nazareth.'

'What? You comforted a Nazarene. But they're—'

Abram held up his hand for silence. 'He told us so many things. We listened carefully. We understood how to end the pain and suffering and my parents and I were baptised by him. Reuben, my mother, father and I are Nazarenes.'

Reuben shrank back as though his friend had told him he was suffering from leprosy. His mouth opened to say something but he could think of nothing to say.

'Pray for us,' said Abram. 'When you understand more about Jesus of Nazareth, and the hope that he gives to the poor people, the downtrodden of this earth, you will understand.'

'You are a Christian! My best friend. You tricked me. You never told me. How could you? They're monstrous. The Christians have pagan rites. They eat babies. They've turned away from *Adonai*. They drink the blood of people they sacrifice. They—'

'No we don't,' shouted Abram. 'We are a faith of gentleness and hope and redemption.'

'I thought you were a Jew. I thought you and I were followers of the Law of Moses. You've turned your back on your people. You're worse than the Romans. You're—' Reuben was lost for words. He stood up, spat on the ground and shouted, 'I hope you die, I never want to see you again,' and started to run away.

Abram cursed himself for having told him. He had believed that he could trust him. 'You swore to keep it a secret,' he shouted.

Reuben stopped in his tracks and turned around, his face full of hatred. 'I will keep it a secret, for my word means much to me. But I hope you are crucified by the Romans. I hope you're caught in one of your hideous rites and the rabbis have you condemned to death by stoning. I hope you fall through a hole in the earth and you're swallowed by darkness and cold forever. I hope you die.'

He turned and ran into the gathering dusk, leaving Abram alone. How little people understood. How easy it was to persecute. But one day, there would be love and harmony in the world and on that day he and Reuben would again walk the hills of Judea as brothers.

CHAPTER 5

In the days following the International Team's announcement of the list, the coverage of the story in the world's media had inevitably changed. Still front-page news, and near the top of most electronic bulletins, speculation now concentrated on its possible effects, and what Jesus might have said in His Testament.

Hypotheses about the Testament's content fell into two general schools of thought—those which followed the Gospel line of Christian orthodoxy, and those which were eschatological, imagining Jesus as a divine prophet seeing into the future, and warning humans of the consequences of their immorality.

Leader writers extolled the unearthing of the Testament as a precursor to the end of the second thousand Christian years, implying a mystical significance far beyond the list's status as an historical document. The popular papers indulged in postulation of what the discovery could do for humankind, collecting together one-liners from pop-singers, actors, television presenters and politicians. The serious media indulged in similar speculation, though at greater length, and with more esoteric experts.

Eirenic churchmen took up the media message, carrying sermons of love and peace into their pulpits. Fundamentalist preachers warned their congregants that the long-predicted Parousia—the Second Coming—was about to take place, a result of the rape and devastation of the planet, the bestiality of the wars fought during most of the twentieth century, and the growth and acceptance of wickedness as a consequence of individual freedom. Even in countries where Christianity wasn't the predominant religion, the story was carried with all the pomp normally afforded geopolitics. And the fact that it was such major news was a news item in itself. Half the media self-righteously criticised the other half for their sensationalism and the amount of space, large or modest, devoted to the story. It replaced the Royal Family in women's sections as the *cause célèbre*. Jesus attained the popular media status of a cult figure.

Speculation paraded as fact. People whose entire lives had been spent in the refined, contemplative interpretation of biblical passages, or in the unhurried fields of archaeology and ancient, long-forgotten languages, were targets for microphone-toting journalists shooting from the lip. It was a worldwide circus in which the reluctant Christians were ensnared by the lions of the media.

Michael Farber opened his eyes after a long and restful night's sleep and saw the *Jerusalem Post* protruding under his hotel room door. He carried it back to bed. Reading through the paper, he came to a large photograph of his friend Ari accompanying an article entitled 'THE CHRISTIAN DILEMMA'. Michael glanced through the introduction, quickly realising it was aimed a general audience, then read on:

... I am caught on the horns of a dilemma. The archaeologist and the biblical scholar in me is ecstatic at the discovery of the list from the Dead Sea Scrolls. That one of the most precious documents of all time may soon be within our reach is a source of great happiness. For a billion people, this Testament is concrete expression of the very word of God.

But then I am also a pragmatist. And though thrilled that a document so precious, so magical even, has been shown to exist, I fear that future circumstances may cause its revelation to prove less than magical.

The discovery that Jeshua of Nazareth, who became Jesus the Messiah/Christ, has left a written document may ultimately turn out to be a matter of the deepest regret for devout Christians throughout the world.

There are dramatic and fundamental differences between the world's three great monotheistic religions, Judaism, Christianity and Islam.

Jews believe that everything has been revealed by God alone through his servants Abraham, Isaac, Jacob and Moses. The Kings, the Prophets, the Judges and their inheritors, the rabbis, to this day have been interpreting the will of God. We believe in one eternal being.

Islam believes in God and the Jewish Prophets and the Christian Jesus but believes that the greatest of its own Prophets, Muhammad, was a man whom God took up to heaven.

Only Christians believe that God sacrificed His Son and that His Son was born a divine being of a virgin mother.

Jews and Muslims are happy in a one-to-one relationship with God. Christians, however, believe in the divine spirituality of their Messiah. The strength, the being, the essence of Christianity is in the divinity of Jesus. Make Jesus into flesh and blood and you risk undermining the faith of a billion souls.

When the Dead Sea Scrolls were discovered in 1947, Jews hailed it as one of the most invaluable finds in our history. It made our past a part of our present. We pored over the words, argued about their meaning, debated their importance. But never once were we unsettled by the thought that the Dead Sea Scrolls could confound Judaism. Add? Enhance? Embellish? Embolden? Yes! All of these. But not detract. The Dead Sea Scrolls were the embodiment of the way our ancestors perceived our religion. Since their day we have changed it by the malleability of our dynamism.

Now let's examine Christianity for a moment. In the space of two thousand years, Christianity has only been put through three fundamental challenges which have affected its future. The first was the Great Schism between the eastern church and the western church. The second was the Protestant Reformation. And the third has been the more recent growing mood of fatalism which has infected the world, creating a feeling that religion is an irrelevance, and nothing, not prayer, not penitence, can change the shape of the future. In this, Christianity joins with Judaism. Only the eschatological, fundamentalist churches have been able to transcend this mood of fatalism.

I believe the discovery that Jesus the Messiah has written a Testament could present the fourth great challenge to the Christian church. A challenge from which it may not be able to recover.

We only know what Christ said and did through his Gospellers and witnesses and the hideous sufferings of the early followers in the circuses and catacombs of Rome. History offers us nothing of the living Jesus. A meagre reference in the annals of Tacitus, written in AD 110; or Pliny the Younger in his letter to Trajan in AD 111; or the historian Suetonius in his letter to Claudius in AD 100 hardly count. Neither can we look towards the Jewish historian in the court of Domitian, Flavius Josephus, who only incidentally remarks about Jesus when talking of the stoning of His brother James in AD 62. Even the pathetic cave art in the catacombs beneath Rome, drawn in desperation by the tortured Christians from the first and second centuries, are a record of faith, not of fact.

And that's it! Not one word proclaims the concrete historical reality of Jesus of Nazareth; all is faith. In the two thousand years since the beginning of the new era, the Christian community has based its belief solely on the strength of this very faith. Christ has been painted by the geniuses of the Renaissance and etched into our minds by the saints and martyrs, but nowhere on earth has there been evidence that is of Christ, or is from Christ. The fragments of blood, bones or the wood from the Cross, pedalled for millennia by charlatans, have long been dismissed as profane trickery on the gullible. Not that I am saying this latest find is a trick, but its effects could be as devastating as finding that a precious reliquary holding some supposedly divine item is nothing more than a sham.

Christians believe implicitly in the accuracy of the interpretations of the Gospels. But if we discover His Testament and it proves them wrong, if it denies the Gospels' claims to His status as Messiah, then where will Christianity be?

Lawyers never ask a question of a witness unless they first know the answer. This may seem to contradict the scholarly approach towards research but in this unique case I think that many more questions need to be asked before the search is undertaken for the answer.

To date, Christ's Testament has not been discovered. My fear is that, one day, it will.

Michael put down the paper and stared at the alien rooftops of the Old City of Jerusalem, capital of the dominance of Judaism over the land of Israel, and still a dominant feature of his life. He was as angry with Ari as he was with the rebellious members of his department. They had abused the trust he had placed in them. Now Ari was doing the same. It was a betrayal, as though his old friend had stripped away his joy and hope for the future. In the cafe, Ari had been cautious about the discovery. He had tempered Michael's rapture by hard-headed rabbinic wisdom, the very wisdom that Michael had denied because of its rigorous dialectic, its incapacity to break away from a set of laws, rather than being part of a rhapsodic way of life. Michael stared at the ceiling and cursed the damned rabbis with their codes of law and their complications. Men who knew the Bible but had little understanding of human needs. Men who had wrapped God in an intellectual cocoon, paying lip service to the hunger of humanity for help in its shortcomings. Rabbis were interpreters, intermediaries between God's Law and humankind. Christian priests, by their training and inclination, were shepherds, whose life's work was to look after the needs and wants of their flocks. It was partly the pastoral shortcomings of rabbinic life which had turned Michael away from his religion and made him seek comforts in another creed.

Why was Ari being so regressive, so reactionary? Why did he think that the entire foundations of Christianity would fall to pieces because Christ's word was revealed? Not through His witnesses, the Apostles, but through His own mouth. And why did he assume that Christ would have written anything other than a message of hope and inspiration that could lead mankind into a new era of peace, harmony and understanding?

He gazed at the cupolas of the Old City of Jerusalem. Ancient muezzins called the faithful to prayer from the tops of their minarets. People scurried backwards and forwards busily living out the pattern of their lives. The world had not changed since the discovery of the list.

But for how long would it remain unchanged? What if Ari was right? Michael stared again at the ceiling and felt the anguish of the words, 'What if'. Why was he cursed by continual insecurity?

If Ari was right, how secure would Christianity remain? What would happen if the very basis for Christianity was disproved? No! That would not happen. Michael's faith, weakened though it was by the inner schisms that were afflicting his life, screamed against the possibility of any further assaults on his certainty. Dear God! Hadn't he suffered enough? His estrangement from his parents, losing Judith, the living nightmare of his son, Deirdre's lack of interest in sex since Christopher's birth, the farce which his marriage had become—he had been punished enough.

If he was weakening, he knew that the Catholic Church would remain strong. Look at the way it dealt with the immorality of the Renaissance popes; at the accommodation it had made over the centuries with the Protestant Reformation and Luther's righteous anger. Look at the way the Church dealt with the findings of Charles Darwin and Sigmund Freud. And earlier, the way in which the work of Copernicus and Galileo were eventually incorporated into Christian thinking. Should this document ever be discovered, the Church would find ways of incorporating it into the creed.

He thought of the Shroud of Turin. For hundreds of years, it had been worshipped as the cloth which had wrapped Jesus after He was crucified. In all those years it had been venerated by the faithful as an icon, a link with the Lord. Did the impression of the Lord's face left on a cloth undermine the divinity of the Messiah? As it happened, recent scientific evidence proved the Shroud was a fake. Perhaps that was for the good, because if science proved the cloth was wrapped around Christ, the cloth itself would continue to be worshipped by the ignorant for having been in contact with Him. Idolatry of the worst kind.

But Michael held no fear this would be the way the devout would worship His last will and Testament. The Testament was clear evidence that the Christ had walked among the people of the earth. Because the Gospellers told the world that in His death, He had taken upon Himself the burden of our sins.

Michael answered the door and welcomed in his breakfast. He poured himself a cup of coffee, thanked the waiter and read the rest of the paper while eating. During his second cup of coffee, he thought again of the article written by Ari. What if? Nothing would be answered until the Messiah's Testament had been discovered.

He ate listlessly, then stood and walked to the phone. He picked it up, flipped through his address book and punched in a series of numbers. The phone had rung twice when he slammed it down. No! Not yet. Not to him, anyway. He was angry with Ari and his anger would come out in a conversation. That was the last thing he wanted. He walked through the room, slid open the balcony doors and was greeted by an enveloping wave of hot air. The reek of petrol fumes and the smells of the Old City made him shut the doors again. He walked back and picked up the phone, his heart thumping. Did he have the courage? Damn it, he did! But what if her husband answered the phone?

It was Judith. 'Am I disturbing you?'

She laughed. 'No. I was actually thinking about you just now.'

'Are you alone?'

'No. Uri's in the apartment, but he can't hear.'

'What were you thinking?'

'Why are you phoning?' she said, sidestepping his conversation.

'Have you read Ari's article?'

'I don't read the *Jerusalem Post*. He told me about it yesterday. I read the draft. I assume it's upset you. He was afraid it would.'

'At first, yes. But then it made me pretty determined.'

'In what way?'

'Not to let the Testament lie unfound. In fact, I've been thinking about what I should do ever since Ari phoned me in Sydney with the news.'

'What are you going to do?' she asked.

'I'm going to search for it.'

'Don't be *meshuggah*. We don't even know if it still exists, and where it might be.'

'Will you help me look?' He was surprised when he heard himself ask the question, it had just slipped out.

'Now you're being seriously *meshuggah*. I have weekly army commitments. I teach archaeology part-time. I should drop everything and go searching with you for something I don't believe in?'

'Yes!'

There was a long pause.

For tourists, the Dead Sea is an idiosyncrasy, an item on an itinerary, as unique to their visit to Israel as the trip to the Grand Canyon or the pyramids. Marauding hordes of lobster-red Americans regularly step out of air-conditioned coaches to gaze in awe and reverence at it for a mandatory five minutes. But Michael felt familiar with its moonscapes and Rift-like valleys. He knew the smell of the vapours which rose from its pestilential waters. He had spent many months here, helping out on archaeological · digs while a student at the Hebrew

University. He spent his precious spare time wandering the deep chasms, and clambering like a goat over the creamy rock escarpments. He most particularly loved the area near to the Qumran community. Despite the pestilence of the Dead Sea, the area was pure. It was clean. It was devoid of artifice. It was there that his first interest in Jesus' teachings had been awoken. He could identify with Jesus' feelings of outrage. Having left the *yeshiva* because he found orthodox Judaism deficient in satisfying his spiritual needs, with its didacticism and professorialness, petty bureaucratic institutions and internecine tensions, Michael felt that Judaism had lost its way, that the purity of the Mosaic faith had been perverted by the rabbinic codes.

As a man in his early twenties, walking in the footsteps of Jesus, he was swept with an overwhelming, an incontestable desire to cloak himself in the warm, enveloping protection of Jesus' mantle. He did not give in to the feelings immediately, but the more he studied Jewish theology, the more alienated he became from it. He took up the private study of Christian theology, and worked at night under the tutorship of a kindly Jesuit who was writing a doctorate at the Hebrew University. Michael's connection with the living Jesus continued with his work as an academic and devout Christian. Any private doubts he may have had about the depth of his faith in later years, about its lack of certainty, he had kept very much to himself.

Michael was acknowledged throughout the world as one of the foremost authorities on the manuscripts of the Dead Sea. His research, as with all other biblical scholars outside of the International Team, was on the original material published a short time after the scrolls were discovered in 1947. No one outside of the coterie had seen the unpublished material until recently.

There really was no need for him to have visited the Dead Sea again. He had been here last year with Deirdre and Christopher. But the announcement drew him back to the lunar landscape, to the huge cliff faces, to the lifeless air. He needed to commune again directly with Jesus, for the Messiah to reinvigorate his faith.

He hired a car in Jerusalem. Driving down the 4000-foot decline to the Dead Sea, to 1300 feet below the level of the nearby Mediterranean, he again felt the joy of isolation, of disconnection from the twentieth century. He became a part of the life and times of the Bible. These were the best times of his life. Whenever he lost his connection with the traumas of the day and became a part of the simplicity of yesterday, he was at his happiest. Not that he didn't enjoy the trappings of modern life; rather that he was more attuned to the unsullied purity, the openness, the lack of artifice of the days when Abraham, Moses and Jesus had walked the land.

The road descended from Jerusalem, from heaven to hell, a falling from God's grace of lightness and beauty, silver and gold, into the fiery dominion of the Dead Sea. In the height of the Israeli summer, its level was already low. Even from the road, he could see bergs of yellow-white salt floating in the milky grey water. This was no Aegean, no Mediterranean, no gentle Pacific lapping talcum sand. This was not a sea. It was a warm soup of festering purulence, a thick pool of salt and potash in which no life-forms higher than a mutant shrimp were capable of surviving. At its most playful, it could support the weight of a grown man, making it impossible to sink. At its most fiendish, it could blind and deafen the foolish. And in its waters, rich tourists frolicked and played around the floating islands of salt like whales in Antarctica, immune to the damage it did to the impoverished. And when the photos had been snapped, they would wash the cleansing mud packs off themselves in the filtered-water showers, relax in the spas and breathe in the conditioned air of buses and cars. The area had been tamed for their needs. Their culture had refined a part of hell and made it into a tourists' paradise. While the Arabs in Jordan and the Bedouin in Israel kept far away from the savage sea, the tourists flocked in droves to experience for themselves the absolutism of nature, the final frontier of the untamed.

Michael turned right, and headed down the coast road on the west bank towards En-gedi and Masada, and ultimately Eilat.

He drove through the pink-blue landscape, towering precipices to his right, grey dead sea to his left, trying to keep his eyes on the road. Green and grey army trucks and tanks rolled towards him, furious dusty cars overtook him, swerving in and out of his vision, as Michael struggled to keep his eyes off the sea. But it was no use. He was drawn hypnotically towards it. The mists beckoned him, the salt bergs insinuated themselves into his mind.

He manoeuvred the car off the side of the road and near the sea. He got out and walked through the brown mud-flats until he came to the top of a rock ledge above the quietly lapping shore. The sun beat down on his uncovered head. He took out a cloth cap, a *Cova Temble*, from his pocket. Michael wondered if Jesus ever covered His head when He walked around this sea. The Bible didn't give those sort of details. What did His disciples say about Jesus? Did they recount the colour of His hair, or His eyes? Did they describe His smile or the way He talked? Did He have a lisp? Did He limp? Was He tall or small?

Was it important? For two thousand years, Christians had been free to colour their own image of Jesus, to place the tiny spectral impressions, stone by stone, until a mosaic was created.

This century, the century of image, had been responsible for a plethora of manifestations of Jesus, from blue-eyed Aryan to jet-eyed Semite, each rendition faithful to how Hollywood's directors thought their audiences imagined Him.

Michael's personal view, idiosyncratic and private, was of a tall spare man with glistening beard and olive skin, floating above the ground on an aura of light. God made man. Man made God.

He looked out over the mists above the sea, as saltbergs glided on the surface, appearing slowly, then disappearing back into the opaque air, like ethereal dancers on a stage, a *corps de ballet* in a Faustian setting.

He felt a cold shudder run the length of his body. Was Christ going to appear to him out of these mists as He had appeared to others? Was he to be blessed with a vision? Did he have the faith, the strength to see? He began to pray for a visitation, a confirmation of his faith. Why did Christ appear to simple fishermen in Galilee, or to a rabid persecutor like Saul on the road to Damascus, but not to him, who wanted so badly to have his faith assured? For half an hour, and more, Michael waited, watching. The sun burned furiously. Insects chirped. Birds high on the cliff-face screamed thinly in the air. The sound of cars and lorries invaded his mind. He tried to maintain his concentration, but the mists slowly began to lift as the sun grew higher. The Mountains of Moab cautiously appeared, like reluctant brides, in the distance. His chance of seeing Jesus had gone.

Deflated, Michael walked back to his car and drove towards Eilat. He soon reached the oasis of En-gedi, where he stripped down to his undershorts and swam in the cool, deep, pure water. Within seconds of leaving the oasis he was dry. He put on his clothes and drove down to Masada. He was soon there. At the bottom of the huge towering cliff was a youth hostel and cafe. On top of the cliff, hidden from view, was the Herodian fortress of Masada. It was the site where nine hundred and sixty men, women and children committed suicide in the year 73 of the first century, rather than be taken prisoner and enslaved by the Romans. It was where Zadokites, Nazoreans, Essenes, Zealots, or any one of a number of other disparate groups may have gathered together in the last days of Jewish resistance to the power of Rome, the sorry remnants of a once dignified people, stripped of freedom and sent into exile as slaves of an unfeeling conqueror.

He looked up at the fortress, perched high on the cliff top. Birds, perhaps falcons, perhaps eagles, maybe even a rare kestrel, wheeled in the sky. He strained his eyes against the glare. High in the hills were caves. Not as obvious as the caves of Qumran; but the trained eye of the biblical detective, the archaeologist, could discern them. They were the caves where the ancients had hidden their precious manuscripts, safe from the unholy hands of the Roman legions under the future emperor, Vespasian. Men who marched to the dictates of pagan gods, who ate the foul flesh of pigs, who placed idols in the temples of the Holy Land, who worshipped a far-off madman called Caesar.

Masada. A symbol of the resistance of the Jewish people to tyranny; to the compulsion of conquerors, from Assyrians to Greeks and Romans to proselytising Christians, to convert the Jews from their religion; to following the religion of the conqueror. Michael wondered why there was this compulsion. Why couldn't people be left in peace to follow their simple, elegant faith, inadequate as it might be.

It was a place to inspire wonder and pity for the tens of thousands of lives destroyed in the names of empires which only lasted a handful of centuries. He thought about the men who had tried to save the remnants of Judaism, its documents, its precious ornaments, from the Romans. Those ancient men must have struggled painfully up these rocky outcrops. Carefully carrying their manuscripts, perhaps in woven straw panniers strapped to their backs, they would have climbed unsteadily from rock to rock, testing a foothold here, a handhold there. And it was not only the terrain that was dangerous. There was the possibility of being discovered climbing the bare rock-wall by a platoon of legionnaires, sent out to reconnoitre the area. And if the ancient had been caught climbing? What would his end have been? What would have happened to the precious manuscripts in his possession, manuscripts which to the Romans contained meaningless symbols of an indecipherable language, yet which to Michael were the expressions of his faith.

Should he climb the rock wall, and peer inside the caves, picked clean by Bedouin and archaeologists? He had Israeli government authority to visit any archaeological site. He could wander wherever he wanted, unlike a tourist, who would soon be turned away by the guardians of the past.

Should he? No! He had seen all he came to see. A year in Sydney clouded his mind to the purity of the Holy Land. Every so often, he needed to get back to the soil, the rocks where his Lord had once trod. Had Jesus visited Masada Himself? Had he walked upon these very paths? Or had some sublime guardian of old collected up his Messiah's Testament and hidden it somewhere among these very rocks, to preserve it for posterity.

Michael knew that he was flawed. He thought of his wife Deirdre, once proud and supportive, now cold and quiescent. Once full of love for him, now only able to devote herself to tending the insatiable needs of their son, a useless infant masquerading in the body of a youth. He closed his eyes. God! Why have You forsaken me? Tell me my sins, that I can repent for them.

And then another image, a more insistent image, began to infuse itself into his mind. An image from a simpler time. The sharply defined, dark-skinned, Semitic beauty, Judith.

Wherever he went, he attracted a crowd, like children gathering around a schoolyard bully. Always surrounded by thirty of his acolytes, Rabbi David Berg marched with other members of the Zion Now! movement from place to place within the walls of Jerusalem, finding a convenient spot to position his dais. He would stand on the curling linoleum, take out his bullhorn and scream an harangue over the heads of the passing throng, spitting out invective to anyone who would stop and listen. Ever since he had come to live in Israel he had practised his militant trans-Jordan Judeo-Zionism in this way. He bemused tourists, terrified inhabitants, exasperated the authorities, made Jews in the diaspora cringe in horror and shame, but delighted his followers.

Today, David Berg felt like a man who had been given an injection of adrenalin. Since the end of the *intifida* and the growing harmony between Arabs and Jews under the euphoric eyes of the pallid Israeli government, Rabbi Berg's invective had been falling on increasingly deaf ears. But the announcement gave him and his followers a new impetus, a new definition.

'And only this afternoon his Holiness the Pope . . . you hear that? Holiness? Some dried up old man in Rome is called Holy! . . . The Pope has announced a week of prayers of thanksgiving for the re-ascendancy and the primacy of Christianity. That's all we need—for Christianity to flex its wings again. Remember what happens every time it does that? Millions of Jews die! Listen to this medieval mountebank, this mendacious moron, this anachronistic buffoon, will you—'

By now, the crowd had swelled from the initial thirty supporters to several hundred onlookers. They had gathered around like iron filings to a magnet, curious at the sudden commotion which was noisier than the normally bustling environment of the Old City. Some stopped as idle spectators, others were genuinely interested in what he had to say, and still others, such as members of the media, had been alerted to his announcement. He was going to give a *drosha*, a rabbinical statement in answer to the ecstasy felt by the Christian communities. The other rabbis of Israel preferred to make no comments for fear of alienating their relationship with Christians. But not David Berg. This was another opportunity to rekindle the fading light of his campaign. Again, he could be the centre of the vortex. Those who were interested in the Bible also stopped to listen, their curiosity having been reawakened by the momentous news of the Jesus Testament.

'Thanksgiving!' Rabbi Berg screamed disparagingly, his voice thin and electronic to all but the periphery of his audience, his tone increasingly mocking. 'You hear this? Wonderful. Think what we can look forward to. A sudden rise in militant Christianity, and who's going to suffer for it? We Jews. Us. The rightful owners of Jerusalem. And Tel Aviv. And Haifa.' He allowed a pause to build up the tension. 'And the East Bank of the Jordan. Even Jericho, given away by a government that sold our birthright for a mess of pottage, a piece of paper. All of Greater Israel. Where God ordained that we Jews should have a home. On both sides of the Jordan. All the land of ancient Canaan that we were promised by *Ha Kodesh b'ruch hu*, from the Tigris and the Euphrates to the Red Sea. Where our forefathers claimed the land after the expulsion from Egypt. Our land! Our birthright! As precious to us as the blood and bones of our bodies.'

The mob shifted uncomfortably. There were no leaders in the throng, no protagonist to contradict him. Their reaction was led by Rabbi Berg's followers who cheered and whistled. 'And now we have some Pope, some *goy*, telling everybody to pray that the whole world might suddenly become Christian. Well, let me tell His Holiness what we Jews think of that! It wasn't Jews that built the Nazi concentration camps. It wasn't Jews that raped and slaughtered millions throughout history, or built the ghettos. It was the Christians. And now this find is going to incite even greater feelings of superiority. We've suffered for two thousand years because of the Christians. Is this Testament going to condemn us to another two thousand? A Testament by an apostate Jew. I'll tell you what we should do with this Testament. We should find it and burn it. What right does it have to be in our land? What right do Christian churches have in Israel? What right do Muslims and their mosques have here? This land was ordained by God Almighty Himself,' he screamed, 'and given to the Jewish people, the Children of Israel, the chosen ones. Not the Arabs! Not the Christians! They have their own lands. There's Rome for the Christians, and Mecca for the Arabs. Let them go find their enjoyment and inner contentment there, not here. Where can Jews call home? New York? London? Berlin? We've been persecuted throughout the ages, and now, for the first time since the time of the Roman conquerors, we've got our own land once again.

Le'heyot am hofshee, b'aretzanu, to be a free people, in our own land. For hundreds of years we were slaves in Egypt, downtrodden, murdered, forced to carry back-breaking loads of brick and mud. To build pyramids for incestuous men with monstrous egos and to fall down dead from exhaustion. And when *Moishe Rabbenu* brought us out of the land of Egypt, out of the house of bondage, he didn't bring us to some five-star hotel where other people were resident in the rooms.' The crowd roared with laughter. 'He brought us here,' he shouted, stabbing at the ground with his free hand, 'to our own house. Our own land. Circumstances have deemed that other people now occupy the land of Israel along with us but we . . . the Jews . . . are the masters of this house, the *ba'alim ha beit.* And we want our house back!'

As the crowd grew larger, the noise of sirens could be heard in the background. The Israeli police were coming to move David Berg away before he caused a further disturbance of the peace. Every time he stood on his now-famous soap box and yelled his hate and anger into his megaphone, he was in contempt of an Israeli prohibition on his appearance in public meetings. Although a member of the Knesset, his disturbances had been so frequent, leading to so many infractions and incidents, that his rights as an individual had been severely limited.

David Berg had grown up in Queens, New York, the son of a Jewish doctor. He had only recently become a rabbi. After qualifying as a doctor of medicine, Berg, a Jew knowledgeable of orthodoxy but professing no heartfelt beliefs, travelled to Israel on a young Jewish American doctors' fact-finding mission. He left the country two weeks later as the most militant, outspoken and idealistic Zionist in the group. Nobody on the tour, especially not he himself, knew what the circumstances were which propelled him into his militancy. He grew a black bushy beard and studied the esoteric aspects of his religion. He was, at first, inclined to become a Hasid, but later shied away from their religious ferocity. He was a compulsive political Zionist, losing the capacity to see the other person's point of view.

When asked by a reporter for the *New York Times* ten years later, he attributed his revelation to his first view of the Wailing Wall. Herod's Temple had had a profound effect upon him. It was his first encounter with the reality of his religion's roots. In America, his Judaism had been an extension of his family and his society. But it was a young land with little history of Jewish tradition. The previous generation of Jews in America looked towards Poland, Russia and Germany for their roots. Berg was a child of the United States and was alienated from the way his parents spoke about 'the old country'. Only when he touched the stones of Herod's Temple, when he walked through the ancient synagogues in Galilee, when he trod the timeworn pathways of cities in which Ezra and Nehemiah had walked, did he realise how little a part America was of his life and how much he was a Jew.

Returning to America, he had joined a variety of right-wing Zionistic organisations until settling upon the Zion Now! movement, a group of rabid Zionists who used their fists and weapons to defend Jews against any hint of a resurgence of persecution.

He rocketed swiftly up in the organisation, at the same time training for and becoming an orthodox rabbi. Friends tried to convince him to become a Hasid but he refused. He did not want to follow the Messianic dictates of the Lubavitcher movement. He followed his own credo, accepting many of the injunctions of the Hasids but sprinkling their ancient superstitious rites with the modern tenets of Zionism. Never wanting a congregation, he concentrated his efforts and aspirations on the activities of the ZNM until he led a raid of a hundred supporters on a virulently anti-Semitic black gang in a Brooklyn neighbourhood. Three blacks were beaten to death. He was arraigned by the police, but they were forced to drop their enquiries for lack of evidence. It may also have had something to do with his lawyer who informed the police that Rabbi Berg was leaving America and taking up citizenship in Israel. Within two years of arriving in Israel he had won election to the Knesset, rallying the extreme right and Zionistic causes under his banner.

As the sirens grew louder, the crowd began to dissolve. One of his aides came up and motioned for Rabbi Berg to leave the platform and to disappear. Before he stepped down, he screamed at the crowd through his bullhorn, 'You know what we're going to do. We're going to find this Testament! And when we do, we'll send it airmail to Rome. And good riddance!' he screamed, trying to be heard above the increasing clamour.

Berg withdrew strategically to a nearby house belonging to one of his supporters, but the morning meeting was merely a prelude to another incident which he had planned the day after the announcement had been made. An incident which, he prayed, would cause a tidal wave of panic among Christians and Muslims, and force the Israeli government into a more militant position.

Two hours later, the crowded dusty streets of Jerusalem allowed the sixty young Jewish men to blend until they became unnoticeable. Approaching the Old City in groups of twos and threes, they entered at different times through the Jaffa Gate, the Damascus Gate, the Dung Gate and the Zion Gate. Berg, head bent uncomfortably between his knees in the passenger seat of an old Ford pickup, entered the Old City through its towering walls. His driver negotiated the narrow dusty laneways turning left past the Gloria Hotel and the Latin Patriarchate and then right towards the Casa Nova Hospice.

Outside the walls in the New City of Jerusalem, the heat and atmosphere were of a different dimension from those inside the walls. It was almost as though the massive yellow stones erected by Suleyman the Magnificent in 1537 created a ghetto, keeping the outside world shut away from the biblical land within.

Looking carefully up and down the road, the driver turned to Rabbi Berg and gave a terse, 'Go.' Berg slipped noiselessly out of the car and secreted himself in a doorway as the Ford drove to the end of the road and then left towards St Francis. Alone on the street, he double-checked that no one was around, and emerged from the doorway walking hurriedly towards the Church of the Holy Sepulchre.

He had chosen the church both for its position within the Old City and its significance. Pope Innocent's announcement of a week of thanksgiving prayers catapulted sites like the Holy Sepulchre into a new and menacing context for Jewish fundamentalists. The churches of Israel occupying the places of Christ's agony and ecstasy in his short life were about to be embroiled in controversy, if Rabbi Berg had anything to do with it.

The Church of the Holy Sepulchre was deep within the Christian quarter of the Old City of Jerusalem where the effects of what Berg was about to do would be felt the most. A swift kick in the guts would make those anti-Semite fascist Catholics realise they could no longer mess around with Israelis and Zionists.

He walked towards the church in the shadows of the buildings. The Christian quarter was the highest part of the Old City. Its population of devout Christians came from as many countries as Christianity held sway in and housed all the major denominations. The houses of the area were dark, closely adjacent to each other and were all crouched around the dome of the Holy Sepulchre like acolytes at the feet of a high priest.

Berg knew with certainty that as he closed in on the church, so too were sixty of his followers, young, fervent Zionists who believed, like him, in the inalienable right of the Jewish people to be the sole inhabitants of the land which Moses had brought them to. For years, he had demanded a cleansing of the Temple area, a repatriation of non-Jews—Muslims and Christians—to their homelands to leave room in Israel for Jews of the diaspora to reclaim their heritage. He was reviled for his views by the liberal establishment, but knew in his heart that he was performing God's demands. A latterday Moses, saying to the enemy, 'Open the doors of my people's captivity so that they are able to live in their own land, gathered in from the diaspora when the land of Israel is pure and inalienably Jewish.' He knew that what stopped most Jews around the world from migrating to *Eretz Yisroel* was their fear of conflict. Cleanse Israel of other races and there would be an ingathering of his people. Then the prophecies of Isaiah and Jeremiah, of Ezra and Ezekiel, of Elijah and Elisha, would be fulfilled and the Messiah would surely come.

Rounding a corner, he passed the Mosque of El Khanqa and saw before him the massive Crusader structure of the Church of the Holy Sepulchre. Christians had claimed this site for themselves, yet Jewish tradition held that the head of Adam, the primogenitor of all humanity, was buried here. Jews called it 'Golgotha', the Romans 'Calvaria', both words meaning 'skull'.

When Christianity was just beginning, a church was built on the site, probably by St Helena, the mother of the first Christian emperor Constantine, but the present church dated from the time of the Crusaders and since then structural alterations had been made through the centuries. It was because of its spiritual significance that Berg had decided to use the church to cause mayhem. Mayhem led to publicity and publicity was the oxygen that he breathed.

He stood in the shadow of the cupola and waited. In twos and threes, they gathered around him. Each was wearing a long jacket to hide the clubs and sticks hidden inside his clothes. Passers-by in the crowded streets didn't give them a second glance. Crowds of tourists following guides were ever-present on the streets of Jerusalem, wandering the Via Dolorosa, standing before the Dome of the Rock, gazing in awe at the Wailing Wall.

Their plans had been discussed at length during the previous days, the strategies argued, the decisions made. Now it was time for action. When the last of the stragglers came into view, Rabbi Berg appeared to stand tall and straight for the first time since entering the Old City. Purposefully, he marched down an aisle formed by his group of followers, who fell in and strode behind him. They began to sing 'Daveed, Melech Yisrael, Chai, Chai, Ve'chai'am'. Only then did people begin to take notice of a small army singing on its way to assault the entranceway of the church.

As they tramped into the huge echoing building, the noise of their songs and marching feet drowned the sepulchral hymns and Gregorian chants coming from deep within the church. To the left of the entrance was the cushioned apse in which the Muslim doorkeepers, traditional custodians of the church's keys, sat. The present incumbent looked in astonishment. The doorkeeper did not even bother to stop them. He grabbed for the phone and dialled the emergency number to call the Israeli police. A lifetime of watching the comings and goings of millions of tourists told him instinctively that these men were evil and out to do harm.

Berg and his followers marched towards the Stone of Unction upon which Christian legend has it that the body of Jesus was anointed. A curt nod from Berg had four men stop at the stone and attempt to overturn it.

A dozen monks from different parts of the sombre building shouted when they saw what was happening and came running out of the darkness to prevent a desecration. Hundreds of tourists gathered in the body of the church turned in horror, realising that they were no longer witnesses of the past but participants in the hideous present. They began screaming and scurried for dark hiding places. Berg and his followers continued inside the church and came to the circular hall with its massive dome-like rotunda. In the centre was the Holy Sepulchre and inside two smaller chapels. As they progressed through the church, Coptic Christians heard what was happening and began running to stop them.

Berg and his followers got no further than the centre of the earth—the Greek Catholicon in which a stone chalice marked the reputed epicentre of the globe. From the deep dark recesses of the church, dozens of priests, monks, officials and even irate tour guides began to run purposefully towards them.

'Ready?' screamed Berg, and his followers let out a mighty roar and began to lay into the defenceless monks with their batons and clubs. Careful not to hit skulls, which could lead to deaths, they attacked the bodies of the defenders of the church, pummelling rib cages, arms and legs. The brawl turned into a melee as the centre of one of the holiest shrines of Christianity became a battleground between Jew and Christian. Men shouted in anger, women screamed and protected their children, dragging them into inconspicuous corners behind columns and iron railings, and even lying on top of them. Men screamed, 'Stop', 'Halt', 'No' in a dozen different languages. Nobody really understood what was happening or why. The priests had one mission—to save their heritage, the objects of their devotion.

For the second time that day, the piercing shriek of police sirens had come to stop the mania of Rabbi Berg. As soon as he heard them, Berg, who had held back from the fray in order to direct it, shouted 'Go!' His men stopped their savage beating, threw down their batons and ran to different parts of the church, jumping over the broken and bloodied bodies of priests, monks, and guides. Men moaned and painfully tried to stand as the invaders disappeared like malevolent spirits at the first sign of light. Berg began his escape but before he could reach the corridor, one of the monks, roaring in anger and frustration, threw himself at him. The old man's fingers missed Berg's body but grasped on to his rabbinical frock coat. He tore the pocket and a small black prayer book fell out. Berg turned in order to retrieve it but saw that the quicker he was away the better.

He was one of the last to disappear down an alleyway but, before he left, he threw down a leaflet. It warned that unless all the Muslims and Christians left the Jewish homeland immediately, there would be more attacks:

Jews have been the subject of persecution at the hands of Christians for millennia. Let all Christians take note. Israel is the land given by God unto the Children of Israel. Finding the false witness of a so-called Messiah will not save you from your fate.

Shulamit Wallenstein opened the door, threw her arms around Michael and pulled him into the room.

She had grown fatter since they had last met. The abundance of children and her life as a housewife, away from the exercise of archaeological digs, had made her put on weight.

They had not seen each other in four years. On Michael's last visit to Israel a year ago, Shulamit had been in Washington.

'I'd forgotten how handsome you were. How's Deirdre?'

In all the times he had seen her, Shulamit only ever asked about Deirdre, never Christopher.

'She's fine. She sends her love,' said Michael, hugging her, and feeling the motherly warmth of her ample body. He handed her a bag containing half a dozen boomerangs he'd bought at the last minute in Sydney airport. 'Presents for the kids. Give them out when I've gone.'

She smiled and understood. Since his son had been born, he found the fuss children made difficult to cope with. As he walked into the large apartment he saw Ari in the kitchen. 'I told you we'd get you here for dinner,' Ari boomed. Michael continued walking until he came to the loungeroom. Judith was sitting in a chair, nestling a drink. She smiled as he entered. He stopped in his tracks and felt his jaw drop.

Ari's voice resonated from the kitchen, 'I've invited Judith. After that article in the *Jerusalem Post*, I thought I might need some reinforcements.'

Michael sat down heavily in an armchair. 'Where's your husband?'

'Uri? He's at home. He doesn't come out much. And he certainly wouldn't come to dinner when I'm talking archaeology.'

'Is that why you're here?'

She shrugged her shoulders. 'Of course.'

As Ari walked out of the kitchen, his body was framed in the doorway and looked too big to squeeze into the living room. If the early Israelites had envisaged a Goliath, Ari would have fitted the bill. He thrust a whisky and soda into Michael's hand. 'I remember what's your poison. So, are you pissed off with me about the article? You have every right to be but it wasn't written for you. It was written for a non-academic audience.'

Michael didn't want to launch into a discussion straight away. He wanted to talk to Judith. But Ari stood hovering, like a boxer at the start of a match. 'I think you said things that I would have preferred you hadn't said. Naturally, I can't agree with you. Imagine if the Ark of the Covenant had been discovered containing the Ten Commandments. Would you feel the same way?'

Judith interrupted. 'Michael, you're being defensive. Nobody is trying to attack Christianity. All Ari was doing was giving his perspective.'

Michael shrugged his shoulders. 'It's all hypothetical, anyway.'

But Ari wouldn't let him off so easily. 'Okay. You hated the article. But tell me what you really thought of the arguments!'

Michael grinned. 'Do you want me to be honest or tell you what you want to hear?'

'Be honest. You've got a reputation for telling people what they don't want to hear.'

'Ari, I thought it was presumptuous, impertinent, arrogant and ill-advised. You're a brilliant biblical scholar but you shouldn't try to impose your views on the faith of others.' Ari looked hurt. Michael immediately regretted his directness. 'Look. What I really mean is—'

But Ari held up his hand to stop him. 'No, you're quite right. I shouldn't have stuck my nose in. I've had a lot of flak from that article. Cardinal Kitzinger has written a rebuttal which will be appearing in a couple of days' time. The editor phoned and warned me. He said it was pretty direct.'

Michael interrupted. 'Don't let it worry you. You said what you thought.'

'I didn't think it would get so much coverage. I've had reporters from all over the world phoning me.' He looked at his friend. 'I was hoping you of all people would understand. You're a Christian and a biblical scholar from a Jewish background. There aren't all that many people with those sorts of qualifications. And you're used to the limelight.'

'If there's damage done, it's already done, so forget about it.'

'But I've hurt people. I've insulted them, disturbed their faith.' His face drooped in remorse like a blood-hound's. 'I didn't mean to. I only meant to sound a warning. A note of caution amidst the euphoria.'

Michael laughed. 'Now you're being arrogant. It's men like Kitzinger who disturb people's faith. Not some bearded giant writing an article in a newspaper.'

Ari sank back into his chair and played with the gold chain around his wrist. 'Have you had any more thoughts about the Testament?' he asked Michael.

Before he could answer, Judith exclaimed, 'Thoughts! You know what this *meshugenneh* did? He phoned me up and asked me to drop everything and come search with him. It's like something out of a Wilbur Smith novel, *Michael Farber and the Search for the Lost Testament*!' she chortled.

Michael was caught up in her mirth. 'I've actually thought of nothing but. The potential is almost unbelievable. If such a thing came to light, imagine the difference it would make.'

'But in my article, I said—'

'Ari, you missed the fundamental point. These are Jesus' words. Whether they're good or bad, happy or sad, it doesn't matter. Would you reject the Dead Sea Scrolls if one of them contained a recipe for making *lokshun* soup?'

'*Mamzer!*' Ari roared laughing. 'Okay, let's say it's there to be found.'

'But that begs the point. Do you think the Testament could still be in existence?' asked Michael.

Ari sipped his drink and contemplated. 'The whole of the Dead Sea cliffs are riddled with caves. I mean, look at the scramble to uncover what else might be in the caves since the Israeli–Palestinian peace initiative, and our fear that we might be banned from the area. Hordes of archaeologists tramping down there. Yet despite that, we've only scratched the surface of what could be there. The area's been combed by Bedouin, scavengers, and archaeologists for the past half-century, but that doesn't mean to say everything's been discovered.'

'My bet would be around Masada. The fall in AD 73 was a cataclysmic event. Flavius Josephus reports that—' Judith commented.

'Aaah! That bastard. Why would you listen to an apostate Jew? One who became a Roman citizen?'

Michael flushed in embarrassment. Ari realised what he had said and apologised.

'You're right, though, Judith,' said Ari. 'It was a land in upheaval. But that doesn't mean it was a time for moving precious documents around the country. Think about it for a moment. The Temple had fallen in AD 70. Hundreds of thousands of Jews were exiled. Thousands, maybe tens of thousands were murdered. Who do you think would have found time to gather up documents, take them to the Dead Sea and hide them in air-tight jars in a cave. I don't think we're looking at the fall of the Temple. I think we're looking at a time much later.'

'Much later?' asked Judith. 'So that's why you invited me. You think it was hidden at the time of Bar Kochba.'

Michael listened quietly and drank a mouthful of whisky.

'Could have been,' said Ari. 'Who knows? Lots of things were happening in Israel at the time. There was still a strong feeling that the end of man's reign on earth was fast approaching and that the Messiah would soon appear. Who knows what could have happened?'

'Bar Kochba?' Michael repeated. He swirled the remnants of the drink around in his glass, considering the possibility of something which had not previously occurred to him.

'Just consider,' Ari continued. 'At the end of the sixties and into the seventies you have Vespasian wandering around with hordes of Roman troops slaughtering and exiling everyone in sight. Even travelling along a road was dangerous. Nobody would risk moving anything precious. So surely it's logical to think that cherished documents would have been hidden in secret places to protect them in those nightmarish days.'

Michael nodded in agreement.

'Okay. Now the area calms down, the Romans send their major legions home and with little or no resistance after the end of 73, Israel becomes relatively peaceful on the outside, but still seethes with hostility on the inside until the inevitable explosion occurs and we have the uprising in 132.'

'So?'

'So, isn't it logical that between 75 and 130 momentous documents, the life and soul of Judaism, could have been transported from hiding places in cities to even safer places such as the caves in the Judean desert?'

'Are you saying that the Qumran documents were placed after the fall of the Temple?' asked Michael.

'No, not those. They were undoubtedly placed there in the first century BC. All the evidence, the potsherds, the style and consistency of the clay, indicates that they were placed there around the time of habitation of the community. But the documents discovered around Masada don't have to date back that far. There's no reason why they couldn't have been placed there in the second century.'

Shulamit, a graduate student of Ari's and an expert in the early Bible, sat down on the sofa and poured herself a drink. She was followed into the room by four of her smaller children. She and Ari were used to the continuous background noise of tiny arguments, hair-pulling, jealousies, giggling and howling. They did not seem to be affected by it. Even Judith willingly accepted a couple of the younger ones on her knees. But Michael felt awkward and uncomfortable.

Balancing a baby in her arms, Shulamit suggested, 'Maybe you should be looking much later in time.'

Both men looked at her in surprise. 'Explain,' asked Ari.

She shook her head. 'I don't think I can explain, it's just a thought. We know that Constantine's mother, Queen Helena, searched all over Israel in the fourth century for the sites of Christ's miracles. She found the supposed spots of the Nativity, the Ascension, as well as what she claimed was the actual Cross. Surely it's not unreasonable to think that she may have known of Christ's Testament and taken it back to Rome.'

'Not possible, Shuli,' said Michael. 'That would be a document of the greatest imaginable importance to the

Christians. Probably the most important document in their possession. It wouldn't have been hidden for thousands of years.'

'Maybe it was destroyed,' she persisted. 'Or was buried in the catacombs. Or maybe it was censored at the time of the Council of Nicea because of what it said, or taken to Constantinople when Constantine moved the Roman Empire to the East.'

'Darling,' her husband interrupted, 'understand, this is not some certificate of membership we're talking about. This is the very turning point of the Church. If it had been brought back by Helena, somebody would have known about it.'

Michael had been thinking while Ari spoke. 'Is that necessarily true though? When you come to think about it, the archives in the Vatican have tens of thousands of documents. Not all of them have been identified. Maybe this was just forgotten. And if it was taken to Constantinople, it would certainly have been destroyed by the Christians in the Fourth Crusade. Nothing was left standing.'

Ari paced the room. His energy wouldn't allow him to stay still for long. 'You're both going down the wrong road. I'm telling you. If the Jesus Testament is still in existence, assuming it's not a pile of dust, then it's somewhere in Israel. The caves around Masada are where we'll find it. Of that, I'm sure. You have to remember what Israel was like at the time of the Romans. It was a land of violence and hatred. Of oppression. These documents were the treasury of the ancients. To them they were more valuable than gold. The people who weren't killed were being dispersed throughout the Roman empire. Our forefathers were willing to die to keep the religion secure and intact. There's no way they would have allowed them to get into Roman hands. No way at all!'

Michael looked at Judith. Her eyes seemed to be invigorated with the conversation, alive to its excitement. In the days when they were lovers, it was the way she looked when they discovered new things together. It was the way she had looked at him in the Jazz cellar at the end of their first date, when she began to perceive the rhythms of the music. That was when he had first fallen in love with her.

CHAPTER 6

Daniel Rhymer knew he was awake because of the insistent throbbing of his bladder. But unlike other men who woke angry at having to go to the toilet, Daniel felt a strong sense of gratitude that Almighty God had woken him up just in time to escape the horrors of his nightmare. He was pulled from the long black tunnel seconds before its walls collapsed in on top of him. Non-believers would have said that his sphincter was the cause of his awakening, that, and the red wine at last night's banquet in honour of St Sebastian. But he knew it was the Holy One, blessed be He, who recognised Daniel's need to be free from his gripping claustrophobia. Daniel was drenched in sweat, his heart palpitating as though he had just run up a flight of stairs.

He swung his legs out of bed, knelt before the crucifix, crossed himself quickly and walked to the bathroom. On his return, he pulled a caftan, a recent gift from an Arab bishop, over his uncombed head, and walked into the sitting room. It was as though he had just walked into the dining room of a five-star hotel. He smiled when he looked at the table. He always smiled. Every morning. Faithful and fastidious, the nuns in his service had heard the toilet flush and rushed a steaming pot of coffee, half a grapefruit, hot crisp Italian bread rolls, brioche, a tray of home-made preserves, and the early edition of *Osservatore Romano* to his table.

Not once in the six months that His Eminence Daniel Cardinal Rhymer had lived in Rome as Secretary of State to the new American Pope had he managed to catch the nuns off-guard, though not for lack of trying. Once early in the piece, he had crept out of bed, glided into his dressing-gown and slippers, and sailed quietly out of the door only to be met halfway by an ill-humoured Sister Maria emerging from the kitchen carrying a tray of everything, proclaiming a disapproving 'tut'. What did they have, these women? Radar? A peephole?

His life-long friend, Pope Innocent, was no help when they were discussing their respective domestic arrangements over a whisky one night. 'Beats me how they know,' Gabby Molloy had said. 'I reckon that the Borgia popes must have wired the entire Vatican for sound.'

Daniel sipped his coffee and straightened out the paper, glancing at the front page. Though fluent in Italian, he sometimes found the smooth reading jarred by idiomatic expressions which he could only grasp by their context in the news item. The whole page was still devoted to the miraculous discovery of a list which pointed to Christ's Testament. Though the entire company was thrilled, ecstatic, Daniel had sounded a note of caution among other prelates at last night's banquet. Many were saying that it was a precursor to the Parousia, a herald to Christ's re-appearance on earth. Others talked of it as a miracle, as though the document itself had been found, not merely a mention of its existence. Only Daniel had asked rhetorically what it might contain. Only he had sounded a note of warning about the dangers which could eventuate if the document was discovered.

Of course, last night had been a night of feasting, not of theology. And Daniel had shared centre stage at the Society for the Promotion of the Works of St Sebastian with jovial Italians and Spaniards, cardinals who knew how to have a good time. The austere, astringent, French, German and Dutch prelates had avoided the occasion, their absence somewhat lowering the theological threshold. So apart from passing observations on the discovery of the list, little debate had taken place.

Daniel opened up the paper and glanced hurriedly through its pages. There would be more time to read after he had said prayers, showered and dressed. He was about to close it and continue with his breakfast when the metallic face of Franz Cardinal Kitzinger stared at him from the pages. Were it not for the crucifix and the collar, the man looking impersonally at him could easily have been a Swiss banker, or a scion of the Viennese aristocracy. His smooth, regular features, his intellectual face and steel-grey hair framed by a close-fitting black skullcap made him seem more portrait than person. But beyond the image was an astute and calculating brain, perceiving the world through hard, determined eyes.

Daniel read Kitzinger's article. It was a rebuttal of Ari Wallenstein's analysis of the find. Daniel recalled reading the rabbi's article in the *Wall Street Journal*. It was a perceptive analysis, even though it was clearly written for a general readership and was obviously written by someone with no theological attachment to the document. It had caused Daniel to think seriously about the need for time in evaluating the implications of the find. Kitzinger, on the other hand, insisted that Wallenstein was biased and that whilst eminently qualified to comment upon the Dead Sea Scrolls, he should keep his rabbinic nose out of the affairs of the Catholic Church. Anybody practised in the subtleties of Vatican diplomacy would know that Kitzinger's article was a barbed condemnation of the Israeli, couched in generous ecumenical terms.

The rest of Kitzinger's article was an analysis of whether a church council should be called to study how best the amazing find should be treated. He, like Daniel and Rabbi Wallenstein, believed that caution was called for, rather than the indecent haste caused by unbridled emotions.

Daniel finished his cup of coffee and re-read the last section of Kitzinger's article. The language was academic and tortuous but a second reading made it apparent that, despite his condemnation, Kitzinger was issuing a warning to every churchman to rein in his followers, to temper the euphoria with counsel. It was as close to a Papal Bull as anything Daniel had read. He shut the paper in anger, wondering at the damnable arrogance of the man.

He buttered his bread roll, then mused as he spread some jam on it. As a man of God, a theologian, a priest who had ministered to the broken souls of desperate drifting men and women, he rejoiced in the news and ached to read the words which might bring comfort and resolution to heal a frantic world.

But as a Doctor of Law, who had seen the neo-Nazis versus the Jews in Germany, Protestant versus Catholic in Northern Ireland, and Muslim versus Christian in the Balkans—that part of him was concerned about the potential divisions the Testament could cause. Men whose minds were in straitjackets, and whose fundamentalism was rigid would grasp the document and pervert whatever were its words to their own cause. It would become a weapon in their hands to prove or disprove whatever obscene cause they were pursuing. And the divisions that Christ's Testament might cause if it was discovered could prove to be of incalculably greater damage than any potential benefit to an already teetering Church.

Daniel wiped his hands and mouth, got up from the dinner table and retreated to his bedroom, where he knelt before the crucifix of the sinless Messiah. 'Please,

Lord, help me clearly to see how to resolve the many problems of the world. Now You have placed me in an exalted position, help me tread the right path. Help me accept the overwhelming stigma of my sins, forgive me for the weakness of my body, strengthen my mind and let me guide Your church from weakness to strength, from division to healing.'

Gabriel Cardinal Molloy, for the past six months His Holiness Pope Innocent, Bishop of Rome, Vicar of Jesus Christ, Successor of the Prince of the Apostles, Supreme Pontiff of the Universal Church, Patriarch of the West, Primate of Italy, Archbishop and Metropolitan of the Roman Province, Sovereign of the State of the City of the Vatican, Servant of the Servants of God, was amazed and bemused.

How had Roncello achieved the impossible? His Eminence Giacomo Cardinal Roncello was Innocent's Prefect for Universal Understanding, a sinecure given to the old man for his knowledge, dedication and humility. He was outstanding. The momentous news had only recently become public and he and Roncello had only then discussed the possibility of using the Sistine Chapel as a setting for the event. Roncello had said that he had gathered so many people that the Sistine Chapel would be far too small and suggested using St Peter's Basilica, which could accommodate five times the number that would be attending. Five thousand people were now gathered inside the vast echoing beauty of the basilica for a Mass with prayers chosen by Innocent himself, a votive offering, a personal paean to God Almighty in thanks for delivering this gift of gifts during his reign. In all the pomp and ceremony of the past half-year since he had become Pope, this was his proudest moment.

Pope Innocent had begun to feel uncomfortably at ease with the Roman love of pageantry. He had tried to humanise the papacy since his coronation, when he became successor to the popes who followed the Polish Pope, John Paul the Second. But the monolith of the Vatican had stood firmly against him and his path of progress. He felt he was single-handedly trying to move two millennia of tradition. He was a latter-day Sisyphus, rolling his rock of modernism up the mountain each day, only to have the cardinals of arch-conservatism wrench it out of his hands and roll it down again.

But the discovery of a list in the Holy Land, a list pointing directly to the last will and Testament of Jesus, the Messiah, well, that deserved the most beautiful of pageantry, as close to a choir of archangels as earthly man could mimic. For once, he and most of the Vatican were in full accord.

The choir of heavenly voices, boys with angelic faces and innocent demeanour, sang Verdi's *Ave Maria*. Pope Innocent had wanted the use of the Sistine Chapel because of its exquisite frescoes. They depicted events from the life of Christ and were a fitting tribute to this holy day of discovery, this epiphany, this day of rejuvenation of the faith; of the final triumph over the agnostics and the dismissal of the atheists. But Roncello had insisted just as vehemently on the use of the Vatican apartments for a small private service for those members of the Sacred College of Cardinals who were present in Rome, and a later public Mass in St Peter's Square.

Gabriel Molloy, the American prelate, had only narrowly been elected Pope by his peers. At six feet two, he towered over the Italian Cardinals, though none were cowed by either his stature or intellect. If he had the energy of New World modernism on his side, they had two thousand years of quiet arrogance and certainty in tradition on theirs. He had wisely appointed Cardinal Roncello as an assurance to the Old World that the New would not be revolutionary, nor intent upon hijacking the faith.

And there was a further reason that the American had appointed Roncello. A reason known only to him and his confessor. Many years ago, when he had just been enthroned as a bishop, Gabriel Molloy had suffered a crisis of faith. He had called his theology into question in an instant, one of those momentary insights into another reality that can doom the minds of even those whose faith is absolute. It returned soon after, but the fear of being without faith, even for a week, had a profound and unnerving effect on him. He remembered the feeling with horror. The solitude, the inexpressible loneliness, was like walking alone through a meadow on the blackest of nights, never knowing if the next footfall would lead to disaster. St Paul had enjoyed a revelation, alone on the road to Damascus. But Paul's experience was a revelation of God. A discovery of truth and light and goodness. Gabriel Molloy experienced a very different insight in a hospital room in Queens. The pain of doubt never fully left him, but so much had accreted to the raw wound that it hurt only in private, in the solitude of his mind, sitting in his favourite armchair. Cardinal Roncello was Pope Innocent's emblem of the innate goodness and constancy of the Catholic Church.

Catholic clergy, nuns, devout laypersons, journalists, representatives of the city of Rome, members of the Italian government and foreign diplomats filled the chapel. They stood in their places wearing lay or religious garb, listening to the melodic harmonies of the choir as voices rose towards heaven. Towards God. As the choir sang the final chords of the Verdi, the Prefect of the Congregation of the Doctrine of the Faith,

Alberto Cardinal Vincenzo, resplendent in voluminous silk, stepped painfully forward. His arthritic legs and gnarled hands supported a body straining under the massive weight of oedema which his personal physicians had not been able to bring under control. Yet his voice was strong and clear. He made the sign of the Cross over the congregation and led them in prayer.

When the prayer was concluded, he turned his back on the congregation and walked weakly towards the Pope. As he began to bend, two acolytes, one on either side, walked forward to help him. He knelt supported under his armpits and kissed the Pope's ring. The cardinal walked back to his place, a signal for two choirboys with the awe of mystery in their hearts and devotion in their eyes, to walk over to the Pope.

Previous popes had dispensed with the use of papal trains and choirboys in processions. But Gabriel, recognising that the future of the Church lay with its children, had invited orphans from third- and fourth-world countries to join him in the Vatican and to participate in ceremonies.

He eased his lean, athletic body, swathed in a canopy of white and gold vestments, out of his chair and slowly walked forward. The children, one from Venezuela, one from India, walked one step behind him. Innocent came to the microphone. He had no notes. He would speak to the congregation in Italian and—why not?—a bit of English. He would tell them his thoughts about this unprecedented find in the desert. He walked purposefully towards the microphones, breathing deeply, concerned that his voice would fail him in the most momentous announcement of his short reign, frightened that the news he carried with him would unbalance the faithful on the tightrope which they trod and cause them to plunge into doubt and despair.

He cleared his throat, made the sign of the Cross, and said in Latin, 'In the name of the Father, the Son and the Holy Spirit.' Then, in Italian, he continued, 'We, Innocent, Servant of the Servants of God, believe that a new day has dawned in the life of our Holy Catholic Church. A list has been found, written by one of the blessed ancients, who walked in the recent footsteps of Christ Our Lord. This list tells us that our Lord left a Testament. Nothing on earth, nothing created by man, of man, is as important to the future of humankind as is the Testament of our Messiah. Therefore, We, by the grace of God, Pope Innocent, do hereby commission the establishment of a new Crusade to the Holy Land.'

There was an audible gasp from the crowd. They had congregated assuming that the Mass would be little more than another thanksgiving ceremony. Innocent glanced at the scarlet vestments of his cardinals and noted the looks of consternation on their faces, one looking questioningly at the other.

'Our Crusade will be termed the Ninth Crusade. It is a Crusade gathered in peace and love, not to spread the Christian message to those who are content in their own faiths but to redeem from the Holy Land of Israel God's Word written for man. The Crusade will determine where our Lord Jesus Christ wrote and laid down His final words to this world. Our Crusade will be a holy endeavour to retrieve this Messianic gift and to usher in a new and glorious age.'

Five thousand faces stared breathless in astonishment at the Pope.

'He's done *what?*' shouted Franz Cardinal Kitzinger, his face livid with anger, matching the red of the piping and buttons on his cassock. 'A Crusade? This is madness.

How dare he, without the permission of the College of Cardinals?'

The tiny priest who had brought him the news moved backwards in fear and deference to the rage which was growing within the normally sedate and self-controlled German theologian. 'He was quite specific, your eminence. He left us in no doubt whatsoever. It's a pity you weren't there yourself.'

The German cardinal slowly turned his patrician head and glowered at the priest. 'I, and most of the other members of the Curia were engaged in other tasks. We don't have time to participate in this American's love of theatricality.' The priest bowed reverentially, a sign of submission and apology. Kitzinger paced his apartments.

He marched to the window and looked out over the panoply of the Vatican. 'Did he give any form to this Crusade? Does he intend to raise an army? Do we send the Swiss Guard out as mercenaries? Just what does our Holy Father plan to do, apart from alienating Catholicism from the rest of the human race?'

The priest shrank further into his chair and shook his head. 'I don't know,' he answered meekly.

Kitzinger dismissed the priest with a wave of his hand and stood looking through the window for several minutes at the domes and towers of the ancient city. How was he going to control this barbarian? Barbarian. What an interesting choice of words, he thought. It was how the geniuses of the Golden Age of Greece referred to people from the recently discovered New World of Europe. The guttural sounds they made sounded like dogs barking. Bah, bah. No! This Pope was not like that, not like the Goths and Visigoths and the other barbarians who brought destruction to ancient Rome; but just as surely, this new Pope was going to destroy modern Rome with his imperiousness and chic ideas.

All that Kitzinger could do was grudgingly concede him a fine intellect.

Yet there was even something about his intellect which frightened Kitzinger. Some indefinable trait, some characteristic which put him out of the traditional square, made him a maverick. Something in his past, perhaps. Something worth investigating. In the meantime, Gabriel Molloy was becoming as terrifying as John Paul the Second, the first pope from outside Italy in nearly five hundred years. John Paul had spent his life travelling around like some cheap politician, doing deals. Why was it that when a prelate was given the mantle of the papacy, the keys to the kingdom, he thought himself no longer a priest, but a politician, able to go on fact-finding tours, pumping flesh, working the crowds?

Cardinal Franz Kitzinger walked to his desk, picked up the phone and dialled a friend in Jerusalem. 'I wish to speak to his grace Hiram Solomonoglou.'

'His grace is currently meeting with a delegation of Coptic churchmen from Egypt. I don't think I can disturb him. May I ask who's speaking?'

'Tell his grace that Cardinal Kitzinger wishes to speak with him.'

The young priest changed his tone immediately. 'Your eminence, forgive me. I will put you straight through.'

After a moment, Franz heard the voice of his gentle friend. 'Eminence, how nice to hear from you. Is this a private conversation? I am in conference with others.'

'No, Hiram. I'm merely phoning to ask you to keep your eye on something for me in your country. I want to know Israel's reaction to the finding of this list.'

'It continues to be in all the newspapers, Franz,' the bishop interrupted. 'It's a reaction of joy and hope and they have assured the world that they will encourage any bona fide groups who wish to—'

'Yes, yes. That's the official line. I want to know what's behind the words. There's a reason for wanting to know. It'll be carried in your newspapers tonight, but I'm warning you in advance that our American friend has instituted a Crusade.'

'What?' the bishop asked, stunned. 'A Crusade! But this is terrible.'

'I know. I thought that would be your reaction.'

'But it will escalate things beyond belief. It will be the spark that ignites the powderkeg that is Israel. For God's sake, eminence, tell him to exercise extreme caution.'

'He has no understanding of caution.'

'What sort of a Crusade?' asked the elderly bishop, his voice drained.

'From what I can gather, not one with swords and daggers. More of an intellectual Crusade—a fact-finding mission.'

Hiram Solomonoglou remained silent, unsure how to proceed with the conversation. After a moment's pause, he asked, 'And how does your eminence view this latest development?'

'I'm terrified of speedy decisions when it comes to matters of the faith. It's something which needs careful deliberation. We can't suddenly rush into the desert like treasure-hunters. We are the Catholic faith.'

'Then dissuade him.'

'He's already made the announcement. The cat's out of the bag.'

'Then what value is there in my interpreting the Israeli government's reaction?'

'Dear friend, the Vatican currently sits at a crossroads between the Old World and the New. If we alienate governments around the world, especially governments as crucial to our faith as the government controlling the holy sites of Christendom, we could find ourselves in limbo. Remember what happened when John Paul unravelled the threads of Communism—internecine war, ethnic cleansing, thousands of women raped by xenophobic madmen. We have to tread carefully. Do as I ask, Hiram, and inform me of the real attitude of the government.'

Hiram nodded, 'As your eminence wishes.'

'I'm begging you not to do this.'

The American Pope looked in distress at the man who had been his friend for the past forty years. 'Don't *you* fight me, Danny. I have enough problems with the others.'

'I will fight you if I think you're wrong in matters of faith and doctrine. And I think you are wrong. Terribly and dangerously wrong!'

'Wrong? How can it be wrong to recover Christ's Testament?'

'It's not wrong to recover it. It's wrong to do it like this.'

'Then I'll change the name. I won't call it a Crusade any more. I'll call it a Holy Mission, a Papal Commission . . . you come up with the right name.'

Daniel Rhymer fidgeted with his crucifix—a habit he developed when he was a monsignor in Chicago. He twisted the tortured body of Christ on His Cross around his fingers, as though they were worry beads. 'It's not a question of changing the name of it, Gabby. That's only tinkering around the edges. What you've done is to invite haste and doubt into the proceedings.'

Pope Innocent wheeled around and looked at him in amazement. 'How so? Three nights ago, there was a momentous announcement. The most important in two thousand years. Yet your counsel is that I should sit and think about it? Dear God Almighty, Danny, do you think Ignatius de Loyola would have sat around for a couple of decades thinking of how to fight the Reformation. He got out there and—'

'And failed,' interrupted Danny. 'Instead of coming to an accommodation, we've had centuries of disputes with the Protestants. Instead of listening to Martin Luther's valid arguments about the moral laxity of the Renaissance church and the selling of indulgences, we ignored him at our peril. Instead of changing the church slowly, we erected a barrier and now there's an unbridgeable divide. You see what I mean, Gabby? In haste, you make mistakes.'

The Pope shook his head. 'Why do you equate speed with error?' he asked. 'If you saw a man drowning, would you sit and deliberate or would you plunge in regardless of the dangers? I'm simply organising the retrieval of Christ's Testament.'

'If it still exists.'

'You have little faith,' said the Pope, and immediately regretted his words. Gabby knew with certainty that Daniel's strength of purpose and beliefs had never wavered or varied. 'Daniel, forgive me for saying that. I've spent the morning speaking to Italian cardinals, English bishops, South American theologians—the whole spectrum. They've all told me what I should and shouldn't do. My mind feels as if it's swimming upstream against doubt and despair. What's happening, Danny? We've just received the greatest news in history. The news that our Christ, our Messiah, has left a Testament for us to follow. And now half the theological community—you included—wants me to slow down and think about it. Well, I don't want to think about it. I want to recover it and bring it to Rome where it belongs.'

'And then?' asked Daniel.

Gabriel Molloy frowned.

'What happens then?' repeated Danny.

'It becomes the centrepiece of our faith,' Gabby told him. 'It becomes the foundation for the next two millennia or until the Second Coming of Jesus. Isaiah said "Prepare ye the way of the Lord". Danny, this could be the preparation for the Second Coming, the Great Day of the Parousia!'

'And if it isn't? If we do find Christ's Testament, if we somehow manage to track it down from this arcane list, what then? What if the translation merely talks about Christ being a man and not the Son of God? What if it points us in the wrong direction? What happens to the faith then?'

'Do you think I haven't thought of that?' said Gabriel. 'I've agonised since the announcement. But I have faith that the words God left us will be the signpost for the future. They're the words we've been praying to read for two thousand years. We can't ignore them now.'

'I'm not saying ignore them,' Daniel said curtly. 'But first we have to consider the theological implications.'

'You surprise me.' Gabriel smiled reassuringly at his old friend. 'Funny thing, isn't it, Danny? I always had the perception that I was the theological conservative in America. Straight down the line. You were the man who was always pushing the faith into new areas of experimentation. What was it they used to call you at seminary? Radical Rhymer?'

Rhymer ignored the quip. 'Gabby, this situation is far too dangerous for humour. Forget theology for a minute. What about this bastard Berg, and what he did to the Holy Sepulchre.'

Innocent felt his shoulders fall. He nodded. 'Yes. It was a vicious and terrible act and I pray for those pathetic men of God who have suffered from his insanity. But blame cannot be sheeted home to me, Daniel. You must realise that! This lunatic would have found any excuse to attack the church, just to further his own bizarre ambition.'

Daniel nodded. 'You're probably right, but it's a horrible coincidence. Look, I know you find this attitude difficult to accept from me, Gabby. We're both Americans and yet for once I'm eschewing my American heritage. I'm asking us to slow down and not go charging ahead.'

'Eminence, I understand your need for caution, for circumspection. But this news means that urgent measures have to be taken.'

'Why?' demanded Rhymer. 'Christ's Testament has been lost for two thousand years. You, as God's representative on Earth, as the successor to Peter, must pray for enlightenment. But if the answer to your prayers was to hide it until a new age of enlightenment dawned, then we have to wonder whether this is the age.' He paced the floor. 'Look at the world, Gabby. Disease, violence, amorality, poverty, lust, a breakdown of values, a lacking of faith. How can you think to impose something so potentially divisive on this maelstrom of confusion?'

The Pope rose from his chair. 'Divisive?' he snapped. 'Danny, this is God's word given to man.'

Daniel turned on him. 'And how do we know that man is ready? This is a different world from the world in which Christ lived. The simplicity of His message has been complicated by man's ego and the speed with which he can communicate messages. His need for material fulfilment and self-aggrandisement. It's been perverted by bigots and fundamentalists and internecine rivalry. Look at the way Catholicism has changed. The schisms, the divisions, the breakaways. Look at the problem Luther created when he protested, look at the debates of the theologians over the centuries, endlessly arguing how many angels could stand on the head of a pin, or whether Christ was poor when he died.'

'That was man's intervention, not God's,' said Gabriel.

'Precisely.'

'And what should we do, Danny? Leave it there for another couple of millennia? When will the time be right? And who are we to judge God's word, or more especially God's purpose?'

'We are the leaders of God's church on earth,' Daniel said quietly. The Pope again sat in his favourite arm-chair. It was the only memento which he had brought with him from America. It had been a present from his sister when he became a bishop. Before she began to hate him.

'My friend, your arguments are persuasive but I have to be against you. I'm the occupant of the throne of St Peter. I was entrusted with the spiritual well-being and continuity of the faith,' said Pope Innocent. 'What you say is a natural consequence of our Catholic Church. It's two thousand years old. It does make decisions slowly and cautiously after great consideration. To rush at things can harm the faith of the pious.'

The Pope glimpsed a vision of himself in one of the gilt mirrors. He was feeling old. He looked away immediately. He glanced at his friend and said, 'There are certain turning points in history where unheralded events are the precursors of great changes. We are at that turning point. I'm sorry you and I are in disaccord, but the keys to the kingdom of Heaven were entrusted to me. I must plan my own path.'

Pope Innocent was tired. 'Eminence, tomorrow you will come to me with the names of experts in the fields of theology, Hebrew, Aramaic and philology, and especially biblical archaeology. Then I will send them out to recover Christ's Testament from the Judean desert, or wherever the hand of God guides them.'

Daniel Rhymer shook his head sadly and began to say, 'The Israeli government will never allow—'

'And there's one final thing, Daniel. You will lead the Crusade.'

'I? But—'

'I want you to go to Israel within the next month. Lay down the ground work. Why don't you drop in and see Francis? For the meantime, keep the visit fairly low key. No receptions or anything like that. Just you and me and a handful of others will know.'

'Gabby, I can't go to Israel. My heart's not in this. It's not fair you asking me.'

'May I suggest, Daniel, that you re-read the Book of Deuteronomy, chapter 18, verses 17 to 22.'

Daniel Cardinal Rhymer was forced to miss his evening meal. He had to do two things. First re-read the Book of Deuteronomy, and second supervise his staff's putting together a list for the Pope. Thousands of superbly qualified Catholic academics were available to the Church. Many held high positions in their countries, either in churches, seminaries, monasteries, universities, or in the laity.

There were experts in all fields, from the sciences to philosophy, the Bible to the arts. For two thousand years, the Church had fulfilled its role as the teacher of humanity, the researcher of facts. The problem Daniel faced was selecting those he considered to be the most theologically sound for the job. He realised that in order for his nominees to be accepted by the Pope, the list he presented must contain men who were both experts and would work within the strictures imposed by the Church.

He needed people well versed in the early Church, on Judaism in Roman times, on Aramaic, Hebrew, Koine, Greek and Latin and on the archaeology of the Holy Land. He needed experts on history, philology, biblical archaeology and Bible exegesis.

It took him four hours to select ten names from a shortlist of over two hundred suitable candidates from four continents. Scanning them, he was satisfied that they would do the job. He looked at his watch. It was 1.30 in the morning. A little late for food. Were he to eat now, he would have another nightmare and feel ill in the morning. Better to fast and wake up with a body cleansed, refreshed. He went to the corner in his apartments where his secretary had set up a crucifix on the wall. There he knelt and said his prayers.

Next morning, after a disturbed sleep, he said his prayers once again, had breakfast and, as he was leaving his room, the phone rang. He answered and a voice said, 'Daniel, you evil old reprobate, how are you?'

Daniel beamed a smile. Francis had been a close friend for years. Daniel always believed that Francis should have been a reporter, he was so inquisitive. Had it not been for the purity of his heart, his inviolable moral goodness, his desire to help and to alleviate the suffering of others, he probably would have been. But he was now living on a *Moshav* in Israel, helping the orphans of Palestinian Christian families, caught in the no-man's-land of Israeli and Arab hatred. He asked for up-to-the-minute reactions to the finding of the list.

'To tell you the truth, Francis,' said Daniel, 'the Vatican is split fifty–fifty as far as I can tell. The liberals are over the moon, the conservatives are cautious.'

'Cautious?' said Francis. 'You surprise me. I wouldn't have thought there was any room for caution. I've spoken to a dozen Catholic priests here in Israel, and they're ecstatic.'

'I understand the euphoria, but I think it has to be tempered with due regard for the security of the faith.'

He heard Francis chuckle. 'Radical Rhymer, the conservative?'

'Francis, you can do me a little service.'

'That sounds Byzantine.'

'Nothing out of the ordinary, just some help with the feeling of the Israeli people, the Jews. Our friend here in the hot seat has made a decision to institute a Crusade.'

'Yes, I read about it this morning. But Danny, a Crusade? What made him think up that name? There's still people here who haven't forgiven the Knights Templar for massacring the Jews and the Saracens.'

'I know, but what I'm interested in is the reaction of the people. We're about to form a group of experts and I want to know how they will be received. I know the Israelis are terribly xenophobic. The last thing we need is trouble in that area. Oh, and by the way, I'll be coming over there in a couple of days. I'll be incognito. A scouting exercise before the public show.'

Francis was delighted at the news. 'I'll do some listening next time I'm up in Jerusalem and get back to you. Mind if I reverse the charges? We're a bit short of cash at the moment.'

'Reverse whatever you want, old friend. Do you need money? Can I help you?'

'No, no. We're fine so long as we keep our expenditure under control.'

'God be with you. See you shortly.'

Daniel walked down the Via de Porta Angelica, past the Belvedere Palace to the Papal Palace.

A member of the Swiss Guard opened the door to the Pope's private apartments. After a few moments, the Pope appeared through the vast, ornately carved white and gold doors at the end of the chamber. He smiled at his friend and asked, 'Have you got it?'

They walked into a small audience room, sat down and discussed the choices.

'I'll write personally to everyone here,' said Innocent. 'Do you think anyone will refuse?'

'I doubt it. There's not one person here that wouldn't crawl on hands and knees for the chance to examine the Dead Sea Scrolls. It's what every Bible scholar has been trying to do for half a century,' said Daniel.

'And do you think we'll have any difficulties with the Israeli government or the International Team?'

'No,' Daniel said, shaking his head. 'We have a right to see a biblical treasure. They wouldn't want to start an international incident. And anyway, it's not as though we're asking for anything out of the ordinary.'

Gabriel poured himself a cup of coffee. Daniel helped himself. Stirring it, Gabriel said, 'Then let the Crusade begin.'

CHAPTER 7

By the time the Chief Rabbi and the Minister for Religious Affairs arrived at Room 4D of the Knesset building, Prime Minister Moishe Rabbinowitz was already in the room, deep in conversation with the Minister for Tourism and the Catholic Archbishop of Jerusalem, Hiram Solomonoglou. They walked straight in without knocking, an indication of the seriousness of the meeting. Archbishop Solomonoglou looked up and nodded as the two men walked towards the table. The minister sat down but the Chief Rabbi walked around to his peer, who stood to kiss him on both cheeks. Each was devastated by the desecration of the Church of the Holy Sepulchre.

The Prime Minister waited for the men to be seated before saying 'Chaim, I've been telling his eminence of our shock and revulsion at what these madmen did yesterday afternoon.'

Hiram Solomonoglou, resplendent in black biretta and robes with a massive gold crucifix hanging at his breast, waved his hand in dismissal. 'Prime Minister, we know that the Israeli government isn't to blame for the action of Rabbi Berg. This situation is different from the slaughter of the thirty Muslim worshippers in the Cave of the Patriarchs in Hebron. By the grace of God, no one was killed in the Holy Sepulchre, though many are still in hospital. The damage we sustained yesterday is more than the broken paving stones or the bones of our priests. The injury is to the spirit of ecumenism which we have been striving to reach for these past years.'

The Chief Rabbi nodded and interrupted. 'We all have madmen on our side. You have anti-Semites, the

Muslims have fundamentalists, we have this chimera, this David Berg, who spits hate and viciousness every time he speaks. But what are we going to do to protect the holy sites of Christendom?'

'And Islam,' said the Minister for Religious Affairs.

The Prime Minister looked at him. 'Do you think that the mosques are in danger? His attack on the Holy Sepulchre was linked to the discovery of the list. My fear is the reaction to the Pope's announcement of the Crusade.'

'That *meshuggeneh*, Berg!' said the Minister for Tourism. 'He'll attack anything that's not Jewish. He was just waiting for an opportunity like this. Till now, his activities have been in the Occupied Territories, now with this Crusade,' he turned and bowed in deference to the archbishop, 'honourable of course as it is, has given him a reason to attack holy sites in the Old City. Do you think he'll just stop at Christian churches? He'll attack Islam next, and for all we know, he'll attack our own Hasidic community. The man's out of control.'

'Then arrest him,' said Hiram.

The Prime Minister interrupted. 'Your Grace, he's been arrested. We locked him up, plus twenty of his followers, at eight o'clock last night. They didn't put up any resistance. They just went singing their way into prison.'

The archbishop looked surprised. 'Why was this not announced?'

'I want to play everything low key,' said the Prime Minister. 'If I move too publicly, I'll make a martyr of him.'

'But surely arresting him stops the problem.'

'No,' said Moishe. 'I wish it were as simple as that. He's like a hydra. You cut off one of his heads and another half a dozen pop out from nowhere. Just arresting him is not going to stop these madmen. He'll direct them from prison, get word out to them, tell them to beat up the poor monks in some other church.'

'Then arrest them all,' suggested the Chief Rabbi.

'We have no idea who his followers are. He claims to have ten thousand in Israel. Shin Bet tells us their best estimate is under a thousand, but there are no membership lists, no cards that they carry. We don't know who they are or where they live. It's like the Mafia. Like some secret society. I'm at my wit's end, gentlemen.'

The Minister for Religious Affairs cleared his throat. 'How is last night's raid impacting on the rest of the world?' he asked.

'I phoned the Vatican last night and spoke to His Holiness,' the archbishop answered. 'He was devastated. He's issuing a statement denouncing the activities and praying for understanding. His Holiness says that, if necessary, he will change the name from "Crusade" to "Mission". He asks forgiveness of the Jewish people for any insult that he may unintentionally have caused.'

The Prime Minister shook his head in defence. 'No, eminence, the Pope has caused us no offence. He talked with me personally before he made the announcement. After his explanation I said I could see no harm in it. After all, as he said, a Crusade means, literally, a movement to retrieve the Cross. We share this land with two other faiths. We're its custodians. His Holiness is welcome to examine anything found in Israel which affects Christianity. But nobody can take into account the prejudices of men like Berg and other fundamentalists, and the lengths to which they'll go to propagate their own brand of hatred.'

A steward knocked on the door and wheeled in trays of coffee, soft drinks and sandwiches. All the men took a break as they were served. When the steward had left, the Minister for Tourism asked, 'So, Moishe, what are we going to do?'

The Prime Minister looked around the table, shrugged and said, 'Any suggestions?'

'Why can't you apply the law against Berg and his followers? They have been guilty of assaults, trespass and other crimes,' said the bishop.

The Prime Minister smiled wearily. 'That would be the most obvious measure. But we haven't got any positive identification that Berg was one of the attackers. And this morning, twelve witnesses have come forward swearing depositions that he was praying with them last night. The bastard's got an answer for everything.'

The Minister for Religious Affairs said, 'If he can abuse the law, then apart from Shin Bet and the police raiding their known headquarters and trying to destroy them from outside, I can't think of much we can do.'

Hiram sighed deeply and shook his head from side to side, fearful of the future.

The tiny cafe in the Old City was crowded. Americans drinking in the atmosphere of the Bible, Jews enjoying the texture of the Arab *shuk*, Arabs enjoying morning coffee. Michael stirred his coffee, Judith sipped her malt beer.

'Why were you so aggressive to me in the valley?' he asked.

'I was angry. I thought twenty years would have buried it, but—'

'Have you calmed down yet?'

She shrugged, her indifference a studied eloquence.

'Are you going to continue snapping at me every time we meet alone? Are we going to be civilised in public only?'

She shrugged again.

Michael became angry. She had opened a wound, but he was damned if he was going to bleed, not after all these years. 'Do you think it's better if we don't meet again.'

She looked at him, searching his face, exploring the lines in it which were new to her, lines which his wife had witnessed developing in the ten years of their marriage. She smiled. It was the first sign of warmth since they had met that morning.

Other people walked into the cafe. An Arabic record of indeterminate male or female voice wailed a song, the ululations inharmonious to their Western ears.

'Are you scared of being alone with me, Michael?'

'No, not scared, but I'm certainly cautious. I can't gauge you.'

'Understand one thing. You're no longer important to me. You're out of my life.'

'Then why did you ring me?' he asked.

She diverted his question. 'Stop looking for a level playing field, because where you and I stand is strewn with rocks.'

'Of my making?' he asked, defensively.

'Certainly not of mine.'

He breathed deeply and looked at the people in the room. Dour-faced, dark-skinned Arabs, their heavily bearded chins and drooping moustaches framed by their *keffiyehs* stared contemptuously back at him. They made him feel an intruder. Yet the tourists thrilled vicariously at their close encounters with the genuine flavour of the Middle East, drinking in the smoky, acrid, alien, dangerous atmosphere.

He was hesitant to broach the subject. Judith was like a dormant volcano, suppressing the next eruption. 'You're acting as if you were the only one hurt.'

At first, she didn't appear to understand. She frowned.

'I was hurt just as badly as you were,' he continued.

'You bastard!' She was livid. 'You ruined my life, your parents', you spat in the face of everybody who loved you, and you have the audacity to say that you were hurt. Well, tough shit. I hope you're still suffering.'

'Yes, I'm still suffering. You haven't figured in my life in years. But believe me, I'm still suffering, as if I'm cursed. I feel like I'm being tested daily by God Himself.'

Her anger suddenly dissipated. She flushed in embarrassment, reached over and touched his arm. 'Oh, Michael. I'm so sorry. I'd completely forgotten. I shouldn't have said what I did, it was cruel.'

One of the tourists stood and walked over to the jukebox, trying to determine whether it was an original model, left over from a former time, or whether it was a modern replica, nostalgically reminding visitors of their American homeland. He was egged on by his friends, as though he were about to undertake some feat of bravery. Michael listened, and envied them their lack of complications. The tourist pressed buttons and immediately a heavy-metal band boomed its cacophony throughout the small room.

Michael stirred his coffee idly, retreating to his corner of the table, wishing that this whole episode in his life would disappear and go away.

'Judith, what do you want me to say? I'm sorry I hurt you. I'm sorry we didn't get married. I'm sorry for a whole load of things. But it's too late to mend. We can only judge each other by our actions today, by who we've become. Can't you just do that?'

She stared down at the tabletop and began to play with the salt and pepper cruet. 'I suppose you're right. I just feel very frustrated, Michael, pissed off with life. I'd got it under control and then you walked back into it.'

'But you phoned me.'

She smiled.

'Why did you?'

'I don't know. I wish I hadn't.'

'But you did!'

She nodded. 'It's a long story. Don't ask.' She seemed to relax and looked at him with a wry smile.

The discussion was getting nowhere, the old ground stony and dry. They sipped their drinks, allowing the peaks and troughs of their passion to subside.

'How long have you been married?' Michael asked. 'What happened to you since we . . . since university?'

'After I graduated, I took a commission in the army. I was patriotic, but still wanted to be an archaeologist.'

'I've read your articles in biblical reviews. You've got some incredible insights into the Bar Kochba rebellion.'

'You never wrote and congratulated me on them,' she said, looking at him distantly.

'You never wrote to me about my Dead Sea Scrolls articles, either.'

'Touché. I always knew you'd become one of the world's leading lights. You have this determination to succeed in whatever you do. Well, most things.'

It hurt, but Michael smiled. 'You know as well as I do that you don't become an authority just on determination. You have to believe with all your heart in what you're doing, devote yourself selflessly to your subject.'

Judith nodded in agreement. They were talking about their professions. It was safer ground. A slight thawing of the ice. An acceptance that wrongs had been done on both sides. Judith drank her malt beer, wiped the foam from her upper lip and again looked at him with something approaching warmth.

'I was down at Masada yesterday,' he told her, 'sitting by the Dead Sea. Thinking back to our student days. I experienced an overwhelming sense of loneliness down there. For the first time since I was a boy in my parents' house, I felt as if there was nobody else in the world. Only me. Against all the elements. As though a primal force had intervened and cut me off from safety and the love of other human beings. I felt as though I was abandoned.'

She ran her finger around the rim of her glass, slowly in deliberate concentric movements, until the glass sang a high-pitched song. Then she stopped.

'Why did Ari want us to meet again?' Michael asked her.

'He knows us both better than ourselves.'

Michael frowned. 'What do you mean?'

'It's not important.'

'Judith!'

'Leave it, Michael.'

'No!' he said. 'I won't. You call me, you open up wounds, you toy with me, then you stick your knives in and twist them. What the hell game are you playing? Is this some eighteenth-century revenge tragedy? Some plot that you and Ari hatched up between you? "Let's get Michael! Let's fuck up his already fucked-up life"?'

The background noise in the cafe stilled as people on other tables stared, but their reactions went unnoticed.

'It's nothing like that. I'm shocked you could have thought Ari would do such a thing! Or me!'

'Then why?' he asked.

Her deep blue eyes searched his face, pondering whether now was the right time. Softly she responded, 'Ari wants your happiness. He loves you.'

Michael shook his head. Nothing was clear. Judith continued, 'And he wants the same for me.'

He stared at her open-mouthed. His mother would have quipped that he was catching flies.

'I love you, you stupid bastard,' she said gently. 'I've loved you ever since that first day you came up to me in the library and asked me where you could find books on Rabbi Akiva. Like I was some librarian. It was such a transparent excuse, but it was cute, gentle.'

Michael's mind raced to find an island of calm in the storm of thoughts.

'When we were together, my love was so strong, nothing else mattered. But when you converted I felt that my heritage was more important than our relationship. I've been regretting it ever since.'

'But you're married.'

She smiled. 'He's a typical Sabra. Cold, hard, precise. He's arrogant, superficial, he has none of the qualities I love in you.'

'Then why did you marry him?'

'Because he wasn't you.'

Michael was close to tears. 'Judith, I love you more now than I've ever loved another human being. Oh God! I'm yearning for you. But it's too late.'

She reached over and touched his hand. 'Not for me, Michael. I'm about to divorce Uri.'

'But I can never divorce Deirdre. She'd never allow it. Her Catholicism.'

They had been walking slowly through the streets of Jerusalem for over an hour. The heat, the petrol fumes, the noise were making him giddy.

They turned into a park in a part of the city he did not know. The park was dotted with clumps of different trees—casuarina, eucalyptus, pine and cypress—casting varying amounts of shade over the strategically positioned seats. Elderly people sat vacantly on the benches, resting, waiting for the time to pass. Michael was terrified of reaching an age when his mind was still active, but his body was worn and tired and refused to respond. Looking at the old men and women reclining against the backs of the benches, heads lolling in a parody of sleep, visions of Christopher trespassed upon his thoughts. As Israeli mothers played with their excited children, he became angry yet again that his ten-year-old son, who should have been playing soccer and fending off the advances of mischievous girls, was imprisoned in a wheelchair, swaddled in blankets, his sightless eyes and perverse ears allowing him no sense of himself, no freedom of thought, no knowledge of the glories of the world around him. Michael fought back tears.

Judith walked over to an unoccupied bench. Michael followed. The noise of the traffic outside the gates diminished when they sat. Around the base of the thicket of trees was a bed of flowers, narcissi, anemones and cyclamen. Two bulbuls and a hooded crow were pecking at insects and seeds on the ground, indifferent to their arrival. A hoopoe, with its extraordinary pointed crest, flew out of the tree and landed at their feet, feeling no intimidation at their presence. It waddled arrogantly away from them, and joined the other birds in the search for food.

'This talk about Bar Kochba,' she said. 'I don't understand it. He seems a bit distant from the Essenes and the Dead Sea Scrolls.'

The shock of her confession had driven away all thoughts of Jesus and the Testament. Suddenly he was catapulted back to the present, to his purpose. 'Last week, I would have agreed with you. We were working blind. But with this new information, I think we have to broaden our horizons. What's that dreadful American expression used by advertising men—think beyond the square.'

She picked up a piece of stale bread, like a white chip of marble, which someone before them must have dropped, and threw it to the birds. They ignored her largesse. 'But why Bar Kochba?' she continued. 'He was around about sixty years after the fall of Masada. To the best of my knowledge, he had no connection with the Essenes. Anyway, weren't the Essenes all wiped out after the fall of Jerusalem?'

'Nobody knows. It's always been assumed that they dissolved into history. Like the Sadducees. Dinosaurs of Judaism.'

'And you think this latest discovery suggests they might have survived?'

'It's far too early to say that. I haven't even seen the list. I can only take the team's word that it's accurate.'

'But how can you be sure that the "Jeshua of Nazareth" this list refers to is the same as Jesus the Messiah. Think about it. There could have been hundreds of Jeshuas who lived in Nazareth over the centuries.'

Michael shook his head. 'No! That's the interesting thing. You see, Nazareth isn't even mentioned in the Old Testament, or in the writings of the rabbis. In fact, the first mention of it is in St John's Gospel, Chapter 1, verse 46, when he quotes Nathanael: "Can anything good come from Nazareth?" It was a small and insignificant place in those days. A tiny village. Maybe a hundred people at most. I'm sure that was a clue left to us by St John.'

'Okay, so it was tiny. But that still doesn't prove—'

'Prove? No! But think about this. We know that there's strong circumstantial evidence to show that Jesus joined the monastery at Qumran. In all the writings that have been found in the caves, there's never been any reference to where one of the community members came from. He came into existence when he was baptised into the community.

'Suddenly, out of the dust of the past, we have a document which tells us that this obviously important man, Jeshua, came from Nazareth. In other words, the librarian or repositorian, or whoever created the list, thought that one and single fact to be of significance.'

Judith was sceptical. 'But you haven't seen the other documents. You have no idea whether they present new styles of reference or not. Surely you have to study this sort of thing before you can go galloping off on wild goose chases. Oh shit! I've just mixed a metaphor.'

Michael burst out laughing. Judith joined in. The birds were startled, and flew away into the safety of the trees. After the conversation in the cafe, after he had recovered from her stunning admission, the anger dissipated, and they drew together. The hardened layers which had accreted over the years, protective laminas to shield their hearts from the pain, were slowly beginning to strip away. Now she was touching him unconsciously, grasping his arm, poking him playfully, skittishly, when he made a mistake. The long-dormant seed was beginning to swell and grow, to burst as a sapling into the warmth of her affection.

Michael sat back and hooked his arms around the back of the bench. Without touching her, she was in the crook of his arm. It was a regression to his boyhood, the sort of trick he used to get up to on the bus riding home from school. The thrill of touching a girl's shoulder without her objection, feeling her warmth, imagining her closeness. Intimacy by proxy. Why was he so shy about touching her?

'Let me put a proposition to you. Shoot me down in flames, but hear me out,' she said.

Michael agreed.

Judith took a deep breath. 'Let's imagine that the Qumran monastery is overrun, or deserted some time after AD 70. The Essenes escape or are scattered to other Essene communities, or join other Jewish groups. The Romans have won and tens of thousands of Jews go into slavery.'

He nodded as she continued, 'Israel seethes under Roman domination during the reigns of Trajan and Hadrian. By the year AD 130, the city had been partially repopulated after its destruction by Titus in AD 70 but Bar Kochba begins to marshal forces. Hadrian crushes the Judean revolt between AD 132 and 134. He's rebuilt Jerusalem as a Greek city, *Aelia Capitolina*. Bar Kochba, Rabbi Akiva and all the rest make their final, glorious stand, grab their weapons, and begin the last part of the guerilla war.' She sounded like a university lecturer.

Michael nodded. He was a willing student. So far, it was an accurate reflection of the facts.

'Say there was a scribe, an historian, a librarian—I've no idea what—whose father was an Essene. He told his son about these incredible treasures in the caves around Masada.'

He would not let her continue. It offended his sense of academic integrity. 'You're going off on a wild flight of fantasy. Where's the proof?'

'No proof. But just hear me out. This is a hypothesis. Now, what do you think would have happened to the treasures?'

'Treasures?' said Michael.

'Temple ornaments, candelabra, maybe the *Urim and Thummim*, documents, wills and Testaments.'

'Okay, Temple treasures, maybe. Things sacred to the Jews. But why some Testament from an obscure first-century apostate who fancied himself as a Messiah? That's where your theory falls down.'

'What if this librarian-type was a convert to Christianity?'

'Bloody hell, Judith,' Michael shouted. 'Enough with the "what ifs". I'm an archaeologist. Not a philosopher.'

'There's one more "what if". What if this Essene who converted to Christianity went to gather the treasures from the caves at Masada. Being a librarian or repositorian, he would have left a list, wouldn't he? Just like a librarian today. They can't bear to withdraw books without leaving a note to say who's taken it.'

'Good God, woman!' Michael groaned. 'Are we dealing here in fantasy or fact? Remember the trouble I got into three years ago with that paper I wrote about the Essenes being vegetarians?'

She ignored the comment. 'You can't get anywhere unless you make assumptions.'

'Assumptions, sure. Schliemann worked on assumptions when he figured out the site of Troy. And Zeitzen worked out the location of Masada. But they had something concrete to go on. This! This is all pure fantasy,' Michael informed her.

'Well, just indulge me for another minute,' she said. 'Put yourself in the mind of that man, or woman. In your possession you have priceless treasures which you want to keep out of the hands of the Romans at all costs. What would you do with them?'

He looked up into the trees and rested his back against the seat.

'I'd probably try to get them to a Jewish or Christian community outside Israel.'

Judith beamed. 'Right! How would you leave the country? Where would you go?'

Michael pursed his lips, and thought back to Israel in the time of the Bible. 'Rome? No. Too dangerous. Damascus? Possibly. Bit close to the Romans. Antioch?

Definite possibility. Antioch was a big centre. You could easily lose yourself there.'

'But you'd be travelling north, right into the lap of Roman power.'

'Okay, how about south? Into Egypt, say Alexandria. Some Roman influence, but not as strong. There was a very big Jewish community there, especially in the upper reaches of the Nile. There was a huge Jewish temple at Elephantine, near the first cataract. You know the rumour?'

She shook her head.

'It's said that the temple was built in Egypt to house the Ark of the Covenant when it left Israel some time between Solomon and King Josiah.'

'You're beginning to get my drift. Treasures would be taken out of the country to safeguard them from the Romans, just like the theories that the Ark was taken out of Israel to protect it from the Babylonian invasion.'

Michael laughed aloud. 'Judith, you've been reading too many of these populist bullshit conspiracy theorists. Everything you've spoken about is fantasy. Not a shred of fact.'

Judith became angry. He felt he had gone too far. He didn't want her anger to return. He drew back apologetically. 'Don't become defensive. If you're going to promote this idea of yours, you're going to meet a lot of criticism.'

She nodded. 'I'm not promoting anything, I'm just trying to help you. But back to where the Testament could have been taken. If it had gone to Egypt, the Jewish community would have given it protection.'

'And interestingly,' said Michael, 'that was where some of the earliest Christian ministries were established.'

Judith reflected, now at the end of her journey. 'Yep. If it were me, I'd go to Alexandria or even further.'

Michael shook his head. 'No. It's too pat. Too convenient. You're forgetting, this is a Christian document. It would have followed Peter and Paul to Rome. I've given it a lot of thought. There are great libraries in the Vatican. Somewhere, assuming it's still in existence, a librarian in Rome has it locked at the bottom of a drawer along with a thousand other unopened scrolls and deeds. That's where it was taken, if it was removed at all. The Dead Sea, or Rome.'

Judith shook her head. 'No. I've also given it a lot of thought. I've gone beyond the square and considered where this mythical person could have travelled if he'd gone beyond Alexandria.'

'If what you say is correct, he would have been crazy to travel on. You mean to Cyrenaica, round the top of Egypt. To Ptolemais, or Cyrene, or Berenice. Those were two-bit towns. Of almost no importance,' said Michael.

Judith was deflated. 'So you reckon he'd have stopped in Alexandria. I don't. I think he'd have travelled on. An early Christian would have run up against the Jewish establishment.'

They remained silent, their thoughts not of the present but of thousands of years in the past. But the past intruded on the present when Judith looked up and saw a young Arabic boy walking through the park, wearing a black and white chequered *keffiyeh*. The boy glanced over to where they sat. His ancestry must have been from the southern climes of the Arab world. His skin was dark, almost to the point of being black. Probably a Muslim of Sudanese or Egyptian origin. Judith was suddenly struck by a thought, something which took her beyond the present, and even the ancient past, enabling her to view the cradle of civilisation from a distant height, seeing obscure races, now long vanished, trading with each other, warring, exploring. She saw land masses, high mountains, pure furious rivers, vast equatorial plains. She saw caravans of ancestral people, proud and rugged, travelling routes carved out of the pool of human experience, people wearing biblical robes, leading camels into caravanserais to escape the infernal heat of the desert. She looked at Michael with the light of inspiration in her eyes. 'My God!'

'What?' he asked.

'I wonder—'

'Don't keep me in suspense. What are you talking about?'

'South.' She said it as though she were giving him an answer to a crossword puzzle.

'South? There was nothing south of Alexandria', he said.

'Oh yes there was.'

Realisation dawned on his face. 'Judith, that's the most fanciful notion I've ever heard. You've not got one shred of evidence.'

'No, but I bet I know where we can get some. I've been working with them since they arrived in Israel.'

He shook his head in wonder. 'The Falashas of Ethiopia?' She nodded.

CHAPTER 8

It was three years and two months to the day since Jonas Watkins had lifted up his hands and been joined forever with Jimmy Wilson. Jonas was the harvest of the slum fields of Los Angeles. When he was twelve, he carried a knife for self-protection, and knew how to use it. At thirteen, he upgraded to a gun. On his fourteenth birthday, his pusher gave him a present of a mobile phone and a Motorola pager. In his wallet he never carried less than $5000. He controlled drug supply for his school and subcontracted drugs to twenty-three other schools in the area. In the early days, when the stars who lived in the Hollywood Hills and their personal fitness trainers were wearing them, he was the only kid in the slums with pump-up Reeboks. And nobody was game to take them from him. Jonas was living life on a high, despite the fears which his mother and father preached every morning and every night. His brother Micah, three years older, was warning him all the while about the danger of what he was doing. But Jonas knew best. Jonas had the touch. Jonas was rich, and wealth was the language of power.

Jonas made more money in one five-minute deal than his old man earned in a week. But his cut wasn't just spent on clothes and music. He bought his mother and father, and even Micah, beautiful things. And they received them with scorn and derision, and put them in the cupboard. Because they knew that one day they would have to give them back. The more he bought, the more he had to buy.

It was the only down-side of his life. The constant trauma within the household. Every day when he came home from the construction site his father screamed and shouted that his son was a no-good bum; his mother wore more and more crucifixes around her neck in the hope that her incantations and mantras would magically cure her son of the diseases of greed and arrogance.

Lieutenant Jose Celebrio cured Jonas more swiftly and completely than all his mother's crucifixes or nostrums. Jonas and his private battalion had decided that the school scene was too small for them and one night went to a neighbourhood bar to do some dealing. They made reasonable money but the following morning a police patrol car screamed to a halt in front of the Watkins' tenement block and two officers pulled the fifteen-year-old off the street. Ten minutes later, their car slowed down sufficiently for them to throw him head first into a back alley deep within Watts. The police car blazed away in a cloud of tyre smoke and petrol fumes, leaving Jonas alone, sprawled on the filthy ground.

He watched the retreating car and wondered what in hell was going on. Nobody treated Jonas this way. He'd kick ass for this, but good. As he picked himself up and dusted down his suede jacket, Levi jeans and rubbed his Reeboks clean on the back of his pants, a voice from deep within the shadows of the alley growled, 'Come 'ere punk.'

Jonas looked around for the source and in the dusty half light of the alley saw a tall, paunchy, muscular man arrogantly sauntering towards him. He walked with a slow swagger, strutting with the confidence of a man who owned the alley. He towered over Jonas. Jonas was petrified. 'What you want?' the boy asked, trying to sound confident, the high-pitched timbre of his voice betraying his fear.

'Youse done a stupid thing last night. I been watchin' youse de past coupla months. Youse doin' all right kid but you gettin' too fuckin' big too quick. You treadin' on de toes o' friends of mine. They ask me to teach you a lesson.'

Jonas stared in horror at his nemesis. For the next fifteen minutes he was beaten and kicked senseless by the huge Hispanic detective. Not one person out of the four hundred who lived in apartments adjacent to the alleyway saw or heard anything. Only after the detective walked away from the prostrate bloodied boy lying in the gutter did a fearful resident call an ambulance.

Jonas was in hospital for four weeks. It took a further month for his bones to mend and wounds to heal. But he was cured of greed and avarice forever. At first, he was desperate for revenge. Swathed in plaster and bandages, he spent hours on the phone trying to track down the man who did it to him. Being street-smart, he knew it must have been a cop. It was then that Micah began to intervene. Cautiously, deliberately, Micah told Jonas that real revenge didn't involve a beating. It came through turning the other cheek. Micah taught him that the beating was God's way of setting Jonas on the path of growth and goodness. Micah spent hours reading to him from the Bible. It was Jonas' introduction to the humility of Jesus Christ. For the first time, Jonas realised that there was a higher purpose to life than Levi jeans and Reeboks. But it was the look of despair on his mother's face which was the catalyst for Jonas' conversion. He had seen grief like that on the faces of parents when street kids had been killed, or had overdosed. But he thought he was immune. Supreme. When he saw that same look on his mother's face, he knew that he had seen his Maker, and he was now in a race for his life. He turned his back on the street forever.

Jonas' grades slowly improved and his mother was ecstatic when he joined her at the First Evangeline

Church of the Witnesses of the Lord. She sobbed as her son walked to the front of the church when Reverend Dr Jimmy Wilson called forth the faithful. The image of her tall, handsome son reaching up and placing his hands firmly into the safe and welcoming arms of the preacherman was burned forever in her mind.

The black sky over the Southern Californian desert blazed with the light of stars, phosphorescence on a velvet canopy. Sprites dancing a numinous waltz. From the vantage point of her bedroom window, two storeys above the arid ground, Annabelle Wilson saw the Milky Way and fantasised that all the planets of the solar system were her special friends, beyond the reach, the corruption, of the vile and putrid earth. Jupiter, Saturn, Venus, Mars. In her boredom, cooped up in the desert, she learned about the stars and planets. They were her allies, her confidants, her constancy. They were always there. They never answered her back, abused her or expected anything from her. Just gave their light willingly, comfortingly.

She began to count the stars as she had last night, and every other night; but only the very bright ones. It was recuperative to lose count. It brought home to her the infinite reach of His hands. Her troubles were diminished by the immensity of the sky, a vast cupola which stretched from one horizon to the other, from the sea to the mountains. And beneath the stellar dome, smack in the middle, like a pustule erupting out of the skin of the desert was the tiny inconsequential Chrome Cathedral. Run by minuscule folk, little people of no worth. People who could not harm her for much longer. Not now. Not with what she knew. One day she would be free. One day soon. Jonas told her so.

The door burst open. Her heart sank. Her throat was paralysed by fear. The neurotic tingling returned to the tips of her fingers and toes.

'Annabelle, honey,' he boomed, full of good fellowship, blustering like an insurance salesman. 'Did you hear me? Did you see the way they looked at me? Why I tell you, I had them reporters eatin' out of my hands. Oh, honey. This is the greatest day of my life.'

Annabelle Wilson slumped against the window, too terrified to turn around. He was in a good mood. He was ebullient. He was happy. He was more dangerous than when he was angry.

'Oh, Jimmy darlin', I'm so glad for you. Such a pity I didn't see you, honey. I was up here, nursin' this headache. It's just too bad. Right when you were in the middle of your triumph.'

Jimmy Wilson walked over to the windows. She could smell his cologne, and the sweat of his success. Involuntarily, her body became rigid. He put his hand around her waist and drew her backwards into him.

'Let's celebrate my triumph.'

'Jimmy, darlin', you know I'd love to, but this darned headache's got me feelin' all giddy. Shoot, I'd do anythin' for you, but I know I'd feel sick as a mutt if I had to lie down right now.'

'Then let's do it special,' her husband said, smiling, 'standin' up.'

She tried to walk away, to turn around, but he gripped her waist tightly. 'No, Jimmy. I can't. You know that hurts me somethin' fierce. I just can't take it like that no more. You gotta understand. Doctor said I wasn't—'

'Doctors,' he laughed. 'What do they know? C'mon, sweets, right here by the window. Under the stars. Bend over, and let me lift your skirt.'

'Jimmy—' She turned her head until she could see his face. She saw that look. When he had that look in his eyes, you didn't argue with him. Not if you wanted to avoid a slapping. Damn her stupidity. Why hadn't she worn jeans? He loved to lift her skirts and pull down her panties. It made him excited. She should have remembered. But everything was a confusion. And it was the Lord's day.

'No, Jimmy. Years now I've been givin' in to your wishes, but I can't any more. It hurts too bad.'

Jimmy looked at her, his face losing its glow of sexual enthusiasm. He frowned, the owner of a recalcitrant pet. 'Now Annabelle, honey, I'm floatin' high on a triumph. Don't give me a hard time. C'mon, honey, just a little comfortin'.'

'No!' she insisted. 'I won't. Not this time. You hurt me too bad inside. Sometimes I bleed, I can't walk properly or sit down!'

Jimmy breathed in deeply. 'Annabelle, you know I get real upset with you when you cross me. Now I'm in a good mood, so I'll overlook this conversation, but do what I tell you—now.'

Annabelle clenched her jaw. Something snapped. She found a streak of bravery. 'No Jimmy. The doctor said last week that I wasn't to any more, and I won't. Not *that* way. Doctor said it was immoral.'

'Immoral? You told the doctor about the way we're man and woman? About our private business?' his voice wavered between the quizzical and interrogative.

Defensively, she said, 'But you know I been seein' Doc Larrimer 'bout my bleedin'. He says I gotta stop doin' it like that, or I'm goin' to get infected.'

'You told him 'bout us? You exposed your husband's private life to an outsider, a stranger?'

'Jimmy,' she said, 'he's a doctor. He's sworn to secrecy.'

Jimmy didn't listen to her. He raised his voice, growling the words, 'You told that quack? How dare you allow strangers to intrude between a man and his wife? And how dare you refuse me, you slut?' He released her, as though she were tainted. Now he was distant, dictatorial, a preacher. 'Need I remind you of the words of St Paul to the Corinthians, "A wife cannot claim her body as her own, it is her husband's." Listen to me, slut, never ever discuss our private life again. Now, if you don't want another beatin', get your fat ass over there by the window and bend over, or so help me, I'll break your head. Now move it, whore bitch.'

'No!' she screamed. 'Not this time. Doctor said—'

And Jimmy snapped. He roared, 'I don't give a tinker's shit what some white-bellied asshole doctor said. Who in the name of Jesus Christ Almighty do you think . . . Git over here, or I'll slap you so hard, you'll—'

She had nothing left. There was nothing more to defend. She was worthless. She lifted her head and cried to the ceiling, 'No! I won't. Not again. You can't make me. You're an animal. I won't do it no more.'

Jimmy clenched his fist, indignation flooding his mind, impelling his body. He raised his hand and swept it viciously across the side of Annabelle's head, knocking her to the ground. She let out a pathetic yelp of surprise as she hit the bed and bounced to the floor, to lie at her husband's feet. Annabelle felt the side of her head, whimpering in pain as her ears rang, and her sight clouded over. She blinked to try to focus. Her head was flaring in agony. Jimmy's knuckles had clipped her ear, which throbbed red and aching. He looked down at her prostrate form, sneering with contempt.

Annabelle began to cry with the hurt and shock, but her plaintive noises unshackled him, driving him further into the corner of frenzied rage. Lying at his feet, all his disgust for those who were unworthy and despicable and base and abhorrent flowed out. He no longer looked at his wife, he looked down at the creatures who hated him, mocked and ridiculed him, and diminished him in the sight of God. He kicked her viciously in the chest, but she held onto his foot, preventing its full impact. She could not bear any more pain.

'Don't, Jimmy. Please. For God's sake, don't hit me no more,' she sobbed, but he struggled to loosen his foot from her grasp, so he could kick her again and again in his volcanic rage. Annabelle raised her arms in front of her face to protect herself, and his kicks landed on her elbows, in her stomach and on her shoulders. With each kick, she sunk deeper and deeper into the floor, shrinking her body, praying she would become invisible. She shrank back against the bed, lying foetus-like, trying to hide beneath the valance. Praying for the beating to be over. This beating was going on for longer than normal. She counted the kicks, trying to keep her sanity. She shuddered each time his feet landed, the excruciating pain jarring her brain. In her mind, one thought—to escape the torrent of feet and venom that was torturing her body.

'No!' she cried from the depths of her body. 'No, please no!'

Finally, Jimmy stopped the assault and looked down at his wife, coiled up on the floor. Breathing deeply, he blinked, focusing his eyes on the poor, hurt lamb lying prostrate at his feet. He bent down to pick her up.

He began to whimper, slowly beginning to realise the damage he had done. God help him for a sinner. God curse him for his temper. 'Oh my God, what have I done? Oh no. Jesus Christ Almighty, what have I done to you? Annabelle honey, I'm . . . I'm . . . God forgive me, I got carried away. What have I done to you? Are you okay? My worst side took over. The devil got loose. You know it wasn't me. I love you. I wouldn't harm you like that, Annabelle darlin'.'

He picked her up off the floor. She was gagging, in too much pain to cry out, to wail to whoever might be listening. Jimmy sat her down on the bed, and gently stroked her hair, as she fell backwards towards the pink and gold eiderdown, which cushioned her fall. Jimmy rubbed her face, shaking his head in horror at what he had done.

'Sometimes the devil grasps hold of me, and makes me do terrible things. Let's pray together, when you're feelin' better, and beseech God to help us with this problem. Will you do that for me, honey?'

Annabelle continued to sob. She knew what was in her heart, but was too frightened to say the words. Last time she'd said them, Jimmy had gone crazy. Hate herself as she would, she knew from hideous previous experience that she had to go along with him. He was still on the edge and if she pushed him too far, the consequences for her could be fatal. When the genie was out of the bottle, it was often out for a long while. She was rational enough to know that these moments of calm and loving could go either way. Jimmy looked at her quizzically.

'What's in your mind? Tell me, honey. Ain't you gonna forgive Jimmy? C'mon, let's not keep this quarrel goin' on. Shoot, this is a prime time for me and you. Money's rollin' in. In no time, we'll give away all this and have enough to retire on, so we'll be able to start a family, and live like any normal couple.'

Annabelle squeezed open her eyes, for the first time since the beating had started. She looked at Jimmy with a mixture of fear and loathing. But she remained mute in self-protection.

'Why don't we forgive and forget, and comfort each other in the way that man and woman are supposed to?'

He put his hand into hers, and gently coaxed her off the bed. She could barely walk, her legs were shaking so badly, her bruises and aching arms throbbed. She didn't dare speak. Jimmy led Annabelle to the bedroom window. She bent down with her forehead resting on the cold window and waited for the pain. Like a child waiting for an injection.

He didn't pull down her panties right away. She closed her eyes and pictured what he was doing. She began to gag, her throat constricting with bile. A disembodied voice shouted in her mind, 'How can you let him do this when he's just beaten and kicked you like you were a disobedient mutt?' She masked her nausea, covering the sounds as though she was experiencing delight. Anything else would have started the beating again. The difference between beating and sex was her response.

She felt him pull down his trousers and move his face to touch her bottom. She knew he would start licking inside her, where she went to the toilet. Grovelling in her shit. Smelling her, like dogs smell each other. He slowly rolled down her panties and spread her legs with his hands. She bit her lower lip. The image of his large penis, erect and violent, red and angry. She squeezed her eyelids as she felt him rubbing himself in her cleft. And as his penis began to enter her, she started to recite the Twenty-Third Psalm. They finished at the same time. When she said 'and I will dwell in the house of the Lord forever', she prayed for the strength to walk out on him. She implored God for Jimmy's slow and painful death.

Jimmy dressed in his black suit, grey shirt and white collar. Annabelle stood by the window. She wouldn't, couldn't sit down. 'I've gotta go down and face the multitudes. I expect you to be down there beside me,' he told her.

'I can't, Jimmy. I just can't. My . . . my head's too bad, and I'm a mass of bruises. I can't come down and face an audience.' She swallowed bile as it rose in her throat.

'Today I had a triumph with the television people. It's goin' out on the national news at six o'clock this evening, coast to coast. We're broadcastin' it in front of a congregation upwards of eight thousand people on giant Sony television monitors. I want you there beside me, and I want you to be lookin' good and smilin' and thinkin' pretty.'

Annabelle's shoulders shrugged in resignation. She was glad that he couldn't see the hatred in her face. 'All right Jimmy, I'll be there.'

'Good, darlin', good. That's the way it should be.' He started to walk out of their bedroom, but as he grasped the handle, he stopped and turned around. 'You know, I'm real sorry 'bout the beatin' I gave you, Annabelle, honey. I don't know what comes over me. Sometimes, it's as if my whole being gets taken over by a demon, and he controls my mind and my fists. I lose control. I kinda snap.' He paused, lost in thoughts of his own weakness. 'I know it's wrong, Annabelle honey. I love you. You're my wife. In all our time together, I've never looked at another woman. You're the only one for me.'

She clenched her fists in anger as he left the room, remaining silent. All that crap about love. And how could she appear in front of a full congregation of God-loving people after what she'd just been through? How could she appear on television in front of an audience of millions, feeling no better than a dog that some sonofa-bitch had kicked and beaten in some alley? Her throat constricted in a sob.

She got up and walked to the door, opened it cautiously to ensure that Jimmy was well down the hall. Then she locked the bedroom door, walked as quickly as her liquid legs would allow around the side of her bed, and opened the closet. She reached down to the third drawer where she kept her tampons and vaginal creams, and searched the back recesses of the drawer. There, she felt a velvet-covered box, small and warm. Her friend. She checked that the door to the bedroom was still shut. Then she withdrew the box. Lovingly, like stroking the delicate cheeks of a newborn baby, Annabelle fondled its lush, black velvet. It was her comfort in times of need. She used it less now than in the past, because the daily nosebleeds and yellow stains of dried mucus on the pillow might alert Jimmy. She would love to freebase. She really wanted to, but it was so expensive that Jimmy would probably start to notice the amount of money missing from his wallet.

Annabelle sat at her dressing table and moved the hairbrushes and combs to one side. She laid her black velvet friend reverentially down, opened it, and took out the sachet of cocaine. She cut a line with the razor and sniffed it deep into her nose through a $20 note. She breathed out through her mouth. Within seconds, she felt at ease. The smells and colours in the room intensified and her pains disappeared. She cut another line. Life was all right. No! it was great. And easy. Look at her. Good-looking, still desirable. Think about Jonas. Yeah! Now that put mustard between her legs.

Think about Jimmy. Dumb fuck. Not that she minded living in a nice house. But she was lonely. She wanted to go out more. See people. Not be stuck in the cathedral all the time. She wanted to see real lights and hear real music. It was Jimmy who was standing in her way. Get rid of Jimmy. Get rid of the problem. Now she could come down and face Jimmy. Now she was at ease. And now she could do what she wanted to do.

By the time Annabelle had snorted two lines of cocaine, Jimmy was walking down the air-conditioned hallway. Down the stairs to the underground corridor which connected his private home to the suite of offices attached to the cathedral. The press conference had been held in the small private chapel into which platinum sponsors of the crusade would be invited to pray in privacy with Reverend Dr Wilson. The chapel was empty now. An hour earlier it had been full of cameras, lights, cables and two dozen people asking questions about his Crusade. How much had he earned from sponsors? When did he intend to go? How many would follow? What was the cost of his Crusade? Was there something fundamentally flawed in calling the expedition a Crusade with its Catholic imagery? Was he repeating what the Pope was doing?

He had handled all of the questions like a master, with wit, humour and the right degree of preaching when he was stuck for an answer. He hadn't quoted the Good Book too many times but had given a solemn undertaking not to return to America until his Crusade had recovered the Testament of Our Lord. A reporter had been stupid enough to ask him to comment upon an article by Professor Ari Wallenstein, printed in the *Los Angeles Times* which had picked it up from the *Jerusalem Post*. Did he, the reporter asked, believe it would be bad for Christians to find Christ's Testament? Jimmy looked at the man in contempt and pity. 'Friend,' he told the reporter, 'our brothers, the Jews, turned their back on the Lord Jesus two thousand years ago and haven't admitted Him into their hearts since that day. I hardly think I need to be told what's good and bad for followers of the Gospel by some Jew.'

It was the closest he came to racism during the entire press conference. Gerald Curtis, sitting inconspicuously at the back of the room, breathed a sigh of relief when Jimmy started to deal with the next question.

At the end of the press conference, after the last journalist had left, Gerald walked over beaming and said, 'You handled that better than Billy Graham. Congratulations!'

Jimmy strode through the suite of offices. Adoring secretaries, fund raisers and direct marketing assistants looked up as he walked past. They smiled at him, trying to catch his eye, trying to establish a rapport. He ignored them. He walked to the office door and into the cathedral vestibule. On the other side of the vestibule, through the Gothic arch and the thick iron-banded oak-veneer door he could already hear the whispered sounds of eight thousand people. The cathedral was packed to capacity. Standing room only. Like Noah's ark, they were sitting two by two, sharing chairs and floor space.

In the vestibule were his helpers. The men who would dress him and escort him through the aisle and to the steps of the platform. Cyrus Vandenplas was a white Harvard yuppie-type. Good for the image, for the middle class southern Californians Jimmy was desperate to attract. Jonas Watkins was a tall good-looking black from the slums of LA. Good for the niggers. He also had an Hispanic. Some guy with an unpronounceable name, all 'Js' and 'Ths' and 'Huhs'. But he was sick today. No matter. Two boys following him would be just as good. One black. One white.

They didn't say a word. That was his preference. He didn't like small talk when he was preparing for an entrance. They helped him into his cloak, his cowl and made sure that he had his Bible, his speech, and his throat sweets. Cyrus took a radio transmitter and placed it into an inside pocket of the cloak. He threaded the wire through the back of Jimmy's jacket and up beyond his neck. Jimmy placed the small receiver into his ear. He would be able to hear instructions from his monitors in the congregation if anybody needed to be picked out for special attention. When he was ready to meet his congregation he walked through the door.

They had been singing and chanting along with the choir for half an hour. And for the past couple of minutes, in anticipation of Jimmy's entrance, they had been brought to silence by an assistant minister.

The congregation came to complete silence when he entered the cathedral. Then an elderly black woman shouted 'Praise the Lord' and Jimmy smiled, turning to her, kissed her on the cheek and said, 'Praise the Lord, sister.' It was the sign the congregation was looking for. They cheered, they whistled, they whooped and a chant began around the huge edifice:

> *Praise the Lord,*
> *Praise the Lord,*
> *Praise Him sisters*
> *Praise Him brothers*
> *He ain't meant for any others.*

The choir on the stage picked up the strain and set it to song, clapping their hands and moving their feet like street rap dancers. Jimmy loved it. The atmosphere was electric. 'Praise the Lord, praise the Lord. The Lord of Hosts, the Lord Almighty,' they sang, dressed in their ballooning purple gowns.

By the time Jimmy walked down the long passageway and ascended the steps, everyone was singing. There was something about niggers and their ability to harmonise.

He climbed the steps to the stage, then held up his arms. The congregation slowly came to silence. Sometimes he preferred to enter from the back of the hall, rather than descend from the clouds. Variety. On stage, he deliberately did not go behind the lectern, where his voice was amplified, but stayed at the edge of the stage, close to his people, and shouted, 'Praise The Lord.'

The congregation screamed back, 'Praise the Lord.'

'This day is our day. Your day and my day. This is the day on which everythin' we believe in will be vindicated and justified. It's the day when the guessin' stops, when the faith becomes reality.'

His words were interrupted by people in the congregation screaming out, 'I've seen the Lord', or 'Praise the Lord', or 'Jesus, sweet Jesus'.

'You'll all have read the papers, or seen the television. You all know what has been found. You all know that out there,' he stabbed the air towards Jerusalem, 'sittin' in some forgotten cave, covered with the dust of ages, are the words of Our Lord. His Testament to us.'

The congregation shouted, 'Let's go', 'Let's find it', 'Praise the Lord'.

'Are we gonna leave it there to gather more dust?'

'No, no. Let's find it.'

'Are we gonna let it rot for another two thousand years until the precious words of sweet Jesus become dust themselves?'

'No. We gotta find it.'

'I say, a curse on them that hid this from us. May their souls be blackened in everlastin' dark. Who was it that hid these things from us? It was the people of Israel. The very same people who rejected Our Lord in the first place. Who told Him they was not interested in His Word. They was too arrogant and stiff-necked to accept Him as the Son of God.'

The congregation remained silent, unsure where they were being led. Jimmy brought them back. 'But it's there, out there, in the land of the Jews.'

'Let's go find it. Let's find the words of the Lord,' they screamed.

'The children of Israel wanted to keep it for themselves,' Jimmy told them.

'Shame!'

'They were scared that we would find it and we would prove—prove, brothers and sisters—that the words of our Lord Jesus will bring eternal salvation for us all.'

'Damn them.'

'They were frightened that we would prove their religion, the religion of the Jews, is wrong. That the Jews now must—I say must—accept the word of the Lord Jesus as the word of God Himself.'

'Yeah.'

'We've gotta find the words of the Lord. We've gotta search for it. We have to go on our hands and knees and scramble through the dust and dirt and heat and flies and insects and vermin of the desert to find the words of the Lord.'

'Let's go. Let's get there. Let's do it.'

'Who's goin' to come with me? Who's goin' to join me in searchin' for the words of the Lord?'

The congregation stood on its feet. It was hysterical. 'I'll go. Let me come with you.'

Jimmy surveyed the congregation and smiled in gratitude at the swaying mass of people, looking like a field of corn ripe for the harvest. He never ceased to be stunned by the ease with which his words could mould a crowd's mood. At the back of the hall he saw the door gently open. Framed by the doorposts was Annabelle. She looked breathtakingly beautiful, especially from afar. Her entry, whether deliberate or not, was timed perfectly. She walked towards him. Her hands were in the pockets of her dress. Only she knew that when she got onto the stage, she would tell the world what the sonofabitch monster did to her. But could she? Since she'd snorted the lines, things weren't so bad. Things were going to be okay.

'And here comes my wife. My support. The staff I will carry with me in the desert, like the rod of Moses and the bough that the Lord Jesus carried with Him as He walked through the hills of Galilee. My dear friends, here is my right hand, my apostle, my soulmate, Annabelle. Annabelle darlin', walk up the stairs, stand by me while I tell our friends how you and me and twenty others lucky enough to be selected will find the words of Jesus Christ the Lord.'

Annabelle walked slowly towards him. Faces turned to her and beamed smiles of love and joy. They loved her like they loved him. They envied her the position by the right hand of their saviour. She looked at their faces as she walked towards the stage. Innocent faces. Faces full of hope and gratitude. And all because of Jimmy. Only she knew the truth. Only she. To tell the truth about him would be to leave these men, women and children bereft. Adrift. Alone. Like her.

Tears welled up in her eyes. Jimmy held out his hands towards her to help her up the three steps to the stage. As the tears began to roll down her cheek, she took her hands out of her pockets, held them up to him and they were joined in his.

'This is even better than I'd expected.'

'No better than I told you.'

'But Jimmy, we've got over forty people wanting to pay a hundred thousand dollars just to come and search with you. That's four million dollars. Put that on top of the six million in pledges and we're up to ten million in the space of less than two days! Once the results from national television begin to hit, it'll be a circus.'

Jimmy Wilson unrolled a throat sweet and popped it in his mouth. No matter how often he preached, his throat always became sore at the end of the day. It was his curse. 'Well, what'll we do? You're the money man, you're the ideas man. You tell me.'

'I think we should break the expedition up into two, maybe even three. You lead one, for which we'll charge a premium of twenty-five per cent. Annabelle can lead another, which will be joined to yours every Sunday in communal prayer meetings. If necessary other church leaders can take an expedition. Just so long as they join together every Sunday, they'll still get the feeling that they're with you.'

'You think you can pull it?'

Harlin Brown nodded. Though Jimmy had once dubbed him an 'Ivy League type', he was actually a street fighter. Gerald Curtis interrupted. 'Don't you think there's a danger of over-exposure here? Ten million dollars is nothing to sneeze at. Twenty million by the end of the week, if we're lucky. That's six months' donations. Aren't we risking killing the golden calf, to coin a biblical metaphor?'

Harlin didn't understand the biblical metaphor and shook his head in disagreement. 'This is a once-in-a-lifetime thing, Gerald. You can't overplay this poker hand. Once in two thousand years something of in-credible importance is discovered. People will have to wait another two thousand years for the same thing to happen again. I'm not worried about overdoin' it.'

Jimmy agreed. Gerald shrugged his shoulders. To argue was of little value. Jimmy Wilson had made him a very, very wealthy man. If it all collapsed now, he would still walk away a multi-millionaire.

Jimmy turned to a young man sitting at the table. Luke Carmody had worked for Jimmy as a front man for twelve months. He was smart as a whip, totally reliable, and seemed to be able to pull congregations in strange towns out of nowhere. 'Luke, how goes it with the Israelis? Any problems?'

'I haven't had an official answer yet, Jimmy, but I don't think they're going to be too willing to let troops of people wander all over their caves. I spoke to the Israeli Consul in LA and he said the prospect of us walking over archaeological sites was not something he enjoyed thinking about.'

'Son, I don't give a shit about what that Jew says,' Jimmy snorted in anger. 'If I can't get permission, I'm goin' over there just the same. Who the hell do them Yids think they are? That's a Christian land. That's where Our Lord was born. Them Jew-boys try to keep us out, they're gonna have the First Evangeline Church of the Witnesses of the Lord to deal with.'

Gerald Curtis cringed.

Jonas carefully applied cooling lotion to Annabelle's rectum. He looked and flinched. It was red and bruised, oozing droplets of blood from the chafed skin. Annabelle was still sobbing even ten minutes after she had told Jonas what Jimmy had done to her. She had come down from her cocaine high.

'We got to do something, Annabelle. We got to stop that sonofabitch from hurting you. He's turning you into a two-bit junkie with all the pain you're suffering.' Jonas found it hard to speak. The anger was in his throat. No man should treat his wife like this. No woman deserved this kind of treatment. The make-up was streaked by her tears and Jonas could see the way in which the skin around her ear was red and raw, where Jimmy had pummelled her. He began to stroke her hair, careful not to touch the site of her pain. She moved her body closer to his, to enfold herself in his lap like a little girl seeks protection with her daddy. And all the while, Jonas stroked her long, blonde, perfumed hair.

'I can't take no more. It's all over for me. He's broken me. He's hurt me once too often. I wanted to expose him back there. Tell the congregation, tell the world what he did to me. But I couldn't. To expose him, I have to expose myself. You know what they'll say, Jonas?' Her words were gasped between sobs. 'They'll say I deserve it. They'll say a woman should do what her husband wants. And they're right! It's written in the goddamn Bible.' She howled in agony, bereft of comfort, devoid of answers. 'I came so close back there. I wanted to see him screw up his face like I screw mine up every time he fucks me like that. When we were first married he used to beat me regular. My momma said I gotta accept that from a man. I was too shamed to tell her about the way we made love.' She laughed bitterly as she said the word. 'For years I've begged him to make love to me properly. He says he doesn't enjoy it that way. Says doin' it this way is nature's contraception. But I know he can't do it the proper way. He can't get it up. He ain't a man. He's a goddamn useless queer.' She looked at him and saw the concern in his face. 'You're scared shitless of him, aren't you?'

'Sure I'm scared of him.'

'Why?'

'I know him. His temper. If I put my foot outta line, I'll get a beating. I can't go through that again. God knows I hate what he does to you.'

'Why you still here, honey? He hates you. He hates all niggers and anybody who ain't white and Protestant. He's a racist, godless sonofabitch. He says horrible things about Jews and blacks and all. And he treats me like an animal.'

Annabelle began to sob, alone and friendless. Jonas held her in his arms and prayed to heaven that soon she would be free.

CHAPTER 9

The music was the breath of angels. Sweet, delicious young voices rising and falling in sensuous harmony, singing with the exuberance of innocence. Unaffected adolescent chords, unconcerned with reward or artifice.

Daniel Rhymer stood outside the door to the classroom, restraining the hand of the headmistress so that he could listen to the singing of the class for a few moments longer. The headmistress smiled. She knew this American cardinal had a love of children. In the six months since he had taken up residence in Rome, he had gone out of his way to visit several church schools, something which other eminences never did.

He smiled and nodded at the end of the song, and the sister–headmistress opened the door. The teacher, another nun, sitting on the table at the head of the class, jumped off as though caught in the act of a minor sin, and bowed low to his eminence. 'Children, stand for our distinguished guest, Cardinal Rhymer,' she said.

As a body, they stood and said, 'Good morning, your eminence.'

'Good morning, children.'

They laughed at his accent. He beamed an infectious grin. Affecting his John Wayne impersonation, which carried even in the Italian, he told them, 'Listen, partners. Just 'cause I'm from the good 'ole US of A, don't mean you gotta make fun of mah accent.'

The class burst into uncontrollable mirth, until the headmistress restored order, explaining to the children that the eminent cardinal had taken time from his extremely busy schedule directing the affairs of state of the Vatican to visit the school, to ensure the children were happy in their lives. Then she invited him to address the class.

He looked at them in awe of their innocence, of their potential. They were all attentive to what he was about to say. Their faces were open and trustful, eager to understand. He felt a stirring responsibility. 'Let me ask you a simple question, and there are no prizes for the right answer. Children, who knows about Heaven?'

A dozen hands shot up. Daniel nodded to one little girl, who stood. 'Heaven is where God Almighty, and His Son, Jesus, are.'

'No!' said Daniel. The headmistress and teacher looked at him in wonder.

Another boy stood up, and said, 'Heaven is in the sky.'

'No!' said Daniel, repressing a grin.

The children began to giggle, and talk amongst each other. 'One more answer, before I tell you.'

A girl taller than the rest stood and uncertainly said, 'Heaven is in the earth and the trees and wherever God is?'

The class looked at Daniel in studied attention. He could no longer repress a laugh, especially looking at the faces of the nuns, who were mystified.

'Heaven, children, is right . . .' he walked over to the front row, and poked a little boy in the chest, then a little girl, then the rest of the row '. . . here. Inside all children. It's in your hearts and heads, in your fingers and toes.' The rest of his words were lost in the roar of laughter, led by both nuns.

Over the ruckus, he shouted, 'There are those men and women in the Catholic Church who would have us believe that God Almighty is an old man in a long white robe, face half hidden by ten years' growth of beard, sitting on a golden throne, surrounded by winged angels, judging your every word and action. But he's not! God is in us. We are made in the very image of God. He—or She—is inside you, and you, and you, and yes, even the young man at the back picking his nose.' The class turned and hooted in hysterical laughter.

'God is not an angry God. He's a God of love and peace and goodness. It's man who has turned against Him. It's man who has created evil, like the Mafia or murderers, or people who go to war. Do you think that God Almighty, or His Son, Jesus Christ, created the Earth and everything upon it to see it destroyed by hatred and crime and terror?'

Tentatively, the children replied, 'No, eminence.'

'No! Of course not. Listen to me, children. There is a process in life. A process which nobody seems to understand. And it begins in every one of you. You are born in love and in beauty. You are taught and cared for by wonderful people, fathers, mothers, your teachers, who show you the best things in life. But something, sometimes, gets in the way. Some of you will be tempted by evil. Tempted to turn from the love and security of the Church and your parents and teachers, and to follow your own path.

'Listen to me, kids. When temptation comes, open your hearts, and say to yourselves, "Should I follow a path which I know is wrong, or should I stay on the path which leads to God and Jesus, and stay happy and content for the whole of my life?"

'Now, with the permission of your teacher, Sister Matthew, and your headmistress, Mother Angelica, I would like to lead you in the blessed Lord's Prayer.'

By the time Daniel reached the Vatican later that morning, Pope Innocent was still feeling irritable, an emotion which was becoming more frequent the longer he spent in Peter's Chair. All his life he had been known to his fellow seminarians, parishioners, colleagues and staff as a man who quietly contemplated everything before speaking. To them, he was, like Pope John XXIII, a saintly man, the sort of whom legends are made.

He had been elected by the Sacred College of Cardinals into the papacy for two reasons. Firstly because after the Polish and French popes, and their alienation of South America, a pope was required who would bond the New World to the Old; and secondly because as a theological neutral, neither extreme liberal nor extreme reactionary, they thought he would not rock any boats. The college knew that he would also carry with him the cautious Rhymer. The majority of the Roman establishment in the conclave trusted that, despite the admission of the New World to the governance of the Catholic faith, the ship of state would proceed smoothly. And there was always the weight of the Curia to calm any troubled waters if the parvenus were over-zealous in flexing their muscles.

Seated before the Pope, dressed in their black silk cassocks with red trim, red buttons and red waist bands were four cardinals. The prelates' resplendence mirrored their sumptuous surroundings as they sat with arrogance and confidence on tapestried chairs. Even the simplicity of their red silk skullcaps gave them a look of superiority.

The setting was glorious. Massive tapestries adorned the walls behind them showing scenes depicting the writings of St Mark and St Luke. Images from the Coronation of the Virgin, showing the Annunciation, the Adoration of the Magi and the circumcision were hung to remind every visitor that the entire edifice was dedicated to the glorification of Jesus and His family, and that the Pope, with all his power and glory, was a servant of the servants of God. On the credenzas were priceless works of the art of the Renaissance gold and silversmith Benvenuto Cellini, from delicate salvers to intricate spice-holders—lattice-works of metal which looked as though they had been spun by a spider. In the corners of the room were massive iron candlesticks, their permanency implicit by the black clinging ivy patterns, with leaves of burnished gold, woven around their stems. In other areas of the vast room were paintings of incalculable value. Leonardo, Tintoretto, Caravaggio, and paintings by the divine Raphael. So much history, such a testament to the enduring brilliance of humankind.

Undoubtedly aware of the history of the room, another intriguer, a latterday Medici, the German theologian Franz Cardinal Kitzinger had been quietly explaining why the Pope could not do what he wanted. Other popes had acquiesced when the Curia brought the full weight of its awesome majesty to bear. This Pope was being meddlesome.

'Eminence, I accept that I have only been Pope for six months. But my word is final.'

'Holy Father, the Doctrine of Infallibility has only been current for just over a hundred years. We Catholics have not yet really come to terms with anyone's word being final except Our Lord's.'

Innocent turned and looked at the man. He wanted to see whether what he said was supposed to be humorous or serious. The theologian merely stared back, far too clever to telegraph his mood. 'But why do you say that this Crusade must not take place?'

'Holy Father,' Kitzinger cleared his throat, 'the Crusades were a part of the church's history which most would prefer to forget. The church militant is not a thing of beauty, and is completely out of touch with the mood today among Catholics throughout the world. They are looking for stability, not challenge. Why, just the other day, a rabbi in Jerusalem burst into our most holy church and clubbed thirty priests. They lay bruised and battered while your holiness was still promoting the idea of a Crusade.'

Innocent winced at the barb which had accurately homed in on his Achilles heel. 'So, I'll change the name. I'll call it "The Quest" or "The Search".'

'It's more than a change of name, holiness. Your spiritual adviser, Cardinal Rhymer, is understood to agree with his Curia colleagues that there is great danger in this search.'

'Leave me out of this,' snapped Daniel. 'I am quite capable of discussing my view with his holiness. I need no spokesman.'

The German nodded. Pope Innocent felt uncomfortable with the growing acrimony in the room.

'But eminence, the Dead Sea Scrolls are amongst the most important biblical finds in history.'

'Only if they accord with and support the authority of the Church.'

Innocent looked at the German in surprise.

The cardinal stood and walked over to the coffee table to pour himself another cup. Gabriel Molloy had been brought up on coffee mugs from Woolworth's stores. When he became a bishop, and was surrounded by sophistication and history, he continued to drink his morning coffee from a mug. Even after six months in the Vatican, he was still ill-at-ease with the delicate porcelain used every day. He watched the patrician German with grudging admiration. The man was so at home in these surroundings, Gabriel was starting to feel like a tenant. The German's three colleagues maintained their seats, allowing him to be their consciences.

'Holiness, who do you think advises the International Team? Where do you think it gets its inspiration? Why do you think that so little of the Dead Sea Scrolls material has been published in the past decades?'

Innocent walked over to his favourite armchair and sat down. The theologian's tone meant that he was in for a shock. It would be the latest in the long line of revelations, none of them divine, since he had become Pope Innocent. If ever a name was apt for the person, then it was the name that he had chosen to define his pontificate. It was eponymous. As an American prelate, he had not previously been privy to the unbelievable machinations of the Roman Curia and its Byzantine politics.

'I think you'd better explain, Cardinal Kitzinger.'

'Seven hundred and fifty years ago one of your illustrious predecessors, Pope Gregory IX, established an office called the Holy Inquisition to apprehend and try heretics, and to maintain the purity of the faith. By the middle of the sixteenth century it had become known as the Holy Office. Today, as your holiness knows, it is called the Congregation for the Doctrine of the Faith.'

The Pope shifted impatiently in his seat. 'I'm aware of all of this, eminence.'

'Holy Father, you may not be aware that before the International Team publishes anything, it discusses what is about to be published with the congregation to determine how the translations of the Dead Sea Scrolls and the other documents found at Qumran and Masada accord with the orthodoxy of the Catholic faith.'

It was another nightmare. But at least this one was not a complete surprise. In recent years, conspiracy theory books had been written about the Church's role in withholding the Dead Sea Scrolls from the scholarly community.

'There has been much speculation over the past decade or so that the Church has been responsible for delaying the publication of the remainder of the Dead Sea Scrolls. You're now telling me that the congregation has been responsible for censoring the scrolls?'

'Censorship, holiness, is a very emotive term. We prefer to look upon it as advice given to the scholars. In the fullness of time the scrolls will all be translated, published and explanations given. But in the meantime we, the congregation, have permitted the world to see only a part of this wondrous find. Be assured, Holy Father, there is much more to come. But we do not believe the world is yet ready to receive the rest of the information from Qumran.'

Pope Innocent stood up in fury. 'How dare you determine what the world will and will not see! You and your brothers in the Curia have gone too far. You may advise me on the doctrine of the faith of our Catholic Church, but you have no right whatsoever to withhold other treasures from mankind. Would you hide Michelangelo's David or the Pieta in a cupboard and keep it just for yourself? Then how can you think of hiding away these masterpieces of the ancients?'

Kitzinger smiled. 'I really do admire the way in which you men from the New World see things so clearly in black and white. I think it's your enthusiasm which makes you such an interesting complex of emotions.'

Years of training in dealing with parishioners and obdurate members of the clergy prevented Innocent from exploding in anger.

'So how does this impinge upon my Crusade?' he asked. 'And why did you permit the publication of this list? Despite your efforts, it appears that you've opened up Pandora's box. Did you make a mistake, eminence? Or was this a carefully planned Machiavellian scheme?'

'Let's just say, holiness, that one of the members of the International Team appointed by the Israeli government managed to get hold of some material, the nature of which was underestimated by the team. He refused to accept our advice, regardless of the pressure we placed upon him. We used every means of persuasion to stop him from publishing but we were unable. That's why Père de la Tour had to come out and pre-empt him.'

'And how can you stop him publishing more material in the future?'

'He will now be given access to no further material of any theological consequence.'

The Pope paced the floor of his private quarters reciting the rosary. It was a self-imposed penance for losing his temper in front of the confident, severe, arrogant men of the Curia.

'For heaven's sake, Gabby, stop pacing. You look like a panther in a cage. This isn't a zoo. You're the Pope. Come and sit down. You've really let them get under your skin.'

The advice from his lifelong friend didn't mollify the Pope. 'It's their sheer bloodyminded despotism which infuriates me. For a thousand years they've run this Church like it was their own private club. I tell you, Daniel, this time they've gone too far. They elected me because they thought they could control me. They thought that I was the new boy on the block and that they could train me in Roman ways, just like you train a puppy to be an obedient lapdog. And the monumental, patronising, totalitarian way in which that German . . .' he searched for a suitable word, '. . . gentleman told me that I couldn't undertake this Crusade to reclaim the Testament.' He banged his chest with his finger. 'My

Lord. Remember that! He's my Lord, Danny, as well as their Lord.'

Daniel Rhymer was concerned for his friend's blood pressure. Though a relatively young and fit man compared to previous popes, he was over sixty.

'Listen to me, Gabby. That meeting was a pain in the butt for us both. It was the Old World versus the New. Them versus us. But you know my feelings. I'm terrified of what could happen if this document negates everything we believe in. I have to agree with the Curia, as I said to you yesterday. I think your decision to commission this Crusade is entirely incorrect. You've gone at it like a bull at a gate. It's probably the first time ever that the Vatican's moved so quickly over such an important matter. Popes don't act overnight. They've sometimes waited decades before moving on a matter. Think about the other monumental issues the papacy's had to deal with in the past two thousand years and you'll see what I mean.'

The Pope sat in his favourite armchair and practised deep breathing. He looked at his old friend and asked, 'You may be against me, but will you do what I ask?'

'Of course,' the cardinal replied without hesitation. 'You're the Pope. It goes with the territory, so to speak.'

'Will you help me plan and execute the Crusade?'

'If you command me, of course.'

'I'm not in the business of commanding one of my closest friends. In a way, you're right about them against us, old against new. I think it's vital that we plot our own course. In my own mind I'm committed to finding the Testament. I know you're not in favour of it because it may open the faithful to doubts. But look around you, Danny. The world is full of doubt. All we can do is bring spiritual clarity to bear on the uncertain. I have absolute faith that Jesus would have given us His

Testament to increase our plerophory in Him, not add to our doubts.'

Daniel Rhymer looked at his old friend. He loved him. He loved his goodness, his gentleness, but most of all he loved his spirituality. It was more than being moral or knowledgeable. More than being good and a loving pastor. Gabby Molloy was a true man of God. If any man was touched with the innate spirit of the Lord, then it was this man. Daniel stood up and walked to the window which ran the height of the room, from the woven tapestried carpet to the crenellated stucco of the ceiling.

He looked down at the roads and squares of Vatican City and beyond into Rome itself. Thousands of tourists walked casually around its Renaissance magnificence. People on holiday, who had bought a two-week package of peace of mind, the privilege to leave their concerns at home. None seemed to have a worry in the world. Men and women, boys and girls, laughed and held hands, gazed and took photos.

He turned to his Pope. 'Gabby, we have to prevent the Church from splitting, end the uncertainty. St Paul said—'

The Pope put up his hand to stop him. 'I don't want another theological argument, Danny. I'm sick to death of theologians. What I want is action.'

Rhymer walked back from the window and said, 'Gabriel, you know I'll support you, whether I agree with you or not. But it terrifies me. The Church has been split enough times in its history. I'd hate to think that you and I were responsible in some way for the fourth schism, between the Old and the New Worlds.'

'Daniel, the schism has already started. The Church has enormous problems right at this very moment, intractable problems. This discovery could be the very cement we need to hold the Church together. Look at what we're facing: liberationist theologians in South America; conservative archbishops in Switzerland and Holland who want to turn back the clock on Vatican Two; priests and nuns leaving the Church because of the issue of celibacy; the question of the ordination of women as priests; the Church's attitude towards homosexuality.' Daniel turned his face back towards the window. 'Daniel, need I go on? I feel like a juggler, sitting in the Chair of St Peter, keeping a dozen balls in the air at the same time. It's a hard act. Now I have something, *deus ex machina* so to speak, which promises to revitalise the faith, strengthen it, make it real again.'

Daniel turned back to his friend. 'You sound as if you're the first person to suffer these problems. Every pope has been confronted with intractable problems. Think of the fourteenth century. What was one of the major issues then? Usury. It was almost insurmountable, but time allowed solutions to rise to the surface. Accommodations were reached. Time, Gabby. Time was needed. Today, we don't even think of usury as a problem. Time is needed now.'

The Pope disagreed. 'In those days, there was no global communication. Messages took months to travel from one part of the world to another. These days, the corridors of the Vatican are full of optical fibres and coaxial cables. Any indecision of mine is carried at the speed of light to the farthest corner of the globe. The problems of the Church aren't isolated phenomena any more, confined to a handful of people until they can be solved. They're spreading like a virus. They'll carry the New World with them in an unbridgeable schism if we don't act now. If we don't give the doubters a new article of faith soon to bring them back into the fold, we'll have lost them forever.'

The cardinal turned and looked at his friend. 'Aren't Matthew, Mark, Luke and John enough any more? Is that why you want to find Christ's Testament?'

'Eminence, a few days ago I asked you to read the Book of Deuteronomy. It was a passage which dealt with the truth from the lips of God and what happens when false prophets lie in His name. I think you should now read another part of the Old Testament.'

Daniel smiled at his friend. 'And what particular part of the Bible is this, Holy Father?'

'It's the Book of Ezra. You may remember, eminence, that after the Babylonian captivity the children of Israel were tempted back into a dry and barren Judah. It was there that Ezra and Nehemiah changed a godless people into a God-fearing one.'

'Holy Father, Gabby, that was five hundred years before the birth of Christ. You surely aren't comparing one with another?'

'No, but think back to what Ezra and Nehemiah did. The Jews were attracted to the glittering pagan world of the Babylonians. Judah was a hard and empty land. By gathering the exiles together and on the Day of Atonement in the year 444 before Christ, reading from the Book of Moses in the Temple Court, they electrified the entire community. Thousands of people listened to the words of God and pledged themselves to His service. Danny, we have millions of people, hundreds of millions even, throughout the world, who have drifted away from the Gospels. To bring them back, to re-establish their faith, we have to give them something new. New hope, new certainties. This miraculous discovery near the Dead Sea could be the instrument we've been looking for.'

Daniel looked down at his feet and shook his head. 'The Church is enough. We have the Gospels. We need nothing more. This Testament could be the undoing of our Church's fabric.'

Innocent walked over and put his arm around his friend. 'Danny, it's my duty to find my Lord's Testament. Please don't fight me.'

Daniel looked at the Pope and put his hand on his arm. 'Gabby, I'll go over there and try to find it for you. But I'm frightened. Terribly, terribly frightened.'

'I don't understand why you're so fearful of the document being found. You're looking at two possibilities. The first is that it confirms our faith in Him, the second that His words fail to proclaim His divinity and we're back where we started, believing in Him in our hearts. I have absolute faith that His words will prove Him to be the Son of God.'

'Gabby, your faith and mine are each as strong as the other. But that's not the reason I'm terrified. For thousands of years the Jewish people have believed in the imminent arrival of their Messiah. This faith has kept them together as a society and as a people. Even through the hell of thousands of years of persecution and decimation, Jews have died with a prayer for the Messiah on their lips.'

Pope Innocent looked at his friend, wondering where his argument was going.

'Our Messiah came two thousand years ago,' he continued, 'and we believe that through prayer and penitence our Messiah will return and bring the Kingdom of Heaven to earth. Can't you see the dangers of this scroll, Gabby? The hope of mankind, of every Christian, be they Catholic, or Protestant, is that the Second Coming will bring peace on earth. Take away that hope and one billion souls will be cast adrift. There'll be a spirit of darkness and disillusion greater than anything we've ever seen, casting its shadow over us all. Christianity will be defeated by the black and evil forces of atheism.'

Innocent wanted to argue but knew that now was not the time. His friend stood up, kissed his ring and walked through the door of his private apartment to return to his own apartment outside the Vatican walls. As he closed the huge ornate doors and walked past the empty papal secretary's desk, his mind became clear. Daniel Cardinal Rhymer, Prelate of the Diocese of Boston in the New World, knew he could not allow the Ninth Crusade to succeed.

Outside the eight-foot-thick concrete and steel walls of the Central Prison, built by the British to house militant members of the Stern Gang and Irgun during the post-war Mandate period, a huge crowd had gathered. Many were settlers from the still-occupied territories who had gathered to support David Berg, their new Messiah. Others were militant Jews—fundamentalist and uncompromising. And there were hundreds of the curious, wondering whether there was an element of truth in the slogans and the anger, but still unable to entomb their heritage as liberal, peace-loving humanists within the bleak coffin of hate. Berg's supporters were chanting Zionist slogans and singing fundamentalist songs. Police cleared a path through the vast organic crowd to allow traffic to flow in two directions but the crowd continually pressed forward to close the gap. When each song was finished, a cheer rose up into the warm night sky and the chant 'David! David! David!' arose, a mantra to the imprisoned rabbi. Inside the jail, the prison governor looked through the window with concern and barked an order to the chief warden, 'Get rid of him or those bastards will break through the walls.'

'Then call the police!' the chief warden shouted, but the governor shook his head and ordered the warden to carry out his instruction. The warden thundered a command into his walkie-talkie. Both men were at their wits' end. They hated Berg with an intensity normally reserved for child-molesters and wife-beaters. And their enmity was made worse by the self-serving contempt he showed both of them, as though they were merely part players in his grand design. The quicker they got the festering cancer out of the prison and went back to dealing with normal criminals, the better.

Rabbi David Berg was escorted by two uniformed officers to the front gate of the prison. As soon as the thick, iron-banded gate opened, a flood of television lights turned the dark archway into brilliant day. A roar of approval met the ebullient bearded rabbi as he stepped through the tiny portcullis, raising both fists to the sky in a gesture of acclamation, appreciation and defiance. When the crowd realised that he was free, they screamed 'David! David! David!' again and again. The rabbi, freed on a technicality by order of the Supreme Court after just two days in prison, fought his way to his familiar linoleum covered soap box and was given his bullhorn.

'They tried to shut me up,' he screamed. He waited for the roar of approbation to abate so that he could continue. 'But we won. This evil Crusade, this invasion of the Holy Land by Papists and anti-Semites, *will be stopped*!' Another roar from the crowd.

'They can jail me again and again. They can jail every one of you for standing up for God's law. But they will never stop the move of Jews towards a pure and unsullied land, free from foreign interference and alien presence.' The crowd drowned out the last few words as they howled and whistled and shouted their agreement. 'Israel for the Israelis,' he screamed. The crowd screamed back.

Two hours later, David Berg, Aaron Merlot and Avi Simons shared *schlugs* from a bottle of Chivas Regal. The mellow whisky burned their throats, as though clearing the taste of prison from their mouths. His lieutenants had been freed just hours after David had been let out of prison. 'How do you gauge the mood?' he asked.

Avi shrugged. 'You've been out of prison longer than I have,' he laughed. David Berg smiled. 'As far as I can tell, David, there's pretty widespread disgust at what we did in the church but that will pass. The mood on the streets seems to be an awakening to the dangers of this Crusade.'

Aaron broke in. 'I think we went too far. Our target is the Muslims, not the Christians. To get rid of them we should be attacking mosques, not churches.'

Berg shook his head in despair. 'Aaron, attack mosques and we'll bring the full weight of the *intifada* back on our heads. That'll drive the government into the peace camp, close down what remains of the building program in the Occupied Territories—but attack churches and you create a tension in the country which won't have a backlash. What it'll do is focus world attention on the morality of our cause. We are as theocratic a nation as is Iran. The world deals with the mullahs with respect. The only way we're going to get respect from the world is to establish Israel as God Almighty ordained.'

'So, what's next?' asked Avi.

'Two days in prison, in solitary confinement, gave me time to think.' An enigmatic smile appeared on his bearded face. Both Avi and Aaron knew that smile. It was the precursor to an escalation in activity.

Aaron said 'So?'

Berg continued to smile.

'Aren't you going to tell us?' asked Avi. 'Invade another church? What?'

'Gentlemen, we're going to cause the biggest headache that His Holiness has ever had.'

CHAPTER 10

The twenty-foot-high image of the Reverend Jimmy Wilson spoke eloquently to the huge audience gathered in his theatre. A curved screen projected the man and his message. His words were carried on banks of speakers timed to deliver the message milliseconds apart to eliminate echo and resonance in the sound-dampened auditorium.

'And how can *you* help me in my quest? How can *you* help deliver this most holy and most precious of writin's into the hands of the God-fearin' American Christian people? Let me ask you somethin' my friends. If somebody was to offer you a priceless oil paintin', the envy of the world, for nothin', would you accept it? And if somebody was to offer you a mansion, a hundred-bedroom palace in the Hollywood Hills, or Malibu for nothin'—no strings attached—would you accept it? Of course you would. Friends, I'm offerin' you the words of God. Better than an oil paintin'. Better than a mansion. Better, even, than the words of the Gospels themselves. These are the actual words of Our Lord, written by His hand in His agony as He was bein' tried, and humiliated and stripped of his dignity and crucified by drivin' nails through his flesh. These are the words of Our Lord.

'Any donation, my friends, will help in our quest. From the most modest gift of money up to as much as you can afford. And naturally, it's entirely tax-deductible under the charitable trust regulations of the IRS.'

Two thousand people in the IMAX theatre saw the flawless open face of Jimmy Wilson grow until it filled the screen as the camera panned in on his vivid blue eyes. As it stopped panning, the camera swept slowly beyond him into the background. His face was replaced by the gleaming Chrome Cathedral resplendent against the deep blue sky of the setting sun in the desert. The picture again dissolved to children happily playing in the cathedral's creche with a lullaby medley beginning to swell up in the background. The final scene was of the resonant all-black choir singing 'Mine Eyes have seen the glory of the coming of the Lord'.

At the end of the singing, the lights were slowly turned up and monitors stationed at every fifth row took out cloth collecting bags and walked from seat to seat as the faithful removed their wallets and placed as much money as they could afford into the hands of the church.

While the congregation was giving, Jimmy Wilson was in his private office listening to a whispered telephone conversation between his wife Annabelle and a man. Jimmy assumed it was a man. The slut was calling him 'darlin'' and 'big boy'. He had assumed that she would not be stupid enough to have an extra-marital affair. He was wrong. She would pay. So would her lover-man.

Annabelle replaced the phone and dressed. She came downstairs and knocked gingerly on Jimmy's office door.

'Honey, wouldn't you know it, I've gotta go out. Anne Tunney's kid Brian's runnin' a temperature and I promised to go over and sit with him. You know what a little demon he is when he's sickenin'. You don't mind if I go and relieve Annie, do you? She was up all last night.'

Jimmy looked at her and smiled benignly. 'Darlin'', you're an angel of mercy. You know, there's not many women that would drop everythin' to go and sit with a sick child. I'm truly proud of you, Annabelle. You don't worry about a thing. I'll grab a bite to eat in the refectory tonight. What time do you think you'll be back?'

'Oh sugar, it won't be late. Couple of hours, maximum.'

She kissed him goodbye and walked out of the office. Jimmy sat with a smile on his face until she left the room. Then he picked up the phone.

'Duane, bring my car around to the front right away. You and three other boys get in another car and follow me.'

'What's happening, boss?'

'Don't ask damn-fool questions,' Jimmy screamed down the receiver. 'Just do what I damn tell you to do.'

As she sped out of the Chrome Cathedral car park, Annabelle waved to Oscar, the black gatekeeper. He waved back, and mouthed the words, 'Have a nice day.' She had arranged to meet Jonas in their small love-nest in the desert. Her body yearned for gentle loving. She drove just below the maximum speed limit. The last thing she wanted was some tightass traffic cop to give her a speeding fine. Jimmy opened her mail. He would ask why she was on this particular road.

By the time she arrived, Jonas was already in the shack. She had chosen a white blouse and lemon skirt. He liked her in pastel colours. He liked to see her fair skin and blonde hair blending together in a vision of purity. He was wearing a tight Lacoste top which accentuated his muscles. His fawn slacks and sandals gave him a look of elegance and comfort. Damn these blacks, she thought. They could look good even if they were wearing a bath-towel.

She closed the door of the shed and walked over to him. This time he wasn't sitting on a chair but lying on the bed. This time he was ready for her. She felt quite heady as she saw his strong, youthful body lying there all ready. She got that tingly feeling. God, this boy excited her. More than the others. More than Duane and Simon and the others. It was more than lust. It was being able to breathe pure air, like living life. Sometimes, she couldn't sleep at night thinking thoughts about lying together and touching each other. Gently. With respect.

They didn't say one single word. Just looked into each other's eyes, knowing that what was going to happen was pre-ordained. She knelt down and kissed him tenderly on the lips. He stroked her fair hair and breathed in her aroma. They removed their clothes, looking at each other's bodies with tenderness and admiration. She straddled his body, rocking gently backwards and forwards in a loving union.

There was no squeal of tyres, just footsteps. Jimmy and his boys waited fifteen minutes in the late afternoon sun so that Annabelle and her lover would be caught in the unholy act. Jimmy's entourage parked at the bottom of the long, dusty driveway. Waiting, they whispered about the coming weekend and what plans each had. They were wondering what was going down. Jimmy had been menacingly silent, refusing to say why they were following Annabelle's car. Jimmy was agitated. When he judged the time right, Jimmy nodded and the five men walked quietly up the driveway.

It was Jonas who first heard the sound of footsteps crunching gravel. He froze. Annabelle held him closer, tighter, whispering lovingly into his ear. Jonas tried to pull her away from his head so he could hear better, but it was too late. The door flew off its ageing hinges and crashed on the floor as Duane's large feet kicked it inside. Brilliant light shafted into the shed, cutting the darkness. Annabelle screamed and turned around, throwing herself beside Jonas onto the bed. She looked at the door and saw four dark silhouettes, spectres from the Apocalypse, bringers of doom. She could not see their faces but she screamed in utter terror.

Jonas pulled the thin woollen blanket over their nakedness, his eyes staring white, and held her firmly in his arms. She screamed again. The four figures at the door silently parted and a fifth, his menacing body awfully familiar, walked down the aisle created by the men and took ownership of the room. She knew who it was, all too clearly. He was strained, standing over them in judgement and retribution, taut and intimidating.

'Slut, adulteress, whore,' he spat.

She found her voice. 'Jimmy, I—'

But he had turned his attention to Jonas. 'You black scum, you've had your filthy thing inside my wife. You've sullied her purity. You . . . thing.'

'Reverend Wilson, I love Annabelle.'

'Don't you dare insult my ears with your foul mouth and words, speakin' of love,' Jimmy shouted in anger. 'You nothin'. I took you in from the slums. I raised you from the depths of depravity and I made you into a man other men could envy—you, a nigger. And this is what you do behind my back.'

Annabelle screamed again.

'Shut up, you Jezebel. You pestilence, you. Harlot. Get out of that niggerboy's arms.'

She whimpered. 'But Jimmy, I'm naked.' She pointed to the other men in the room.

'They're pure,' shouted Jimmy. 'They're men of God. They're white. You've exposed your nakedness to this nigger. Get out of bed, slut.'

She pulled the blanket over her breasts and left Jonas naked on the bed. He covered his penis with his hands. Jimmy walked over to her and ripped the blanket from her hands. She screamed again and covered her breasts and her pubis with her arms. Jimmy flung the blanket to the floor at her feet. He hit her with the back of his hand. She flew backwards, hitting her back against the wall with a dull thud. The shed reverberated. Tin cans rocked and fell with a clatter to the ground. Duane closed his eyes, praying that the nightmare to come would soon be finished.

Jonas roared with fury. He sprang up from the bed, arms outstretched towards Jimmy's neck, but the four men rushed from the doorway and grabbed him before he could avenge her pain. They forced him down into a kneeling position on the floor at Jimmy's feet, his lips kissing Jimmy's toes. Nobody noticed Duane grimacing, eyes shut tight against the horror.

'Lift him up boys. Hold him good. I want the nigger to see this. If he closes his eyes, force them open.'

For ten minutes Jimmy Wilson beat Annabelle to a pulp. Her nose was split open, blood and mucus seeping from the crevice. Her mouth, eyes and lips oozed blood and slime. She had deep lacerations in her cheeks from where the soles of his boots had ground her face into the splintered wooden floor of the cabin, which turned a sickly red. Her ears swelled up and were deafened by the claps of his hand as he hit her repeatedly across the side of the head. Nothing of her frail body was left unsullied. He kicked and punched and tore at every orifice, grabbed every part of her body where he could claim a handhold.

Even her fingertips were bleeding from rough cracks in the floor as she tried to crawl away. But every time she moved towards the door, Jimmy came up behind her and kicked her hard in the anus, felling her, splaying her across the threshold.

The four men holding Jonas no longer restrained him. His body was limp and he was crying in sorrow and fear. He was ashamed of his impotence. Duane also felt shame, digging his fingernails hard into his palm to stop himself from screaming. He was inert, incapable of preventing any more damage to Annabelle, to the woman who had helped him into manhood. He walked surreptitiously out of the shack, unable to witness the violence any longer.

Annabelle's body slumped against the wall of the shed. She didn't have the energy left to moan. What she could feel of her body was hurting too badly. But every time she lapsed into unconsciousness, Jimmy would revive her by filling a rusty jug from a corroded tap and throwing water over her face.

When she was too bruised and battered to be recognisable, he stopped. He looked at his boys and smiled. Three smiled back half-heartedly. From the door, Duane forced a smile, fighting back vomit. Jonas thanked God that Annabelle's retribution was over. Jimmy walked over to the tin basin and ran the single tap. He massaged his hands and washed them under cold water.

'That's her done. Now, let's take this one out into the desert and do unto him as he would do unto others.'

Jonas struggled but the four men held him firmly and dragged him by the arms past Annabelle's unconscious body, through the door and into the yard. They pulled him down the long driveway, his naked feet scraping painfully over the rocks and dust and bundled him into Duane's car.

Jimmy and Harlin drove away from the shack first. The other car followed. They turned right, not left. Eventually, the road became a track and the track became bumpier and rockier. When there was no sign of civilisation, when the citrus groves had long since given way to the arid desert, Jimmy began to relax. They continued to drive until the road was indistinguishable from the land. They talked of the church, the Dodgers, the coming presidential election, anything but what had happened and what was going to happen.

Harlin looked across at Jimmy and saw him sucking his knuckles, which were bruised from the bashing he had just given Annabelle. He appeared to be relaxed, in full control of his senses. For the first time in their relationship Harlin was frightened of him. Up till now, the preacher had been a cash cow, earning Harlin more money than he knew what to do with. Harlin wondered whether Jimmy would soon bring the edifice of the church crashing down around their heads.

Jimmy looked vacantly through the windscreen and asked, 'Tell me, boy, with all your Harvard education, you ever heard of a science called telegony?'

'No, sir.'

'Well, I think you ought to know about it, so you'll understand my anger and what I'm doin'. Telegony isn't somethin' they teach you in medical school or in the Baptist Theological College, because its so explosive, so incredible, that it'd blow the whole fabric of the United States apart.'

'Sir?'

'It's the proven theory that when a woman has relationships with a man of another colour, the rest of the children she bears throughout her life will be infected with that man's influence. See, boy, now she's had that nigger's thing inside her, I can never again have a relationship with her, for fear that my offspring will be contaminated with his seed.'

Jimmy looked as though he was in a trance, as if he was trying to come to grips with new and overwhelming circumstances which diverted his life's plan. 'The authorities in Washington and in our great universities know the truth, but they're hidin' it from us. Lyin' about some of the most important things which face us today. Only one man had the guts to speak out about it, and in 1939 the world went to war to shut him up.'

Harlin stared transfixed out of the window.

In the car following, Jonas was crying and begging but the three men were deaf to his pleas.

'Reckon this is a good enough place?' asked Jimmy.

'You ain't gonna kill him, are you?' Harlin asked in trepidation.

'Hey, would I do a thing like that?' Jimmy laughed. 'I'm goin' to teach him a lesson he's never goin' to forget.'

They dragged the screaming naked man bodily over the rocky ground, tearing the remaining skin on his feet. Night-time was coming to the desert and the temperature was dropping dramatically.

Arms outstretched, they held him rigid. One of the men grabbed him by the hair and pulled his head upwards, so that he could see Jimmy's face. Jonas' black face was impassive. He was too scared, too full of hate, to show emotion. Last time he'd been this scared was in front of that chicano police detective who beat him half to death. Jonas knew what to expect. He prayed he would survive the beating, so he could wreak retribution on the Antichrist.

'Jonas,' said Jimmy, 'there's two things I could do to you. I could give you a thrashin' and leave you here. But that would only hurt for a couple of weeks at the most. You'd get over it. But you've sullied my wife. You've made her impure by your act of impurity. By your depravity, you've forever prevented me from enjoyin' her comforts. You have transgressed against the order of God. You must be taught a lesson.'

Slowly, letting Jonas see every movement, he took out a hunting knife. Duane staggered, his knees too weak, then supported himself by clutching onto the boulders.

'Why don't you boys hold the nigger down with his belly up,' said Jimmy.

The three men spreadeagled Jonas on the ground. He struggled and strained but lying with his back on the desert floor, arms extended, he did not have the strength to fight.

'Open his legs,' ordered Jimmy.

Jonas screamed. '*No!*'

Jonas' penis and testicles were exposed to the cold desert air.

'Say goodbye to 'em, niggerboy. That's the last time you'll ever put that thing into a fine white woman.'

Jimmy grasped Jonas' scrotum and penis in one hand and with a rapid motion cut them off. Jonas shrieked. Blood gushed out from the open wound, pumping onto the desert floor. It was absorbed immediately. Jimmy threw the penis and testes far off into the desert to be eaten by wild animals. As Jonas screamed, Jimmy quietly rubbed his hands into the dust of the ground in case he had been sullied by any of the blood. He vowed to throw the knife away when he returned to the church.

The three men let Jonas go. He doubled up his body, screaming in agony. The three men stood. Duane opened his eyes and gulped air to stop himself from vomiting. He swallowed and, when he saw the writhing man on the ground, closed his eyes again. Jonas kept screaming, like a wounded animal. Two of the men were grinning as he writhed on the cold desert floor. Duane couldn't hold it in any longer, and his vomit sprayed over a rock as he retched.

'Well, that's that done. Now let's go back to the cathedral,' said Jimmy.

As they walked to the car, Duane caught hold of Jimmy's sleeve and sobbed, 'Boss, you can't leave him like that, he'll bleed to death.'

Jimmy looked at him quizzically, wondering why Duane was concerning himself with a man like Jonas. Jimmy worried about Duane. He was weak. 'Isn't that rather a matter for the Lord?' he replied.

The air smelt of antiseptic. Figures in starched white uniforms bustled about. Nurses walked over to the mummy-like object on the bed, tapped drips, checked charts, turned knobs and recorded measurements. She was not a woman. She was a patient. The battle-hardened doctors of the emergency room who spent years treating the wounds of Los Angeles' urban theatre of war had seen many cases like this, but still classed it as bad. Her face was unrecognisable, her bones broken, her skin lacerated and suppurating. The difference between her unconscious and conscious states was marginal. Her mind wandered between the rational and the irrational. She had been brought in late the previous night by a young man who gave his name only as 'Shane'. He said he had found her on a street in the slums of Watts. He said he didn't want to get involved.

They had stitched her wounds, bandaged her face and body, encased her broken limbs in plaster. They pumped her full of pethidine and antibiotics. They tested her for AIDS, Hepatitis B and C, and for evidence of drug use. They swabbed her vagina. At the end of the tests, she was recorded as a white woman who had been the victim of repeated anal intercourse. Her nasal passages, linings and the damaged septum between her nostrils indicated lengthy continuous exposure to cocaine. She was probably the plaything of some coke dealer who got her fingers caught in the till.

The police lieutenant from the nearest station saw her before she was bandaged. Forensic took photographs of her naked unconscious body. She could not have looked more dead were she in the morgue. When they had finished, the police left and she was dressed in hospital nightwear and put into the intensive care unit. They hooked her up to monitoring machines. She was breathing of her own accord. She needed rest, quiet and a chance for her body to begin to heal itself.

Annabelle opened her eyes as the light in the ward increased with daylight. She felt no pain. She was happy. Her mind was free and floating. She remembered the beating. She didn't care. She loved life.

'Good morning. You're awake? Don't try to talk. How are you feeling? Just nod if you're able.'

Annabelle nodded. She was feeling fine.

'The pethidine will help you, honey. You'll probably feel quite light-headed, maybe even a little drowsy. What I'm going to do is to reduce the dosage somewhat until you start to feel a little bit of pain. Now the moment you do, you hit the nurses' call button. Just that we've got to reduce the dosage for your sake as quickly as possible.'

Annabelle nodded, then drifted back to sleep.

In the chill hours of Wednesday morning, when the only noises in the ward were the electronic beats from the life-support machines and coughs from sleeping patients, the serenity of the ward was broken by a rending scream.

'Leave me, please leave me—'

Nurse Joyleen Thomas was not used to this sort of thing. This was the women's intensive care ward. She turned and walked rapidly over to the bedside of the patient who was doing the screaming. Before even looking at her, Nurse Thomas checked the vital signs, the IV drips and the drains in her pelvis and nose. Everything seemed to be okay. She looked at the woman's face. God, but she'd taken a terrible beating. Carefully she prised open the swollen eyelids. Her eyes were still badly bruised. She shone a torch in the pupils to see if they'd contract. They did. Sure that nothing was going wrong with the treatment, Nurse Thomas smoothed the woman's hair and whispered in her ear, 'Calm down, honey. You're having a nightmare.'

The patient moved fitfully in the bed. She mumbled. Nurse Thomas knelt down to hear what she was saying.

'No, Jimmy. Stop. Oh, for God's sake, stop. Jesus, stop. You're hurtin' me. Don't kick me no more, Jimmy, stop kickin' me.'

Nurse Thomas continued to stroke her hair until the woman fell back into sleep.

Jimmy Wilson was the model of indignation as he strutted about the ward, whispering menacingly.

'I may be a man of God, doctor, but I swear to you that the man who did this to my Annabelle will pay. The good Lord said "Vengeance shall be mine", but I shall demand retribution at law of the animal that did this to my wife.'

Dr Segal nodded. 'I don't want to distress you unduly, sir, but I'd say that she must have suffered a beating over a period of hours. I think you might have to prepare yourself when she recovers. It appears that she may have been subjected to a certain amount of forced anal intercourse. There's also evidence of some damage to her nasal linings, some minor bleeding. Type of thing usually associated with cocaine use.'

Jimmy gasped in horror and looked down at the floor. 'My God, how can . . . it's beyond my comprehension.

Don't worry, doctor, she's in the bosom of the church and she'll be safe with me when she recovers.'

The two men shook hands and as the doctor walked out of the ward, Nurse Thomas called him over.

'Doctor, in the middle of the night Mrs Wilson was screaming out in a pethidine dream. She kept on begging "Jimmy" not to keep kicking and beating her. I was just thinking that the Reverend Jimmy Wilson—'

Dr Segal stopped in the doorway. He turned and looked at Jimmy gently stroking the hand of his comatose wife. Having worked in Casualty and Intensive Care for five years, there was nothing that Dr Segal hadn't seen. He knew Jimmy Wilson's reputation as a rabble-rousing fundamentalist preacher. The Beth Din in Los Angeles wrote complaints to the newspapers about him. Dr Segal was no admirer of the Reverend Wilson. He turned to Nurse Thomas.

'Joyleen, when you come back on duty tonight, two things I want you to do for me. One, reduce the pethidine. She's a coke addict, so we might have to vary the types of painkiller she's taking. Second, you keep a very careful watch on Mrs Wilson. I want you to write down whatever she says. Will you do that for me?'

Two days later the hospital had balanced the pain with the pethidine and was monitoring Annabelle's drug dependencies.

Jimmy had been to see her three times. He was solicitous, even unctuous the first time. But in subsequent visits he cautioned her against saying anything to the police. He told her she'd been found beaten to a pulp on the streets after her car had broken down on the way to visit her friend Anne Tunney. A kindly stranger had brought her in. Jimmy was working late in his office with four associates when the beating took place. There were at least six other witnesses whom he could call.

Nobody would believe her word against that of all those churchmen, especially now there was this surprising evidence that she was a coke addict.

He told her that he would accept her back into his family provided he was able to keep a closer eye on her. For her benefit, he would give her a full-time servant, to help her out in her busy lifestyle. Jonas had been the subject of a brutal attack. His body had been found in the desert.

The last visit had taken place this morning. Not a word was said about the beating. Jimmy accompanied the police for an interview at her bedside. She told the police her car had stalled in Watts. She had been robbed, beaten and held prisoner for hours. The police promised to make every effort to find the perpetrator.

'Joe? Arnie Segal. How're you going? Got a story for you. Woman was brought in a couple of days ago with the shit beaten out of her. She claimed it was a stranger who raped her in Watts and did her over like a dinner. She's the wife of Reverend Jimmy Wilson.'

Joe Deakin, religious affairs writer for the *Los Angeles Times*, wondered why his friend Arnie Segal was telling him about a story which crime reporters usually covered.

'You want me to introduce you to someone on the crime beat?'

'No, this one is for you. I'm ninety-nine per cent certain that she wasn't beaten up by some member of a street gang. I think her Bible-bashing prick of a husband half-killed her.'

'Why doesn't she report him to the police?' asked Joe, becoming suddenly interested.

'She's shit-scared of him. I have to give her valium half an hour before visiting time.'

'Why didn't you tell the police?'

'Because if she's not going to testify against him, I'm not going to get involved.'

'But you want me to?'

'Kid, it's a story.'

'It sounds like a great one to me! Thanks, buddy. I'll come around this afternoon. What ward's she in?'

At four o'clock that afternoon, Joe Deakin dropped by the ward and went over to Annabelle's bed. He was a tall, athletic young man, who had worked for the paper for four years. The son of a minister from a middle-class suburb of Chicago, he was interested enough in religion to specialise in it as well as handling baseball when the season was on. His editor was glad he handled religion. Nobody else on staff was willing to and the editor hated the way that non-journalist religious specialists wrote. All patronising, holier-than-thou bullshit.

Annabelle looked at the young man and wondered who he was. He introduced himself. She thanked the Lord that she was covered in bandages. She would hate for him to see the way she looked right now.

'Mrs Wilson, I'm really sorry to see you like this. I heard that you'd been beaten up. Working on the religious desk of the *LA Times* I thought I might come over and have a chat to you.'

'I'd rather not talk about it, sir. I was beaten by some coloured man when my car broke down in Watts, but I don't want it in the paper.'

'Ma'am, nothing's going in the paper without your permission, so don't worry about that. But if you don't warn people how dangerous it is driving in ghetto areas, then it could happen to other women like yourself.'

She shook her head. 'Please, Mr Deakin, I don't want anything in the paper. Nothing at all, please.'

'Mrs Wilson, you really don't have to worry. I'm not here to upset you or frighten you. You've been through enough. Anyway, maybe the police will be able to identify this man, Jimmy, the guy that beat you up.'

Her body shrank away from him. The bandages prevented him from seeing the terror in her eyes.

'What are you talking about, "Jimmy"?' she gasped.

Innocently, he told her. 'The whole ward knows about it, Mrs Wilson. Every night in your sleep, you've been screaming out, "Jimmy, don't do it", "Jimmy, don't beat me". We all assumed that the man who did this to you was a man called Jimmy.'

'No sir, you've got it wrong. Please, for God's sake, you've got it wrong. It's not Jimmy. He wasn't called Jimmy. I don't know what his name is. He never told me his name, but it's not Jimmy, I swear to you. Oh God, please don't put that in the paper, I'll get killed if you do.'

Joe reached over and held her hand. 'Who's going to kill you, Mrs Wilson? Is Jimmy going to kill you? Now why would Jimmy Wilson want to kill his own wife?'

She stared at him in horror. 'Get out of here. Get out of here, right now, or I'll call the nurse. You print one word of this and I'll be dead. Oh my God, I'm begging of you, begging. Please—'

But the rest of her sentence ended in sobs. A nurse came over and told Joe to leave.

He had a story! What he needed to do was get the facts.

'Of course it's big!' his editor screamed. 'I know how fucking big it is. Some hotshit preacher spreading love and God's word on Sunday beats shit outta his wife Monday. But ya ain't got the facts.'

'I'll get 'em, Ben,' Joe shouted back.

'So what you got right now?' asked the editor. 'You got some bullshit theory about a woman whose husband is some bullshit preacherman who beat the shit out of her. You've not got one word of evidence. They've already picked up a perp, some Mex, charged him with the assault. She's out of her skull on pethidine, laughing fit to bust with the fairies at the bottom of the garden, and you seriously expect me to let you follow this up?'

'Yep!'

Ben Brady looked at the reporter with amusement and fatherly admiration. 'Do you think I'm completely stupid? You're on a fishing expedition and I won't have you wasting my time. You've got two days to get me the evidence. If it's strong, we'll run the story. Till then, don't fuck with my time.'

'You gotta give me longer to get the evidence, Ben,' demanded Joe.

The city editor sat back in his chair and began to calm down. 'I'm not going to give you all week. Look, this guy is one of the true assholes of California. He's a racist who masquerades as somebody loving the family of man. You think I haven't been following his career? He's more than a fundamentalist. Yes, I know, he's got an audience full of blacks and Hispanics but you and I both know that he's a loudmouth bigot. But that's still no reason to invent stories about him. There's plenty of other sons of bitches in this state that commit real-life crimes. You've spent too long on your religious rounds. You've lost your perspective.'

'They've hauled his ass into court three times at the beginning of his ministry. Three times, Ben!'

'Remind me.'

'Couple of times for defamation against the Jews and once for leading a violent demonstration against a homosexual film festival. But Ben, he's only big with blacks and Hispanics because they're his power base. Trust me. I've spoken to some people who knew him in the old days. If you'll let me follow this through, I'll give you a story that will hit the front pages of papers all around the country. I'll prove that sonofabitch beat the shit out of his wife.'

'Don't tell me how to run my paper. You think I don't know a front-page story when I smell it. I'm not talking about the quality of the story, I'm saying that your facts are empty. You give me some hard facts about other people he's beaten, about complaints made in the church, stuff like that, and you can crack the bastard wide open. So far you ain't got zilch. Denials from the wife and the police. Get me some facts!'

Joe Deakin sat back in the broken armchair in his boss's office, put his hands behind his head and stretched his long legs beneath the coffee table. Of all the reporters on the *LA Times*, Joe Deakin seemed to have more confrontations with his boss than any other. Perhaps Joe came to grief so often because the subject he was writing about tended towards the spiritual, and spirits didn't buy newspapers.

'Boss, tell you what I'm going to do. I'm going to spend a couple of days around the Chrome Cathedral talking to Wilson, interviewing parishioners. I'll tell him I'm writing some articles about fundamentalism in America. Or I'll tell him it's to do with the new Dead Sea Scrolls material and this search party he's organising. I'll ask him how it's going to impact on the church. Let me see what I can come up with.' He got up and started to leave.

The city editor smiled and shouted after him, 'Make sure you haven't joined his wife on the pethidine next time you speak to me.'

CHAPTER 11

'Tiberias? Why do you want me to *schlep* to Tiberias?'

'When I want to think, I have to get out of Jerusalem. I go to Kibbutz Ein Gev and walk around to Tiberias. Then I get a boat back. It's wonderful.'

Michael thrilled at the enthusiasm in her voice. In all their conversations since he had arrived in Israel, there had been a pronounced stress. Now her voice was free of strain, open, willing.

'You have to think? What about?' he asked.

'I can't think in Jerusalem. I need to clear my mind. Go to Tiberias.'

Two hours later, they parked their car in the old Jewish quarter, close to one of the waterfront fish restaurants. She had been quiet since he had collected her from outside her apartment block, saying only perfunctory things. Different from how she had been on the phone.

They began to walk by the shore, ignored by the dozens of shoppers and tourists.

She closed her eyes, and inhaled deeply. 'Don't you feel it?' she asked.

He also breathed in the rich atmosphere. The air was hot and dry and carried the distant smells of pollen and fruit trees, blended with the tangy aromas of fish from the nearby sea. He felt again the zest of life which he had once enjoyed.

'Yes, I feel it. I feel youth.'

She looked at him in surprise. 'I thought you'd—'

'What?'

'I brought you here so that we could be transported back to the time of Christ. You can't do that in

Jerusalem. Too many tourists. But places like Safed and Tiberias for me are straight out of the Bible.'

They walked around the coastline and sat on a bench with a commanding view of the distant mountains.

'I've been a complete and utter bitch to you.'

She said it so matter-of-factly, with no reference to anything which had been said previously, that it took Michael a moment to digest it. He remained silent.

'I'm glad I phoned you in Sydney. It's good that we've stopped avoiding each other. But I'm really sorry I said things which hurt you. Sometimes I can be very direct, and quite cruel. It was wrong for me to tell you my feelings. Wrong to say I still loved you. I know you can never leave Deirdre and Christopher. I shouldn't have said a thing.'

She turned to look at him and smiled, waiting for a sign from him of forgiveness. And Michael smiled, sheepishly at first, but then openly, realising that some major turning point in their friendship had just been reached, but not knowing what had instigated the change. A massive pressure was lifted from them. She threaded her arm through his and entwined their fingers, something which she used to do when they were lovers.

'Tell me, how much time can you spend in Israel? When do you have to get back to your family?'

'I haven't really got a schedule. Term's almost over. I was just going to spend the holidays doing up the house a bit. Nothing that can't be delayed, provided there's a good reason.' He waited in excitement for her offer. All the way to Tiberias, and now holding his hand, Judith was planning something.

'I have a really good friend, a sociologist in the Hebrew University. He's made a special study of the customs and traditions of the Falasha Jews—the ones who were airlifted from Ethiopia. He said something interesting. Apparently, there's a timeless superstition among the Ethiopian Jews that they were the recipients of the treasures from the Temple of Solomon, just before it was destroyed by King Nebuchadnezzar.'

He listened in astonishment, but allowed her to continue.

'Well, it appears that there's talk among the tribespeople of hidden treasures and unknowable information and initiation ceremonies which apply only to one or two boys each generation—as though they were chosen for a special purpose.' She stared at him, not knowing how he was receiving the information. 'I think we should investigate the Falashas together, find out the source of these tales. Find out if there's any truth to the stories of hidden treasure.'

If it had been anyone else, Michael would have dismissed it, but Judith . . . He looked at her, then he pulled her towards himself. The heat of her breasts, the perfume she was wearing, the smell of her hair evoked overwhelming memories of youth and freedom. Suddenly he ached for her. As she ached for him.

He drew her closer to him, tightening his grip. Her body was soft and fluid. Their eyes stayed open, looking questioningly at each other, instinct overpowering reason. She put her arm around his neck and drew his head down until his lips pressed onto hers. He had forgotten how soft a woman's lips were, how moist, how warm, how willing. Kissing her, the bitterness of his life, the hardness of the intervening years, melted away, and he was young and potent once again. The heat of her body was a deluge, engulfing him in warm, baptismal security. He was reconsecrated, gaining in strength and manhood as her fingers entwined themselves through his hair, willing him to be closer, until they were a unity.

They kissed breathlessly, fluidly, whole moments lazing by as they gripped each other and renewed the joyous memory of a once-and-only love. And then it was over.

'I'm glad we've done it,' said Judith, somewhat matter-of-factly. 'It was something that was coming between us. A sort of a blockage. Now we can be friends.'

He was startled. 'I—'

'Michael, you have a wife and a son.'

It was such a stunning turnaround that he felt unbalanced, as though teetering on the edge of a precipice. 'Then why did you kiss me?'

'There are some things that are too hard to explain.'

'Oh no,' he said angrily, 'don't crap me off with that sort of a throwaway line. You know all about my life. It's a desert. Then you come back into it, and kiss me, and then—'

She placed a finger gently on his lips. 'I won't come between you and your wife.'

Michael frowned. 'Because of Chris?'

'Because of everything.'

'Judith, my marriage is over in everything but name. I don't want to go into the physical details but the moment Chris was born Deirdre turned off sex. She and I haven't—'

'I don't want to hear it, Michael. I'm not a home-wrecker.'

'But you love me. And I love you.'

She put her arm protectively around his shoulders. 'You know, you're not the only one with problems. I met Uri a month or two after we split up. He was studying electronics. I was on the rebound and he caught me. I was raw and angry. He was an outlet for me physically. And damn good, too. Still is. But there's a wintry coldness there. A closed-off sort of marriage. I feel I'm treading on eggshells when we're together. I'm stifled by him. I have to get out. He thinks it's another man. He can't accept it's him.'

'Then why can't we—'

'We can. We will. But only sex. Nothing permanent.'

He was so shocked by her openness, he was lost for words. Western women were usually more reticent. He had forgotten how open Israeli women often were. When life was lived on the knife-edge of momentary extinction, there was no time for sophisticated pleasantries.

'If you don't want to,' she added, 'I'll understand.'

'Judith, of course. From the day we parted, I've dreamed about the way we used to make love.'

She laughed. 'Dream no more. I've booked us into a hotel. It has a lovely view of the lake.'

'You planned all this?'

'Of course. If you don't plan, nothing ever gets done.'

A gull swooped down and landed at their feet. 'And when did you start planning?'

'The moment I put the phone down after calling you in Sydney.'

'Ari?'

'Just a catalyst.'

'But he's a rabbi. How can he condone—?'

'He doesn't want to know, but he loves us both and knows we'll each be happier together than apart.'

'A bit naive.'

'Ari sees everybody as he sees himself and Shuli. Larger than life, genial, accommodating, capable of anything. I'll never know why he became a rabbi, or an academic. He should have been the host of some TV game show.'

Michael burst out laughing. They held hands and she led him from the swerve of the shore, up the hill and into the hotel. They made love.

They lay in bed, staring at the ceiling fan, which rotated hypnotically, sending down cooling air like a pleasant wave washing over their bodies. It was as if the years had never passed between them, as though they were still young and fresh and desperately in love. As though the pain of unfulfilled marriages or broken children had never been. As though there had never been a gulf between them, a gulf which only the other day, had seemed unbridgeably wide.

They lay in each other's arms, sweat-drenched and expended, hoarse and replete, the sheets tangled and awry as though their passion was anger, their love nothing more than physical.

'You certainly haven't forgotten what to do,' she quipped, licking her lips.

'I had the world's best teacher.'

She reached over and grabbed a glass, drinking some water, then offering it to him. 'Michael,' she said as they lay, now recovered, 'say we do find the Testament. One in a million, but say we do.'

'Uh huh.'

'What will we do with it? Where should its home be?'

'Depends. If I find it in Rome or Alexandria or somewhere, then it should probably stay there.'

'And if it's in Ethiopia, where the Falashas used to live?'

'I think it should come back to Israel. That's where the Falashas have come to live.' She nodded. 'Or maybe the Vatican. What do you think?' he asked.

'I haven't given it any thought,' she mumbled. But neither of them believed what she had just said.

They were visible long before the stench of their exhausts and the discord of their air-conditioning units disrupted the harmony of the desert. There were not many of them, but the clouds of dust heralded their arrival like a stampede of bulls. And as they drew closer, spearheads of technology racing out of a mayhem of their own making, the two Egged coaches reminded the young Israeli soldiers of Crusader knights, charging into battle, lances ready to impale any heathen in their path. The brilliant midday sun, scorching the thin air and arid landscape, was reflected in dazzling scintillas from their windows. It was the tenth bus tour in the past three days. Things were getting out of hand.

The young lieutenant, a car mechanic by trade who was doing his monthly army service, had been warned that the buses were on their way. He called over General Dov Baer, who had been sitting in his staff car since 9.00 a.m. waiting for an incident to happen. Like every other senior officer in the Israeli army or security forces, Dov Baer made sure that he was in the front line whenever there was trouble. Israel won its wars because so few of its officers were desk-bound; instead they led their men into battle. Israel had one of the highest casualty rates among officers of any army on earth.

But unauthorised tourist coaches were only part of the problem. The whole military establishment was on alert because of the rise of activity of the Jewish fundamentalists, led by Rabbi David Berg. Since his release from prison, Rabbi Berg had been ominously dormant.

Standing with his small contingent of troops beside an army half-track, Dov turned to the young lieutenant and nodded. The young man picked up the radio and pressed the intercom button.

'Jericho One, two buses approaching. We're positioned across the road. I'll report in following contact.'

'Base to Jericho One, we've just received word from the army ministry that you are to be firm, but not to cause an international incident.'

Dov smiled. It was one of those no-win situations. He watched the buses approach and when the drivers saw his army half-track positioned like a road block, they came to a stop. As soon as the dust had started to settle, he walked forward to mount the first bus. He indicated to his second-in-command to walk towards the other bus. He decided to get on the bus to contain the visitors rather than allow them to spill out onto the roadway and confront his troops.

The driver looked at him in concern. He recognised the chevrons of an Israeli general. '*Shalom Aluf. Ma Shlom'cha*?' asked the bus driver. Dov switched to English for the benefit of the American evangelists. He addressed the bus party.

'My name is General Dov Baer. I'm in charge of security. Would you tell me who's leading this group, please?'

The bus driver nodded to a man in a clerical collar. His face and confidence said that he was American. He had the lean, earnest look of a man who clutched the Bible as a weapon.

'Good day to you, sir. I believe it is your intention to visit the Qumran area and search the caves.'

'We are here to seek the Testament of Our Lord.'

'You have been informed by the Ministry of Tourism that this is temporarily a restricted area. You do not have permission to be here from the Ministry of Religious Affairs.' He turned to the driver and said in Hebrew, 'And don't you bother smiling! You'd better have a bloody good explanation for why you disobeyed our instructions.' The driver flushed. His risk hadn't paid off.

The minister smiled patronisingly at Dov and turned to the rest of his group. He declaimed, 'Young man, we are here in your wonderful country on a month-long pilgrimage to the holy sites of Christendom. We've been to the churches in Bethlehem where our Christ was born in a stable. To Nazareth where Our Lord grew up and trod the very streets, and to Jerusalem, up yonder, where he kicked the moneychangers out of the Holy Temple. It was a miracle that while we were all here from Georgia, this momentous announcement was made.'

Dov began to get impatient. The group spokesman added, 'No sir, we do not have permission from your government to visit this area. But then, neither did Our Lord when He trod these very pathways.'

The entire bus 'Amen-ed' and 'Hallelujah-ed'. Dov ignored them.

'I'm very sorry, reverend—'

'Bishop!'

'I'm sorry, bishop, but this is a sensitive area both geologically and religiously. As would have been explained to you in Jerusalem, we've had to restrict visits until we sort out priorities. You'll have to return to Jerusalem and try to obtain permission from the relevant ministry.'

'Son, we've gone to the trouble of hiring your buses to come down here. We've halted our itinerary. At considerable expense, I might point out. Now, we don't want to go back and ask some civil servant for permission. We're not going to do any damage, we're just going to go around this area and hold a prayer meeting, asking the good Lord for divine guidance in order to find His Testament.'

'Bishop, you will not be going into this area. It's a restricted zone for archaeologists and for people with government permits. I must ask you to turn this bus around and go back to Jerusalem.'

Dov turned to the bus driver and said to him in Hebrew, 'Get this bloody thing out of here before these religious madmen start another war.'

The driver smiled and turned the ignition.

The bishop stood. 'Now hold on a minute. Just you wait right there, Mr Bus Driver. You turn that engine off, boy. My people have paid four times the usual hiring fee for this bus and you go where we tell you.'

He turned aggressively towards Dov. 'Son—'

'General!' Dov smiled.

'General, I don't want to quarrel with you. I'm sure you're a God-fearing man yourself, although of the Jewish persuasion. But I'm also certain that you don't want an international incident which will be reported back home in the East Coast newspapers. It'd be bad for your country's reputation. And we know that's taken a battering recently. I hardly need remind you about the Occupied Territories, need I?'

Dov bristled. The bishop realised he'd gone down the wrong track and withdrew. He gave an avuncular smile. 'We're not getting heavy or aggressive, but there's no harm in us people having a meeting in this area to pray for deliverance of Our Lord's words. Now, is there?'

Dov was getting impatient. He needed to be in Jerusalem for a meeting. There was an obvious solution, one which he had discussed with the ministry earlier that morning. 'Bishop, two miles down the road is the Monastery of Qumran. There's a car park next door to it. It's an archaeological site which must remain closed to you until you have permission. But why don't you go with us to the car park and pray there. It's just a stone's throw from where you wanted to go anyway, and no one will get into trouble. You can actually see the Qumran caves from where your buses will be parked. It's probable that Jesus Himself walked in the area. And you'll be quite private, I promise you.'

The bishop turned to his congregants who all nodded eagerly. 'Son, I think that's a sensible compromise. It's the Old and the New Testament working together, hand in glove, like our good Lord Jesus wanted it to.'

As the soldiers drove in the half-track with the buses following, Dov reported in to his headquarters.

'Amos, it's Dov Baer. These lunatics are going to be holding a prayer meeting in the middle of the desert. I'm escorting them to the Qumran car park. In future, that's the way we'll confine them. Okay?'

Amos laughed. 'Sounds good to me, general. Do you think you can get them to buy stuff from the kiosk? At least let's profit from their *meshuggass*.'

For Archbishop of Jerusalem Hiram Solomonoglou, the stress of being the head of the Catholic Church in the Holy Land for four years was beginning to tell. It was a position he had accepted only with much soul-searching and he missed the simple life of the Catholic ecclesiarch.

He had been recommended to the post by his dear friend in the Vatican, Franz Kitzinger. His brief was to hold the fortress against the wave of ecumenism threatening to dilute the purity of the Christian faith in the Holy Land. The Church of the Holy Sepulchre was a polyglot of religions from Ethiopians on the roof, to Armenians in the basement; his tenure as pastor was notable for maintaining the rigorous standards of the Catholic faith. His reward was his elevation to the archbishopric of Jerusalem.

But the tension which he felt today was of a new order, greater by degree than the burdens which he had carried in the past. He had just put down the phone to the Archimandrite of the Russian Orthodox Church in Israel who had expressed his fears for the safety and sanctity of places of Christian worship and complained that the Western Orthodoxy was doing too little in the way of security. Hiram Solomonoglou begged him to understand the need both for security and free access for the tens of thousands of worshippers and tourists, but the Russian was unimpressed. Dealing with the Russian was like treading a tightrope at the best of times. As a Bulgarian, he had been hounded out of his native Sofia because of his proselytising of Catholics against the dictates of the Communist rulers. Of course, the Russian patriarch was no Communist, but he was still a Russian and had that deep throaty resonance in his speech, the same speech patterns as the NKVD officer who had tortured Father Solomonoglou before partisans had arranged his escape.

It seemed as though his entire life had been spent in dealing with fanatics who were trying to destabilise his religion. First the Communists, then the Arabs in mandated Palestine, then the Jordanians who held sway over the Old City, then the Israelis after 1967 and now Jewish fundamentalists. Would there be no peace in his life? Would there be no time when he could ensure that his day would be free of the trials and tribulations of politics? When he could simply devote himself to the sanctity of his God?

He picked up his pen intending to write a letter to his old friend Bishop Bosco Szakisk, the President of the Pontifical Commission of Sacred Archaeology. He and Bosco had cried on each other's shoulders dozens of times in the past when life seemed unbearable. He knew that he could pour out his wrath and agonies in a letter which would be read, shared and understood, even if no letter came in return. It was the ultimate confession, an expiation of problems, a sharing without the qualification of repentance.

Before he had a chance to address the letter, there was a commotion outside his office door. Shouts, anger, furniture knocked over. Archbishop Solomonoglou frowned and started to rise from his chair to see what was going on but four men wearing balaclavas burst in through the heavy cedarwood door and ran towards him. The intruders grabbed him by his arms and pulled his large body from behind his desk and through the door. Solomonoglou struggled to keep up, his feet dragging against the resistance of the heavy carpet. He was an elderly man, in frail health. His heart could not tolerate this type of roughness. He gasped, shouting, 'What are you doing? Who are you?' but they ignored him and pulled him through the office vestibule where the bishop had only a brief moment to see his secretary lying alongside his desk, his head cut with a hideous gash.

The intruders dragged him roughly out into the brilliant sunshine of the courtyard, where a car was waiting with its engine revving. They pushed him into the back of the car, which sped away with a roar and scream of smoking tyres. A blindfold was placed over the old man's eyes. He lay still in the back, struggling for breath, his large body squeezed between two lean, hard men.

For the entire zigzag journey which lasted for half an hour, he continued to plead with the men to allow him to go free. But their silence was more threatening than any threat they could have uttered. It was obvious that they were not going to respond no matter what Solomonoglou said and so he prayed silently for his own life and for the safety of those who had toiled on his behalf in his secretariat.

The car came to a halt and the archbishop was pulled into a building. He heard the door slam and sensed the difference in heat between the outside and the inside. Another series of doors told him that he had been taken deeper into the building. He didn't know whether it was a house, a factory, a warehouse, a church. All he saw was black. All he felt was fear.

He was taken into a room and let go. Then a door slammed and locked. He stood still, shaking in his robes, scared. He tried to breathe deeply and bring his mind and body to rest. Once he had got his breathing under control he listened carefully for the sound of movement but heard none. He took off the blindfold and blinked at the dull light in the room. There were no windows to tell him where he was and the only furniture was a chair, a table and a bed. The archbishop moved slowly over to the door, reaching out to touch the handle as though it were a religious object. He moved it gently up and down and felt that it was locked securely. It was a stupid thing for him to do. Of course it was locked! The archbishop walked over and lay down on the bed in order to recover his composure. He stared at the ceiling and looked around for a crucifix in order to pray. But there was none. He took his personal Christ off his neck and hung it on a peg on the wall. He kneeled down and prayed to Almighty God for his safe deliverance.

Outside the room, four men sat at a coffee table drinking Arak. Before his first sip, one of the men said a *b'rucha*. He threw the aniseed liquid to the back of his throat and wiped his lips and his beard with his fingers. He stroked his long beard and smiled with satisfaction at his three colleagues.

Michael was one of a handful of world authorities lucky enough to have been granted permission to examine the list found amongst the newly published Dead Sea Scroll material. His attempts to see the scrolls immediately had been deflected by their custodian, Romain de la Tour.

After his earlier decision to write and demand access, his allocated time, given to him by Romain's secretary, eventually came around and Michael dutifully presented himself at the offices of the International Team. He signed a document promising not to reproduce any material which he was about to be shown, as all material had been copyrighted by the International Team. At the appointed hour, he went by taxi to the Hebrew University, where he was admitted to the holy of holies.

Touching this ancient brown leather fragment was like touching something blessed by God. Its awesome majesty, the secrets it had revealed, were beyond his wildest comprehension. The beginning and end of the document were serrated, lost to the ravages of dust and age, but the faded middle portion spoke to him through the aeons.

He re-read the list for the twelfth time:

I, Abram, son of Raphael, son of Eliezar, have taken into my keeping the following, which are the words of God Himself as written in the days of the desert people called the Essenes, from the cave of Machpeler,

one silver bell

one golden pointer

one book used by the anointed in the Holy Place within Jerusalem for the service of the Levites

one book used by the anointed in the Holy Place for the service of the Cohanim

and Testaments of the anointed for the afterlife of the following

Isaac the Blessed

the Teacher of the Holy Congregation

Nahum the Librarian

Azriel, the teacher of Women

Jeshua the Nazarene

Samuel the Just
Abraham, the Teacher of Children
Abimelech the Good
and these treasures with loaves and fishes have I taken to
    the people

The rest of the document was part of the dust of the cave. The conclusion was inescapable. To cite 'the Nazarene' indicated that this man from the inconsequential village was extraordinary. No mention in any Dead Sea Scroll was ever made of where an Essene came from. To place this man 'Jeshua' in a geographical position meant that he was an outstanding figure. Carbon-dating had placed the creation of the fragment from between the fall of the Essenes in AD 70 to the fall of the last Jewish resistance to the Romans by Bar Kochba in AD 135, and meant that the Jeshua mentioned was almost certainly Jesus.

The list gave credence to the existence of Jesus, doubted in recent years for the lack of contemporary evidence. But it was tantalising. The list did not contain Jesus' actual words, just a sign that His words, the Testament He had written, had been removed from where it was originally placed, and had been hidden somewhere else. Hidden by a man called Abram. Who was he? Where was he from? What did he look like? Who sent him? Was he an early Christian, burning with intensity, with love for the just-dead Messiah? And who were 'the people' he had taken these treasures to? The people of Rome? Of Antioch? Of Alexandria? Or further afield. Could Judith be right? Could myths, whose origins were buried by the millennia have a basis in fact? It was so tantalising, so exciting.

As evening fell, Michael left the hall in the Hebrew University where the manuscripts were stored. As he walked into the vestibule, along with half a dozen other scholars, he was accosted by a young man whom he had seen on several occasions.

'Professor Farber. I'm Yitzhak Aviman. I'm a reporter with the *Jerusalem Post* and I'm also the local stringer for the *Los Angeles Times*. Can you spare me a minute?'

Michael didn't like speaking to journalists. They distorted reality in their quest for sensationalism. But he was distracted by the joy he had experienced during his afternoon's work and unwittingly agreed. They sat on a couple of chairs in the vast, echoing chamber.

'I'm just doing some wrap-up work before I file a comprehensive story for the States. I haven't spoken to you yet about the find. You're a friend of Professor Wallenstein, aren't you?'

'We're all friends in this business,' Michael said, smiling, 'or hadn't you worked that out yet?'

The journalist grinned. The rivalry between biblical scholars, especially in regard to the Dead Sea Scrolls, was legendary.

'Professor Wallenstein says that the reference in the list is almost certainly to Jesus Christ, but that the Testament will probably never be found. What are your views on that?'

'I suppose that academics in the 1930s and '40s said that we would never be able to prove the existence of the Essenes. It wasn't luck that led to their discovery but brilliant archaeological detective work.'

'So you think that the Testament of Jesus may some day be discovered?'

'Certainly, if it hasn't been destroyed by the ravages of time. It's just a matter of working out where it was put to rest.'

'And you think it's right here in Israel? Maybe near to the shores of the Dead Sea?' asked Yitzhak.

Michael shook his head. 'I'm currently working on a different theory. I believe that the Testament, along with the other items mentioned on the list, were spirited away from the country because of the danger of the Romans finding and destroying them.'

The reporter became interested. He took out his notebook. 'Any idea where?'

The moment the notebook came out, Michael realised that what he was saying could be misunderstood. He was far from an innocent in these things. Much of the controversy which surrounded him was because his carefully crafted statements in the intellectual and academic media were picked up and distorted by cheap-shot sensationalism. Others in biblical scholarship had been ruined by the media. He was in an embarrassing position. Publicity often helped an academic career, but only non-controversial publicity. Not this sort. Yet he couldn't afford to alienate this reporter. This was the *LA Times*.

'Not a clue, I'm afraid. Could have been anywhere; perhaps Rome, Antioch. Maybe even Alexandria. Only time will tell.'

Michael excused himself and started to walk out of the building. 'Oh, professor, just before you go, one last question? What's your opinion on the kidnapping of the Archbishop of Jerusalem by the Zion Now! movement? Do you think the Pope should cancel the Crusade he's planning?'

Michael turned back in surprise. 'Kidnap?'

'Yes, the same guys that busted the Church of the Holy Sepulchre. They've kidnapped the archbishop. They published a demand this afternoon for the Pope to halt the Crusade or they'll kill the archbishop.'

Michael said, 'I . . . I'm sorry. I've been in here all afternoon. I haven't heard the news. It's terrible. I'm sorry, I have to go.' He would have to phone Ari. The prophecy that his friend had made was coming true, even before the Testament had been found. God! What other problems would happen as a result of this find? Michael dreaded to think.

Yitzhak Aviman phoned in his story. The last paragraph, picked up later by syndicates as far afield as Rome and Tokyo said:

> *And as academics ponder the fate of what must be considered the world's most priceless missing document, theories as to where it is are beginning to surface. Dr Gerhard Kremnizer of the University of Cologne said he thought it may have been buried deep in the Temple foregrounds. Another, Professor Mario Brusccone of the University of Milan, thought it could have been part of a geniza (storage area for sacred texts), destroyed when Jerusalem was destroyed. Yet another, Professor Michael Farber of Phillip University in Sydney, believes that the document may have been carried out of the country altogether, perhaps to Rome, Antioch or even Alexandria.*

Daniel Cardinal Rhymer put down his copy of *Osservatore Romano*, the Vatican's own newspaper, and stroked his chin. He knew of Michael Farber and Brusccone. But he had never heard of Kremnizer. Farber was an interesting man—a convert who had once considered becoming a Catholic priest. The two men had never met, but Daniel knew the Australian's formidable reputation. He re-read the quotation. Outside Israel? What a fascinating concept. Perhaps it could be buried along with the thousands of unattended documents within the Vatican's libraries and repositories. Stranger things had happened. The Vatican had been the centre of world politics for hundreds of years. Maybe this document had been overlooked, or its significance not realised.

No! It was highly unlikely to be in Rome. Its importance would have been recognised by the early church fathers. More likely to have been taken, as Farber suggested, to one of the early centres of Christianity. Alexandria? Antioch? Ephesus?

Daniel would pay a visit to Professor Mario Brusccone, as well as to Professor Michael Farber. Courtesy calls. In the not-too-distant future. But first, he had to deal with trying to free Archbishop Solomonoglou. How could they kidnap such a godly and innocent old man? What type of people were they? It was as bad as America, as bad as his diocese of Boston or New York City or Los Angeles, where hideous crimes were committed. It was a harsh reminder of the land he lived in when he was growing up.

Sipping a pina colada on the balcony of his mansion overlooking the desert, Jimmy Wilson read the *LA Times* with interest. He must look up these academics to give some credence to his quest. He read their names again. Kremnizer a German, Brusccone an Italian and this Michael Farber guy. See what they're all about.

The telephone rang. Jimmy put down his drink and muttered to himself that there was never any peace.

'Yes!'

'Dr Wilson. I'm real sorry to disturb you sir, but there's a reporter from the *LA Times* on the phone.'

'Well, put him on to Luke, he's the director of public relations,' he said testily.

'Reverend, I've tried that, sir, but he says he has to speak to you. He won't tell me what it's about.'

'Put him on.'

'Reverend Wilson. Joe Deakin from the *LA Times*.'

He put on his most patronising voice. The *LA Times* had been critical of him in the past and anyway, Jimmy's preferred medium was television. 'What's so important that you have to speak to me personally, young man? Why can't my director of public relations assist you?'

'Dr Wilson. I really must have your personal assistance on a quote which I'll be using for a major article I'm writing. It's scheduled for Saturday's newspaper. It concerns the Jesus list. I know that you're going to Israel to search for the Testament, but in view of this morning's article I'm wondering if now you might change your mind.'

Jimmy froze. Any hint that the Testament might not be in Israel could destroy the expedition. And hopes of a multi-million-dollar coup. He changed from being patronising to being unctuous.

'And what article is that you're referring to, Joe?'

'What Professor Michael Farber from Australia said about the Jesus Testament being outside Israel. Maybe in Antioch, or Alexandria.'

There was no way he could get Americans to pay for a trip to an Arab land. This was trouble!

'Friend, we have one lone voice, crying in the wilderness. All other voices, experts from around the world, have said that Our Lord's Testament is within the Holy Land. That's where it is; and that's where I'm going to look for it. As to this Farber gentleman, I have no idea where he's coming from.'

'Dr Wilson. I phoned Professor Farber just an hour ago to ask him to expand on his theory. He shut up tighter than a clam. Be interesting to investigate him, wouldn't it?'

Jimmy frowned. 'What do you mean "investigate"?'

'Well sir, the *LA Times* has people in Israel who could see what he's up to. Find out what he knows.'

'Joseph, it wouldn't take you long to get out here to the Chrome Cathedral. Why don't you drop round here for dinner tonight? If you have no alternative arrangements, of course.'

Joe smiled to himself.

Jonas Watkins' coffin sat majestic on its catafalque before a predominantly black congregation of three hundred people. At the front in a position of honour normally occupied by church elders were Jonas' parents and his brother Micah. They looked drawn and haggard. When Jonas had failed to return home four nights earlier, Micah had been concerned and had phoned people at the church who told him that Jonas had not come back to work after lunch. By late evening, the family was worried enough to contact the police, who fobbed them off and said to call back the next day if he hadn't appeared. The next morning, Micah sat in the secretariat of the church, begging to see Dr Wilson, but was told he was too busy and had no idea where the young man was. Apart from that, the Reverend Dr Wilson was also concerned that his own wife, who was supposed to be visiting a girlfriend to look after her sick child, did not arrive and was lost to the forces of the night.

They found Jonas' body the following day. A Mexican worker on a citrus farm sent to find a place to plant left-over lemon trees came across the body. He thought it had been savaged by animals. Its skin looked like a dried up grapefruit that had been left out in the sun too long. The body fluids seemed to have leaked out of the gaping wound in the boy's pelvis. The sun had done the rest.

The police allowed only Micah and Jonas' father to view the body before it was interned in its casket. His mother, they reasoned, would be haunted for the rest of her life if she saw the body.

As the choir swelled, Jonas' mother gripped tightly on to the arm of her remaining son. Micah stood rigid, as the anger swelled inside him. No one, especially a good, decent God-fearing boy like Jonas, deserved to be treated in that way. Someone would pay. Justice might be mine, according to the Lord, but Micah would ensure that God would be given every assistance to bring retribution against those who had destroyed his mother's hopes.

CHAPTER 12

Pope Innocent held his arms out at right angles from his body. The morning light flooding in through the window cast a shadow of a cross on the floor of his private apartment. He saw himself crucified in the shadow and smiled.

The valet finished dressing the Pope and bowed reverentially, walking backwards towards the door. No matter how often he asked his staff not to bow and scrape like Victorian servants, they never listened to him. The tradition of their lives held greater weight than the commands of a pontiff, the temporary inhabitant of the permanent seat of Peter.

Dan Rhymer was amused at the scene. There were few men less suited to the role of overlord than the present Pope. A man of painful modesty and humility, he worked himself to exhaustion to avoid other people working on his behalf. His generosity, spirituality and faith, and the immeasurable popularity he had earned, rather than commanded, was responsible for his elevation to the highest ranks of the Catholic hierarchy. His papal role, making decisions of incalculable importance, having to command underlings and play the game of palace politics, did not suit him well. But he was learning. Dan Rhymer's pontifical gift when his friend became Innocent was a copy of Machiavelli's *The Prince*. It sat, well-thumbed, and ever-present on the Pope's coffee table.

Innocent turned to his friend as they walked out of his private apartments for the forthcoming audience. 'I was looking forward to this last night, but now I'm not so sure.'

Dan Rhymer nodded. 'They won't ask any questions about the kidnapping of Hiram Solomonoglou. They've already been briefed not to. Is that what's causing your problem?'

Innocent said that it was only partly what was worrying him. 'I get the sense that it's all starting to go wrong, Danny. It began as such a pure and innocent idea, such a devotion to the future. The Lord's Testament and what it could do for mankind. Yet already it's being captured by those who want to stifle it. You included.'

'It's only a scrap of parchment, Gabby. A list. That's all,' countered Daniel.

The Pope turned on him, eyes gleaming in passion. 'But you're wrong, you're so wrong. It's a link. It's our very first positive concrete link to God-made-man. In all of history, there's never been anything which has been of such moment. We've got a direct link to the Saviour, to God. Don't you understand, you of all men?'

Daniel again felt acute embarrassment. Nobody could expose his sins with such directness as Innocent. 'So why is it all going wrong?' he asked in a subdued voice.

'Because of the reaction of the godless. Because of the criticism against my Crusade from both within and without the Church. Because of poor Archbishop Solomonoglou, rotting in some foul airless room, held captive to the prejudices of fanatics, humiliating a sick and humbled old man to force me to change my mind.'

Daniel nodded in understanding. 'Do you think the announcement you're going to make will be any less momentous? You haven't discussed it with the Curia, with anybody in the world of theology, except me. Do you think that this decision of yours will be any less controversial? You're going to set half a billion Christians adrift.'

'No, I'm going to release them. I'm going to put them in charge of their religion for the first time in their history. I'm going to free it from all of the constraints.'

'Like Martin Luther?'

Innocent bit his lip at the insult. But it was the type of remark he would have to wear. It was a spiritual coming of age, and many people wouldn't like it. 'There is a view, Danny, that Luther wasn't fighting the Catholic Church, but rather the growth of humanism. He saw the leaders of the Catholic community treading the same path as the humanists.'

Daniel disagreed but remained silent. After hours of arguments, he had said all that he could say.

'Ready?' he asked.

Together the two men walked from the Pope's private study into the pontifical antechamber within the Medici Apartments and were met by the Pope's Prefect for Universal Understanding, Giacomo Cardinal Roncello. Roncello bowed and kissed his Pope's ring.

'Ready?'

Roncello nodded.

'Are they all there?'

'Everyone,' Roncello said.

'Not just the usual Vatican media? *Izvestia* as well?'

'Especially *Izvestia*,' he said with a wicked grin.

The Pope nodded and smiled. 'Good. Then, to the fray.'

The three men slowed their pace and walked towards the door which led into the audience hall of the Medici Apartments. This was the hall where popes for hundreds of years had met world dignitaries, where private audiences were conducted, where deals were done, treaties arranged, agreements made.

As they reached the door, the three stopped. Roncello walked forward a pace, tapped gently on the door and stepped back in line with Cardinal Rhymer, one step behind the Pope. At their signal, the two Swiss Guards on the other side of the door reached back and opened it, their halberds crossed. As the doors slowly opened, they uncrossed their halberds in order to allow the Pope and his small entourage through. The background noise in the room instantly quietened and the thirty journalists rose as the American Pope walked in.

The reporters were seated in rows before a dais on which three chairs were placed, the large chair in the centre for the Pope, the others smaller and on either side for his advisers. A cynic might have compared the placement of the chairs on the dais to the crucifixes on Golgotha, and there were a few cynics in the room. Present were people who represented news media from around the world, asked to a private audience with the Pope to be told what Roncello described as 'momentous news'. Some faces were familiar. Others he had not seen before.

The Pope had asked the various heads of pontifical commissions within the Catholic Curia whether they wished to be on the platform with him but all except Roncello had declined. Not through any malice, they assured him, but because this was his announcement and should be made by him alone.

The Pope and his two advisers walked processionally towards the chairs on the stage. Each man and woman in the audience stared closely at the pontiff. Only a few of them had come this close to the supreme spiritual ruler, the vicar of Christ for the worldwide congregation of Catholics.

The Pope walked forward and shook the hand of each reporter. Half felt they were touched by God. The other half were flushed in awe. As he shook hands, he quietly asked, 'And where are you from?' With each answer—

'*The Times* of London, your holiness', 'The *Washington Post*, your holiness', '*France Soir*, Holy Father'—he nodded and made a comment about the reporter's city or newspaper in the language of the reporter's country. Just enough to make the most hardbitten and cynical journalist feel as though the Pope had personal knowledge of the people whom the newspaper represented. When he had done the circuit, he walked to the stage, picked up his chair and carried it down level with the others. The sceptical reporters could not help but smile at the common touch, the patent openness of this spiritual man.

'Ladies and gentlemen,' said Daniel Rhymer, 'his holiness wishes to make an announcement in regard to the recent discovery by the International Team of translators and researchers who are currently working on the Dead Sea Scrolls in Jerusalem. His holiness will not make a formal statement but will speak personally on the matter of how the Catholic Church views this discovery and what we intend to do in its regard. You may ask questions of the Holy Father when he has finished his address. Even though the Holy Father is speaking to you personally, he is speaking with the authority of the Catholic Congregation.'

Lights were switched on, buttons pressed. The Pope cleared his throat and addressed his audience.

'For two thousand years, Christians have believed in the perfection and divinity of the life of Jesus of Nazareth. Until now, He has lived for us only though the immutable writings of the holy saints, Matthew, Mark, Luke and John. Christian faith has never doubted the existence of the Son of God, the man born of the Virgin Mary who suffered the pain of crucifixion in order to redeem our souls. Faith alone has sustained us as a Christian community for all these years because there has not been one shred of scientific evidence which can be relied upon to offer proof of the existence of Our Lord.

'And there, ladies and gentlemen, is the conundrum. For Christians, He lives. But sceptics, in an increasingly fatalistic world, require proof. The religious Christian community has only been able to offer faith and hope as proof.'

Newspaper reporters furiously scribbled the Pope's words. Sound recordists checked levels. Cameramen panned across the audience and zoomed into a full face close-up of the handsome Pope.

'The discovery of the Dead Sea Scrolls in 1947 offered a challenge to Christianity. For Jews, the scrolls proved once and for all that the Torah and the words of the Books of the Kings, Prophets and Judges have come down to us from the time of the Bible virtually un-changed over these last two thousand years. But for followers of the simple Nazarene, the Dead Sea Scrolls offered challenges. For many, they threw up even greater obstacles to the belief in the Messiah. The scrolls presented an even more splintered cross on which their faith was tormented. They appeared to say to us, through the mists of two millennia, that Our Lord Jesus was a member of a monastic desert community called the Essenes. There were strong similarities between the Essenes and the early Christian church. Christian intel-lectuals throughout the world were concerned that placing Our Lord amongst the Essenes might call into question the two-thousand-year-old record which we have accepted from the Gospels.

'And now a fragment, a list, a scrap of leather has been found which is contemporaneous with Our Lord's mission on earth which records His having written a Testament.'

The Pope could see that he was beginning to lose his audience. Everything he had said to date had been written about in the last few days. He would now come to the point.

'My friends, Our Lord's Testament must be found. I am not concerned, as others have been, that Our Lord's Testament could compromise our faith. I have absolute and abiding belief that Our Lord's Testament will act as a signpost left by Him for us to follow into the future. It will be a document of love and of reconciliation. Its discovery will end hostilities between men. It will end jealousies, hatreds and pettiness. The discovery of the Word of God on earth will usher in a new age of love and peace and reconciliation in which all men and women, regardless of their faith, will, in the eyes of Christians, become brothers.'

He had their attention back again. Now he put on his pontifical voice: 'On 25 January 1959 the Blessed John XXIII, Angelo Giuseppe Roncalli, assembled the Second Vatican Council. It did more to modernise the Holy Catholic Church than any other decision in the past thousand years. We, Innocent, Servant of the Servants of God, Successor to the Prince of the Apostles and Supreme Pontiff of the Universal Church, announce the creation and assembly of the Third Vatican Council.'

Thirty faces looked up into the Pope's eyes, jaws slack in astonishment. The Pope smiled. Nearly forty years earlier, Pope John XXIII had stunned the Catholic world by announcing the Second Vatican Council.

'Our Jewish brethren have long accepted that the story of the creation in the Old Testament is a brilliant and beautiful metaphor for man's origins. They have accepted the Tower of Babel, the Garden of Eden, the story of Joseph's coat, Sodom and Gomorrah and the turning of Lot's wife into a pillar of salt as figurative ways of experiencing the abiding condition of humankind. Only a handful of radical creationists around the world believe that these charming metaphors are absolute literal fact.

'Yet not since the earliest days of Christianity has the Holy Catholic Church itself examined the Gospels of Matthew, Mark, Luke and John to determine which of Christ's miracles are myth and which are fact. In light of the discovery of this fragment and its ability to give concrete form to the reality of Jesus Christ Our Lord, it is time that we Christians applied modern thinking to the Gospels.'

The Pope cleared his throat again and said, 'I have not discussed the Third Vatican Council with any member of the Curia. Like the decision of my predecessor, John XXIII, it is my decision as the supreme pontiff, and my decision alone. But the matter of the Crusade is different. That matter I have discussed with many members of the Curia. It would be foolish and naive to suggest that every member of the Curia accepts the need for a Crusade. A number are worried about the use of the name, believing it will cause fear and resentment. Yet more are concerned about the failure of an expedition and what that will do in dashing the hopes of the faithful. They would prefer a quietly conducted search, but I believe that this discovery heralds a new dawn at the end of a long dark winter's day in the life of mankind. I do not want to give false hopes, yet I fervently wish for a swelling up of faith in the hearts of Christians throughout the world. I believe that our announcement of a Crusade will give to modern, sceptical and fatalistic mankind what he has sought for so long—a faith in the future.'

'A sort of *fin de siècle* present,' quipped the reporter from *Paris Match*.

The assembly laughed. So did the Pope. Daniel failed to see the joke. It was the very problem which was splitting his mind.

'You know,' said the Pope, 'you could be much closer than you believe. We are approaching the end of the second millennium. At the end of the last century, a wave of *fin de siècle* . . .' Innocent searched for the appropriate word, 'excitation spread throughout the world. The 1880s, '90s and the turn of the last century were accompanied by anxiety and uneasiness which led to a mood of play, impulse and self-indulgence.' The Pope scanned the congregation of reporters to see if they were still with him. It was vital that they put his Crusade into an historical, rather than a sensational context. 'As we approach the end of the second millennium, I sense the same mood to be growing. Today there is a move towards the irrational and against certainty, against enlightenment, against intellect. But the move is not towards faith. It is towards temporariness and against permanence. We have lived through an age of greed, deceit, corruption and immorality in both private and public lives. But what have we entered?'

The reporters began to fidget, unclear where the Pope was leading. 'An era of despair, of fundamentalism and of rejection. Our Crusade will, I believe, be the movement which leads all humankind back from the brink.'

At the end of the press conference, Pope Innocent walked slowly back to his apartments. Now would be the most testing time in his life. Daniel Rhymer realised the problems and remained silent.

The Pope suddenly broke the silence. 'I want you to leave tomorrow morning and fly to Israel. I want you to talk in confidence to the members of the International Team. I want to know what hope there is of finding the Testament.'

Desperate for the privacy of his apartments, as he walked out of the Vatican Palace Daniel felt close to weeping. The tensions in his body were threatening to rend him apart. He had kissed the pontifical ring, sworn allegiance and obedience to the Chair of St Peter. Daniel was about to betray his oath, not for personal gain or grandeur, but to protect the only rock of stability in his life, the security in his faith, a bulwark against his own weaknesses.

As he was flawed as a sinner, so his faith was strong. As his body trod the road to eternal damnation, his mind was anchored on the rock of absolute dedication to the sanctity, the purity of the creed, the creed which his mind daily abused. No matter what the consequence to himself, he would protect the faith, build a stone wall around it and repel the invaders. A Christian knight: pure in mind, sullied in body.

The Reverend Dr Jimmy Wilson read the front page story in the *LA Times* and sneered at the young man sitting opposite him.

'Can I say something off the record, Joe?'

Joe Deakin nodded.

'Now, you're sure you ain't going to quote me on this, 'cause I'd be greatly embarrassed if you did.'

'Reverend, you have my word as a Christian gentleman.'

Jimmy Wilson nodded. He slapped the paper with the back of his hand. 'These goddamned Papists, who the hell do they think they are? Their time has been and gone. They had the opportunity to accept the Reformations of Luther, Calvin, Wesley and Knox and all the rest of them ancient people. But they stuck to their guns and they ain't moved a skerrick since.

'It's us that's carrying the torch of Christianity. Me and the Pentecostalists, and the Southern Baptists and other God-fearing Christians like us. This is where Jesus is at. This is His home. He ain't in Rome. He gave that a miss five hundred years ago. He's right here in California, and New York, and Chicago and Washington. Oh no, sorry, He ain't in Washington. He's where congregations gather to sing His praises. Now I don't want you to go quoting me on this. You gave me your word, but ain't no way I'm gonna let a bunch of red-hat Catholics, dried up old men in silken gowns, get the word of my Lord.'

'Amen to that, Reverend,' said Joe, nodding vigorously.

Jimmy eyed him with affection. 'You know Joe, I gotta tell you, I was surprised to find a man like you in the *LA Times*. From what they've written about me and my ministry I thought that they were just a bunch of Communist fellow-travellers and atheist carpetbaggers. So tell me, what's a God-fearing son of a Christian minister doing working in a whorehouse like that?'

'Sir, when I was a boy my daddy made me promise that I'd devote my life to helping other people see the light. When I was at journalism school with all the atheists and Communists and non-believers, I felt myself to be the only man of morality in a pack of degenerates. When the position came up as religious reporter of the *LA Times*, I thought I could truly do something for the godless. Now, it's not all been my way. Very often, I've had to bury my inclinations to the dictates of those people above me. But slowly and surely, Reverend Wilson, I'm getting my message through.'

Jimmy Wilson listened to the young man in admiration. 'Son, I don't mind if you call me Jimmy while we're in private.'

Joe Deakin had to force himself not to burst out laughing.

In the refectory later that afternoon, the two men were joined by Jimmy's assistants Harlin Brown, a good-looking Chicagoan, and Luke Carmody, a stringy youth from Texas. Both men still viewed the reporter with deep suspicion despite the fact that he had been Jimmy's guest for the last three days.

Stirring his coffee, Joe asked the group, 'How many men and women will you be taking over to Israel?'

Luke answered. 'We're hopeful of taking a minimum of fifty but it could be up to a hundred if applications keep coming in at the rate they are.'

'And how much does each expedition member have to pay?' he asked.

'What in hell business is that of yours?' snapped Harlin.

'Now, Harlin,' Jimmy intervened, 'we're not making a secret of it. Joe here is a reporter and has the right to ask questions. As it happens, each person on the expedition is paying one hundred thousand dollars to defray our expenses and as a contribution. As you'll appreciate, Joe, it's money that goes to the many good works of our church. To our Bible classes, the missionary and out-reach programs, our hospital and aged-care institutions, the medical insurance we have for our parishioners, the day-care centre for the children, and many other God-ordained projects.'

Joe was about to ask another question when there was a commotion at the entry of the refectory. A figure seated in a wheelchair, head bandaged down the left side, arms encased in heavy plaster, was being wheeled through the door.

Jimmy reacted in shock. He turned and softly spat at Harlin, 'I thought I told you to keep her upstairs.'

Harlin shook his head, not fully comprehending what was happening. Joe looked at the doorway. Jimmy beamed a smile. 'Darlin', how wonderful to see you out and about. Come over here and meet a new friend of mine.'

Everyone in the refectory looked at the pathetic figure in the wheelchair being pushed along by her newly appointed attendant. Joe stood to greet the arrival of the patient as Jimmy introduced him. 'Mr Deakin is going to assist us in giving proper reporting to the good works that we're doing here.'

Joe was stunned by the look of Annabelle's face. In the hospital with all the bandages, he had been unable to see the full horror of the beating she had suffered. As she sat in the wheelchair, he witnessed her face as a contusion of blue swollen skin and scabs healing over stitches. Her lips were still puffy and her eyes showed discoloration from where her husband's boot had kicked her. With the exception of her arms which were bandaged, the rest of her body was covered by a dressing gown.

In the past three days Joe had been wheedling his way into Jimmy Wilson's confidence. The church was merely a gigantic money-making machine, a fraud designed to fleece the flock, and he was working on ways of finding where the money collected ended up.

Seeing Mrs Wilson in the wheelchair brought back to him the prospect of Jimmy Wilson being a sadistic wife-beater as well as a con-artist. The fear in her eyes at seeing Joe sitting with her husband spoke of a woman in terror for her life. Joe felt a sudden revulsion in being in the same room as Jimmy.

'Mrs Wilson, it's nice to meet you. I heard about your terrible attack. I'm very sorry for what happened to you. I'm so pleased that they've arrested the culprit. I hope you're feeling a lot better now.'

She looked at him with questioning eyes. He searched them for a meaning but he could not detect anything other than pain and humiliation.

Through swollen lips, as though speaking in an hypnotic trance, she said, 'I'm glad you're with us, Mr Deakin. I hope you're not going to print anything about us which is untrue.' Her voice was thick, indistinct. She was on heavy tranquillisers.

Joe looked at her pitifully and smiled reassuringly. 'Ma'am, I promise you nothing will be reported that will hurt you.'

'Praise the Lord,' Jimmy chanted.

'Praise the Lord,' said the other two dozen people in the refectory.

When Daniel Rhymer returned to his rooms outside the Vatican Palace, he found a note waiting for him. He ripped it open and read it.

Danny, I'm not used to being a spy. Running around the streets of Jerusalem in a deerstalker hat, meerschaum pipe and magnifying glass does not suit the elevated ranks of a member of the clergy. I'm sure you've got a good reason for wanting me to follow this hapless professor and I've done what you asked. Why, I don't know, but since you've been in the Vatican I'm sure you've become just as Byzantine in your affairs as everyone else becomes in that great and holy palace.

I don't know what to tell you. He's staying at the King David Hotel in Jerusalem. He enjoys coffee and croissant in the morning. He is often in the company of a woman who I believe is an Israeli native.

Yesterday the two of them went to a neighbourhood of Jerusalem called Ein Hod. I had to be particularly careful here because I could easily have been spotted.

Danny, what have you got your old seminary friend into? And does his holiness know about this or am I committing a sin by proxy? Anyway, after a couple of hours he left the house and I didn't bother following him back to the hotel or wherever he went. I thought you might prefer for me to find out who he visited. It appears the house belongs to the Ministry of Absorption and has been allocated to an elderly Jewish gentleman and his family who have recently arrived from Ethiopia.

Do you want me to keep following him or have I done my job?

Your brother in Christ, Francis

Daniel smiled as he put down the letter. He, Francis and Gabriel had been the very closest of friends at the seminary. Of them all, Gabriel had been the most obviously successful. You didn't go higher than being Pope. And with the lifelong affection for Gabriel, Francis held a position of love just as large within Daniel's heart. He and Francis were as close as brothers. When Francis chose to follow a missionary life and devoted himself to working in an orphanage of Christian Arab children in Jerusalem, the two men had not lost touch. Daniel missed Francis' good humour, irreverence and plain common sense. He could have used him in these last six months in the Vatican.

He re-read the letter a second time with affection. Ethiopia? Now why would Professor Farber be talking to an Ethiopian Jew?

'Are you sure?'
'Absolutely.'
'Ethiopia?'
'That's where he was from.'

'Well, what did he ask?'

Joe Deakin shook his head. 'I don't know, reverend. Our guy in Jerusalem said that Professor Farber met with three or four Ethiopian leaders again this morning. The stringer didn't say anything other than that. I can get the names of the Ethiopians if you want.'

Jimmy nodded. 'You do that, Joe, I'd like their names, so that when I go over there I can maybe talk to them.'

Judith sipped her beer. She and Michael had been to visit another three Ethiopians that afternoon, each visit arranged by her friend at the Ministry of Absorption. The three families had been chosen because one was a rabbi, one a musician, and one a chronicler of oral histories of his peoples; each was knowledgeable in Falasha history and traditions; each had been a disappointment. At the end of a tiring day, they retreated to his hotel room to recoup. 'Did you find out anything in the library this morning?' she asked, flecks of foam sticking to her upper lip.

'Very little, most of it contemporary history and custom,' he said, fishing in his briefcase and taking out his notebook. 'How much do you know about their history?'

'Quite a bit,' replied Judith. 'They were discovered by Portuguese and Spanish travellers, but the rest of the Western world first heard about them in the late eighteenth century. They were air-lifted to Israel in the mid-1980s when their Judaism was confirmed.' Michael nodded and she continued. 'They were brought here to escape Colonel Mengistu, who was trying to convert them to Communism. The airlift was called Operation Moses. The Falashas made representations to the Israelis and thousands of Jews around the world petitioned the government here about the activities and dangers of the Marxist dictatorship. The Israeli government eventually decided to offer them a new home here.'

'Anything else? Say about their history?'

'They claim to be descended from King Solomon and the Queen of Sheba. They lived in a place called Gondar Province in the mountains of Ethiopia, undiscovered by Europeans for thousands of years. When they arrived in Israel, they were investigated by anthropologists and ethnologists. Some fascinating stories emerged. They believed that the son of Solomon and Sheba, Menelik, was their ancient primogenitor. Their history tells them that his Hebrew lineage was carried down by them to the present day. Even the Emperor Haile Selassie thought he was descended from Menelik. He called himself the Lion of Judah. A bit confusing, because the former Sephardic Chief Rabbi of Israel declared that the Falashas were the remnants of the Tribe of Dan. There are persistent rumours that the Agau people—that's their name for Falasha—'

'What does "Falasha" mean?' Michael interrupted.

'Stranger or outcast. Another possible meaning, according to the books I've just read, is "exile". It ties in with their perception that they became the chosen people when the children of Israel began to worship idols and other graven images in Solomon's Temple during the reign of King Manasseh in 642 BC.'

Michael shook his head.

'I know this is delving into the realm of the fairytale, but I've got a feeling about this.'

He smiled at her, reached out and took her hand. 'Judith, you're more expert on the Jews of Africa. In all the time you've been studying them, have you ever come across any reference to the Dead Sea Scrolls?'

She shook her head. 'Never. Not once.'

He sighed. 'Then we really are in the realm of fantasy.'

'What if we could turn speculation into fact?' Judith asked. 'You know how often archaeology has been speculation until a discovery turned it into fact?'

They sat and gazed at the darkening sky over the Old City. He was about to suggest they have dinner when she said, 'I think I'd better be going. Uri will be waiting for me.'

'Can't he wait a while longer?'

She smiled and imperceptibly shook her head. Heart pounding, he walked around the coffee table and gripped her by the shoulders.

'Michael, not now, please.'

He pulled her closer to him and felt the heat of her body through his thin shirt. Again, as in Tiberias, he was aroused. They started to kiss. The phone rang.

'Damn,' he said, picking it up. His face paled. 'Hello, Deirdre.'

Judith quietly left the room.

CHAPTER 13

Abram sniffed the air in disgust. Never before had he smelt a smell like it. Its odour was of the medicinal balm his mother used on his skin when it erupted in boils and pustules. When she used it on him as a boy, the unguent's acrid smell had stayed in his nose for days afterwards. He sniffed the ground and the seashore. The smell seemed to come from a yellow powder. Looking around, he saw that the rocks near to the sea were tinged with yellow. Perhaps this was the source of the awful stench. And the rocks themselves, he had never seen rocks like them. They seemed to glisten in the sun, as though they were composed of the chips of marble or the precious stones found in the jewellery of Roman ladies. He realised that the rocks were covered in salt. This was the place that fathers warned their children they would be sent if they were evil. This was once a fertile, blissful valley, like the Garden of Eden, until the residents of Sodom and Gomorrah had turned their backs on God. And God had punished them with fire and torment. The yellow powder must have been the brimstone he smelt in the air. Abram looked around in sudden and abject terror. Now he knew for certain that this was the place described in the Books of Moses, the downfall of Lot's wife and the site of God's wrath against the unrighteous, his feeling of bravado evaporated. The man who had journeyed from northern Galilee down to the shores of the Sea of Salt was a boy again, uncertain and insecure, yearning for the comforting reassurances of his father and mother. Heart pounding, he searched the crags and shadows of the nearby rocks and hills, terrified of the devils and evil angels hiding in shadows.

Abram stood on a promontory overlooking the huge expanse of the lake. He could barely see the opposite shore. The highlands were far easier to see, huge majestic cliffs rising almost vertically out of the water. These must be the Mountains of Moab, as foretold by John of Syracuse. Abram took out his map. It was a necessary diversion from his fear and an opportunity to rest after the long, tortuous walk down from the City of Jericho. So far, since leaving his home he had been on the road for four weeks. He had lost weight and felt as though he had grown taller in stature. Certainly his beard had grown. He could now tease the bottom of it to touch the top of his ribs. But it was still scraggly around his cheeks.

According to John of Syracuse, this place was dangerous for many reasons. Not danger from the Romans, or from the Jews, or even from the evil spirits which Abram could sense in every fissure, but danger from the land itself. In the height of summer, the sun and atmosphere in the surrounds of the Salt Sea could exhaust a grown man in hours. John had told of merchants travelling from Eilath up to Jerusalem who had been found dead, still strapped into the saddles on their camels. John had made him promise to fill up his goatskin to capacity before beginning the descent to the sea. There would be no fresh water before the oasis of En-Gedi. And the water of the Salt Sea could be used neither to wash nor to drink. For in the water, floating white and stiff, turned into solid salt, were the souls of the damned from the towns of Sodom and Gomorrah. Who but a madman would drink of that water? And if he drank, he would surely turn mad.

He stepped down from the promontory, hoping to skirt the sea within seven days. Any longer and he could be in trouble, especially if the oasis at En-Gedi was dry.

He was not used to travelling in the desert, but knew enough to fear the season, and the real prospect of the oasis being without water.

He walked down to the shore of the sea and breathed deeply. If this place was to be his home for the next week or so, he might as well get used to the smell straight away. His lips curled in disgust. Beginning the long walk south towards Masada, he wondered for how long he could stand it. Every breath hurt, every step was painful, as though he was walking alongside one of the infernal furnace devices of the Romans.

By the end of the day, he was close to dropping. It was much more difficult to walk in this stinking broth than in the warm, pleasant breezes which danced over the hills. He felt as though he had sunk into the bottom of a cauldron, or into the nether regions of the Hell that St John spoke about in his Revelations. Was this where the demons lived? Was this the home of *Ba'al Zevuv*, the Lord of the Flies?

He had no idea how far he had travelled. Ten leagues? Twenty? It felt like one hundred. The sun was beginning to sink below the imposing mountains to his right. Soon, he must seek shelter. A cave, or somewhere protected below a rock. He looked up to find a suitable place, and his eye caught the entry to a canyon. He knew the local name was *wadi*. His father had told him. He thought it meant valley. At the top of a wadi, he often found hollowed out areas which could protect him from the elements. There were no tracks leading into the wadi. That was good. He wanted to be alone. Strangers or animals in this environment could, would, mean trouble.

After several minutes' walk, he approached the blind end of the wadi. He surveyed the ground and noted that there were no recent tracks of animals or humans. He looked back at the wadi's entrance. From halfway in, he realised that it was not nearly as deep as he first thought. He felt safe enough within its steep walls to look for a cave.

Abram rounded a large boulder and his eyes were forced downwards. He recoiled in horror, screaming in fear. The scream rose up and echoed like an obscene laugh from wall to wall, rebounding back to ridicule him. On the floor of the wadi were human bones. Attached to the bones were old, dry rags. There was no flesh left. The bones had been picked clean by birds or animals, or had rotted, and been carried away by ants, beetles and scorpions. He felt revulsion at being alone in this awesome and fearful place.

He looked carefully at the bones, went over, and removed the last scraps of rags which were trapped where the pathetic man or woman had fallen. With a bleached-white stick Abram found nearby, he poked and examined the skeleton and saw that it was virtually intact. No broken bones. From the looks of the bones, the man or woman must have died many years, possibly decades ago. What could have caused this pathetic son or daughter of God to have wandered up this wadi, so far from the warmth and comfort of others? Would somebody wonder the same about him in ten or twenty generations?

Abram decided to bury him and say the proper prayers. Those he did not know, he would make up. He began to scratch the dust on the wadi floor to make a shallow grave. Soon it was deep enough. Carefully, reverentially, he rolled the skeleton over and it fell with a pathetic hollow clatter into the grave, its gaping skull staring upwards. At least it would be able to look at the sky from now on, rather than stare remorselessly into the earth. He said a few blessings and looked down at the human being that had once walked and talked. What was it doing at the top of a hostile wadi? Looking for shelter, like him? Maybe it was a sign from Jesus that this place was cursed and he should not stay here.

He glanced down and for the first time he noticed an arrow head, firmly implanted inside the skeleton's breastbone. It was Roman, that much he could see. And from the look of it, it was very old. The shaft of wood must have rotted away years ago. Poor, poor person. To have been killed by an arrow in the back, with no chance of escape. And no one, except the cruel Romans, to see. Abram shovelled dirt on top of the bones, said another prayer, and turned to leave the wadi. There would be other wadis. This one he would leave as the eternal sanctuary of the pathetic soul mourned by nobody.

Pope Innocent cupped his hands and buried his face. When would he be free to do the things which he so badly wanted to do? Get out into the badlands and raise up the downtrodden, the impoverished, the abused. This was the work of the Pope, not to be imprisoned in the Vatican by silken ropes and tapestried walls.

He stared around him at the magnificence of the edifice. He felt like the Pharaoh Khufu, surrounded in his chamber by gold and precious stones, buried by the millions of tons of rock of the Great Pyramid. All this must change. He hoped his decision to institute the Third Vatican Council would breathe new life, new hope into the Church.

He stood up and massaged his aching back. He had been at his desk for most of the day and desperately needed to relax before night. He sat in his armchair and touched the familiar curves, felt the worn fabric, ran his fingers over the friendly wood. And every time he sat in the chair, his mind sped back to Bernadette and her agony.

'Ready, my lord bishop?'

'Not you too, Mikey. For heaven's sake, don't you start. Its hard enough keeping my feet on the ground without having the likes of you calling me "my lord bishop".'

'Gabriel Molloy! You'd better get used to it, because, from now on, every two-bit politician and hustler in town is going to want your endorsement. You're big time now, Gabby. Monsignors are ten a penny, but a real, live bishop. Now that's something out of the box, my lord bishop!'

Gabby Molloy smiled at his chaplain. He was a lovely young man, the very best that the Irish community in New York could produce. He would never make it to the top in the church—he'd found it hard enough to make it to priest—but his heart was in the right place. He had a love of people, a pure faith in God, and if his grey matter didn't allow him to distinguish between the philosophy of Bob Dylan and Immanuel Kant, well, so what.

Mikey placed the crozier in Gabriel's hand, straightened out his train, and ensured that the mitre was firmly fitted before gently knocking on the door to let the choristers know that the brand new bishop was ready. As they walked processionally to the door, the organ swelled and the choir led the congregation in Verdi's *Ave Maria*. As he walked slowly towards the apse between the hundreds of people who had packed into the cathedral for the solemn enthronement, he saw his mother, crying softly into her handkerchief. She'd cried at his graduation, cried when he was ordained a priest, cried when the bishop had selected him to be the youngest monsignor in the history of the American Catholic Church, but she'd made him a faithful promise that on this one day of days, she would hold back the tears. His father, beaming an ear-to-ear smile, was fighting to retain his dignity, but losing badly. Gabby knew that behind the grin was a dam holding back a reservoir of pride and humility. Then there were his brothers and sisters, winking, blowing secretive kisses, mouthing blessings and wishes. Such a wonderful family. Gabby thanked God Almighty for his luck at being born into such a warm and blissful Catholic household.

And at the end of the row, as close as she could get to where the cardinal would enthrone Gabby, was Bernadette. Dear, sweet, blessed Bernadette. She smiled at him. He smiled back.

America's newest bishop, Gabriel Molloy, stood in front of the body-length mirror, beaming to himself. He adjusted his mitre and swept the air with his crozier, as if to fight off the enemies of the Church, or to row its boat through turbulent waters. He felt no degradation at committing the sin of vanity; on this one day of days, this day when he was elevated into the apostolic succession, he knew God Almighty would forgive him his minor peccadillo. A soft rap on the door brought him back to the present. Standing there was his housekeeper, behind her a police sergeant.

An hour later, he was standing outside the door of a room in New York's City General Hospital, talking to a doctor. He entered the room and recoiled in shock at the sight of Bernadette. She lay like a cadaver, ghostly pale, stiff, staring intently at a spot on the ceiling.

He walked over to the bed and sat in the chair. He stroked her shoulder. It was cold and white, mottled like alabaster.

She didn't turn, or respond in any way. Not even her breathing altered. It was as if she were adrift in a boat and couldn't hear the cries of those offering help from the shore.

'He hurt me, Gabby. He hurt me so badly.' Gabriel strained to catch the words, whispered to the ceiling. 'He pulled me into that filthy alley and pulled me down behind dustbins where the dogs and rats had been.' Gabriel remained quiet. 'And he pulled my dress up. I had that dress made specially for your enthronement. He just pulled it up and tore it as if it had no value.'

Gabriel bent until his forehead touched her arm and began to pray silently to himself to shut out his sister's words. He could not bear to hear her pain. They cried together.

A week later he received a call from the police. They had arrested a forty-eight-year-old Cuban on a narcotics charge who matched Bernadette's description of her assailant.

'May I see him?' asked the bishop.

'It ain't usual,' said the detective, 'but seein' how you're a man of God, I don't see why not.'

Gabriel Molloy made the sign of the cross over the head of the man who had raped his sister and stood quickly. He left the cell and walked up through the long, resonating corridors until he reached the open air and the blessed light, God's light of day.

He walked the long way home.

Later that afternoon he visited Bernadette in the hospital. It had been eight days since the attack.

'How are you feeling, Bernie?'

'I'm okay,' she said.

'Doctor tells me you're still washing six or seven times a day.'

'I just feel dirty, Gabby. I feel so filthy every time I touch myself.'

'What did the psychiatrist say?'

'Oh, he was fine. Musn't blame myself. Put it behind me. Get away on holiday. Talk to other girls that have been raped and share experiences.'

'Sounds sensible,' Gabby said. 'It would be good to get you out of here, back to the family.'

'Every time I get out of bed, my legs just collapse under me. Knowing it's hysteria doesn't seem to help. My biggest single fear is that I'm carrying that monster's baby. I tell you this, Gabby, if I am, I'm going to have an abortion, as God is my witness.'

Gabriel recoiled, the horror of her words ringing in his ears. 'Bernie, don't even talk like that.'

She laughed. It was an empty laugh. 'Why? Because it's murder? You think I want his brat in me? What's better? To give birth to something like that or to kill it before it claims a foothold in my body?'

'Bernie.' Gabriel shook his head and bowed towards her.

'Oh don't worry. You'll be the last person to know. I wouldn't dream of compromising you or your blessed faith. I'll just take myself off to a quiet corner and get some doctor to do it.'

'Bernie, please. What do you mean, *my* faith? It's our faith, *your* faith, a faith you were born in. How can you even—'

'How can you even advise me?' she spat, her mood changing from distance to anger. 'You don't know a thing, Gabby. You have no idea what it's like to be forced to the ground by some stinking, leering, evil man. To have him pull your dress up and pull your pants down and force your legs apart.' Gabriel wanted to shut out the horror of what she was saying. 'What's the matter, your grace? Can't you take it? I thought you priests were trained to listen to the horrors of the world.'

'Bernie, please, let me get another priest to talk to you. We're too close. This is too painful for both of us.'

Her eyes were full of tears. 'So you don't want to know what happened out there in the alley? In the filth. You don't want me to tell you what he looked like, what he smelt like, what he did,' said Bernadette, her words like daggers, sheathed in anger.

'I know what he looks like. I know what he smells like. I know what you've suffered.'

'You know?' she whispered quizzically.

'Yes, I know. I've been to see him. I had to. I needed to share your pain.'

Bernadette looked at her brother in astonishment. 'When?'

'The police phoned me this morning. They told me that they'd caught a man. I went to see him.'

Bernadette breathed deeply in anger, the hostility and fury that she had barely suppressed for the past week rising in her throat, threatening to strangle her. 'Did he show any signs of contrition?' she hissed. 'Did he apologise? Did he ask for my forgiveness? What did he say, Gabby? Tell me every word he said. Don't miss out a syllable, not a single sound. I want to know everything he told you. Everything.'

Gabriel held his breath. She looked at him, allowing the moments to pass, weighing like lead between them, hanging around their necks. She was surprised by his silence. But she looked intently at him. And then she knew. She knew with an absolute horror that her nightmare was to be continued, that her pain was to be doubled.

'You've heard his confession.'

Gabriel remained silent, looking at her. But his eyes betrayed him.

'You've given him absolution, haven't you?'

Gabriel stayed silent.

'You've forgiven him, haven't you?'

Gabriel mumbled a prayer into the void.

'Haven't you?' she breathed.

Gabriel couldn't talk.

'*Haven't you!*' she screamed.

'Yes,' he whispered, almost inaudibly.

Bernadette fell back rigid into her pillows. She raised her head to the ceiling, the ligaments in her neck knotted like coiled ropes, and screamed '*No!*'

It still resonated inside Gabriel's head.

Annabelle Wilson twisted her neck to see behind her. It was painful, but necessary. 'Now look you, Miss Iron Lady, you get your goddamn stinkin' hands off my wheelchair, you hear.'

Joyce had never been spoken to that way before. Not in all the years she had spent on the wards. 'Mrs Wilson, the Reverend Dr Wilson gave me strict instructions.'

'I don't give a tinker's shit what the Reverend Dr fuckin' Wilson told you. I said I wanted to be by myself and that's exactly the fuckin' way I'm goin' to be.'

Nurse Joyce recoiled in horror from the wheelchair. Nobody spoke to her that way. 'Don't you dare swear at me, you slut. I know what kind of a woman you are. It's all over the church. Some say you deserved that beating.'

Annabelle reached down to the cold steel rims of the wheels, twisted them viciously, and wrenched the wheelchair out of the nurse's hands. Joyce jumped back in shock.

'No one deserves to be beaten like that,' she spat. 'What in the hell do you know, anyway, you cold tightass bitch? You don't know nothing. Get outta my sight.'

'Whore! I'm going to tell Reverend Wilson right away.' Joyce turned on her heels, muttering imprecations under her breath and marched back to the Chrome Cathedral. As she watched her retreat, Annabelle breathed deeply in the hot dry air. Now she could experience the joy of being alone for the first time in days. Jimmy would scream his guts out at her, but what the hell? She couldn't give a damn any more, and right now Jimmy was rousing a congregation to give more money. That gave her a couple of hours of solitude.

She slowly reached down and felt the steel rim of the wheels once again. She hadn't done much freewheeling since she left her bed and turning the wheels made her shoulders and armpits ache. But the ache was nothing like the pain of being constantly in the company of Jimmy and that damned starched woman with a steel ramrod up her ass. She wasn't a nurse, she was a guardian, a custodian, a woman whose job it was to stop Annabelle doing things.

She wheeled herself further down the path until she came to a bank of peonies which she had planted last spring. They were dying in the heat of summer despite the constant watering they received from the church's computerised irrigation system. Before she was beaten, she would have plucked the dead heads from the flowers and crushed their desiccated remains back into the earth. Death bringing forth life. Some of it would have blown away as dust into the desert. Some would have been reabsorbed when the water wet the earth. But today she couldn't even reach down. She continued to wheel herself along the path until she came to a vast flowering cedar.

When Jimmy had been looking for land to build his Chrome Cathedral, he'd been attracted to this block on the edge of the desert because of the cedar. But today, the softness of the tree was overshadowed by the unrelenting hard-edged post-modernism of the building. Nobody knew where the tree had come from or who had planted it. It was lost in the mists of time. Maybe some Lebanese who had migrated to California to grow oranges had planted it. Maybe it was an itinerant worker or one of the monks who used to wander up and down the concatenation of missions that stretched from Mexico to Oregon, San Diego, San Luis Obispo, San Francisco and San Clemente.

She wheeled herself to the trunk and looked up as far as her neckbrace would allow. The sun was dappled through the tree and scintillas of light filtered through. It was as though the sun was raining all over her body, pure, medicinal light dancing over her damaged form. Her bruised fingers reached into the inner folds of her light summer dress, painfully undoing two buttons on the bodice. She looked back along the path to ensure she was alone. It hurt to twist her head too much. She craned her neck as far as the pain would allow to make sure that no one was around. She opened the fold of her dress and reached inside her brassiere. Flattened against the soft, supple skin of her breast was a plastic sachet. It had taken her ten agony-filled minutes to extricate it from the back of her personal hygiene drawer.

Annabelle opened the top of the bag, careful not to spill any of the white powder. She took a $20 bill from her other pocket, nearly dropping it in the pain of holding it between her fingers. Annabelle rolled it as thin as she could. She put it in her nostril and stuck the end of the note in the plastic bag and sniffed. Then the other nostril.

Within a few minutes, her mind was floating in living vivid colours, feeling relaxed and confident. Her body didn't hurt nearly so much. The aches had gone from her joints, her butt didn't hurt as she sat on the air cushion on the wheelchair. In fact, nothing really hurt so much any more. In fact, life was pretty good. In fact, she was happy.

Annabelle began to feel stronger, better. She breathed in the hot dry desert air and felt its restorative powers.

Jimmy held Annabelle's hand and gazed into her eyes. 'Are you sure? Are you absolutely sure, because this is a big step we're takin', and I wouldn't want you ever to regret it.'

'Darlin',' she told him, 'I've never been surer of anythin' in my life.'

'Your momma and poppa can always have time to think about it. I mean, this is a mighty big decision.'

She dug him playfully in the ribs. 'Now you just stop it Jimmy Wilson. You know we're goin' to get married and there's nothin' you're going to do to stop me. I'm the luckiest girl in the county and quite frankly I think you're pretty damn lucky too. Ain't that you're the first to ask me. I've had lots of young men wantin' my hand in marriage and I've said no to them all because they didn't even begin to measure up to the likes of you.'

'But Annabelle, honey, you've only known me for six weeks. Shoot, I can't bring you anythin'. I ain't even got a job.'

'Jimmy, don't be so silly. Preacher like you is going to be offered jobs all over the country. There's a thousand congregations that would give their back teeth for a man like you. Tall, strong, good-lookin', sexy as hell.'

Jimmy laughed. 'So far, you ain't said nothin' about my fear of God.'

'Oh honey, that's taken for granted. You're a God-fearin' man. I've listened to you up on the pulpit. You know how to stir a body. Jimmy, there's times when you're up there talkin' and I can hardly control my emotions.'

'Anythin' else you can't control?' he said, digging her in the ribs. Annabelle flushed crimson and he was sorry. 'I shouldn't be talkin' like that. It's just that you stir my blood.'

She put her hand on his elbow and squeezed tenderly. 'No, don't you go apologisin'.'

They walked on beneath the trees by the bank of the Alabama River. She turned to him, her eyes revealing the depth of her passion towards him. 'Jimmy, I—'

He took off his jacket and laid it down for her to sit on. Jimmy sat beside her and lay down, his hands behind his head.

'I love you, Jimmy. Every time I hear you in front of a congregation I get all these stirrin's in my body. Natural stirrin's. Like I've got a river inside me and every time I see you up there declarin' the word of the Lord, the river starts to flow hot blood.' She lay down beside him and stroked his chin with a blade of grass. Jimmy smiled. She tickled his lips. She moved closer and kissed him tenderly. 'I can't wait for us to be married, Jimmy. To feel the heat of your body in mine. I—'

'Annabelle, you know where this is goin' to lead. I think we ought to desist.'

'Just once. Here, in the open, under the trees. Nobody's around. Make love to me, Jimmy. I so badly want you. I'm burstin' for you, honey. Jimmy—'

'Annabelle, it's wrong. You know it's wrong. You say there's no one about. God's about. And His Son Jesus Christ who died for our sins. I don't mind kissin'. That's natural, but I ain't going to break the chastity that you were born with and that you were given as a precious gift by the Lord Jesus and which you should keep until our marriage day. Annabelle, I love you but I ain't goin' to do it to you until we're married.'

Annabelle rolled onto her back and stared up through the dappled leaves. Her body ached for him but her mind knew he was right. Quietly, almost in a whisper, she said, 'God bless you, Jimmy.'

But she couldn't see the tears welling up in his eyes. Tears of self-loathing and shame at his inadequacies.

CHAPTER 14

Avi prayed for someone to enter the room and break the monotony of guarding the old bishop. He had watched the same fly climbing the dusty window pane for half an hour and was beyond boredom. The smell of stale body odours in the hot and airless room was overpowering. Avi counted the minute before his relief came.

They still had another two full days left before they would toss the old bishop back on to the night-time streets of Jerusalem to show the Christian world that they were in control of the Holy Land. It was a brilliant scheme—a kidnap with no ransom, no threats, nothing, just a clear unmistakable message to the Pope and a billion Christians throughout the world that you can't fuck around with Israel and get away with it.

Finally Aaron arrived. They took balaclavas from the pegs outside the room and slipped them over their heads. Silently they unlocked the door and opened it. Solomonoglou was on his knees before a crucifix that he had hung on a peg on the wall.

Avi walked over to the old man and touched him gently on the shoulder. The body fell sideways, its eyes staring into infinity. Aaron reached down for his pulse but felt nothing. He pulled off his balaclava and said, 'Oh shit. This fucks things up.'

Avi pulled off his balaclava and asked, 'What the hell are we going to do now?'

'I don't know. Get David in here.'

Five minutes later, the four men were standing around the old priest, whose body was frozen in a foetal position. David Berg was quietly contemplating, walking up and down the room in an effort to think.

'We can deposit him late one night in the streets around Jerusalem. He will be found and that will be end of it. A post mortem will show natural causes. We'll just deny any knowledge,' said Vladimir.

Berg turned around. 'That destroys all the work we've done. Then his kidnap becomes a useless waste of time and effort.'

'Pin a note on his body explaining what happened,' said Avi.

'Nah!' said Berg. 'We've got to capitalise on this.'

'Capitalise?' asked Aaron. The others looked on in incomprehension.

'Yes. Capture world headlines.' They remained silent. 'Let's do something which will be on the front pages of every newspaper throughout the world. Let's make the *goyim* sit up and take notice. Do to them what they did to us!'

'What are you talking about?' asked Avi, shaking his head.

David Berg smiled. 'Let's crucify him.'

The others recoiled in horror. 'Are you crazy?' said Vladimir.

'No. The man is dead. A post mortem will show that he died of a heart attack, or something similar. All we're doing is symbolising what happened to Christians in Judea at the time of the Romans. What the Saracens did to the Crusaders; what the Christians did to the heathens. It's a violent, unforgiving land. We're just the latest to be unforgiving!'

Avi was sickened at the thought. 'What are we? Nazis? Fascists? Animals? Have you forgotten the reprisals since that madman killed the Muslim worshippers in Hebron?'

David Berg persisted. 'Just listen to me for a minute. He's dead. It wasn't our fault. Nobody can blame us for an old man dying, but death serves as a symbol for what will happen if this Pope goes ahead with his obscene Crusade. It will be an object lesson the like of which hasn't been seen in two thousand years.'

'You're mad. I'm having nothing to do with this,' said Avi, and turned to walk out of the door.

'Avi,' said David, 'so far nobody has connected you with this kidnap. Don't force me to tell the police it was you. I have a perfect alibi. I have three members of the organisation who will swear that I was with them for these past two days. What alibi do you have?'

The blood drained from Avi's face.

Three hundred people in Ben Gurion Airport arrivals hall looked round in surprise as two tall men, both wearing the clerical collars of Catholic priests, ran towards each other. The men hugged amidst a maze of suitcases, slapping one another on the back, talking animatedly. People smiled. Anxious security guards relaxed and looked in other directions. Catholic tourists arriving or departing from Israel looked in shock and disapproval. Their disapproval would have turned into open condemnation had they known that one of the men was a prince of the Church, swearing like a trooper.

Ignoring everyone else, the two walked arm in arm, like animated schoolchildren. They reached the taxi rank and sped off.

'My dear brother, how are things in that place?' asked Francis, conscious that the taxi-driver might be listening. And in Israel, there was always the possibility that the driver might speak Latin.

'As always, Francis,' said Daniel Rhymer. 'More . . . what was the term you used? Oh yes, more Byzantine than ever. I tell you, if it wasn't for those Italians, the Church would be a wondrous place indeed.'

'How's our friend?'

'Weighed down by the cares of office. The German is giving him a lot of trouble. I tell you, I don't trust that man at all. God forgive me for saying so, but his vanity outstrips his fidelity. He sits in conclaves with the rest of the Curia gathered at his feet, talking in whispers out of the corner of his mouth. He worries me, Francis. He worries me greatly indeed.'

'And Gabby. What does he think of all this? Surely he was used to intrigues in his old diocese.'

'No matter what experience of Machiavellian plots one has in one's diocese, one is never prepared for the world of the Vatican. There are more twists and turns in the mind of one Italian prelate than there are in all the streets of San Francisco. Thank your stars that you chose a teaching order in preference to a curial life.'

Francis, who had left the seminary to go to Loyola University to obtain a further degree in Classical Philosophy, had abandoned the life of a university lecturer in preference for a missionary life of service in an orphanage in Israel. His mission was to rescue orphans of Christian Arabs of Palestinian descent from the refugee camps into which they were born. It was a common fallacy that all residents of the camps were Muslim. The Christians were a small minority and were treated mercilessly by the Muslim majority.

Since Francis had begun his mission at an abandoned *moshav* a few miles from Jerusalem, the original twenty orphans had been joined by a hundred more. He now employed the services of five other teachers, as well as a housekeeper and cook. More and more of his time was spent in begging money. The Israeli government gave him grudging assistance and allowed him to bring bona fide orphans across the border.

Francis nodded as he thought about the friend whom he had not seen in nearly a decade. Gabriel Molloy had been his bosom friend in the seminary in Boston. Francis considered him the closest thing to a saint currently walking the earth. Even the normally acerbic *Chicago Tribune*, not noted for its friendship towards the Catholic Church, once called him 'the nearest thing America has produced to a Mother Teresa'. While Francis and Danny were studying, Gabby would be out in the streets, picking up drug addicts and tramps and delivering them to relief agencies. While they were off at a movie, Gabby would be assisting an order of nuns at a field kitchen, feeding the poor and homeless. And they would only find out what he had been doing when a brother or sister delivered him back, exhausted, to enable him to catch a few hours' sleep before Matins.

Nor was anybody particularly surprised when Gabby graduated with highest honours from the seminary. Francis had never met, nor was he ever likely to meet, a finer person than the man now sitting on the throne of St Peter. He asked, 'But is all this ecclesiastical politics affecting his capacity to run the Church?'

'He tries to rise above it,' Daniel Rhymer told him. 'He uses goodness, generosity and decency to undermine their intransigence and hostility. Only on a few occasions have I seen him fearfully angry. And usually when dealing with Kitzinger.'

The taxi bounced along the roads until it reached the outskirts of Jerusalem, where the driver turned left towards the foothills. Heat hazes over the dusty land gave the view a feel peculiar to the Middle East, or other areas where the desert was beaten back by the inventiveness of man. The heat and dust of summer was punctuated by luscious fields of crops, or intense orchards of oranges, grapefruit, avocado and lemon trees. And between them, the ubiquitous olives trees, bushy lush trees of dull green, bursting with ripe clusters of olives as they had burst since time began. Every centimetre of land was used by the people to grow something. As the taxi weaved its way along the road, at regular intervals a heavy mist of water vapour hung in the air from the irrigation jets, constantly fighting against the sun and dust.

They were not going to rise into the city sacred to the world's three great monotheistic religions, Judaism, Christianity and Islam. Rather, they were skirting the base of the mountain and travelling from one collective community to another. On the right and left of the road were the farms which had enabled Israel to gain self-sufficiency in agriculture since the once-malarial swamps of this outpost of the Ottoman Empire had been drained and made fit for habitation. The farms were of two sorts—*kibbutzim*, the collective communities based on communistic lines, and *moshavim*, less egalitarian than *kibbutzim*, in which free enterprise based around the need for communal interests had met the desire of people to own private property.

The taxi skidded to a halt on the dusty road. Facing Daniel was a collection of tin huts which looked more like an Ohio share-crop six months after it had been repossessed by a bank. Weeds between buildings, overgrown flower beds, and ancient rusting vehicles gave testimony to the lack of resources of the community.

Francis saw the look of disapproval on his friend's face. 'It's not exactly the Medici Apartments, but for us it's home.'

Daniel cringed with shame. How could he pass judgement on the man and his work by the look of the place in which he lived? Had he forgotten all his vows of humility since he took up residence in the Vatican?

'Francis. Please. I was admiring the—'

'It's a full-time job to make enough money to pay for food, clothes and medicine,' his friend said, interrupting him. 'We don't have the spare cash for gardeners. And don't forget that the people we look after are children. They're not strong enough to do heavy manual work.'

They paid the driver, unloaded the cardinal's luggage, and walked into the shed entitled 'OFFICE'. A pre-Second World War desk on spindle legs, a couple of armchairs devoid of stuffing, and two rusting filing cabinets whose white paint still adhered in patches were the sole occupants of the room. There was no carpet, no curtains, nothing to give a feel of either luxury or permanence. Dust from the outside had found its way under the door, the ripped flyscreen and made dendritic patterns on the splintered wooden office floor. Daniel began to make plans to assist Francis financially.

As the two men put down suitcases and moved chairs to take ownership of the shed, the door opened and a woman walked in. She looked in her mid-fifties, but the energy she radiated belonged to someone in their twenties. Francis beamed a smile.

'Danny, this is the heart and soul of Moshav Yeladim, Pazit Fine. Pazit, I'd like you to meet an old friend of mine from America, Father O'Malley.'

The woman smiled and shook his hand.

'Father, welcome to Israel.'

'So, Mrs Fine, you're the life and soul of the party.' He treated her to his broadest smile.

The penetrating look she gave told him she could be a formidable adversary.

'Without Pazit, this place would collapse,' Francis enthused. 'She's cook, matron, treasurer, mother, father and disciplinarian to our hundred and some charges.'

Daniel nodded, impressed. 'And how did you come to be connected with the orphanage?' he asked. 'It seems like a labour of love.'

She dismissed his comment with a wave of her hand and laughed. 'I was with the *moshav* before it went bankrupt and Francis bought the place. I've been here ever since, like an old mattress or a sofa, left to gather dust on a porch.'

'And we hardly pay her a nickel. She says she stays because she loves children, but I think she's secretly in love with me.'

'You wish!' said Pazit, bursting into laughter. 'Dried-up old relic like you? I wouldn't waste my time.'

Pazit picked up Daniel's case and began to walk out the door. He snatched it away from her. 'Please, Mrs Fine, let me take that.'

'Don't be silly. You've just had a long journey. Stay here and talk to Francis and I'll bring you some coffee.'

'Remarkable woman,' Francis said when she had left the room. 'Jewish. Her children have all grown up and left home, so now her husband's off gallivanting around, she's really got no one. So she treats everyone here like they were her own. But she's a typical Sabra.'

'*Sabra?*'

'Native-born Israeli. It's the name of the fruit of the desert cactus. It describes the children born in this country. Tough and bitter on the outside, but soft and sweet on the inside. Her husband was desperate after the financial collapse and went off the rails chasing women. She basically kicked him out. Trouble was, there was no money, so she was left stranded.'

'How can a whole community collapse?' asked Daniel.

'The *moshav* collapsed through bad management. It tried to introduce modern farming techniques, bought a fortune's worth of sophisticated equipment from slick salesmen, and couldn't make the place pay. All the equipment was repossessed. Everyone drifted away. Pazit had nowhere to go. I fed her in return for her looking after the initial crop of kids I brought here from the Lebanon, and she's stayed ever since. Ten years.'

'And *is* she in love with you?' There was humour and seriousness in his question.

Francis smiled. 'Danny, I love her and she loves me. We're a team. But is it physical? Of course not. She could do far better for herself than me. Anyway, she goes off into Jerusalem every Tuesday evening and comes back Wednesday morning with a gigantic grin on her face. I once followed her, with malice aforethought, but she knew it was me and managed to give me the slip in the Old City.'

Daniel smiled.

'Did you like the Father O'Malley bit? I hate dissembling, but I assumed that you didn't want all Israel to know that the Vatican was in town.'

'Good enough. Now, after coffee, why don't we discuss the reason I'm here. I want to set up meetings with Father de la Tour and other early Bible experts. People who may have a gut instinct for where the Testament could have been placed. Oh, and I want to see what we can find out about Professor Michael Farber and this strange visit to the Ethiopian.'

Judith shook her head sadly. Michael nodded. The old man would give them no help. It was the fifth—or was it the sixth, or seventh—rejection they had suffered in the past three days. And during the week they had suffered at least a dozen more.

The old man looked like the biblical Joseph, with colourful clothes of reds, yellows and blues. They were vibrant, magnified in intensity by his coffee skin. He smiled innocently at Michael. He had a look in his eyes that Michael had seen in the eyes of many of the other Falashas. A look which said that he would like to help the nice young couple, but he simply didn't know the answers to the questions they were asking.

Judith stood and nodded vigorously. After interviewing at least twenty Falashas, she knew that the men observed the age-old pre-Talmudic tradition of not touching women who were not their wives. She did not reach out to touch his hand.

Michael reached down to where the old man was sitting on the mat, and proffered his hand. The old man grasped and kissed it. Still holding it, he pressed it to his forehead. It was endearing, an age-old symbol of acceptance, a custom developed in the deserts of the Bible. Was this the way strangers had said goodbye to each other before Christ was born? He was of the very people from the Five Books of Moses, the Book of Kings, and the Books of the Prophets.

Nomadic shepherds gathered at night around a desert oasis, camels roaring and growling, goats bleating, men talking quietly with each other as the sparks from their fires flew heavenwards in the cold dry air, women on the periphery of the camp repairing clothes, or preparing meals, telling tales of their forefathers, of battles and victories, of great wanderings and hardships. They were living relics of an ancient and noble past. Colonel Mengistu and his Communist fanatics had a lot to answer for.

They walked from his house back into the late twentieth century, feeling the terrible disappointment at yet another avenue of investigation leading nowhere.

After the initial excitement of discovering the Falashas, Michael's morale sagged as he and Judith hit walls of resistance. More and more, he thought that Judith was wrong. That the Testament would be found, if still in existence, hidden in a long-forgotten drawer in a library, somewhere in Damascus or Alexandria or Rome. No Falasha seemed to be able to help them make the connection between Christ's Testament and the possibility that it was in the possession of their race.

'I think we're barking up the wrong tree,' he said to Judith as they walked out into the sunlight.

'How so?' she asked.

'All these rumours about the Falashas . . . I've heard some of them before. They crop up from time to time and come to the notice of biblical scholars and archaeologists like you and me. Mind you, always in the context of Solomon's Temple riches, nothing to do with Jesus.'

'But that's the whole point,' said Judith. 'The rumours that the Falashas were the possessors and guardians of Temple riches have been around for at least a couple of hundred years.'

'Prester John?'

Judith smiled. 'Very good. I'm impressed. Of course, nobody knows whether the guy was an explorer or a ruler, was from the Middle Ages or the Renaissance, was from Ethiopia or India. Apart from that, he's a pretty reliable source. Still, there are persistent rumours tying him in to the area. I still think it's worth travelling a bit further down this road,' she said.

As they walked, she linked her arm through his. A taxi came round the corner, slowed to see whether they wanted a lift, but drove off quickly when they ignored him. Judith waited until a convoy of cars and buses had passed and the traffic noise had quietened down before going on. 'There was an undisputed line of Jewish presence in Ethiopia from, say, 500 BC onwards. Now, you just don't get a huge community in one of the richest trading areas of the then civilised world without having trading relationships. Do you realise that, in Byzantine times, Ethiopia was the third most important trading nation in the world. The third! Think about that. It had fantastic resources—minerals, precious stones, spices, food, timber, just about everything.'

As she became more animated, she increased the speed at which she was walking. Michael had to struggle to keep up with her. 'Ethiopia owed far more of its trade and commerce, its trading relationships, to the Red Sea and the Arab areas than to Egypt and Africa in general. We've lost sight of how important it was because for the last fifteen hundred years Ethiopia has more or less contracted in on itself. Its economy has been swamped by the rise of Europe. But in those days more than half of the entire population of the country was Jewish. That's why, with the growth of Christianity, it became isolated and introspective. With the defeat of Judaism in Israel by the Romans, it started to wither on the vine. But think back to the time of Christ when the religion began to spread. Look at the way Paul was able to proselytise the Gospels and early Christianity after Christ's death. Communications were already very well established, especially through common religious groupings.'

Michael wondered where she was heading. Judith continued, 'So it seems fairly likely that there was communication between the Jews of Judea, Arabia, and the whole of North Africa, even the Horn of Africa.'

'So?'

'So we're not talking about Old Testament times. David, Solomon, Saul. We're talking about a much more sophisticated people. Alexander of Macedon, Ptolemy and the Romans had opened up the entire known world, spread its boundaries, established trading routes.

People were wandering all over the place, taking boats to far distant shores on trading missions, visiting relatives, going on religious missions.'

Michael was getting frustrated. 'So?'

'So it's not outside the realm of possibility that before AD 200 a well-meaning Jew could have rescued Christ's Testament and taken it to somewhere safe, like a major centre of Judaism such as Axum in Ethiopia.'

'But it was a Christian document!' he shouted in exasperation.

'Not at that time,' Judith stressed. 'The early Christians probably considered themselves as successors to the Essenes. Their founder was an Essene. Their teaching was based in the philosophy of the Essenes. Their early approach was contemplative, like the Essenes.'

'Judith, that's so speculative.'

'Michael,' she shouted as another semitrailer thundered past, 'all archaeology is speculative until you discover the evidence.'

Two thoughts were competing in Michael's mind as he listened, each fighting for attention above the din of traffic. It was wholly illogical that treasures of incalculable importance such as the precious objects from Solomon's Temple, or the Essene documents, could have been hidden in the possession of this people for so long. Surely they would have told someone. Word would undoubtedly have spread. The fables surrounding Troy, Masada, and King Solomon's Mines had become realities with modern archaeology. Then why not the most fabulous treasures of them all?

On the other hand, if the Falashas had been made the repositorians of these treasures in the days of the Bible, and had subsequently lost contact with the world for nearly two thousand years, it was just possible that modern archaeology had not caught up with them.

Maybe Judith and he were the first to have made the connection between the Falashas and the New Testament. Maybe they were the Heinrich Schliemanns of Christ's Testament. Maybe the Falashas were their City of Troy. Michael looked at Judith and felt guilty and depressed. They walked on in silence.

Judith felt his dejection as they continued walking in Jerusalem's frenetic rush-hour. 'What did you expect? You surely didn't expect it to fall into your lap, did you?' she said.

'Of course not. But it would be nice to have at least one person we interview know what we're talking about. All we get are quizzical looks.'

'Oh, I don't think that's absolutely true. The first man we saw, Benawie, the tribal leader, was very helpful. He told us not to expect anything much, but at least he gave us the names of dozens of people to interview. And let's face it, if we hadn't been put on to him by my friend in the Ministry of Absorption, these people would have shut up tighter than clams. They only talk to us because we have Benawie's imprimatur.'

'Judith, don't think I'm ungrateful, but we seem to be no better off today than we were last week. If the people we're seeing are the community leaders, and they know nothing, it seems fairly forlorn to hope that people lower down in community status would know anything.'

The traffic noise grew even louder as they walked closer to the heart of Jerusalem.

'Why don't we go back and see Benawie? When you come to think about it, he didn't actually say whether he knew anything or not,' Judith said finally.

Yitzhak Stein, the local stringer for the *LA Times*, was good at getting people to divulge secrets. If appealing to their vanity or greed didn't work, he had been known to resort to lies and, on the odd occasion, blackmail. He had no idea why Joe Deakin from Los Angeles wanted him to follow Professor Michael Farber around, but so long as he was being paid . . .

Having carefully removed any insignia which could identify him as a cardinal of the Catholic Church, Daniel washed, freshened up and got back into the car for the first of a number of appointments which Francis had arranged for him. Daniel had asked for interviews to be set up with Israeli experts who could identify a possible connection between the Black Jews and the Dead Sea Scrolls. While not an expert in the Essenes or their writings, Daniel had a reasonable knowledge of them and their teachings.

But in all of his readings about the Essenes, no one had mentioned the Falashas—the pre-Talmudic, pre-Christian Ethiopian Jews. That was why he couldn't understand Michael Farber's visit to the old Falasha leader. His throwaway line to the *Los Angeles Times* about the Jesus Testament being outside the country was imaginative and exciting; but why the Falashas? Why wasn't Professor Farber speculating about possible hiding places in other Middle East areas connected with the Roman occupation?

Daniel had been to Jerusalem many times. While a student in Rome, he had often visited Israel, where he attended advanced courses in theology. He loved the purity, the sparseness, the feeling of the Bible, and had enjoyed spending time on retreat in some of the Catholic missions in the Holy Land. He had toured the length and breadth of the country, walked in the path of the Lord, touched the stones He might have touched, and felt that he had come closer to his Messiah. But the mission for which he was called by God was to aid the inner cities of decaying America and he had not returned to Israel for over twenty years. Nothing, and yet everything, had changed in the timeless land. It still smelt and felt like the land of the Bible, ancient and irreducible; yet among its white rocks and jagged horizons, it sported bright new towns with straight, clean, geometric lines.

The car laboured up the hill, heaving with exhaustion. Younger, imperious Asian cars flew past the old Mercedes, which coughed and spluttered like an old man with consumption. Francis looked at his old friend in apology. Remembering how his face had betrayed his feelings when he first arrived, Daniel smiled broadly and laid his hand on his friend's shoulder.

At the top of the hill sat Jerusalem, immutable and precious. White stone buildings standing stark against the powder-blue sky, the razor-sharp horizontal lines of today living in absurd harmony with the ancient ragged minarets, spears which defiantly lanced the air, towering closer towards God. Domed cupolas of gold and blue and silver. Friezes and mosaics. Crosses held proud against the skyline proclaiming the foothold which Christianity claimed on the city. And gold, silver, and stone *Magen Davids*, one of the oldest and most revered icons of humanity were silhouetted in greater prominence, asserting native status, as though the crescents and crucifixes were parvenus. During the twenty years since he had last set foot in this awesome city, Daniel had forgotten how Judaism, Islam and Christianity lived side by side, tolerant, forgiving, mutually respectful. It was the xenophobic, political influences which had entered the religious environment that had poisoned the respect in which each should hold the other.

The Mercedes struggled around the Old City, with its Caliphate walls, until it reached the university. Driving into the grounds, the gatekeeper saw the old car and cheerily waved it on. Obviously Francis was well known here. He explained, 'To make ends meet, I lecture one night a week in Catholic mysticism to second-year students in the Department of Religious Studies.'

They walked through the air-conditioned passageways of the building, until they came to a sign saying 'JEWISH HISTORY' in Hebrew, Arabic and English. Francis knocked on a door marked 'Ari Wallenstein'. Daniel knew the name. He was a foremost authority on pre-Christian Israel, specialising in the Herodian period. The door opened, revealing a Gargantua in height and girth.

After introductions and telling him they were interested in the religious history of the Falashas, Ari asked: 'Why are you interested in them, Father O'Malley? I'd have thought they were a bit obscure for you.'

Daniel wasn't used to lying. The dissembling about the Irish name was bad enough; now he had to compound the lie by supporting it. 'Francis and I were corresponding about the prospect of where Our Lord's Testament might be, and we thought it could perhaps have been taken out of Israel.'

'Yes, father, but why the Falashas?'

'We read an article quoting Professor Michael Farber. He thought it might have been taken to Alexandria or even beyond.'

Ari burst out laughing. 'Look, Michael's a brilliant scholar, the most brilliant student I ever had. Not as good as me, of course, but then nobody could be,' he said laughing. 'But with all his brilliance, he gets these *idées fixes* in his mind.

'If Michael is looking towards Alexandria, then I'm sure he thinks he's got a very good reason. Me? I know where the Testament is. It's in Israel. Somewhere around the Dead Sea. Let Michael go to Ethiopia if he wants. He's always been a bit of a *meshuggeneh*, an individualist, that one! He marches to the sound of his own drum. If it wasn't for his genius, it would be safe to ignore him. He's sometimes had a flash of insight and been right, but he's also had lots of flashes and fallen flat on his arse. Typical of the man—every couple of years, he has these amazing gifts of perception which open up a whole new field of thought. Listen, Michael and I are great friends, but I wouldn't follow him to the end of the street, let alone the ends of the earth.

'I've honestly no idea why he's interviewing Falashas. Maybe because they have a colourful past? When he and I were last talking, he said—' Ari frowned. 'Oh dear, he may have wanted our conversation to be confidential. Maybe I'd better check with him before I tell you.'

Daniel nodded vigorously, to prove he had nothing to hide, but added, 'Look, don't tell us what you two talked about. Could you just tell us anything about the Falashas, and what possible connection they might have with the Dead Sea Scrolls.'

'None,' said Ari, shaking his leonine head slowly. 'There's severe doubt as to whether the Falashas are even proper Jews. The Sephardic rabbinate called them Jews for humanitarian reasons, because they were being massacred by that madman Mengistu—you know, the Communist madman. And it's not even definite that they've actually been practising Judaism for the past three thousand years. There's a very interesting doctoral thesis by a young woman from America who spent years studying their liturgy and songs. She says that their canticles and prayer songs come from the Christian monks of the fourteenth century, and not the other way around. Interesting, no?'

Francis could not see the relevance. 'Monks?'

'Don't you see?' said Ari. 'If these so-called Ethiopian Jews, these Falashas, date back to the Middle Ages, they can't have any connection with the Dead Sea Scrolls.'

'How likely is it that what you say is correct?' asked Daniel.

Ari shrugged his huge shoulders, his black casual clothes rising and falling as though on pulleys. 'Who knows? They've got almost no written documentation, very little archaeology dating back to before King Lalibela in the 1100s. I think they're just charming stories.'

Daniel and Francis were now completely confused. Ari realised from the looks on their faces that they felt despondent. He smiled. 'Sorry, gentlemen, but in my opinion the Falashas have nothing to do with the Dead Sea Scrolls.'

Francis asked, 'Then why is Michael Farber so interested in them?'

'Ask him.'

'Professor,' said Daniel, 'what about the persistent rumours that the Falashas were given the Ark of the Covenant, and other sacred ornaments from Solomon's Temple, to look after?'

Ari grinned. 'Father, don't you think you've been watching too many Harrison Ford movies? *Raiders of the Lost Ark* is a fairytale. And that's precisely what Michael Farber is chasing.'

Benawie nodded in acknowledgement as the white man and woman were ushered into the tiny living room. As the community leader of the tens of thousands of Falashas in Israel, he was a man who held rank among his people. His word was law. He was of even greater importance than the religious leaders of the Falashas, who were still not recognised by the Israeli Beth Din, the court of the rabbis. The priests of Benawie's people, who had administered the rites and led the ceremonies of their people for thousands of years, had been told by Israeli rabbis that they were unsuitable; unqualified according to the Israelis to lead religious ceremonies.

He had not expected the man and woman back so soon. He had warned them. He had said they would find little information from his community about the ways of the Strange Ones. Even Benawie did not know too much. Knowledge of the Strange Ones, the Guardians, was something which had been hidden by the people of the Agau for thousands of years. He wasn't about to divulge the secrets of the Guardians to anyone, even though he was in a new land. He rose from his squatting position on the ground to greet them.

'*Haverim*, so soon? You have had no *mazzal* in finding out what you need to know?'

Michael found it hard to follow the strange intonations in the Hebrew of the Ethiopian. But Judith followed it and quickly translated into English.

'Master,' she said, 'we have had no *mazzal* at all. Every avenue was like a track blocked with rocks, leading nowhere. We've returned to the source of wisdom to see if your shining mind can shed light on our problem.'

Benawie nodded sagely. The girl spoke well. He was impressed. She spoke to him better than the man had spoken. When they first came to see him, she should have done the talking.

'Child. Again, what is it you wish me to tell you?'

'Master, we search for the truth. As you know, a great discovery was made in the desert. The man Jesus, who followed the Bible and was of the line of King David and King Solomon, left a Testament. Many experts believe the Testament and many other precious objects of the Jews have been hidden in a cave within the Negev desert. We—my brother Michael from Australia and I—believe that in the time of the Righteous Ones who tended the Temple, someone removed it from its hiding place and took it out of the country to avoid the Romans. We believe that he may have taken it to the people of the Agau.'

'Woman, you told me this when you first came to see me. Then, I told you I had no knowledge of it.'

'And your excellency was kind enough to give us the names of other important people in your community, whom we have visited. People like priests and those who guide your community in the great books of your people. But they too have no knowledge.'

'Then nobody knows,' said Benawie, smiling.

'Or nobody is willing to tell us?' she asked.

Benawie shrugged his shoulders, still smiling.

Judith decided to try another tack. Dealing with Benawie was more difficult than dealing with leaders of the Arabic community in the newly independent Palestinian state of the West Bank. Their hostility was palpable; his was couched in friendship.

'Master,' Judith continued, 'what method should I use to encourage one of your community leaders to tell me more of what he knows?'

'Explain what you mean, child,' said Benawie, frowning.

'Master, not only am I with the Israeli army, but I am also, like my brother Michael, an archaeologist. I am a person of worth. Within my gift are many things; I can provide benefits to one of your community who helps me.'

'Benefits?'

'Fame. He who helps me will be recorded in the pages of history as he who helped find the greatest treasure of all mankind. He will be famous throughout the five continents. He will be asked to sit with kings and presidents and prime ministers and tell them of his part in finding the Testament of Jesus. He will talk before great audiences about his actions in all the countries of the world.'

Michael forced himself not to look at her in astonishment.

Benawie nodded and stroked his chin. 'But he will be accused of treachery if he reveals the great secret of the people of the Agau. What is the value of fame, if one is despised?'

'Let me assure you, master, that he who gives the secret to us will not be despised. Not by the Israeli government, nor by the leaders of the other great religions whose home is in this country. He would be revered.'

Benawie nodded, 'What you say may be true, child, but this man must also live among his people. What value would all this be to him if he is spat upon in his own house?'

Judith considered his words, according them respect by not replying immediately. 'The people of the Agau have entered a new world. Old allegiances are of another land. Your allegiance is now to Israel, its people, and its needs. Israel needs one of your community to help it.'

'Israel, or your brother Michael and yourself?'

'Both Israel and us,' she smiled.

He picked up a glass and drank. Out of respect, they also drank. When they had drained their glasses, Benawie's wife appeared and refilled them all. Benawie waited until she had left the room before saying, 'Suppose a man of my community was to help you. This man does not know whether or not there is a Testament. But he does know who knows. It would benefit this man, and his community, if his stature rises in the eyes of the world.'

Michael and Judith remained silent. The wrong word, or an insistence or intemperate remark at this stage could lose everything. He thought for a full minute, then slowly leaned forward and whispered, 'Children, let me tell you about a small sect of men we call the Guardians.'

The librarian looked intensely at the two men and motioned both to stop speaking so loudly. Daniel had no idea that they were causing annoyance to others. In part it was the glory of studying with Francis again. Their mandated time in the library had been a relief from the rigours of seminary life, a regulated existence of prayer, study and contemplation. Not that they had been reprobate. They would borrow books, take them to their rooms, and study hard until late at night. But the official schedule gave their minds no time off. The seminary library had been their escape valve.

Francis looked at his friend and smiled. Both hid their eyes from the glare of the librarian, a Germanic-looking woman who wore her confidence like a floral hat on the lady mayoress' head.

Sprawled all over the desk, like spoils of conquest, were books about the Falashas from the Hebrew University's library. They had been gleaned from the sections on history, ancient Judaism, Jewish racial geography, ethnology and modern sociology. Since the disappointment of their interview with Professor Wallenstein, Francis and Daniel had decided to raid the library to see if they could determine what might have led Michael Farber to the Ethiopians.

Having spent the afternoon reminiscing about old times and searching the books, the two clerics concluded that there was little they didn't already know about the discovery of the Falashas and of their religion. Modern works concentrated on Operation Moses, the airlift which had brought them to safety, and how they were being integrated into the Israeli community. There were the usual learned theses dealing with Falasha history and the current situation and there were numerous texts identifying Prester John and later explorers as having found the tribe of Judah. Some books were devoted to determining whether the Queen of Sheba was an Arabian or Ethiopian monarch; whether her son Menelik had stolen the Ark of the Covenant; whether the Ark was hidden in one of the ancient Christian churches built into the mountains of Ethiopia. But none dealt with any subject linking the Dead Sea Scrolls with the Falashas, or a subject which could lead Francis and Daniel closer to what Michael Farber might be doing.

Looking up from one of the books, Francis said, 'You know, I always thought that the Falashas were little more than an historical oddity, but they really do have a very interesting history. Look here,' he said, pointing at a section of the book and pushing it over towards Daniel, 'the part where it deals with the Falashas' own independent kingdom.'

Daniel read it quickly. The author identified the mountains of the north-west of Abyssinia as having been one of the largest Jewish kingdoms outside Israel for thousands of years until they lost their political independence at the hands of the Emperor Susneyos in 1616. 'I suppose you and I have always been led to believe that Christianity took over from Judaism with the death of Christ. According to this, Ethiopia was the last independent Jewish state from the time of the Roman conquest until the founding of Israel in 1948. The problem is that there are no written records on which to base firm conclusions about their origins; but the Falashas' own version is that they are descendants of the lost tribe of Dan which, after its exile in Babylon, somehow found its way into Ethiopia.'

Francis turned and looked at the librarian to see if she was still scrutinising their activity. He put a finger to his lips and told his friend to keep his voice down.

Daniel continued in a whisper, 'Before the beginning of Christianity, Judaism had spread all around the Mediterranean and Red Sea basins, and along the valley of the Nile. Then it went deep down into Africa, and up through the Rift Valley into the plateaus of Ethiopia. You know, Francis, I was taught that after the destruction by Nebuchadnezzar, the Jews struggled back into Israel and stayed there for five hundred years until the second exile by the Romans. I had no idea they had established colonies so far afield.'

'See here,' said Francis, scanning the pages of another book. They turned as the librarian came over to them and said, 'This is a library. There are other places to discuss. Please pick up the books and take them to a conference room which you will find down the corridor.' Like a couple of errant children, they gathered up their books and walked away under her stern gaze.

When they had settled themselves in the conference room, they continued reading until Francis came to a particularly interesting section in another book. 'Listen here to what this author writes. It says that Judaism came to the Falashas from south-western Arabia, where a large and impressive Jewish community existed from the time of the destruction of the second Temple in AD 70. But a contrary hypothesis says that it reached Ethiopia by way of the Jews who had established a trading post before the fifth century at Elephantine, an island in the Nile, opposite Aswan in Upper Egypt, as well as from other settlements in the Kingdom of Meroe, which was known in the Old Testament as the Land of Cush.'

Francis put the book down. 'You know, all this is very interesting, but it doesn't really help us in discovering the relationship between the Falashas and the Dead Sea Scrolls. What in the name of heaven do you think Farber is up to?'

'Come on,' Daniel said. 'Let's get out of here and talk about it.'

As they left the library, the librarian 'tutted' in disapproval.

In a hall which normally resonated with the sounds of as many as six or seven thousand people, the minuscule congregation hardly made an impact. Overawed by the majesty of their surroundings and the sheer size of the setting, the sixty parishioners sat whispering to each other in the front pews. They were people of substance. People of position in normal life. Yet here, sitting in God's house, they were mere acolytes.

On the stage was the entire Congregational Choir of Heavenly Voices, huge black women in voluminous purple silk robes. They sat there, beaming everlasting smiles at the congregation, who smiled back and then avoided looking up again. Everyone waited on the Reverend Dr Jimmy Wilson. As one, the entire choir rose to its feet, the front row stepped one pace forward, the organ began to play and the front row sang out, 'Mine eyes have seen the glory of the coming of the Lord'.

Every man and woman in the tiny congregation joined in the stirring, swelling sounds. This place was theirs. It was more than most had dreamed of in their entire lives. As the hymn rose in pitch and fervour, so did the singing of the congregation. They forgot that they were alone in a vast auditorium. They did not mind that seven thousand, nine hundred and forty seats were unfilled. This was their day. They had paid their dues, and now they were reaping the reward.

And at the end of the last verse, as the voice of the organ was disappearing into the vast ether of the auditorium, Jimmy appeared out of a cloud of vapour on his heavenly chariot. No matter how many times they had seen him do it, each and every one felt an intimacy with their Maker as their preacher descended towards them in his pulpit. He stepped off the platform as the organ played a solitary chord and walked down the three steps from the stage to be among them. He walked up to every man and woman in the congregation, and shook their hands, whispering softly for their ears only, 'Thank you very much', 'God Bless you', 'Christ will bless you for this'.

The emotion was held in the right balance. Enough for each person there to feel personally touched by the magnitude of the occasion. As though each was visited by the Heavenly Spirit. Women pulled out handkerchiefs to dry their eyes; men couldn't talk. The closeness, the love, the feeling in the audience that each was a participant in a great and glorious event was overwhelming.

He ascended the steps back into his pulpit and spoke to his followers: 'Good people, friends, brothers and sisters in the Lord Jesus. You have been selected to join me and my ministers in our holy mission to the land of Our Saviour.

'Yes, folks, we've been inundated by requests from people all over the country to join with me in rescuin' the Testament of Our Lord, Jesus, the Messiah. But you people represented here are like the Apostles, and have been selected to join with me. You have qualified to rescue the most precious gift of God that has ever come into the hands of man.

'Just as sure as we Americans sent rescue missions to North Vietnam to rescue our boys from the clutches of the godless Communists. Or to Iran to rescue decent God-fearin' American boys from the hands of the Ayatollah Khomeini and the other fundamentalist madmen from the Muslim world.

'Our Lord's Testament is in the hands of the heathen. I'm talkin' about anybody who doesn't believe in the evangelical word of Christ Jesus. Who professes another religion from the one given to us on the Cross by Jesus of Nazareth Himself. The religion handed down by Him in His death agony, as He was crucified with rusty iron nails driven through His hands and feet. Now, I ask you folks, would Our Lord have willin'ly died, if He hadn't wanted the entire world to follow in His footsteps? No, 'course He wouldn't. So it stands to reason that anybody who follows another religion is laughin' in the face of Our Lord. Laughin', brothers and sisters! Laughin' and mockin', as the Jews laughed at Our Lord strugglin' up the steps of the Via Dolorosa on the road to Golgotha, bowed and broken and bloodied, to be taunted and ridiculed and humiliated by a stiff-necked people who said: "Go 'way, Jesus. Scat. Get outta here. We don't want none of Your religion here. We're doin' all right without you."

'And who are these people? Why, the Jews, of course. And who is it that's hidin' Our Lord's Testament? The Children of Israel, and the hierarchy of the Catholic priesthood in Rome—that's who! Who is it built a church and took possession of the place where Our Lord was buried and was resurrected shortly thereafter, the place called Golgotha? The Catholics, with their Church of the Holy Sepulchre. Men whose ambition is unto themselves alone, and not to the everpresent good of Christian folk. Men whose intention it is to prevent the Testament of the Messiah from fallin' into the hands of those charged by God Almighty Himself to take care of it. You and me, brothers and sisters. You and me.

'I doubt whether there has ever been a more vital and pressin' mission which any group of people has been charged with undertakin'. When we succeed—and succeed we shall—we'll bring the very words of God back to our church, right here in California. I have today issued an instruction to our architects to begin plans for the construction of a proper and fit restin' place for this treasure from God Almighty Himself.'

The audience 'amened' and 'praised the Lord' at the end of every sentence. But when they heard of the new project, their supplications grew louder. Rising to their approval, Jimmy continued, 'It will be a vast complex, spreadin' over twice the existin' area which our cathedral currently uses. There'll be adequate accommodation for pilgrims from all over the world, with special facilities for families to leave their children and old folks while they participate in pilgrim services. These will be called the Cedar Rooms and will be built over that old cedar tree yonder, soon as the land's cleared. It will be a sight of splendour and wonder in the desert.

'It'll be a family-oriented destination. We're even talkin' to the city authorities about makin' special windowless transit buses available from LAX, so pilgrims don't have to sully their eyes with the heathen things which are all around us.'

Even three members of the choir, normally silent while Jimmy was speaking, were transported in delight and 'praised the Lord' along with the audience.

Jimmy was still riding an emotional wave as he sat back in his office, surrounded by his staff and the now regular presence of Joe Deakin. Joe was accepted by most of the support staff, except Harlin Brown who reserved judgement until a favourable article appeared in print. Jimmy called him the 'Doubting Thomas'.

'This new pilgrimage centre, it's for real?' asked Joe.

'Thought that would impress you,' Jimmy smiled. 'Sure it's for real. Idea came into my head as I was descendin' into the congregation from my Heavenly Pulpit. Disneyland and Movie World attract tens of millions of visitors a year, but what attractions they got? Fun rides and that garbage. We'll have the Lord's handwritten Testament as our central attraction. Can't get much bigger than that, now can you?'

Joe couldn't help admiring the audacity of the man. 'But Dr Wilson, what happens if you don't find it?'

Jimmy shook his head, amazed at the limitations of the people around him. 'Son, for two thousand years, people have been goin' on pilgrimages to visit sacred sites, or to see the supposed bones of saints and splinters from the Cross. We're about to go to the Holy Land.

Place is brimmin' with sacred things. I'm absolutely confident that if our prayers are loud and sufficient, the Lord will direct us to the right place.'

He leaned forward in a conspiratorial whisper. 'With your help, and the assistance of the *LA Times*, we can make the place an overnight sensation. But naturally, it's vital that we find Our Lord's Testament first, or somethin' of equivalent value. Now, any further news about this professor from Sydney Australia, and his idea that we should be lookin' outside the Holy Land?' he asked with an unmistakable sneer in his voice.

'I heard back from our stringer in Jerusalem just a couple of hours ago. He's been following Professor Farber around. seeing where he's going. Also, I've had our people check him out in Australia. Appears he started life as an orthodox Jew, but saw the light, and converted to Catholicism.'

'He's a Catholic,' said Jimmy, 'one of the whores of Babylon.'

'Sir?'

Jimmy calmed and asked, 'Is he for real?'

'Apparently. At one stage. he was thinking of becoming a priest, but became an academic instead. He's very well respected as an expert in the early Christian period.'

'So he's a convert, is he? Saw the light. Like Saul of Tarsus on the road to Damascus. Praise the Lord. Well, don't keep me in suspense, Joseph. What's our convert been up to?'

Everyone in the room listened with interest as Joe took out his notebook. It was a ritual. Joe had only scribbled down a couple of sentences from the telephone conversation, but reading from a notebook gave one greater authority. Only Harlin looked at him quizzically.

'Our stringer has been following Michael Farber all over Jerusalem. It seems he and a lady companion have been visiting an awful lot of people in one particular area of the city. An area with a large population of newly arrived immigrants from Ethiopia.'

'Ethiopia?' Jimmy burst out.

Joe closed his notebook and nodded. 'Yep, there's thousands of Black Jews called Falashas who were air-lifted a couple of years back to escape the Communist regime in Ethiopia. Farber has been visiting dozens of them. We don't know why yet, but we're making every effort to find out.'

Jimmy Wilson shook his head in consternation. If the Lord's Testament was in Ethiopia, he could kiss goodbye to the twenty million pledged so far. No American would go on a pilgrimage to Ethiopia, a famine-stricken land full of niggers. But was that the case, he wondered on reflection. In some ways, maybe it was better there than in Israel. The Holy Land would be full of archaeologists scouring the land. His chances of finding the Testament were close to zero. In Ethiopia, he would have to contend with a hostile government, but he could buy any official that stood in his way. And he would have to beat Michael Farber to the draw. But what chance did a university professor stand against him?

Jimmy looked at his group. All were waiting his reaction. 'Boys, Joe, I find it interestin' that he's investigatin' Ethiopia. Very interestin' indeed. I think we should find out more about these Ethiopians. A whole lot more. Joe, somethin' I've been meanin' to ask you. Do you think your editor would find it in his heart to allow you to visit the Holy Land with us? As a sort of a chronicler of our pilgrimage.' Joe looked deeply into Jimmy Wilson's face. Innocence was written all over it. He wondered what was behind the mask. He smiled.

'Dr Wilson, I'm sure I can persuade my editor to let me come.'

Harlin Brown looked down at the floor in fury.

Franz Cardinal Kitzinger was incapable of anything but dignity. Born in Germany of Polish parents, he had been twelve when his mother and father were taken away by the Gestapo. His parents begged their landlord to hide the child, which he did, until he could place young Franz in a hostel for Catholic orphans. But even there was not safe. The orphanage was closed down by orders of the *Gauleiter* of Hamburg, and the children fostered out to good Aryan families for Nazification.

After the war, in his eighteenth year, Franz searched Red Cross and American Occupation records to trace his parents. To this day, he did not know whether his mother and father were alive or dead. Every day of his life, he prayed for them.

When the stain of Nazism was removed from Germany, Franz joined a seminary. He absorbed the knowledge of which he had been deprived and quickly came to the attention of the Novice Father, who championed him. He was sent to Rome, where he excelled in philosophy and theology. His teachers had nothing but praise for his intellect and dedication; but reservations were expressed about his pastoral abilities. In the four years of tuition, he had made no close friendships or allegiances, and dominated others with his brilliance rather than any innate qualities of leadership.

When his fellow students left Rome to preach and teach abroad, he stayed and became a tutor. He soon became recognised as an extraordinary thinker and was encouraged to study for a licentiate. What normally takes two years took Franz a mere twelve months. After his graduation ceremony, Franz was visited by the head of the Gregorian University in his room and offered a place to study for a doctorate. If he had created a record in the time taken to gain a licentiate, his time to be awarded a doctorate staggered even the most jaded of academics. His thesis, a seminal rebuttal of existentialism, was widely circulated among clerics and was published as a book.

He was offered a teaching post at the university but declined in preference to returning to the Vatican as an official in the Congregation for the Doctrine of the Faith. This role gave him little to do in pastoral care and plenty of time to think, write and publish. Pope Paul began to consult the young theologian as a rebuttalist of the growing trend towards humanism, and asked him to research and counter the liberationist theologians coming to power in South America.

His brilliant career saw Franz appointed cardinal in the early 1980s, an *éminence grise* in the Curia. Ultra-conservative, intellectually arrogant and supremely confident, he was the rallying point in the bastion against radicalism within the College of Cardinals.

Franz had bitterly opposed the appointment of the American Pope in the conclave, but had lost out to the weight of numbers who wanted a change towards dynamism. Now, his job was to ensure that the Church moved forward slowly and cautiously.

His meeting with the two liberal Italian prelates was one of three meetings he would hold that day, constantly in caucus to propagate his views.

'So, eminence, the Crusade?' he asked Cardinal Luchetta.

'Brother, I am distressed. No matter what our Holy Father says, the use of the word "Crusade" will not sit well with our followers throughout the world.'

'Certainly, brother, but forgetting its name for a moment, what of its implications? Do you see any harm coming from it?'

'If I may answer,' Cardinal Braschia intervened, 'I really can't see a difficulty with searching for Our Lord's Testament. Finding it would be the greatest accomplishment since our Church was founded by the blessed St Peter.'

'And would our Church have been founded as successfully if St Peter had carried a copy of Christ's Testament in his pocket? Our Church is built like a castle in the air. On faith and trust. Whenever we Catholics rely on physical expressions of our faith, we come crashing down. Think of all the relics of the saints, the bones, the shrouds, the bits of wood from the Cross. Throughout our history, charlatans masquerading as God-ordained clerics have been seducing the faithful like insurance or real-estate salesmen. Are we to enter another age of indulgences, and testaments for sale?'

'Brother eminence,' Cardinal Braschia laughed, 'you go too far. Would you allow the words of Our Lord to continue to rot in the desert?'

'Rather they remain hidden than they destroy the faith of the followers. How do we know if the Testament was written by Christ Himself. It may be a pseudepigraph, or palimpsest. And worse, what if Vatican Three goes ahead and it denies the veracity of the Apostles, or signifies an acceptance of the Jewish faith. The Catholic Apostolic Church is facing a severe test to its existence from those Dead Sea Scrolls which have yet to be published. Finding this Testament could be our undoing.'

Cardinal Braschia shook his head vigorously. 'Brother, I am getting reports back from priests known to me of increased attendances at church and increased donations. Surely, your eminence is not forgetting the shortfall in revenues this year, which is likely to exceed one hundred million American dollars.'

Cardinal Luchetta smiled and nodded his agreement.

'No, eminence, I am not forgetting any of those matters. Our congregations are swelling on faith and hope, brothers. And on these two ethereal factors alone will the Holy Church succeed.'

The two remained quiet while Cardinal Kitzinger continued, 'And all the while, our American Father and his friend are treading dangerously closer to damaging that faith and hope.'

'Where is Brother Rhymer?' asked Luchetta.

'He's gone to the Holy Land on a secret mission for the Pope,' said Braschia.

Kitzinger smiled and shook his head. 'He has gone on a secret mission, but I'm not sure how much is for the Pope. His Holiness told him to interview the International Team. What he's doing is renewing his friendship with an American priest. And my sources inform me that they are running around Jerusalem like Sherlock Holmes and Dr Watson.'

'Does the Pope know?' asked Braschia, shocked at the possible deception.

'Who knows what the Pope knows?' said Kitzinger.

The two Italian prelates 'tut-tutted' disapprovingly. But neither wished to show his ignorance by asking who Sherlock Holmes and Dr Watson were.

A feeling of security descended upon the Chrome Cathedral the day after Jimmy Wilson, Harlin Brown, Luke Carmody and the group of wealthy parishioners flew from LAX to New York and to Israel via Rome. Jimmy had organised for the sixty donors to be picked up from their homes by white stretch limos and transported in one of the biggest motorcades that LA had seen. The motorcade was covered by every television station in the city and Jimmy's press conference had caused a scene unprecedented at the airport since the arrival there of the Beatles. Annabelle was not allowed to go to the airport to say goodbye, especially since she had misbehaved so badly with her minder. Jimmy had made it patently clear that if she ever pulled a stunt like that again she could expect another beating.

Secretaries looked out of the church windows to see if they could glimpse the 747 as it rose above the cathedral before swinging to the east to fly to New York. Even Oscar the gateman began chatting amiably with a young black man who pulled up to ask him questions about the construction and the purpose of the Chrome Cathedral.

An hour after departure time everyone sat back and relaxed into their work. Church wardens walked the corridors whistling as they went. Deacons and acolytes who ministered to the needs of the congregation sat in the refectory reading or playing cards. The oppression, the intrigues, the palace politics had evaporated as soon as Jimmy's entourage roared off in clouds of dust towards the airport. The whole church now felt in a holiday mood. On the following day, people passed each other in corridors or walking into and out of rooms and smiled. There was time to ask about family and friends. There was freedom to ask about plans for weekends and holidays.

Duane was left in charge of the day-to-day running of the church and was answerable to Gerald Curtis. In the past few weeks Duane had become introspective. Nobody could explain his change of mood.

Annabelle's change of mood was easier for everyone to understand. Jimmy's domination had increased since he brought her out of hospital, almost as though she was responsible for her own thrashing. But nobody had been willing to intervene on her behalf. Nobody wanted to cross Jimmy.

It was shortly after breakfast when an ageing Ford Mustang drew up to the gatehouse. Oscar looked at the cathedral and saw it was safe. The tall young black got out. 'How you doing, Oscar?'

'How you doing, Micah?'

'Got your call.' Oscar looked again at the cathedral. 'Worried?' asked Micah.

'Sure, I'm worried. Where's an old nigger like me gonna to get another job if I gets fired?'

'You ain't gonna get fired.'

'I shouldn't have even been talking to you these last two days. They pays my wages. I got a duty to them.'

'C'mon, Oscar, you and Jonas was buddies. You told me he was the only one who treat you right. I been trying a week now to get something outta the church and I got sweet fuckall. Shit man, if us niggers can't stick together, what hope we got?'

'Don't you come niggerin' here with me. You told me you wuz my friend. You gonna use the information I give you 'gainst my employers.'

'You don't know that. All I want to find out is who killed my brother. Police won't help me. Now the preacherman's gone, maybe someone will talk.'

'Well, if you get into trouble, I ain't never heard of you.'

Micah got back into his car. 'You got a deal, brother.' He drove his Ford into the empty car park of the church, stepped out and walked purposefully towards the vestibule. He wanted to talk to Annabelle Wilson. Jonas had mentioned her many times. Said she was a sweet, decent woman. Maybe she would help.

He spoke to a receptionist. 'I haven't got an appointment but I'd like to see Mrs Annabelle Wilson. My name is Micah Watkins.'

The receptionist paled. 'You're Jonas's brother, aren't you?' The young man nodded. 'I want to tell you that I knew your brother real well and he was a fine young man. We're all truly sorry about what happened to him.'

Micah nodded in appreciation.

'I'm afraid, however, that Mrs Wilson is too unwell to see anybody. Perhaps you'd like to talk to one of the deacons. He might be able to help you.'

'I really would like to see Mrs Wilson,' said Micah, shaking his head. 'I tried to get to see the Reverend Wilson before he left but he was too busy to see me. I know that Mrs Wilson was badly assaulted but I must talk to her. I have to find out what Jonas was doing on the day he was murdered. The police are just giving me the runaround.'

Behind him, there was the noise of shuffling. 'You're Jonas' brother?' a hoarse voice whispered.

Micah turned around in surprise. He saw a woman supported by a walking frame, arms encased in plaster and legs swathed in bandages, approaching him. Her face showed signs of recovering from a hideous beating.

'Mrs Wilson?'

'I'm Annabelle Wilson. You're Jonas' brother?'

'Yes, ma'am. I wonder if you can spare me a few minutes? I know you're in pain but I'd dearly like to talk to you.'

A woman aged in her forties stepped from behind Annabelle and interposed herself between the two.

'I'm afraid Mrs Wilson is too tired to talk to you, but—'

Annabelle shuffled her walking frame and pushed her aside.

'You just get out of my way, you interferin' bitch. I've had it with you, listenin' to my phone calls and tellin' me who I can and can't see and where I can go.'

The woman smiled confidently. 'Annabelle, my dear, you know Jimmy had words to you last night about your treatment of me. Now I'm under strict instructions to report to Jimmy about this sort of thing. If you don't want me to report you, then I suggest that you let this young gentleman here get back into his car.'

'Don't you dare call me "my dear". Jimmy's gone and won't be back for three weeks. I'm firin' you as my assistant. Now you pack your bags and get out of here, you bulldyke bitch.'

'Don't you dare talk to me like that, you foulmouth slut. You can't fire me. I don't work for you. I work for the Reverend Dr Wilson.'

Micah looked at the two women in concern.

'Mrs Wilson, perhaps I can come back another day.'

'It's perfectly fine now, thank you Mr Watkins. I'd very much like to go for a walk in the garden. I haven't been outside this air-conditioned hellhole in two days, and I sorely need some fresh air,' she said, hissing the last two words in the woman's direction.

'I will not be spoken to in that way by you,' said the woman. 'I'm going to go right away and see Duane and inform him of what's just happened.'

When she'd gone, Annabelle began to walk slowly out of the vestibule into the fierce heat of the mid-morning sun.

'I didn't want you to get into trouble on my account,' he began, but she interrupted him.

'I'm in trouble up to my ass. You ain't goin' to make a puppyshit of difference.' She laughed. It was a hoarse laugh, as though she was suffering laryngitis. As they walked down the path towards the irrigated garden, she said, 'Your brother was a fine young man. He was a man of God and a man everybody loved. I hope before God one day that they catch the devil that hurt him so bad.'

'Mrs Wilson, can you tell me what he was doing on the morning that he disappeared? The police have interviewed people in the church and everybody says he was just working normally. They said sometimes he went off for lunch instead of eating in the refectory but that he always came back by two. This time, he just didn't come back.'

She looked at him through her painful eyes. 'I'm really sorry, Mr Watkins, but I have no idea what he was doin'.'

'Do you know if he was meeting anybody? If he was friendly with somebody?'

'He was friendly with many people here, maybe he was meetin' a parishioner. I don't know. He was responsible for bringin' many many people into the congregation, especially black people who were on drugs or down and out.'

'So you have no idea?'

Every step was still an agony for Annabelle, but the hot desert air made her skin feel alive again. She turned to him, 'I'd love to help you, I really really would. It's just so unfair what happened to him. After that first terrible beatin' he took as a boy, why, such a thing just shouldn't have happened twice.'

'How did you know about the beating? That was years ago.'

Annabelle didn't answer for a moment. 'He must have told me about it.'

'So you knew him well?'

'Not terribly well, no.'

'But well enough to know that he'd suffered a real bad beating.'

She remained silent as she continued to walk. Micah walked slowly beside her.

'Why don't you tell me the truth, Mrs Wilson? You'll feel better if you tell me from your own lips. Jonas told me all about you and him.'

'He told you about us?'

'He told me all about you. Do you want me to go into details?'

She became vacant, lost in glorious memories.

'Did he tell you how it was when we were together? How we'd just look into each other's eyes for hours on end?'

'He said you was the best thing ever to happen to him. He said you smelled sweet like flowers. That you was warm and passionate. He told me how much he loved you, ma'am.'

'He said he loved me?' She fought a sob, and blinked back tears as she allowed the painful memory of Jonas' strong, young body to re-enter her mind. 'I want you to know this. I loved him, Micah. I loved him with all my body and all my heart.'

And she began to cry.

CHAPTER 16

Some priests lived their ministries in kraals in the heart of Africa, others in huts in the highlands of New Guinea, still others in rat-and-cockroach-plagued slum tenements in the decaying hearts of affluent American cities. Some spent their lives ministering to the dying in the mortuary streets of Calcutta, or praying for the souls of those killed fighting fascists in South America. But Franz Kitzinger lived his entire ministry surrounded by the opulence of the Catholic Church's Renaissance grandeur and pageantry.

Since his late teens, Franz had lived his life in isolation from such squalor. The seminaries where he was inducted and trained in the priesthood following the Second World War were converted monasteries or mansions. His first appointment as priest was to a post within the Vatican. While his accommodation was an unembroidered one-room cell outside the Vatican walls, it was within sight of the epicentre of the Holy City, and from the first moment when he opened the shutters of his bedroom and gazed out on the eternal scene, he knew with absolute certainty that he had arrived where he belonged.

After his academic life as a philosopher, when he joined the staff of the Bishop of Siena, Franz Kitzinger lived within the bishop's palace, a Mozart at the court of Count Colloredo. As he climbed higher on the ladder of ecclesiastical success, his apartments grew increasingly sumptuous. They became his second skin.

His appointment as a prince of the Church was a fitting tribute to a man of his brilliance. While avarice was one of the deadly sins for some people, humility was a sin for Franz. His credo was simple. The Church retained its standing in the eyes of its worldwide congregation by holding them in thrall of its power. And power came both through its word and through the Church's appointments—its buildings, regalia, ceremonies, conventions and paraphernalia. It was what held the Church apart from and above mankind. In that way, the Church could act as intermediary between God and man. If the Church became man, it lost its mystery. If it became removed from man and aspired too much towards God, then it became little less than a gigantic monastery in which a devoted coterie excluded the uninitiated. By his early twenties, Franz Kitzinger had determined the way the Church should be. All his life he had worked to ensure that the Church remained in its ordained stratum between God and man.

It had been the same in medieval Europe. Why were Gothic cathedrals built on such a vast scale, with spires which could be seen for miles across a landscape of hovels? It was to show the total dominance of the Church over every aspect of a peasant's life.

Franz Kitzinger had been one of the first to recognise the Church had slipped dramatically in its authority. Priests openly questioned the eternal dogma of the faith, the laity no longer treated the clergy with the respect due to God's anointed. The East was separating from the West. The North from the South. The appointment of a Polish Pope had signalled the beginning of the end of Roman authority.

Cardinal Kitzinger never aspired to be Pope. The true power of the papacy lay not with the Italians, but with those who could exercise control without being accountable to the masses.

In the late hours of Friday night, when most of the Vatican was asleep, a member of the Swiss Guard escorted a visitor into his apartments. Kitzinger rose to meet his friend. They had known each other for nearly half a century, yet as Kitzinger stepped down from his chair he held out his hand to compel Père Romain de la Tour to bend and kiss his cardinal's ring.

'My dear friend, thank you so much for coming. I felt it important we meet face to face. Not even the Vatican's phones are absolutely secure. I had to see you because of the Pope's action in sending Cardinal Rhymer to interview you and the other members of the team.'

'Please don't worry. I enjoy coming to the Vatican. I've spoken to those members of the team I control and assure you that they will give him nothing more than information which is already in the public domain.'

Kitzinger breathed a sigh of relief and kissed his friend on both cheeks. 'It's good to have you here.'

'It's good to be out of the hothouse of biblical scholarship for a while. You know, Franz, I didn't think the simple error in giving our Israeli colleague the list to translate would have had such serious ramifications.'

'That's all in the past now,' said Kitzinger, dismissing it with a wave of his hand. 'With tens of thousands of documents, it's surprising that more unauthorised material hasn't reached the world before now. The truth is that you've done a brilliant job in keeping the lid on the scrolls for all these years. Romain, you're to be congratulated.'

'I'm not sure congratulations are necessarily in order, with what's just happened to poor Hiram Solomonoglou.'

Kitzinger grimaced in distress. 'An atrocity, an obscenity. I never thought even the most fanatical of our Jewish brethren would stoop so low.'

'Well, you know the Jews—'

Kitzinger turned and glared angrily at the diminutive priest. 'Jews have suffered at the hands of Christians for two millennia,' said Kitzinger, with a snarl. 'We've forced them to convert to our will. In all that time, save for the very early days, no Christians have suffered at the hands of Jews. It's as a result of our Holy Father's irresponsibility that this situation has come about. It's nothing to do with the psyche of the Jew.'

Romain bowed his head in apology. The two men walked over to the coffee table and each poured a *demitasse* from the Georgian silver coffee set which had been Kitzinger's choice of gift on elevation to the cardinalate.

'What will you do about Hiram's kidnap?' asked Romain.

'What can we do? It's in the hands of the Israeli authorities, but I intend to go to Israel in the very near future to lead the prayers of the Christian community and intercede on his behalf with whoever has kidnapped him.'

'You know who's kidnapped him. This maniac Berg.'

'It's inconceivable that a man of God, an orthodox Rabbi, could be so fanatical as to commit an act of obscenity like this,' said Kitzinger.

Romain wanted to tell his eminent friend that it was typical of the duplicity of the Jews, but he had just received a sharp reminder of Franz's disapproval of his feelings towards the Semites.

'May I draw you back to the reason for my visit? How much longer do you think we can prevent the publication of the rest of the scrolls material?' asked Romain.

Kitzinger looked at his friend and smiled. 'Another decade, perhaps. I don't suspect we can keep them quiet for much longer. The biblical community is baying for the blood of the International Team, and since the publications by the Huntingdon Library in California, there's intense speculation about what else you have hidden up your sleeves.'

'Are you sure we can keep them quiet for another decade, Franz? There have been several books already published from unauthorised photocopies. Others are bound to follow, and then the Israeli government may have no option but to impound the remaining documents.' He massaged his aching knee. 'You know, I really do detest these Americans. They're in clear breach of copyright. I've sent them the usual letter threatening legal action but it hasn't impressed them. I got one curt letter from a scholar at Harvard telling me he would welcome legal action, so things could be exposed to public scrutiny through the courts of law.' Romain strangled a laugh. 'Can you see me in a courtroom in New York with some glib-mouthed American attorney trying to make me give evidence about the scrolls.'

'I have the same thing here every day with the Americans,' said Franz. 'They have the gift of tongues but they're unconvincing and unsophisticated. Molloy's theology is contemptible and his appreciation of Church history nothing short of bankrupt. Why else would he have created this absurd Crusade and opened the Church to the dangers of Vatican Three?'

'Do you think there are dangers?' asked Romain.

The tall prelate spun. 'Dangers! Look at what happened to the Church after Vatican Two. Schisms, discontent, disruption. Do you want all that to start again? And so soon. My God, the last thing we need at this perilous juncture is a questioning of the faith.'

It was the first time that Kitzinger had spoken so openly about the inside workings of the Vatican.

'And what about the other one, Rhymer? What's he like?' asked the scholar.

'Oh, bright enough, I suppose. Rhymer is theologically sound and, I gather, a conservative. His faith is very strong. I just wish the Pope's sanctity was devoid of a need to change, to modernise, to update. When we have completed the process of bringing him back into the fold, then I will help him. I will offer him love and devotion.'

Romain wanted to ask more questions about life in the eyrie of the Vatican but the look on Kitzinger's face told him not to.

Kitzinger continued, 'What unauthorised publications are planned about the scrolls? How damaging is the material they'll be publishing?'

Père Romain de la Tour shook his head and wandered back to the tapestry-covered armchairs set either side of the marble fireplace. 'Of themselves, not terribly important. Bits from an earlier version of the Book of Ezekiel. Some new stuff from the War Rule. A couple of interesting thanksgiving hymns and four or five new apocryphal psalms. They aren't particularly revealing but one thing that does worry me somewhat is a new version of the Genesis Apocryphon. It's dramatically different from the one published in 1956 by Yadin and Avigad. The differences appear to be in an association between the Genesis myths and the birth myth of a Messiah. Doubtless the gullible will believe that the writing refers to Jesus.'

'Serious?' asked the cardinal as he sat down to face his friend.

'It's hard to say. They're like pieces of a jigsaw. First we had the discovery. Then the wild flights of fancy about Jesus being an Essene and the Teacher of Righteousness having pre-dated Christianity by a couple of hundred years. Then we had the denials and since then we've effectively managed to keep a lid on this obscene association between the Old and the New Testaments and the origin of Christ. And that damn woman, with her publicising Jesus as being little more than an ordinary politician. These Australians . . . first her, now Michael Farber—'

Kitzinger cut in. 'I know of this Michael Farber. He was a student in the Vatican, a convert from Judaism. How good is he?'

'Prima facie, one of the best. No question. Brilliant mind, astounding insights, but uncontrollable. Certainly not the sort of person we would want on the team.'

'Why couldn't you control him?'

'He's arrogant, self-righteous, he has the zeal of the convert. Very dangerous if uncontrolled.'

'I see,' said Kitzinger, 'but do you think that, despite your efforts, the rest of the scholars, those not on the International Team, will be able to fit these pieces of jigsaw together? After all, there are people like Professor Wallenstein of Israel and excellent men in Rome, Germany and the United Kingdom.'

'Some day, yes. We're not dealing with fools.'

From a distance a bell tolled. One of the dozens of churches in central Rome was calling its faithful to late-night prayer.

'Is there any more material of importance since the last drafts you showed me?'

'Franz, I suppose it depends on how you define the word "importance". As a biblical scholar, every word, even every letter, is important to me. It's a portal into the past. It shows me what those great minds in Qumran were thinking when Our Lord was beginning His ministry. But in the context of any endangerment to our faith, I suppose the answer depends on how our faith is viewed.'

'Explain,' demanded the cardinal.

The little biblical scholar stood up and walked towards the window to look out over the rooftops of the Vatican. The domes and cupolas blended into silhouettes against a dark, starless inner-city sky. He turned to face his old friend. 'I fear that this could associate us too closely with the Jews.'

Kitzinger became visibly agitated. 'Don't start that anti-Semitic diatribe with me again. You know the trouble with that.'

'Eminence, dear friend, I wasn't going to say a word against the Jews, I promise. But it cannot be dismissed. The Jews were responsible for the death of Christ. They were the original persecutors of the Apostles.'

Kitzinger stood up and walked towards the ornately carved mahogany *credenza* to pour himself a glass of *schnapps*. He must not get angry. Only by commanding with authority could he quieten de la Tour. He had nearly lost his control over the scrolls because of de la Tour's imbecilic and gratuitous anti-Semitic outbursts in the past. It had taken phenomenal negotiation on his part with the Israeli government to maintain Romain de la Tour's leadership of the International Team.

'Father de la Tour, our decades of friendship do not entitle you to speak in that way about our brothers, the Jews. I have a long and wonderful relationship with the rabbinate in a dozen or more countries. I have hundreds of Jewish friends. I have attended *Seder* services at Passover time and addressed Jewish congregations in America, England and all over Europe about the wonder of the ancient Hebrews. I will not permit you to disparage the Jewish race in that way. We Christians have done their race enough harm in centuries of persecution.'

Romain de la Tour flushed red in embarrassment. No man in the world could belittle him as conclusively as Franz Kitzinger, yet there was no man whose friendship and respect he craved more highly. 'Forgive me, dear friend, my anti-Semitism is not real. The words I use are from my childhood vocabulary, they are not from the heart. But that does not detract from the danger of associating Judaism too closely with Catholicism. You know my own view on this matter, which you share.' He took out a handkerchief to wipe his forehead, and joined his friend at the *credenza* to refresh himself with a Perrier water. 'Allowing the intimacy between the Old and the New Testament to become public would be to undermine the uniqueness of Catholicism in the eyes of our flock. It would give vicarious pleasure to Protestants, Jews—' he glanced apologetically at Franz, 'Muslims and atheists. It would breach the mysticism which is the glue holding our Church together. From that point of view every word which we prevent from being published is important. But if you're asking me whether there is a gun which will shoot Catholicism in the head, the answer is *"no"*. But I've discovered so much explosive ammunition that I'm not sure a gun *per se* is necessary.'

Kitzinger sipped his *schnapps* and continued to scrutinise his friend. What a rich relationship the two men enjoyed. From the day he had become a young adviser to the Pope, he had managed to steer Vatican thinking in a direction of conservatism. His influence enabled him to have appointed as Chief Biblical Scholar and head of the International Team his young and brilliant friend Romain de la Tour. He and Romain had studied philosophy and biblical exegesis together. Their views were common, though their career paths vastly different. Franz the eclectic philosopher, a masterful German who had risen to the upper heights of the hierarchy, Romain an aristocratic Frenchman who devoted his life to the understanding of the early Bible documents.

Yet despite divergent careers, both had maintained an intimacy through correspondence and holidaying together, sparking each other's appetites with new thoughts, new approaches to old problems and the posing of unanswerable questions. Romain was the closest friend Franz possessed, but even the intimacy of friendship was not allowed to intervene between his estate as a prince of the Church and Romain's modest office as a clerk in holy orders.

'Tell me, how seriously do you view Michael Farber? Be more specific, if you can.'

'Farber?' said Romain. 'Why are you so interested in him? He's just one of many hundreds of scholars.'

'I read in an article in *Osservatore Romano* that he thought the Testament of Our Lord Jesus might be found outside of Israel.'

Romain laughed again, dismissing it with an indifferent wave of his hand. 'Pure speculation. Not a shred of evidence. Typical of his brand of modern scholarship. He comes up with an idea, broadcasts it to the world to make an instant reputation for himself, sees if anybody's interested, and if he gets a good response, then he sets about proving it.' He sipped his Perrier water and settled back into the opulent comfort of the chair. 'If it wasn't for this trait, he would be much more highly respected. As I said, Farber is a very clever man. If he'd stop running off at the mouth, he'd be one of the best scholars in the field.'

'Better than you?' asked Kitzinger with a smile.

'There's real zeal in Farber. A passion which I find frightening. Me? I lost my passion years ago. All I'm concerned about now is the purity of the faith.'

'And does Farber pose such a serious threat?'

'Yes, unquestionably, and not just because he's a maverick. It's also because he's both Jew and Christian. Because he sees things from both sides. He's a devout Catholic now,' Romain continued, 'but one can still see the Jew in him. He's almost Talmudic in his writings and in conversation. He's currently racing around Jerusalem talking to leaders of the Falashas.'

'Falashas? The "Lost Tribe"?'

'Yes, the Jews of Ethiopia. My reading of it is that he believes Our Lord's Testament may have been spirited away to Africa. Maybe Alexandria, maybe even to the Falashas.'

'How do you know?'

'Franz, I have spies everywhere in Jerusalem. I have spies in the government, in the Ministry of Antiquities, in the Hebrew University. Everywhere. Some are Catholic, some are Jewish. In another day, I could have been a Renaissance prince, or a Christopher Marlowe.'

Kitzinger burst out laughing again. He had a heavy thunderous laugh, different from the high-pitched nasal whine of Romain de la Tour.

'And is there any possibility he's on the right track?'

'Not a hope in Heaven. Masada, the Dead Sea, Qumran, are riddled with caves. We wouldn't have excavated more than ten per cent. We walk into a cave, have a cursory glance around and walk out again. Yet, buried under a foot of dust and rubble, could be half a dozen scrolls which may never see the light of day. One of these could be the Testament of Our Lord. And if ever it's discovered, God help our mother Church.'

'I wonder.'

Romain looked at his friend.

'I wonder if that's why Rhymer has gone to Israel. Could that be the reason he's gone to see this missionary friend of his? Maybe he too thinks the Testament has left the country.'

Romain de la Tour shrugged. 'I didn't even know Cardinal Rhymer was in Israel until you told me.'

'What happened to all your spies?'

'I said I have a lot,' Romain chuckled, 'I didn't say they were particularly competent. But why would Rhymer go to Israel? Is he on a mission for the Pope?'

'The Pope's told us one thing, but I have no doubt that he's doing another. I wonder if he's meeting with Professor Farber and offering assistance in finding the Testament. My God, if the Pope puts money into the search, I can't control the consequences.'

'It's not a matter of money, Franz. It's a matter of luck. You can spend ten million dollars and come up with nothing. Or take a package tour to Israel and stumble on the Testament. Money won't buy results in this case.'

'But an association between the Vatican and Michael Farber is not something I'd encourage. Within the next day or two, I intend to go over to Israel on behalf of the Vatican. My mission is to represent the papacy with regard to Hiram Solomonoglou's kidnap. However, while I'm there, I think it would be well for me to call upon his eminence Cardinal Rhymer and find out what he's up to. Perhaps away from the panoply of the Pope's munificence he will be more inclined to unburden himself to me. And if I can't call upon his loyalty to the Church, there are other methods of persuasion which can be used.'

A change in wind velocity forced the Pan Am 747 to change landing runway minutes before its scheduled landing time. The pilot explained to his passengers that because of a *khamsin*, a desert wind blowing in from Saudi Arabia, the plane was being diverted by air traffic control from the north-south runway to runway 4, east-west. That meant the plane needed to fly further down the Mediterranean coast to avoid over-flying Tel Aviv and to wheel over the Negev desert in order to land.

Within the plane the first and business class sections were entirely occupied by a group from the fundamentalist First Evangeline Church of the Witnesses of the Lord. Led by the Reverend Dr Jimmy Wilson, they had driven the stewardesses crazy. The group of nearly seventy people had spent the three and a half hour flight from LAX to Kennedy singing hymns, kneeling in the aisles and being preached to. For the first hour, the stewardesses were amused. But when the prayers continued into the time reserved for food service, when compliant passengers were normally getting bored, the good humour of the cabin crew changed to irritability. Jimmy Wilson castigated two of the stewardesses for their 'un-Christian'-like attitude towards pilgrims flying to Israel to retrieve the word of the Lord. The captain, concerned about potential litigation, came downstairs personally to apologise to Jimmy.

During the in-flight movie, in which semi-naked men and women posed as drug-dealers on the Miami beachfront to infiltrate themselves into a vicious gang of narcotics importers, Jimmy stood at the front of the cabin and, as images of the film danced over his body, shouted a vituperative harangue against the evils of Hollywood, the debasement of womanhood, the propagation of the glamour of a drug culture to young people and the evils of unbridled lust and sexuality outside the confines of a family group. Losing patience, and spurred on by complaints from other passengers in other parts of the plane who could hear the sermon, the chief steward asked him to sit down and allow the film to continue.

Jimmy was outraged. 'I'm gonna write to my congressman and tell him of the filth and pornography which you're peddlin',' he said, to the cheers of his supporters.

As the aircraft was about to land in Israel, the group again became animated. Flying over the harsh yellow solitude of the Negev desert, a murderous expanse of rock and wasteland, Jimmy looked down and shouted to his seventy followers, 'See here, down below, is where Our Lord Jesus trod and suffered for forty days and forty nights, wrestling with the Devil in this very desert. My friends, we are soon to be walking in the very footsteps of the Lord. I want you all to kneel down and silently pray to Him for forgiveness for all the sins that you have committed in your lives.' Seventy people dropped to their knees as the stewardesses tried to bring around cold washerettes to refresh the passengers.

As the giant plane finally shuddered to a halt, the group sang the hymn 'Onward Christian Soldiers', drowning out the stewardess's welcome to Israel in English and Ivrit.

It took an hour for the entire group to collect their baggage and to line up outside the customs hall to be met by the air-conditioned bus which would take them to the Regent Hotel in the New City of Jerusalem.

As the bus climbed the foothills leading up to the city, it passed dozens of burnt-out tanks, half-tracks and passenger cars left by the side of the road. Some were garlanded with flowers, others with signs. The bus driver explained that the fight to relieve the siege of Jerusalem by the Jordanian forces in 1948 had been vicious. The burnt-out vehicles were the remnants of the battle, monuments to the hundreds of martyrs who had died to save their starving brethren. Only a few in the bus were interested.

When the coach pulled into the driveway of the hotel, Jimmy emerged and a battery of lights burst into brilliance. Two reporters thrust microphones into his face.

'Dr Wilson, I'm from NBC. I'd like you to comment on your mission to rescue the Testament of Jesus from the Israelis.'

The other reporter shouted over him, 'Dr Wilson, I'm from ABC America.'

Jimmy turned to his group with a confident smile and settled down to a ten-minute interview while the bus-driver was unloading the luggage. The two reporters asked questions about the itinerary, about what the group hoped to achieve, and the chances of success.

'Why don't you reporters talk to some of my people here? These are like the Apostles of Christ, who have followed me and will be travellin' into the desert with me to find the word of Our Lord.'

The reporters smiled and moved into the crowd, thrusting microphones into faces at random. Hotel security officers looked on with bemused indifference.

When the reporters were lost within the thick of the group, Luke Carmody sidled over to Jimmy and whispered in his ear, 'Nice touch, huh!'

'Who are they?' Jimmy whispered back.

'Coupla actors I picked up. Came dirt cheap.'

'And the equipment?'

'Rented for the day.'

'What's the matter, Luke,' Jimmy asked, 'couldn't you get the real media to cover us? I would have thought this would be a big news item.'

'Boss, I reckoned that media coverage would be more useful later on in the trip. When we got something important to say about what we might have found, if you get my meaning. I didn't want to wear out my welcome with the local newsboys. It was my call. If I'm wrong, I'll apologise.'

'No, no. I'm not sayin' you're wrong. Fact is, this should get the tour off to a fairly impressive start. NBC and ABC. Good thinkin', boy.'

After the television crew had their fill of interviews, they cordially thanked everybody and the reporters, cameramen, light men and sound people packed their equipment. Jimmy collected up his group, who piled into the hotel reception area, ready to rest before the first prayer meeting in the ballroom later that night.

Francis' elderly Ford pick-up backfired, coughing out a cloud of black oily smoke as its wheels spat stones and dust in Daniel's direction, and turned right out of the *moshav* onto the dusty service road to make its long trip up the road to Jerusalem to buy supplies. In less than a minute, the dust settled, the noise disappeared and the sound in the air returned to the buzzing of insects and the mechanical hiss of irrigation sprinklers.

Daniel remained standing, watching the dust cloud behind the car disappear into the horizon. He ambled back to the shed laughingly referred to by Francis and Pazit Fine as 'the office'. On a *moshav*, any room with a telephone was designated as the office.

The interior of the tin shed baked in the heat. The light which angled in from the windows mixed with particles of dust. Only the telephone and the plastic chairs prevented Daniel from imagining he was in a Bedouin tent in the middle of the Arabian desert. The smells of animals, the acrid irritation of the dust, the timpani of the flies and beetles were those of Abraham, Isaac and Jacob. They were the currency of the early Israelites wandering nomadically through Sinai, or the peasant shelters of peoples who had disappeared from the memory of history millennia ago, people such as the Hapiru, the Edomites and the Nabateans. People who would have been lost from the memory of human experience were it not for their deeds being recorded forever in the august pages of the Old Testament.

As he entered, an eddy of dust flew in and danced a circular motion on the floor. Pazit Fine looked at him and said, 'Father O'Malley, you look just like a priest desperate for a cup of coffee.'

Daniel smiled. His conscience told him to tell Pazit that he was not just a priest but a prince of the Church.

'Pazit, that sounds like a wonderful idea. Won't you please call me Daniel?'

He followed her from the office to the refectory, where the cooks were preparing lunch. Two teachers had groups of boys in a classroom and those not being taught were working in the field under the supervision of older boys. It was like any day in any boys' school and any orphanage throughout the world. Daniel stirred his coffee thoughtfully and looked at Pazit. Her hair had been transformed from grey to a healthy and attractive black and was curled in a fashion not so wildly different from the style created at vast expense by hairdressers in Rome. She wore a red short-sleeved blouse and an attractive blue skirt which clung tightly, but not too tightly, to her body. Her battered Reeboks were replaced by an attractive pair of black moccasins. Perhaps this was the day she was due to go up to meet her lover in Jerusalem.

'It's my day off today. I was wondering if you'd like to spend some time having a look around the area? I'd be delighted to show you.'

'That would be wonderful, Pazit,' Daniel said, and smiled gratefully, 'but I thought that you normally spent your day off in Jerusalem.'

'I can give it a miss this once.'

'If you're sure you don't mind, I've not really had an opportunity to have a look over Francis' school since I got here. We've been too busy up in the capital.'

'What are you doing up there? He's become very secretive.'

'We're doing some research on a matter in which we're both interested.'

Pazit nodded and drank her coffee. When he was ready, he would tell her. Half an hour later, Daniel had changed out of his dog collar and lightweight grey suit into a Lacoste top and jeans. He walked across the courtyard to where Pazit was standing beside the 1963 Mercedes.

'You're a very attractive man out of your dog collar.'

Daniel was shocked by her directness. He had almost forgotten what it was like to be spoken to as though he were a normal, regular human being. Even if she knew he was a cardinal, he doubted whether she would speak to him in any other way. It was refreshing and invigorating.

She drove him around the borders of the orphanage estate. It was much smaller than Daniel had envisaged. But then everything in Israel was on a smaller scale than most people realised until they visited. The greatest work of intellect and philosophy which had been handed down from God to mankind, the Bible, was so thick with detail and contained such glimpses into the society of the Israelites and the early Christians that one would think the events took place in a land the size of America. Yet Jesus' travels around Galilee and subsequently into Jerusalem could be replicated by car in no more than a couple of hours.

From the school she drove north to the nearby village of Ma'ale. 'Do you want to stop for a cup of coffee?' she asked.

'No. Is it possible to drive down the escarpment towards Jericho? I remember that to be one of the most fascinating views in all Israel. I'd love to see it again.'

She laughed. Her laugh had a singular clarity like the tinkling of a bell. 'Daniel, I'll guarantee to get down there. But I give no guarantees about getting back up that hill in this old heap of shit.'

They drove north to the road which skirted Ranallah and continued towards the village of Silwad and then down the long winding escarpment towards Jericho.

He envisaged the area around Jericho as being central to the relationship between Jesus and John the Baptist. He was interested in seeing it through the eyes of a simple priest, rather than escorted around as a dignitary of the Catholic Church.

As the car drove closer towards the city, Pazit asked, 'Would you like some lunch before we go touring?'

'What did you have in mind?'

'Well, there are some charming little Arabic restaurants where you're guaranteed a cheap meal and food poisoning. Or I could buy us some bread, *houmous*, *t'china*, *kebbe* and *beira schora* and we could have a picnic in a little spot I know north of the old Allenby Bridge.'

It was unseemly for a cardinal to be picnicking with a divorced Jewish woman. He knew he should say no. 'I think it would be a lovely idea to have a picnic.'

The tray of sandwiches in the Cabinet room of the Knesset building was left virtually untouched. None of the twelve men in the room felt like eating, although stewards had been supplying pots of coffee for the past three hours. The Prime Minister nervously clicked and unclicked the point of his ballpoint pen.

'Well, I don't think anything more can be gained by just talking. I have to put out a statement. Just give me a summation from Shin Bet's point of view, will you, general?'

General Dov Baer reviewed the vast number of facts and condensed them into a few terse sentences to enable the Prime Minister to marshal his thoughts. He did not envy the man who would have to leave the Cabinet room and go to face a hostile world media. 'David Berg has gone to ground. We have raided the homes of fifty men and women who are known supporters, but no documentation or information has been found about the archbishop's kidnapping. We've been interviewing them all night and haven't been able to extract one shred of information. I'm one hundred per cent convinced that this operation was carried out on the sole orders of Berg, in conjunction with a maximum of four of his Zion Now! movement members. They kidnapped the archbishop, assaulted his secretary, rushed him into a blue General Motors stationwagon which is registered to one of the group's followers and Berg, the other kidnappers, the archbishop and the car have disappeared from the face of the earth.

'I have hundreds of men scouring every inch of every city, town and village in the country. We didn't have an inkling that this incident was going to happen because it was held so close to Berg's chest. That's all I can tell you, Prime Minister, until we get a breakthrough.'

The old man shook his head and looked at his Cabinet colleagues. 'And no one saw the car disappear or on the road? No one saw an old man being bundled into a building?'

'No one,' said General Baer. 'You've all heard the appeals we've been broadcasting every hour on the radio and television. We've offered massive rewards. We've got full-page notices appearing in all the newspapers in four languages. Every journalist in town has printed our request for information. It's as if he's just vanished into thin air.'

'But he can't have!' shouted the Prime Minister, banging his pile of papers. He looked in embarrassment at his colleagues. He hated losing his temper in public. It was a sign of weakness in leadership. 'This is going to cause the most terrible repercussions between us and the Christian community. As if we don't have enough trouble with Arabs demanding more of our land for their new state, this bastard Berg has opened up a Christian front.'

The young Minister for Trade, Jonathan Benyamin, asked, 'I still fail to see what Berg can gain. If he kills this archbishop he'll be imprisoned for murder. If he releases him he'll be imprisoned for kidnapping. The Pope's not going to bow to blackmail.'

'Who knows what goes through the mind of a *meshuggeneh* fanatic?' answered the Prime Minister. 'Every time I try to understand the mind of Berg, I keep thinking of the other bastard who killed the Muslims praying in Hebron. It's beyond my comprehension.'

'I think I may have an idea of what is going through his mind,' said the general. All the ministers looked at him with interest. 'Normally, in a kidnap situation, a ransom note is received within the first twenty-four hours. So far, there's been no ransom. The only reason that we assume it's Berg and the Zion Now! movement is because of what he did to the Church of the Holy Sepulchre. But what if he's really smart? What if he doesn't admit in public to having kidnapped the archbishop?'

He was interrupted by a howl of protests: 'But it's obviously him', 'Of course it's him. We all know that.'

The general raised his voice to be heard above the interruptions. 'We're assuming it's him. We have to prove he did it, to the satisfaction of a court of law. Capturing the archbishop is an implied threat to the

Pope to halt this Crusade idea of his. And that may or may not work. But this bastard's really clever. Look at the way he was released from prison after he desecrated the Holy Sepulchre, using a technicality in the judicial system. If we can't pin this kidnap on him, then there's no way that he will go to prison for it. I think he's trying to get the rest of the world to jump to his tune and he's got some scheme up his rotten sleeve to walk away from it, free as a bird. Knowing he did it is one thing, proving it another.'

Two days after they landed, the sixty wealthy parishioners and the support staff gathered in the ballroom of the Regent Hotel. Jimmy Wilson, dressed in a 1990s version of the safari suit, bounded down the aisle between the chairs and onto the stage. His followers whooped and hollered as he sprang onto the dais, arms high in the air, and shouted, 'Do you feel the power, the magic in the air? Do you feel the electricity, the positive vibrations around?'

They yelled out that they did.

'This is goin' to be *the day*, my friends. It's D-day. Discovery day.' More shouting and hollering. 'The day the Lord's goin' to bless us. Outside, I've got two air-conditioned coaches. They'll be taking us to Masada. We've got official permission from the Israeli government to go to the area and see what we can find. Who's gonna find it?'

They all shouted, 'Me!', 'I am!'

'Who's gonna bring it back and place it with their own hands into a new temple, which is right now, right this minute, being built beside our Chrome Cathedral?'

As one, they told him they would.

'Then let's go,' he shouted, jumping down to more hooting and hollering, running through the audience like a motivational speaker at a salesmen's conference. As they mounted the buses, Jimmy was pulled aside by Luke.

'You sure this is such a good idea, boss?'

'Son, I give the orders. You follow 'em.'

The buses left Jerusalem and trundled out into the glaring light of the desert. Even through the darkened glass, the elderly parishioners had to fan themselves and squint against the incandescence. The road through the desert towards Masada split, one fork leading to the Dead Sea approach to the mountain fortress from the east, the other through the desert, enabling visitors to ascend the hilltop by a ramp or a funicular from the west. Jimmy chose the shore, because the caves were more easily visible. After three hours, just before eleven o'clock, the coaches arrived and parked on the roadside looking up towards the cliff-face.

Everyone trooped out and gasped at the stupefying heat. The air burned in their throats, they grimaced at the stench from the Dead Sea, sweat broke out on their florid faces. Jimmy was delighted with the reaction. No one would want to risk staying outfor too long. They formed up beside the coaches, a straggly platoon of red-necked, rich, elderly Americans, in the alien environment of the man they called their own.

Like a field marshal, Jimmy said, 'This is where and when our search begins. I've prayed to Jesus Christ Almighty to show us a sign. Who knows, brothers and sisters, today He may be walking beside us.'

He directed the assembly into two parties, one under Harlin, the other under Luke. The plan was to wander the roadside until inspiration, the divine insight, struck one of the group. Then that team would climb to the cave and examine it.

Twelve o'clock, then one, then two. The straggle of elderly people, forced to return regularly to the coach for rest and refreshment, was beginning to lose hope and inspiration. Jimmy suggested a new tack—south along the road, rather than north. With renewed vigour, they set out again, latterday adventurers, US marines on the shores of Tripoli.

They rounded a bend and took a track up towards the escarpment. On either side, the rockface rose hundreds of feet sheer into the white sky. An elderly lady from Texas looked up and saw a cavemouth, twenty, maybe thirty feet above the path, hidden by a cleft in the face. Had she not peered up she would never have seen it. Her heart pounded in excitement and a dull light seemed to illuminate the deep shadow which hid the cave from all but the most observant.

'Look,' she shouted, pointing upward. 'There. The light. Do you see the light?'

The group stopped and looked up in silence. Jimmy forced his way through the throng, impelled by the urgency. 'Where?' he demanded.

Ten people pointed upwards, chattering excitedly. He looked from the cave, into the eyes of the woman from Texas. 'Mary Beth, do you feel anythin' unusual happenin' to you? Did you feel that somethin', some inner voice, has entered your body or your mind and caused your face to look upwards? After all, that cave ain't easy to see!'

'God bless you, yes, Jimmy. I felt the Lord descend and say to me to look upwards.'

'Praise the Lord,' Jimmy shouted and fell to his knees in the dust of the path. Uncertainly, the others in the party fell to their knees and Jimmy led them in prayer. After a minute, Harlin stood and said, 'Dr Wilson, who do you think should climb up into the cave?'

'Who here,' said Jimmy standing, 'feels worthy? Mary Beth, naturally. I should go, as Christ's disciple. You, Harlin, because of your youth and vigour.' He looked around and nominated nine of the younger members of the troop. As the rest watched, the twelve men and women climbed the rocky face, the older people, such as Mary Beth, helped by Harlin. Jimmy helped some of the others. One by one, they climbed into the cave. Harlin took out a flashlight to aid further illumination, though there was sufficient light in the cave to see most of the surface, except the nooks and crannies. They spent ten minutes giving the cave a cursory overview. They found nothing. Mary Beth became despondent.

'Honey, don't get upset,' Jimmy said to her. 'If it would have been easy, God would have led us to it sooner. Before we go, why don't we have one further look around. Say further down in the cave.'

'Careful of the floor,' warned Harlin.

The twelve followed the light of the torch, unsure where they were going. Mary Beth seemed to discover new strength as they walked deeper into the darker, cooler atmosphere.

She shone the torch on the roof, the side walls and the floor. She walked to crevices and investigated whether something might be hidden in them. As she walked with the torch away from the group, she plunged them into darkness. She explored like 'an inquisitive puppy, poking here and there. The rest of the group let her alone. And then she squealed with shock and delight. 'Here. Here. I've found it. I've found the Testament of Our Lord.'

The eleven others ran towards the light. There, on a tiny rock shelf, was a fragment of parchment. It was lying beneath thick layers of dust, but the edge was protruding. It was this edge that the torch beam had picked up. The eleven stood aside for Jimmy, who reached out, with trembling hands, and touched the edge of the parchment.

'The word of the Lord! I have touched the word of the Lord!' he shouted. 'Hallelujah, bless God Almighty. I am reborn! I am blessed! This day, I have touched the word of the Lord.'

The power of his prayer electrified the other men and women, who began to shout out praise to Jesus. Harlin reached over and, with his hand, carefully brushed away the chalky dust, uncovering more of the manuscript. It was obviously ancient, the script faded, the letters Hebrew or Aramaic.

Jimmy reached over and lovingly lifted it from the ledge. As though he was carrying a child to a baptism, he held the document in his hands and walked processionally to the entry to the cave. Looking down, surrounded by the eleven who had climbed up with him, he stood high above the path and announced that he, guided by the inspiration of Mary Beth, had recovered a document of the ancients. One which he would take back to Jerusalem so the experts could examine it and if, as he believed and prayed, it was the written word of God, he would lead the visitors back to California and install it in pride of place in the new Temple of Christ.

Everybody down below on the path was ecstatic. Everybody but Luke. He was worried about the effect on the group when the document was shown to the experts. Jimmy had told him yesterday their disappointment wouldn't last more than a couple of hours. That it would impel them forward with renewed confidence. But Luke wasn't that sure.

CHAPTER 17

Abram felt the sun searing the back of his neck as his leaden legs carried him further south, deeper and deeper into the wilderness beside the Sea of Salt. He was a man without will, walking stiff and aimless as though he was drunk or suffering a fever. Yet his mind was aware and alert to the danger from which he could not extricate himself.

It was as though he was in the bottom of a huge well of warm spit, surrounded on all sides by steep white walls. And the thick, acrid, pustulant water at the bottom of the well, warm like blood, white like death, was the only moisture in the whole damnable area. Water which he could not drink. Water which was deadly to the touch. Water created from the lowest regions of the bottom of the tomb of hell, the place where idol worshippers and pagans and men who committed abominations against the eyes of the Lord were cast down when they had been judged by God. Abram imagined demons and evil spirits looking at him from behind the hideous shapes of the rocks.

John of Syracuse had told him that travelling would be difficult but the old man didn't say how difficult it would be. Every footstep made him feel as though he was wearing boots with lead in the soles, as though his feet were covered with some sticky gum from a tree. The air was so heavy, even breathing was an effort. His muscles were tense and tired.

For the eighth time that morning, Abram looked in his sack, as though a miracle could occur and he would see again the ripe fruits and mouth-watering roasted meat that he had carried with him and eaten. All he saw were the dry remnants of his starvation. Why was he so hungry after eating so well just days ago? Perhaps that was it. Before En-gedi he had slowly run out of food and water and his stomach had got used to it. Then he had eaten like a lion and now he was hungrier than ever.

He did not know the distance from the rock where he was resting until he reached Masada. Neither did he know the distance from Masada to the southernmost tip of the Salt Sea. And there was still a long and dangerous walk uphill until the Gulf of Aqaba.

An hour later, two hours, and already the sun was beginning to weaken its grip. Flying high above were large birds. Vultures? No, they were too beautiful for vultures. Perhaps they were kestrels. Birds of prey, but noble, magnificent, not like carrion-eaters.

A kestrel plunged from the sky, falling like an arrow towards a rock ledge. Abram's eyes tried to follow its path but lost the bird as the background sky gave way to the sheer rock wall ahead. And as its path traversed the top of the cliff, Abram involuntarily called out a cry of joy. On top of the cliff, standing like an ancient monument against the sky was a series of towering buildings. Herod's Winter Palace. He was at Masada.

He faced south and started to walk. After a thousand paces, he stopped and examined the map again. High in the cliff were a series of caves. Three, four, eight, nine. Nine caves in all. John said that the Temple treasure was hidden in the third cave from the south. It was called the cave of Machpeler. Abram looked north and south along the road to ensure no one was watching.

He placed one hand carefully above the other and found secure footholds, aware, from his childhood experience of climbing rocks in his valley, of the danger of loose stones. Painfully, slowly, handhold by handhold, he found his way to the bottom lip of the cave. The white dust on the cave floor grew grey and dark as the cave flowed backwards into the hillside and out of the blinding light of the afternoon sun. He sat on the edge of the cave to rest and to recover his breath. Aware that he would be easy to spot from many leagues away, Abram rolled into the cave and hid in the shadow.

When his eyes adjusted to the dark, he stood and walked cautiously into the inner recesses of the small cave. As John predicted, they were there. Dun-coloured jars, like the jars the Romans sometimes used, with lids encased in black pitch to protect them. Excited, he counted how many. There were eight jars altogether. Jars half his height and as thick as the circumference of the grip of his arms.

He looked around for candelabra, gold and silver breastplates and the dozen other ornaments that John told him would be there, but found none.

He took out the knife he had been carrying and wiped it on his cloak. Carefully he cut into the hard, stone-like pitch and worked his knife around the lid of a jar. Using the thick end of the blade, he levered the lid off and looked inside. Other much smaller jars, similarly sealed with pitch stood inside the mother jar. These had writing on the outside. There were also several scrolls without protecting jars around them. He took one out, opened it and read the title. *These are the rules of conduct for the master in those times with respect of his loving and hating.*

He put that carefully back and searched through every other scroll within the jar. They were the same. Some, he recognised, were of the Prophet Isaiah, Jesus' favourite, some of psalms, some of tributes. None were of the Testaments that he had been told to find. He opened another jar and searched but was disappointed, for that too contained manuscripts which were of no interest to him. And the third, and the fourth, and the fifth jar.

But it was when he opened the sixth jar that his heart leapt. For this was different from all the other jars he had opened. The others had contained large scrolls used by the ancients in their prayers, but the sixth jar, the one which stood apart from the others, contained nothing but other small clay jars.

He put his arms around its neck and dragged it across the floor of the cave until it was close to the entrance where the light was better. The morning sun revealed a treasury. He took out the first jar from within and read its name: *The Testament of Nahum the Librarian*. Abram's throat constricted in excitement and his mouth felt dry. Nahum the Librarian. John of Syracuse had told him that Jesus' Testament would be amongst those of others within the community. People such as chief priests, teachers and librarians. Abram laid the testament reverentially on the floor and pulled out a second. *The Testament of Abimelach the Good*. Abram closed his eyes and tried to imagine a community in which Christ Jesus was surrounded by men like Nahum and Abimelach, before he left them and found the blessed twelve Apostles in Galilee. He placed the scroll beside that of Nahum.

Anxiously he took out the next and the next until only a handful of jars was left. His hand was sweating despite the dryness of the cave. He reached in and touched a cold metal object which tinkled. It was a silver bell. He took out another object. It was a golden pointer. He took out a small jar, different from the others, as though it was special. He read and re-read and read again the words on the outside: *The Testament of Jeshua the Nazarene*.

The small jar was tied with a leather strap buried in the bitumen seal of the lid. Abram re-read the name. *The Testament of Jeshua the Nazarene*. With trembling fingers, he held it to his lips and kissed the name. He cradled it to his bosom. He rocked backwards and forwards on his knees, incanting ancient prayers. Words from the depths of his memory, blessings connected and disconnected. It made no difference, for he was in rapture. For Abram held the very word of the very Son of Almighty God.

John of Syracuse had forbidden Abram to tamper with the Testament. He was not permitted to open the lid. He was permitted only to take it to the people of the Agau in the mountains of Ethiopia, from whom, one day, it would be recovered when Judea was free from the crushing heel of the Romans and the Kingdom of Peace had settled upon the earth.

He kissed the jar again and tenderly put it into his sack. He gathered up all the other small jars. John of Syracuse had insisted that he make a list so that, should a follower in the future seek to find his Lord's Testament, he would know that Abram had taken it and made it safe.

He had argued with John of Syracuse. Why make a list? It would mean that anyone wishing to find the Lord's Testament could do so easily. But John had smiled at him. 'Understand,' he had said, 'that on the road you tread many will also tread. But in your footsteps will follow only the faithful who understand our symbols. After you will come those who believe in the Word of the Lord. Only they will know that it is the Testament of Christ you have taken; only they will recognise the symbols; only they will follow. How are they to know where to look for our Christ's Testament if you do not leave a sign?'

John of Syracuse had explained how to write the code so that it could only be understood by the followers of Jesus. He was also told not to make the list too obvious.

Only a follower of the Nazarene must realise that the Testament he sought had already been found.

He took out the stylus and tiny ampoule of ink which he had carried and guarded since he left home. On a leather parchment given to him by John at the start of the journey, Abram wrote:

I, Abram, son of Raphael, son of Eliezar, have taken into my keeping the following, which are the words of God Himself as written in the days of the desert people called the Essenes.

From the cave of Machpeler,

one silver bell

one golden pointer

one book used by the anointed in the Holy Place within Jerusalem for the service of the Levites

one book used by the anointed in the Holy Place for the service of the Cohanim

and Testaments of the anointed for the afterlife of the following:

Isaac the Blessed

the Teacher of the Holy Congregation

Nahum the Librarian

Azriel, the Teacher of Women

Jeshua the Nazarene

Samuel the Just

Abraham, the Teacher of children

Abimelech the Good

and these treasures with loaves and fishes have I taken to the people of the Agau in the mountains of Abyssinia for safe keeping.

When he finished writing, he re-read his list. He had placed the name 'Jeshua the Nazarene' in the middle. Any Christian would know this was Jesus born of Nazareth who was the Messiah. If there was any doubt, the reference to loaves and fishes would be a signpost to the initiated, yet meaningless to Jews and Romans. He read the list a third time to ensure he had noted everything and put the leather fragment into the empty jar. Abram replaced the lid and laid the jar on its side so that it should not fall and break.

He carefully placed the bell and the pointer from Herod's Temple, and the scrolls and jars containing the Testaments into his sack and walked towards the cave entrance. Checking that there was no person on the road far below him, he climbed from the lip of the cave downwards to the Salt Sea. With a happy heart and invigorated steps, he walked south with his priceless treasure on his back towards the Gulf of Eilath.

His eyes bulged with tiredness and dehydration. His lips were swollen from the harsh sun. His legs ached from the joints of his toes to his thighs. Every step he took brought more pain. The sack he carried on his back seemed heavier and heavier on his shoulders. Yesterday he rested for an hour in the morning and an hour in the afternoon. Today he was resting every couple of leagues. He was no longer hungry or thirsty. That had passed days ago. His head was light and spinning. Every few steps he was forced to correct his path for he was wandering off the track and into the desert with increasing frequency and he knew without any doubt that were he to wander into the desert and not be able to find the path again, he would be dead within hours.

He shuffled like an old man, weaving from side to side like a drunkard. Maybe he was travelling ten leagues, maybe a hundred leagues a day. Or maybe he was merely walking a hundred paces before his body gave out in exhaustion, and his mind started to play tricks of distance. Maybe Masada was only just behind him and he would die on the path, visible to the ghosts who played still in King Herod's Winter Palace.

He forced his eyes upwards to see where the broiling sun was sitting within the sky. In the old days, in the days before Moses, man had believed that the sun was a god shining down on the crops and giving new life to the ground. But in the desert it was a merciless god. A god which killed. Why was he being tortured like this? Why was he being shrivelled like a raisin, starved like the skeletons he had heard about in the Roman dungeons in Caesarea Philippae? What had he done to deserve the punishment he was receiving? Why had John of Syracuse sent him to his certain death and why did not the Lord Jesus his Messiah, very God of very God, send down one of his angels or cherubim to give him food and drink so he could continue in his task and save the Lord's Testament for all time?

Abram struggled ten, twenty, thirty more steps. His knees buckled like a snared animal and gave way. He tumbled face first onto the ground. His face was buried in the sand and stones of the path. And as he breathed in, tiny grains of sand lodged in his nostrils. He coughed but there was no one to hear him. He was so tired. All he wanted to do was rest. To sleep and sleep. And to wake up the next morning in his cool bed beside the family's kitchen table, on his comfortable mat of straw and sheep's wool, and to see his mother smiling at him as his eyes opened and offering him a cup of herb water. To smell the delicious smell of freshly baked bread. And to see the pot of honey sitting on the table ready for him to assuage his ravenous hunger. He closed his eyes and the dream became a reality. He was back at last in his parents' home. He smiled as the sun beat upon his head and neck and arms and legs. He closed his eyes and fell into a deep, peaceful sleep.

He was still smiling when the small caravan from Jericho found him an hour later. The ten camels and twenty people gathered around the prostrate body and turned it over gently. The leader, ibn Saud, an Edomite, knew all about bodies found under the hot desert sun. He lifted up Abram's eyelids and saw that the eyes were still alive, though barely. He called for a flask of water and dipped the bottom of his *keffiyeh* into it. Softly, gently, he held the wet cloth over Abram's lips and squeezed a few drops. Like rain falling onto parched ground, it seemed to be absorbed the moment it touched his swollen, flaky skin. He squeezed a few more drops gently and with the rest of the damp *keffiyeh*, washed the boy's face.

He continued to squeeze tiny amounts of water into the boy's mouth for several minutes, cradling his head in his lap and ordering the rest of the people in the caravan to stand around to provide shade against the sun. Ibn Saud began to worry. The boy showed no response. Perhaps it was too late. Perhaps the gods had deserted him and taken their life force elsewhere. Perhaps the boy would soon be dead. But there was a momentary flicker in his eyelids and his body seemed to shift weakly in the cradle of ibn Saud's arms. The leader of the caravan looked up and smiled. Everyone understood.

Two hours later, Abram was well enough to be strapped to a camel and gently transported along the road to Eilath. Every five minutes a young boy who was walking beside the camel offered him a rag soaked in water to refresh the inside of his mouth. Ibn Saud knew that any food at this stage would kill the boy. Even water could be harmful if it were given in too great a quantity.

By nightfall the desert began to lose its heat and the caravan made its way into a wadi to stay the night. By this stage, Abram was able to sit up. He heard his own voice for the first time in weeks. It was harsher than he remembered. Communication between him and the group was difficult but they found the common tongue of Aramaic, which neither side spoke with proficiency, but well enough. One of the women found dried fronds and dead wood and was able to light a fire. In his honour, they slaughtered one of the few remaining sheep they had brought with them. Ibn Saud explained that as they were nearing the end of their journey and would be in Eilath the following day they could afford to eat well that night. The fire, the first Abram had enjoyed since En-gedi, was like a welcoming friend. The last few nights had been bitterly cold and had drained him of energy.

'Are you well enough to tell me why a boy travels alone through the desert?'

'I'm on a journey to Eilath. My parents could no longer afford to keep me at home and so I seek prosperity in Arabia.'

Ibn Saud nodded. He knew the boy was lying, but Edomites must not insult a guest at their campfire. 'And the sack you carry with you, it contained no food?' Ibn Saud knew it contained only old jars of no value and a few silver trinkets of some worth in the *shuk*.

Abram pulled his sack close to him for security. 'I ran out of food shortly after leaving Herod's Winter Palace at Masada. This contains nothing but old clothes.'

Again ibn Saud nodded. 'And what will you use to buy passage to Arabia?'

'I cannot afford to buy. I'm hoping to work on the ship in return for the captain carrying me.'

'If the gods will it, so it will be. This God that the Hebrews pray to, He did not look after you on your journey?'

'On the contrary,' said Abram, 'he brought you to me.'

Ibn Saud nodded again. The young boy pleased him. It would be a pity to sell him into slavery. When he recovered his strength, perhaps he could work for the caravan. But then, maybe not. A strong boy would fetch a good reward.

CHAPTER 18

The phone call was enigmatic. It had been late at night, and caught him off guard, otherwise Michael Farber wouldn't have agreed to meet this American minister for breakfast. He had read much about Jimmy Wilson in recent days in the news media. Fascinated by what the Pentecostalist would want with him, Michael had agreed to the meeting at Jimmy Wilson's hotel.

The waiter led him over to Wilson's table. He was seated with four or five others, some young, clean-cut college-looking boys, others older with the look of rich, conservative red-neck Americanism about them. All looked like the sort who thought they could purchase their place in Heaven with a chequebook. Jimmy looked up and saw a man approach. He beamed a greeting. 'Well, Professor Farber, how good it is of you to join us for breakfast.' They shook hands. Wilson had a strong, claustrophobic grip. He quickly introduced the other people around the table, speeding over the credentials of someone called Luke and someone called Harlin, and extolling the importance of Mr Larry Sarkin, a Californian computer millionaire and Mr Randy Nielstrop, a Louisiana rape-seed magnate, and Mrs Mary Beth Yablonski, widow of the Texas oil king.

Michael sat down and asked the waiter to bring him a cup of tea and some toast. He refused the pleas of the others to try the pancakes and hash browns. 'Reverend Wilson, what can I do for you? You said on the phone there was a matter you wished to discuss with me.'

'Professor Farber, I know you. You may think that odd, but believe me, sir, I know you. I know your work. I know your stature in the Bible community and I know that you're a convert from the children of Israel to the one true Christ.'

Michael was immediately irritated. He knew all about Jimmy, his radical fundamentalism and his noted anti-Semitism, but he kept quiet, and listened to his host.

'I'm sure you realise we share a mutual interest in the word of the Lord.' Jimmy didn't bother waiting for a response. 'Professor, I'm here today in Israel with sixty extremely influential, very important and financially secure American true believers in order to retrieve the word of the Lord from the desert and to repatriate it to California, where we'll build a shrine to house its great and glorious words. I heard you believe that the Testament is outside Israel—in Ethiopia—but I think this proves you wrong!'

Michael was careful not to let his astonishment show. How in God's holy name had this right-wing holier-than-anybody bastard learned about his and Judith's closely guarded hypothesis? He must have been followed when visiting the Falashas. From now on, he must be on his guard.

Jimmy reached down and opened his briefcase, which was on the floor next to his chair. He withdrew an ancient document which, with gentle motions, as though it were confetti about to blow away at any moment, he put into Michael's hands.

Michael looked at it carefully. The material was leather or ancient vellum or papyrus. On it was faded writing in old, probably Talmudic-period script. It was interesting, nothing more than could be picked up for a substantial sum from an antiquarian in the Old City of Jerusalem. Instinct told him it was genuine, possibly fourth or fifth century, maybe as late as eighth century, when Safed began to become prominent again. He read the faded script:

You ask why. It is because the Lord has borne witness against you on behalf of the wife of your youth. You have been unfaithful to her though she is your partner and your wife by solemn covenant. Did not the one God make her, both flesh and spirit? And what does the one God require but Godly children? Keep watch on your spirit and do not be unfaithful to the wife of your youth. If a man divorces or puts away his spouse, he overwhelms her with cruelty, says the Lord of Hosts, the God of Israel. Keep watch on your spirit and do not be unfaithful.

'I'm afraid, Dr Wilson, lady and gentlemen, that this document is from the Book of Malachi, one of the somewhat minor Prophets. How it came to be in a cave in the Negev desert near Masada is anybody's guess. It's an interesting, indeed a valuable document, but similar to many which can be picked up for the right price in the *shuk*.'

Mrs Yablonski and the other pilgrims seemed overcome with distress. Not Jimmy.

'Professor, you're an eminent scholar. I don't doubt you're right. Naturally, I'll have your view verified by other experts. But it don't alter one iota what it is we're doin' here. See, findin' this document, hidden in the dust of time, where,' he raised his voice to give solemnity to his next few words 'no one before us has been, tells me that the Lord Jesus Christ is guidin' our footsteps.

'Look at it this way. We found, sorry, Mary Beth found the document. The Lord God guided her hand. Now that means that His Only Begotten Son, Christ Jesus, is on our side and in His own good time, He'll lead us to His Testament. Look on this find as an initiation, a proof that we are His chosen vessel to find His Testament.'

The three rich Americans said, 'Amen.' The two younger men responded shortly after.

'Reverend Wilson, how do you think I can assist you in this task?'

'Naturally, we have examined biographies of every biblical scholar, from your friend Professor Wallenstein, to members of the International Team itself. Our view, Professor Farber, and this I believe is shared by each and every one of us at this table,' they all nodded, 'is that because of your origins as a Jew, and your later conversion to Christianity, you are the most eminently qualified person to help us in our mission. We'd like to offer you a substantial reward if you'll join us and assist us simple pilgrims in our God-ordained task.'

Michael tried not to laugh. 'Tell me something, Reverend Wilson. Which do you think will give you a greater chance of finding this document, paying me a hundred, a thousand or a million dollars?'

Michael looked at the younger men and saw them frowning. Jimmy smiled, appreciating the argument. 'Oh sir, I know that the amount of money we pay you makes no difference to our success. Knowin' the sort of man you are, you would do it for nothin'. What I'm sayin' is that you'll be searchin' anyway, but if you join us and lead the search with my party, you'll be searchin' with substantial material resources.'

'And what precisely will you do if we find Christ's Testament? Oh, forgive me, you've just answered that. You intend to repatriate it back to California. Do you not think the rest of the world deserves a look at it before you and your church become its keepers? You see, my vantage point is that of the scholar and the academic. Certainly, I'm a man who believes deeply in God, and as you quite rightly say, for the last nearly twenty years I've adopted Jesus as my personal saviour. But I have no greater insight into the workings of my Lord's mind than does any other man or woman alive today. My interest therefore is that of the public historian, not of the trader in the marketplace.'

Jimmy bridled at the insult. Harlin jumped in to prevent the situation becoming ugly. 'Mr Farber, it wasn't ever our intention to exclude the manuscript from the rest of mankind, but if it's money that will help to pay for its recovery, then we're the source of that money.'

Michael sighed deeply, wondering how to extricate himself from the encounter. There was only one way. Forgoing his tea and toast, he stood and said, 'I believe, if you read the first letter St Paul wrote to Timothy, you'll find something apt. The blessed saint said, *"The love of money is the root of all evil things, and there are some who in reaching for it have wandered from the faith and spiked on many thorny griefs."* Be careful, Dr Wilson, of thorns in the desert!' He turned on his heels and walked out of the restaurant.

The coaches had travelled from the Jezreel Valley in the north down the length of the Sea of Galilee to the ancient city of Jericho. Glimpsing the Dead Sea from the tortuous road which led down to the lowest point on the earth's surface, Jimmy had instructed the drivers to turn around and to take the entire party back to Jerusalem. 'Our unique and glorious first discovery, in which we simple God-fearin' folk beat hands down all the so-called experts and archaeologists, has astounded the world. We beat them all with sister Mary Beth's remarkable discovery of a priceless document in the caves in the formidable Negev desert where Our Lord Jesus wrote His Testament. We're goin' to seek guidance from Almighty God Himself as to where, in this small but glorious land, His only begotten Son might have placed His Testament.' With renewed vigour, the coach party whooped and hollered. Jimmy repeated the same message when he transferred to the second bus.

The coaches snaked upwards to the city and parked in tourist bays close to the ancient quarter. The Wailing Wall deep within the Old City of Jerusalem had stood as a silent sentinel to the passing folly of mankind for two thousand years. The ancient structure, peppered with prayers on folded scraps of paper where once the stones had lain flush together, was built by a man who was despised by the entire ancient Hebrew nation. The alien King Herod the Great, master builder, tactical genius and political intriguer, ascended to the Jewish throne in 37 BC, put there as a puppet of the Roman rulers, who had been trying to quell the recalcitrant Jews for a quarter of a century. Herod married the Hasmonean princess Mariame but, once secure, murdered his wife, her two sons, her brother, her grandfather and her mother. He installed puppet priests to the fury of the religious Jews and rebuilt the Temple of Solomon to cement his authority within the Jewish law.

Destroyed by the Romans after the first Jewish uprising in AD 70, the only structure remaining of the Second Jewish Temple was the western wall, which became known throughout the Jewish diaspora as the 'Wailing Wall', a symbol of sorrow and remembrance for an exiled, deracinated people. It was a symbol of the rawness of Jewish suffering and one of the few examples of Jewish architecture which survived from the times of antiquity until the beginnings of repopulation of Palestine in the late nineteenth century.

Leaving their air-conditioned buses, the sixty followers of the Reverend Dr Jimmy Wilson and his supporters walked to the Wailing Wall.

Within a stone's throw of each other stand the three great monuments to the great monotheistic faiths. The Via Dolorosa, in which the Christian Messiah struggled, tormented, with His cross to His crucifixion; the Wailing Wall of the Jews; and the gold-domed Mosque of Omar, the last place on earth where the Muslims' Prophet Muhammad rested before flying to heaven on his horse, touch each other at this pinpoint on the earth's surface. They are tangential in the centre of the Old City, structures beating within the old heart of God on earth. Jews, Christians and Arabs in Jerusalem have learned over generations the value of accommodating each other's professions of faith. Only on rare occasions have their conflicting emotions bubbled over and been used as fuel for the cauldron of Middle Eastern politics.

And Jimmy Wilson, better than even the most skilled of Middle East troublemakers, knew how to stir up trouble. And trouble meant publicity. And publicity meant new converts. The buses pulled to a stop on the ramp to the east of the Wailing Wall, overlooking the Kidron Valley, and the seventy fundamentalist Christians walked out, quietly chanting to themselves, 'Jesus is our Saviour.'

A crowd of children from a nearby *yeshiva* dressed like seventeenth-century Russian farm boys, looked at them with disdain. Every day, tens of thousands of tourists flocked to the Wall to destroy its peace and harmony and to take thousands of photographs. The students' *melamed* hustled them back inside the building to continue learning their *Talmud*.

The sixty parishioners and nine support staff followed Dr Wilson down the long ramp to the huge cleared expanse of ground in front of the Wailing Wall. There is no restriction placed on entry to the Wailing Wall by either the Jewish or the Israeli authorities. Any person is permitted to approach close to the Wall, though generally only Jews do so. Tourists usually stand back and take photographs.

But the Jewish faith demands a separation of men and women in prayer. Men prayed to the left and women to the right. Every Jewish couple who walked towards the Wall separated, the men to form a *minyan*, the women to join their sisters in prayer. The two huge areas of prayer in front of the Wall were separated by a screen known as a *mehitzah*. To the orthodox male Jews praying at the Wall, a woman encroaching upon their territory was an affront to their religion.

Jimmy had been told of this the previous day by Luke Carmody. The phalanx of fundamentalist Christians, men and women, walked confidently, heads high, behind their leader towards the Wailing Wall. The area was already full of devout Jews praying to their God. Nobody noticed the approach of the large group of men and women until they were already well within the confines for men only. Jimmy formed his small army into two lines and they marched singing 'Onward Christian Soldiers'.

The Hebrew incantations and prayers were interrupted by the hymn. The Jewish voices rapidly became silent, leaving the voices of the American Christians dominant. The silence of the Jews spread throughout the entire prayer areas of both men and women. People put down prayer books, men took their prayer shawls off their heads, women their scarves. Everyone turned around from the Wall to see what was happening. The Jewish silence continued, punctuated by the Christian hymn. Suddenly there was a crescendo of anger and the hymn was drowned by a hubbub of shouts, whistles, condemnations and shaken fists.

An elderly, grey-bearded rabbi handed his prayerbook to a young boy praying beside him and walked purposefully towards Jimmy. 'No, no, you can't come here. Not with women. You must go back. Go back now.'

Jimmy stopped and smiled at the old man. 'Brother, we are all children of God. We have as much right to pray in your area as you have to pray in ours. This holy site was once a place where our Lord Jesus of Nazareth, the Christ Messiah, walked into the Temple to turn over the tables of the money-changers and argue with your predecessors, the doctors of the law. And to claim this site as a site for Christian folk throughout the world.' His group behind shouted 'Amen'.

The rabbi didn't fully understand. 'This is *haKotel haMa'aravi*. Is for Jewish prayers only. You are *Noz'rim*, Christians, *goyim*. You cannot come here. This is for us only.' The old man began to raise his voice. His instructions were not being heeded.

'I don't want to quarrel with a brother under God,' said Jimmy. 'We both have our different ways to reach the Almighty. Ours is through the Lord Jesus. Yours is your own way. But brother, we have as much right to be here as you, and it's my intention to conduct a Christian prayer meetin' right here, right where the Lord Jesus Himself prayed to make the Jews see the error of their ways.'

The old rabbi continued to shout. A crowd began to move towards the strangers. It caught the attention of a handful of religious Israeli army soldiers in the crowd, as well as the hidden and deadly effective sharpshooters placed strategically on rooftops overlooking the Wall.

Israeli security, though often clandestine, was never far distant from sites of potential danger. When the alert went out and security forces started to move in, the orders were overheard on the jeep's intercom by General Dov Baer, who was on his way to a meeting in the Ministry of Defence and was taking a short-cut through the Old City. Knowing full well from previous experience how tinder-dry was the fuel of religious ferment, he arrived quickly to defuse the situation. As soon as his jeep pulled up, he leapt out and signalled to the twenty soldiers gathered on rooftops nursing sniper rifles that more should come down to reinforce the troops already on the ground. He marched over to the tall Westerner arguing with the elderly rabbi and said to him, 'My name is General Dov Baer. What's going on here?'

Jimmy turned and looked at the man. He also saw the dozen or so soldiers coming through the crowd.

'General, I'm the Reverend Dr Jimmy Wilson and I arrived in your wonderful country recently from Los Angeles, California. You may have read about our recent miraculous discovery in the desert. We're here on a mission to find the Testament of Our Lord Jesus. Before I take my group again into the Judean wilderness where Our Lord travelled, it is my intention to hold a prayer meetin' to gather further inspiration, here by the Temple where Our Lord Himself walked and overturned the money tables. Last time, we was so close. Next time, the Lord will guide us to the exact spot.'

'Reverend Wilson, we have dozens of churches in Jerusalem where you can happily hold a prayer meeting. This site is sacred to Jews. It is not appropriate to hold a Christian prayer meeting here.'

The rabbi nodded and began to speak in Yiddish to the general, who politely held up his hand to quieten the old man.

'General, I'm truly sorry, sir,' Jimmy continued. 'I'm a man of God, not a man of politics. But it is my intention to do what I said right here and now, and I will lead my followers in a prayer meetin' to pray to the Lord for guidance so that we can find His Holy Testimony. We have been guided by Jesus Christ Himself to pray in the very Temple which He tried to cleanse two thousand years ago.'

The paratroopers now stood behind the general.

'Dr Wilson, if you hold a prayer meeting here, you will be assaulted by Jews. If you attempt to go inside into the Mosques of Omar and Al Aksa, you will be assaulted by the Muslims. It's also very likely that the Orthodox Christians in Jerusalem will assault you for upsetting the fine balance of this place. Before you do any damage, I'm ordering you to leave now. You will immediately take these women out of this place for men only. You will go to any church that will accept you and you will pray to your heart's content. But you will leave now.'

Jimmy said nothing. Luke had promised that there would be television coverage of the incident. Television had not arrived. Instead, out of the corner of his eye he saw a young man take a black box off his shoulder and remove a camera. At least there would be newspaper coverage. And with Joe Deakin here, something might appear in the *LA Times*.

'General, you and I are at loggerheads. I respect your views. But you don't respect mine. If you'll excuse me I'm goin' to take my group over to the Wailing Wall.'

He turned back towards the Wall and pushed forward past the rabbi, who began to shout and spit. Jimmy's congregation followed him. The reporter and cameraman from the *Jerusalem Post* followed, taking pictures and recording the scene.

Dov Baer shook his head in wonder at the man's stupidity. Jimmy did not walk more than a dozen steps before the general barked a handful of commands. The soldiers broke into two groups and ran through the gathering crowd to interpose themselves between Jimmy and the Wall. When they positioned themselves, they formed a phalanx, their Uzi submachine guns slung over their backs, and raised riot-control pick handles to shoulder height. The murderous line of tough Israeli paratroopers faced the Christians. They stared at the pilgrims unflinching, waiting for an order from General Baer.

Jimmy's resolve began to fail him. He stopped and his group stopped behind him. General Baer walked forward slowly and stood in front of his men.

He said in a voice of command, 'Reverend Wilson, I'm giving you ten seconds to turn around, go back to your transport and leave this place. If you fail to do so, I will order my men to march towards you and force you out physically. You and your party will undoubtedly be injured. Then I will arrest you and your group for disturbing the peace. If you put up resistance, I will have you handcuffed and manacled and you will be dragged off to prison. Please believe I am very serious.'

The group huddled together in fear. The determination which they had enjoyed at the prayer meeting in the conference room of the Regent Hotel in the early hours of the morning evaporated in the face of stern-faced men with pick-axe handles and Uzi submachine guns. The crowd of orthodox Jews whistled and shook their fists and moved closer, menacing and threatening the group with physical violence. General Baer shouted an instruction to the crowd in Hebrew. They quickly responded by stopping their forward movement. Some retreated.

Jimmy Wilson shouted out, 'If it were just me, you could shoot me, and my soul would ascend to Heaven, pure as driven snow, singin' the words "I am walking in the glory of the footsteps of my Lord". But I will not let you Israelis harm Christian people who have come here with the God-given task. of retrieving Our Lord's Testament. You, General Baer, will get your reward in Heaven when you are judged by Jesus Christ Himself.'

The group, made defiant by his words, shouted 'Praise the Lord' and 'Amen to that'. They stood there facing each other for the ten seconds allowed by General Baer. Still Jimmy did not move. General Baer gave an order to his troops. He asked one of the paratroopers to give him his two-way radio and ordered two detachments of police into the area.

Jimmy turned to his group, held his arms outstretched and intoned, 'Now is the time for us to retreat in the face of a powerful and unrelenting enemy, as Jesus Himself would have done. Tomorrow will be our day. Brothers and Sisters, back into the coach.' They turned and walked away.

That night, the story was carried by the evening newspapers and was mentioned on Israeli television, using stock pictures of the Wailing Wall and a library shot of Jimmy Wilson. By the following morning there were headlines and pictures throughout the world of the first Christian assault on the Temple of the Jews since the time of the Crusades.

It was four in the morning when the black, dusty old lorry rolled out of the streets of Afula and took the little-used road to Mount Tabour. The lorry carried a load of oranges collected from a nearby *kibbutz*. The lone driver, a cigarette stuck to his bottom lip, unshaven and with sleep in his eyes, wore a blue *koua tembel*, the conical hat of the *kibbutznik*. The dim headlights of the old lorry did little to pierce the darkness more than twenty metres ahead.

The lorry trundled up and down the slopes until it reached the junction of the Haifa to Tiberias road, which it crossed on its way north to Safed. When the lorry reached the intersection of the Akko to Capernaum road, it turned right towards Lake Kinneret and left the road to struggle up a nearby hill, a hill which overlooked the ancient Sea of Galilee. The driver stopped the lorry, ensured that the brakes were firmly on so that it didn't slip down the hill, and cut the engine. He looked around to ensure that there were no lights in the vicinity, either from cars or houses.

He listened carefully for any noises or other human sounds, but there were none. Just a gentle sighing wind which rustled the grasses and made the branches of the nearby trees sway in rhythmic motion. The driver knocked on the back partition and got out of the cab, carefully closing the door without slamming it. Two men stood up and lifted a huge wooden cross from the bottom of the lorry, where it had been covered over with oranges. They passed it down to the driver, then jumped down to help him carry it up the hillside. The driver reached back to the cabin and took out a pick, shovel and crowbar. He ran back to where the other men were standing and began digging a narrow, deep hole in the ground, narrow enough to take the wood of a vertical cross. When he had excavated three feet down, he nodded to the other men. The two men allowed the driver to take a draught of water before they climbed back onto the tray of the lorry. From under the huge pile of oranges they excavated the dead body of Hiram Solomonoglou, his face stiff and waxy in the moonless night air, his clothes dusty and stained from the oranges. They carried the dead man's body to the cross, where they tied his arms to the horizontal beam with thick ropes, and his feet to the vertical beam. Struggling under the heavy weight, they manoeuvred the base of the cross above the deep narrow hole and as they raised it into the vertical position, it slowly began to slip in, accelerating as they levered it higher and higher until with a final thud, it came to rest. It was held by two of the men as the third filled in the hole and trod down the earth until it was firm around the base.

The three stood back to view their handiwork. Avi shook his head in disgust and self-loathing. He hissed at David Berg, his voice carrying in the pre-dawn silence. 'You're a despicable man to have conceived of this idea. Call yourself a man of God! I call you a man of the devil.'

'The end, Avi, justifies the means. Would you not have done the same thing against Adolf Hitler, or Saddam Hussein?'

'This man is no Hitler. Unlike you, Berg, he was a real priest.'

David Berg ignored the remark and muttered a silent prayer into his beard while Vladimir begged them to turn back to the lorry. They drove away south to Tel Aviv, praying they would not meet any Israeli police patrols or road blocks. As the lorry left the hillside and entered the road, the noise and dust from its wheels slowly settled, leaving the dead eyes of Hiram Solomonoglou closed to the obscenity of his crucifixion.

That morning the body was discovered by a farmer and the area cordoned off. General Baer personally flew by helicopter to the area and supervised the removal of the archbishop's body.

His revulsion at the obscenity threatened to overwhelm his need to be dispassionate. He also needed to calm the loathing of the men under him, who were noisily swearing oaths and threats against Rabbi Berg and his followers. The man had to be caught and brought to justice. Above all else.

CHAPTER 19

Jimmy Wilson sat up with a gasp, sweating, his pyjamas clinging to his body. He searched the blackened bedroom for the source of the noise. The phone by the side of his bed rang again. He felt as though he was suffering from a fever. He would remember the dream if he could, but the phone ended the delicious night-time thoughts. Angrily he reached over and snatched it off its cradle.

'Yes?' he grunted, his voice dry and rasping.

The momentary delay told him it was an international call. And there was the familiar echo as he heard his own voice a fraction of a second later.

'Is that Reverend James Wilson?' asked a deep voice, thousands of miles away.

Jimmy's mind, a moment earlier a confused fog of sleep and dreams, was now awake. 'This is Jimmy Wilson,' he said. 'Who in hell is this callin' me? Do you know what time it is, for God's sake?'

'James Wilson?'

'Jimmy Wilson! Who in hell are you?'

'Detective Curtis Munroe, LAPD.'

'Who? Who'd you say it was?' Jimmy's mind was aware of reality even though his body was still numb after sleep.

'Curtis Munroe. Los Angeles Police. I'm a detective with homicide. Are you Reverend Jimmy Wilson?'

'I am he,' said Jimmy, now wide awake. 'What you want, Munroe? You sure you know who you're phonin'?'

'Jimmy, I'm currently investigating the murder of a man name of Jonas Watkins.'

'Who you callin' Jimmy?' he asked angrily, but the officer repeated.

'It's about the murder of Jonas Watkins.'

'I've given statements to your superior officer. A captain! I've nothin' more to add to what I've already said about that poor dear man and the person who killed him. Whoever that was.'

'New evidence has come to light, Jimmy, which makes it fairly imperative for me to talk to you.'

'What new evidence?' asked Jimmy, as the phone froze in his hand. He felt prickles under his armpits.

'I don't want to go into that over the phone. Let's just say that enough new evidence for me to bring a murder charge against you, a man called Harlin Brown and another man called Luke Carmody, as well as two other white dudes whose names I don't currently have.'

Jimmy's voice failed him. In the silence, the American detective continued. 'Now you can do one of two things, Jimmy. Either you can come on back to LA and answer my questions or I'll fly over to you and investigate you on the spot. You hear that, boy?'

'What new evidence is this?' Jimmy asked, his voice returning. 'Don't you play games with me! How dare you accuse a man of God of so heinous a crime? And who's given you this evidence? And who in hell you callin' "boy"?'

'Come on now, Jimmy,' the detective laughed. 'You may think we're all stupid dumbass hillbillies, but we're not. You don't seriously think I'm gonna tell you who our source is so you can do to him what you done to poor Jonas, now do you? See, fact is Jimmy, I could have done this real quiet and had my friends over in Israel just simply come and arrest you, or I could have got an extradition order and come over there for you myself. But I thought that a couple of gentlemen like us could deal with this nice and quiet over the phone. See Jimmy, over here, it's the middle of the night. Ain't nobody listening to what I'm saying, or who I'm saying it to. And the best news, Jimmy, is that my phone ain't tapped. Wonders of modern science, old buddy. This is a cellular phone.'

Jimmy listened in rapt attention. What in the hell was this man talking about? Arrest? Extradition? Did he know or was this a fishing expedition?

'Now you listen to me. I don't know who in hell you are. And I don't want to know. If you think you've got some proof of my involvement in the death of that pathetic boy, then you present it to a court of law, but if you don't get off this phone right now, I'll have you busted down to a rookie.'

'Jimmy, here I am trying to be nice to you, trying to help, trying to get you out of a fix and you're putting on an attitude. Now that ain't nice, is it, boy?'

'Stop callin' me boy!' he screamed. 'And what do you mean "tryin' to help"?'

'You're a really well respected man, Jimmy. You got a bit carried away, that's all. Way I was told it, first you did over your wife. She deserved it, adulteress and whore. Then you kicked shit out of that poor niggerboy. Now I understand why you done over your wife. Woman shouldn't fuck a nigger. Not a white woman. But the nigger? Jimmy, that was a real bad thing to do. But like I said, you're really well respected in California and in the rest of America. And here you are over in Israel trying to strike it rich for the USA, doing the good Lord's work. I don't want this to get out of hand, Jimmy. I'm sure we can contain it and come to some arrangement.'

'And what sort of arrangement is that, Munroe?' asked Jimmy, starting to feel relief drain the tension from his body.

'That's something you and me can talk about when you get back here, Jimmy, but I'd have to say I'd be wanting at least six figures. There's going to be a lot of expenses, keeping your name outta this.'

'If I agree, I want the bastard's name.'

'You'll get the name, Jimmy, soon as I get the money. You can deal with him personally if you want. After all, he's a good friend of yours.'

Jimmy gasped and clutched the phone tighter. 'Duane?' he whispered.

'No, not Duane. I spoke to Duane. I spoke to your wife. They shut up tighter than clams. No, somebody else in your church, someone you know and trust. Anyway, Jimmy, I think we understand each other well enough now. Should be coming up to first light where you are. See if you can catch another couple of hours' sleep before you get back to searching for what it is you're looking for. Oh, and Jimmy, if I die, all the information I got's safely sealed away in the offices of a couple of attorney friends of mine. Know what I mean?'

The phone went dead. Jimmy looked out of the window and saw the sun beginning to rise over the mountains of Jordan. He put the phone down and picked it up immediately to speak to Luke Carmody. If he moved quickly enough, he could contain the damage and there would be one dead detective in Los Angeles that night. That bullshit story about the attorneys was straight out of a TV cop show.

And when he'd dealt with Mr Curtis Monroe, he'd begin a witchhunt throughout the church to establish who it was that knew. And the witchhunt would make the trials at Salem look like a Saturday night TV quiz.

Thousands of miles away in California, Micah Watkins disconnected his mobile phone. The call was untraceable. He looked at the taut face of Annabelle Wilson anxiously sitting in the corner, her body huddled into itself through strain. Her face was beginning to return to its original shape and the bruises and welts were slowly disappearing.

He looked at her and smiled.

'Well?' she asked.

'After what that sonofabitch did to my brother, I'm gonna take him for all he's got. He's so shit-scared, I'll get my momma and poppa set up for life.' The huge man smiled. 'You know, all my life I've avoided getting involved in drugs, and armed holdups, and that shit. Now, listen to me, talking about extorting money.' He laughed dryly. 'Who'd have believed it?'

'But Micah, honey, you ain't takin' money from an innocent. That man won't never go to prison and fry for the murder he done. He'll buy the best damned lawyers and judges in town. Only way we can make that sonofabitch suffer is to take away the thing he prizes most. That's money and his goddamned church. You take him for all he's got. You pay your momma and poppa for their grievous loss. For me, honey, I don't want nothin'. I don't want his filthy blood money. I just want to be rid of him. I'll let you get the money and then I'm goin' to call the police. Tell them what that motherfucker did to me.'

Micah nodded. 'I ain't sure 'bout all this blackmail. Maybe we should both call the police. If you're with me, they might believe us.'

'No, sugar. You get what in hell you can out of him. Take him down for everythin'. *Then* I'll call in the cops.'

'To think that Jonas loved that man.'

'Loved and hated. He loved him 'cause he took him out of the slums. He hated him for what he did to me. And for the hypocrisy.' Annabelle's eyes became moist. 'Oh, God, what're we gettin' ourselves into?'

'You havin' second thoughts?' he asked.

'Some. I just don't know if I've got the guts for all this. Maybe . . . maybe you should forget about me and go to the police straight away. Maybe that's the best thing to do.'

'Ma'am, I live in a town that beats niggers to death for traffic violations. They ain't gonna believe me. Mr Wilson's too well connected for me to do things proper. This is a case where I gotta take the law into my own hands if I'm gonna get justice.'

Pope Innocent lay prostrate on the floor of his private chapel. He prayed for the Holy Spirit to imbue him with that same quality of faith as was enjoyed by Daniel Rhymer and the other good men of Catholicism. He had been born into a God-loving family, not a God-fearing one. As a child, he had faith. Every night and morning, he would commune with Jesus, discuss matters with him, wander down the road to school talking about the difficulties he was having with his work, praying with Him to intercede on behalf of his large and loving family.

Faith in Jesus had been part of him when he entered the seminary, forgoing forever the joys of creating his own family and the ineffable comforts of a wife and children. And there was no diminution of faith when he took the vows of priesthood, and listened to the confessions, some great, some small, of the people whom God had given to him as his flock.

But his faith had been dealt a severe shock on the day he became a bishop. He had even been prepared to walk away from the Church, turn his back on Jesus. But his cardinal had begged him not to. Implored him to make no decisions for a year, just do the job, get on with life,

and put to one side the burning issue which was engulfing his heart. He had taken the cardinal's advice. After a
year, his faith started to return, but it was never as deep,
as unqualified. There was no longer that intense clarity,
that absolute certainty. Would he ever be rewarded by
God with a return to a burning faith? Perhaps this
miracle in the desert would be the long road back to the
way he used to be. Perhaps this was God's signpost to
him and to those others whose faith had been side-
tracked along the way towards God

As he lay on the floor, Pope Innocent prayed for that
wisdom which had turned so many of his predecessors
into the spearhead of the Catholic Church. As the time
he had held the papacy grew longer, as the workload
increased and the decisions became harder, Gabriel
Molloy, Pope Innocent, felt increasingly unworthy of his
ascension to the Chair of Peter and felt unworthier still
as he steered the vessel of his Church through the shark-
filled waters of Vatican politics.

The rest of the world could take care of itself. He
could come to terms with liberationist priests in Chile
and Argentina or with ultra-conservative bishops in
Holland and Switzerland, or the Jesuits or the Maronites.
He could quell the wildly beating hearts of the Irish and
the Filipinos. He could debate with kings and princes,
Anglican archbishops and rabbis, witchdoctors and
voodoo workers. But God protect and save him from his
own advisers within the Vatican. The Italians versus the
Germans. The Spaniards versus the Asians. The blacks
versus the whites. The forces for conservatism versus the
forces for liberalism. The pro-contraception lobby versus
those who demanded anti-contraception. The schisms
went on and on. Irreconcilable, enervating. And he, as
supreme pontiff, as Bishop of Rome, as tenant of the
Chair of St Peter, as the man with the keys to the

Kingdom of Heaven, was supposed to have all the answers. And no one knew that he was an empty vessel, faithless, hollow. Did they not realise that he was just a man? That because he was elected six months previously he was no more than he was when he was a cardinal and a bishop before that. And once a simple parish priest.

He called upon his old friend and mentor, Jesus of Nazareth, to lay His hand upon his head and bestow upon him the wisdom that He had shown in dealing with the doctors of law and the Pharisees within the Temple. Was it so much simpler for Jesus? Were things easier in His day than they were today, or was Gabriel Molloy a man of such little value that he could not solve the simple questions besetting the ship of which he was now captain?

He continued to lie, arms outstretched, on the chapel floor, his forehead touching the deliciously cold marble mosaic, while his personal retinue sat respectfully waiting in the dark shadows of the cloister. They ached to show this simple, godly man that their love for him must allow them to aid him in his tasks. He had already earned the love and devotion of millions of the poor throughout the world. Now they must show him how to earn the love of the powerful. The more they tried to help him, the more he smiled and blessed them and told them that he would rather do things than impose them upon others. He was working himself to death, yet nothing any of his staff said would convince him to share the load. Not even his closest friend Daniel Rhymer was capable of convincing him of the need to delegate.

His staff were joined by two of the most senior cardinals in the Curia. The young men stood as the prelates silently walked in but the princes smiled and waved them back into their seats. Everyone gazed at the prostrate form of the American on the hard floor of the chapel and admired the Pope's silent devotion. They recognised that this was not a man whose devotion was put on for public scrutiny but was from the very depth of his heart, from his being, from where his faith began.

After ten further minutes of prostration, Innocent got up from the marble floor to kneel before the crucified Christ high above the altar. Then he turned towards the apse which would take him back to the rest of his private apartments where his day would begin. As he turned, he saw Cardinals Braschia and Luchetta. He flushed in embarrassment. He walked over to them.

'Eminences, good morning. I was just praying. Will you join me for breakfast?'

Sitting in the Pope's private apartment, with its frescoed walls and its Aubusson tapestries, it was easy for the two cardinals to forget that this Church reigned over the lives of a billion people, most of whom were impoverished and millions on the point of death from starvation. But the Pope did not forget. He would have loved to sell some of the treasures of the Vatican to give the money to the poor; but the plan he put up was dismissed out of hand by the Cardinal who controlled the Pontifical Commission for Preserving the Patrimony of Art and History.

'So, eminences, to what do I owe this unexpected but delightful surprise?'

Innocent's Italian was excellent, though his American accent was appalling. Braschia looked questioningly at his colleague. Innocent was surprised. He would not have expected subterfuge from these two. They were widely regarded as jovial, liberal, good-natured clerics.

'Holiness, my brother cardinal and I are troubled. We wish to seek your advice.'

The Pope nodded, willing him on. Braschia cleared his throat.

'Let me ask you a hypothetical question,' he asked. 'Assume that a family, say a poor American Catholic family in the backwoods of Florida, has parents with many children. And say that three of these children get together and begin discussing the affairs of the father.'

The Pope nodded. Luchetta picked up the theme and continued, 'Let us now say that one of the brothers was trying to influence the others to act against the father's interests. He believed that he was acting for the good of the family, yet the other brothers believed that the father was the one who should determine the direction in which the family should follow.'

'And your question?' asked Innocent.

'Should the two brothers inform on the third?' Braschia answered.

'Have the two brothers sworn an oath of secrecy?'

'No, holiness. Not an oath. But before the conversation started, the brothers gave the assurance that their conversation would be held in confidence.'

'Then a confidence cannot be broken,' the Pope nodded sagely. 'But I'm sure this American father is perceptive enough to keep open his eyes and his ears to listen for the sounds of disharmony and dissent within his family. Any good father knows in advance when problems are arising. With the aid of the entire family, no problem is so great that it cannot be adequately handled. And the miscreant brother will soon be made to see that the majority of his family is opposed to his conservative ideas.'

The two cardinals smiled at the Pope. 'Eminences, another cup of coffee?'

When the two Italians left the papal apartments, Innocent reflected on what had been implied. After careful deliberation, he went to his delicately sculptured maplewood writing bureau.

Innocent regretted his inadequacy, sitting at the desk, the very desk at which the saintly John XXIII wrote the Bull *Pacem in Terris*, extolling forever the dignity of man. What was that wonderful line from Coleridge's 'The Friend': 'The dwarf sees farther than the giant, when he has the giant's shoulder to mount on.'

How true that was of him. A dwarf from the New World, with its brashness and superficiality, pontificating to the Old World which resented its institutions being confronted. He turned and again marvelled at the Renaissance frescoes, the flowering of minds steeped in a thousand years of culture and tradition. What could his New World offer? Energy? Innovation? Perhaps, but surely what was needed was a diminishing of the barriers. There should be no 'New' and 'Old', just as there should be no 'East' and 'West' or 'North' and 'South'. These were artificial barriers created not by geography, but by politicians.

And men like Franz Kitzinger.

Innocent picked up his pen to write to Dan Rhymer, warning him of what Kitzinger was up to. But he put down the pen, deciding to pray first, in order that his words might accurately reflect the situation and that God might guide his thoughts. Gabriel Molloy was used to living with doubt. He had suffered two other tests during his life. In both he had failed, shown himself to be unworthy of the offices which Christ had thrust upon his shoulders. The first was his failure to help his sister; the second, fully to reconcile his lack of faith. His faith had once been so strong, but how could he believe as fervently in a Church which forced him to treat his sister in that way? To put the interests of a rapist above the interests of the pure and darling girl.

He'd walked away from the filthy cell of the filthy man feeling unclean within himself, defiled by his act of forgiveness. Yet, it was what the Church demanded, what he had been trained for—to give forgiveness to the sinner as Christ forgave the iniquitous. But he was no Christ. He was more like a doctor in a clinical white coat, telling anxious relatives to put their faith in God, then expunging their grief from his mind and dealing with the next body, getting on with the next job. That's all it was. A job! His faith, once so burning and impatient, had devolved into well-explored phrases, happy little confidences, easygoing homilies. His impotence over his sister's suffering made Gabby realise that he was little more than a travelling salesman of faith and hope, a carpetbagger, wandering the byways of frantic humanity, offering a bit of consolation here, a morsel of forgiveness there. A hollow man.

He wailed to his cardinal, but not even his assurances came close to breaching the gap which had grown between duty and faith. It was all he could do to keep sane. He was riven by guilt and paralysis—guilt because the Church had forced him to chose between the well-being of his sister and the spiritual needs of a depraved denizen from Hades, paralysis because he wanted to destroy the man who had destroyed Bernadette, but his hands were bound within the straightjacket of his vows.

He had to get away. Escape was his only recourse. He didn't dare face Bernadette again, not so soon, not after she had denounced him as vehemently as Savonarola condemned the heretics. She had raised an impenetrable barrier between them.

Gabriel had wandered far away in body and spirit. He hung up his bishop's vestments the day after his ordination and drove north towards Canada. He just kept driving, seeing nothing, speaking to no one. On the second day, he was sitting in a run-down drive-in foodbarn which served bitter watery coffee. He'd been sitting there for three hours. The waitress kept bringing him more coffee. The manager was about to call the police. The guy looked like a bum on drugs, unshaven, eyes glazed, staring for hours at a saucer. Then he moved. He took the tiny crucifix from his lapel, left it in the saucer and got back into his car. The manager shrugged. Bums! You never could tell. He put the crucifix in the cash register, in case the bum came back to collect it.

Gabby communicated with nobody. He didn't pray, go to church, confess or attend Mass. He was so utterly bereft, so beyond the help of the Church that had turned its back on his sister, that he wanted nothing more to do with the institution.

After a month of driving all over northern America, sleeping in barns, or in small hotels where the owner didn't ask questions, he arrived at a tiny hamlet. It was a small, impoverished backwoods community on the Canadian border. Gabby was running out of money. He easily found work as a janitor in a fly-blown motel. His body was relaxed, but his mind was still riven by irreconcilable forces. Yet it was in the inauspicious hamlet in the middle of nowhere, under the auspices of an old, stolid and forgetful priest, that the future pontiff of the Catholic Church slowly began to conflate duty with creed, and return to the bosom of the faith he had once held so close to his heart.

The motel owner happened to be a Catholic and, over coffee, told his old priest that there was a new man in town. 'No,' said the motel owner, 'I don't know whether he's Catholic or Protestant. Could be a Muslim for all I know.' Sitting alone in his room, staring at the peeling wallpaper, Gabriel Molloy was visited by the local parish priest, an elderly asthmatic who wheezed his way on a bike through dispiriting woods and roads in all weathers to tend to his parishioners. The priest visited Gabby in his tiny room above the kitchen. Gabby welcomed him in. He admitted that he was a Catholic but that his faith had wandered.

'Something bad happen to you, did it, my son?' said the priest.

'Not me, father. It happened to a relative. I'd rather not go into it.'

'Why are you taking it out on God? He's here to help you.'

'Because I can't any longer bear the immorality of man. How can there be a God protector who allows such evil to be rampant on the earth which He's created? Wasn't Jesus sent down by God to expiate our sins?'

'And who are you to tell God how to behave? How do you know what His purpose is? Maybe He sent this evil thing to test you. To make you into a stronger person.'

'Please, father, don't use such simplistic arguments with me,' Gabriel said. 'I've been driving around, thinking about nothing else. I can't resolve it in my mind. Paraphrasing naive philosophy isn't going to help.'

'Naive, is it? Well, Mr Smartpants, if it's so naive, how come some of the greatest minds ever to have lived believe precisely in what I'm saying? Minds like St Luke, St Mark—'

Gabriel sat up in his chair and stared at the priest. All the vehemence which had been growing in him during the past month of solitude erupted. 'And what help are the blessed saints when it comes to starving orphans and widows? When decent men and women are brutalised in wars fought in the name of our God?'

The old man shook his head in sadness. 'St Paul said—'

'I know what St Paul said, father. And it no longer helps me. And I know what Descartes and Spinoza and

Locke and Epictetus and Plotinus said about the Divine Nature in itself. God for God's sake. Well, not for me! Not right now, anyway. I've got a lot of thinking to do for myself, not the second-hand philosophies of men who never experienced a world like the one we live in. Who never witnessed the bestiality of mankind.'

'And you can't do your thinking within the bosom of the Church, where you've got people who care for you, worry about you?'

Gabby smiled at the old man's innocence. As a monsignor, he'd had responsibility for dozens of priests within his bishop's diocese. Men like this old priest were two a penny. Burnt out with work, weary from a life-time of tending the needs of others, perplexed from lack of bodily comfort and warmth, driven to drink like Graham Greene's whisky priest because the bottle pro-vided a more ready and accessible comfort than faith. Yet men like him were the pillars upon which the estate of the Church was built. Gabby could demolish his arguments in seconds, quoting arcane and formidable philosophy that the old man would never have read, let alone understood. But to do so would be the act of an intellectual bully. And the old priest had what Gabby, with all his knowledge, lacked so badly—unquestioning faith.

'Father, one day I may come back to the Church. When that day will be, nobody can foretell. Let's just maintain our faith in eschatology.'

A silence descended on the room. 'Bit of a philoso-pher, are you then, my son?'

'I know enough philosophy to know that it's of no use against the barbarity that we see every day in the world. That while the great philosophers were idly contem-plating, they closed their eyes to the hideous realities which were going on around them.'

'And what can we bring to bear in the fight against barbarism if not reason, goodness and truth?'

'Oh please, father, you sound just like a Superman story. Truth, justice, and the American way. Well, there is no Superman. Not even Nietzsche's.'

'Go back to your philosophy, son. You'll find the answer there.'

Gabriel laughed. 'I was reading a work of philosophy on the day that I realised the Church couldn't help me or someone I loved when we most needed help. It was,' he searched his mind, back to the hideous hours after his enthronement, '*The City of God* by St Augustine. Ever read Augustine, father?'

The old priest coughed apologetically and said, 'Many years ago, son. When I was in the seminary.'

Gabriel was concerned about embarrassing the priest, but continued, 'Augustine spent much of his life after his conversion preoccupied by the nature of evil. *The City of God* is an apologia of human history seen in a spiritual light, a rebuttal against paganism. It wasn't until just now that I wondered why he'd wasted so much of his time.'

'I'm not with you, son.'

Gabriel sighed. 'An animal, a filthy rapist destroyed my sister. He raped her. And I couldn't comfort her. I had to follow the dogma of the Church. That evil man's wanton actions showed the world which St Augustine wanted to re-create on earth to be pretty ineffectual. And I'll tell you another thing, father. Just six months ago, I was reading René Descartes' discourse about the intellect of God. That was a time when everything was going right for me and my family. Before the disaster. D'you know what Descartes said? Let me quote, as best as I can remember, "I shall then suppose, not that God who is supremely good and the fountain of truth, but some evil genius not less powerful than deceitful, has employed his whole energies in deceiving me; I shall consider that the heavens, the earth, colours, figures, sound, and all other external things are naught but the illusions and dreams of which this genius has availed himself in order to lay traps for my credulity."

'Interesting hypothesis, isn't it, father? What if God hasn't created the world, what if Christ wasn't his only begotten Son? What if we're pawns to an evil genius, Descartes' genius? What if we're all fossicking around down here, trying to do good, but the real people, the *cognoscenti*, are the evil ones among us? What if evil is right, and good is wrong? Look around you, father. You see evil everywhere and it's triumphant and ascendant. Now, tell me that good is right and evil's wrong. You can't, can you? We're all like wolves, baying at the moon on a cold, cloudless night.'

The old priest coughed in distress. It was a novel experience for him, sitting in a run-down room with a hobo, talking about Augustine and Descartes. Holy Mary, he hadn't picked up a copy of Descartes since he left the seminary in the early 1950s and he'd never understood Augustine's *Confessions*. This bum was way over his head.

'My son, you're a troubled soul. Why don't you pray for understanding?'

'Oh, I understand, all right, father. I understand that I don't understand, and nothing, not prayer, reflection, insight, chanting mantras, fasting, or anything will give me that understanding.'

'You sound so certain. You're an arrogant fellow. Clever, golden-mouthed, but vain. You spout philosophy, yet you have no faith. I don't understand your philosophies, son. They're way over the top for a simple parish priest, worn out trying to minister as best I can to the inadequacies of those about who need me. But I do have faith, something which you're sorely lacking.

'And you talk about people being destroyed. How do you know your sister's destroyed? Look, son, you haven't told me the full details of what happened, just that your poor sister was violated. You need to share it. Maybe it was ordained by God to make her into a better person. Or maybe to make the person who did it to her into someone who becomes God-fearing. You can't define the nature of God's mind. You have to accept what God does in loving faith.'

The priest had remained quiet for many minutes looking at Gabby's open honest face. Gabby stared far into the distance, beyond the confines of the small room which smelled of the kitchen. The old priest had rightly defined the difference between them. Gabby had become a dry intellect, faithlessly following the creed. But the old priest had lived a lifetime of faith. What did it matter if he didn't understand philosophy?

Gabby felt strangely warm talking to the old man, a feeling that he hadn't experienced since his days in the seminary. Was this the way back into the Church? A month of isolation had failed to clarify his thinking. Maybe the clarification would come in the future years, years spent within the establishment, working to make it more human, less institutionalised. Right now, he was angry. But he could only assuage his anger, fix up the mess, by working to make the Church system better.

For the first time in weeks, he no longer felt so angry. In place of his anger, he felt an enormous weight of sadness suddenly descend upon his body. A sadness which clutched his chest and constrained his breathing. He abruptly realised that, despite himself, warm, salty tears of grief were trickling down his stubble-ridden cheeks.

The priest knew that something momentous was happening in the mind of the younger man. Cautiously, the old man stood and approached the penitent on the bed. He stood over him, like a loving father stands over his sorrowing child, and put his hand on his shoulder. Then he enfolded him in his body, and Gabriel Molloy sobbed his anguish into the old priest's shoulders.

Eventually, Gabby looked into the rheumy eyes of the old priest and said to him, 'Father, will you hear my confession?'

The old man smiled and kissed Gabriel on the cheek. He didn't know what he'd said, or what had countered the young man's righteous anger, but something had happened. The old man said, 'Welcome back, my son.'

Daniel walked side by side with Pazit, stepping carefully around a small mound which was near the edge of the pathway. Inside the mound was a small black entryway, which Pazit explained was the open end of a mole's burrow. He thought of the animal family, lying in the cramped, dark, airless tunnels far below ground and shuddered.

Dan Rhymer was enjoying himself immensely. He hadn't been this physically active since his college vacations. He was determined not to let his exhaustion show while following this woman around in her effort to strip the orchard of grapefruit. Apparently she was used to it. She propped the ladder against the tree, scampered up it like a child at play, and pulled down each large yellow orb in her reach. Then she tossed them down. His job was to catch them and put them in the panniers. But the strain of bending, stretching and carrying was exercising muscles that a genuflecting cardinal rarely used any more. His back and legs ached, and he had lost feeling in his shoulders soon after morning tea.

He looked up the ladder and saw her stretch for a grapefruit which was tantalisingly out of the reach of her fingers. Holding onto the ladder with one hand, she put her foot on a distant branch and extended her body to its limits. Her shorts lifted high onto her thighs, and her T-shirt came away from the elasticised waist. Clearly visible through the bottom of the shirt were her breasts. And he also glimpsed the delicate curvature of her buttocks.

A powerful surge of excitement galvanised his body. He could not take his eyes off her bottom, or her breasts, firm round breasts with small nipples. He felt a prickling under his armpits and a movement in his groin, but still he could not look away.

Pazit solved his problem by grasping the grapefruit and throwing it backwards at him. It hit the ground and she looked down. His eyes were traitors to his thoughts. She grinned, and said, 'When you've finished looking, perhaps you could pick up the grapefruit.'

He flushed a deep crimson, as deep as the crimson he wore as a prince of the Catholic Church. He stuttered an apology, but Pazit interrupted, 'Don't be silly, I'm flattered. A bit surprised that anyone would still want to look at my old bones.'

'Please be assured that I wasn't. My thoughts were elsewhere, I promise you.'

'Right now, mine are on food. Hungry? Okay, then, we'll take a break and have a picnic.'

Ten minutes later, their blanket was spread out beneath the shade of a grapefruit tree, and Pazit laid out a typically Israeli picnic lunch of sour cream, yoghurt and cucumber, *humous*, *t'china*, *felafel*, *pita* bread, olives, pickled onions, tomatoes, and the famous malted black beer, *beira se'chora*. Pazit tore the *pita* in half, and filled it with the *felafel* and other accompaniments. She didn't ask whether he would prefer to do it himself. Decades of looking after little children had made her into an eternal mother. He ate hungrily, and drank his fill from the black bottle. She too ate as though it were her first meal in days. The outdoor life gave one an unholy appetite.

When they had eaten their fill, Dan insisted he clear away the food. Pazit smiled gratefully and lay back on the blanket. Daniel realised once again that he was staring at her and felt the same guilt he had felt when she was on top of the ladder.

'Does it upset you, being here with me?' she asked.

'Why should it? We've become good friends. It's a blessing for good friends to be together. And we're doing God's work, feeding the orphans.'

'God's work, huh?' Pazit laughed. He loved her laugh.

Daniel smiled. He had dissembled and the guileless woman picked it up immediately.

'I'm sorry, just a priest being sententious and coming out with pithy sayings and maxims because we're too scared about getting to the heart of things.'

'And if you were to get to the heart of things, what would you find there?'

Daniel did not answer immediately. Many priests gave in to moments of bodily weakness and repented eternally in their own personal hell.

'There, Pazit, I would find God Almighty.'

She shook her head, understanding the message. 'And whose God would that be, Father Daniel O'Malley, your God, or the God of the Jews?'

'Isn't He one and the same?'

'That's a deep philosophical question which I'm not qualified to answer. All I do is help a particularly wonderful Christian missionary called Francis look after a bunch of little children whom God, your God or mine, seems to have forgotten. But then, these aren't the only group of forgotten kids, are they? There are kids in Africa, South America, China, all over Asia, even in your fabulously rich country, that the good Lord Jehovah seems to have overlooked.'

Daniel shifted uncomfortably on the blanket.

'Forgive me if I'm saying things that offend your ears, Daniel,' Pazit continued, 'but you probably come from a rich diocese in prosperous America. Francis and I are working in enemy territory here. My brother and sister Jews don't like us being here. They think their resources should be used for Jewish orphans, and God knows there are enough of them. They say that the Arabs should care for their own. Francis works his guts out and gets no help from the Vatican, where all the bloody money is.'

Daniel was swept with shame and stared down at the blanket. But if he thought the diatribe was over, he was wrong. She continued, 'Do you know how poor we are? Remember how he picked you up by taxi from the airport? He was too scared to take the car in case it broke down on the way and caused you problems. That taxi cost the adults on the *moshav* a meal for the night. Thanks to you, we all ate bread and jam.' Her laugh was hollow, humourless.

'All he had to do was to ask. The Vatican would have come to his assistance immediately.'

She turned on him angrily. 'He thinks this wonderful God of ours will provide. He thinks that asking for help is taking money and resources away from people who need it more.' She took another deep drink of the black malt beer. 'Christ, he's even got a best friend in the Vatican. Thinks the world of him, but he's too important to remember poor Francis. He's some "Mr Big" up there in his rich palace, juggling money and careers, while Francis is down here slaving away saving souls.'

Daniel prayed for an archangel to appear and carry him away from the righteous condemnation of this woman. How far he had strayed from his calling as a priest! He had taken a holy vow of celibacy and obedience. Yet because of his arrogance, and his unholy enjoyment of intrigue, he had been able to rise to power within the American Church and ultimately to sit at the right hand of the papal throne itself. He had thought that his only sin was against the vow of chastity. Pazit made him see he had also sinned against poverty and obedience.

How had the unworthy risen! Here he was, a prince of the Church, brought down to size by a middle-aged Jewess. Would she speak to him like this if she knew he was a cardinal? Daniel reflected for a moment and smiled involuntarily. Yes! Of course she would. Pazit was one of these rare people whose lives were uncontaminated by artifice and the cloaks of power. When she spoke, it was her heart which led her mind. What she lacked in diplomacy and sophistication, she made up for in the brutality of her innocence.

Would God, would Pazit, would Francis ever forgive him for his indifference and isolation? Could he possibly atone for his sins of omission without offending his friend? And how could he make Pazit understand that while her need was manifest, he dealt with problems like hers every day on an international scale. Throughout the world, there were men and women like Francis, struggling to keep alive children born into poverty and abuse, tiny innocents whose lives were debased before they were able to comprehend what was happening to them. And there was an injustice and inhumanity abroad with which the creaking institutions of the Vatican were slowly trying to cope. The Catholic Church was universal, yet could not get its own house into order; and while its prelates and bishops and clergy and theologians were arguing moot points of dogma, Francis and thousands like him were scratching the fallow ground with bleeding fingers, seeking sustenance for those they loved.

An anger born of frustration welled up inside him. All his life, the Church had sustained him, nurtured him, equipped him to argue succinctly with people such as Pazit; yet now he was in her territory, the grandeur of the edifice, the majesty of his arguments, began to look uncomfortably superficial.

He reached over to hold her hand, to apologise, to make amends.

She opened her fingers and threaded them through his. Without thinking, without artifice, she manoeuvred her body close to his. They lay beneath the shade of the trees, looking up through the leafy canopy as the sun fell dappled on their bodies. Pazit reached over and tenderly kissed him on his lips.

He closed his eyes. Her kiss was her acceptance of him as a simple, goodly man, a sign that she had forgiven him for his trespasses. She kissed him again, tenderly. She stroked his hair. His body was relaxed, pliant. He felt as though it was part of the earth, a warm, vital extension of the trees and the grasses among which it lay. He made no move to kiss her. She understood. Slowly, tenderly, like a mother undressing her baby, she undid the buttons of his shirt, his trousers, and the rest of his clothes. He let her do it. He let her defrock him. He looked up into the trees, his mind confused, frozen into inaction. His body followed its own path, undulating to the rhythm of its desires.

She looked closely at the strangely coiled-up man. Though his eyes were tight shut, a tear forced its way beneath the lids, reflecting the sunshine, as it ran down the side of his face. Pazit shook her head in wonder, and pulled him closer to her, cradling his naked body as she cradled the pitiful children who craved the warmth and security of her breasts. She enfolded him in her soft warm arms and enclosed him with her body.

CHAPTER 20

'We got trouble,' Harlin Brown said, entering the hotel suite. He walked over to the bench and poured himself a cup of coffee. He was a worried man.

Jimmy Wilson looked at him in irritation. He hated sentences which hung in mid-air. 'What sort of trouble, for God's sake?'

'Real trouble. Serious trouble. I just got off the phone to my contact in the LAPD and he said there's no Detective Curtis Monroe in Los Angeles, Dade County, San Clemente, San Diego, or anywhere south of San Francisco. Says he knows just about every detective in Homicide, and ain't anyone with a name closely resembling that.'

Jimmy shrugged. 'Maybe he's usin' a false name 'cause he knows I'll be comin' after him.'

Luke Carmody nodded in agreement, but Harlin shook his head. 'Jimmy, you don't understand. There's no one on Jonas Watkins' case except the detectives who were there at the start. And they've got this Mexicano in the cells in Watts who's coming up before the Grand Jury for what he did to Annabelle. That's it, Jimmy. They ain't got no leads at all about Jonas. They've closed the book on him.'

'So what's the problem?' Jimmy said, frowning. 'If they ain't got nothin', why we in trouble?'

'Jimmy, the guy on the phone said he knew all about you, me, Luke, and what we did. He gave you chapter and verse, for Christ's sake. If it ain't the police, who in fuck is it?'

'Don't you go usin' those foul gutter words at me,' Jimmy told him.

'Jimmy, listen a minute. When I got off the phone from the LA police, I put a call through to Duane to see what was doin'. He tells me Annabelle's fired that minder-woman you gave her. Sent her packin' days ago. He was too shit-scared to phone and tell us about it. Annabelle got one of the security guards to pack her bags and haul her ass out of the place. Duane went off his tree, but he said Annabelle was real determined. He was jumpin' up and down, tellin' her he was in charge, but she told him to stick it up his ass.'

'She did what? Who in the hell does she think she is? I'll kick her butt for this, good! And why in the name of sweet Jesus didn't Duane phone and talk to me about it?'

'I told you! He said he was too scared. Apparently, Annabelle's changed completely. She's been walkin' into offices givin' staff the mornin' or the day off. Turnin' on music all over the cathedral. Givin' out free food and drink from the refectory. Tellin' women they could bring their kids to work free 'stead of puttin' 'em into our daycare centre. We been gone a week, and already she's turned the place into a holiday camp.'

'I'll kill her for this,' yelled Jimmy pacing the floor like a tiger. Waves of anger burst on the shore of his mind. 'Get onto Gerald. Tell him to get his ass in there and sort the mess out. Fire Duane. Useless sonofabitch. I left him in charge and the place is goin' to hell and back. Shit. By the time we get back, there'll be no church left. Bitch is undoin' twenty years of hard work. I should've done for her in that hut in the desert. Millstone round my neck since the day I married her.'

'Jimmy,' said Harlin, 'Annabelle's not the problem. For God's sake, listen to me for a minute, will you. Like I said, I spoke to Duane. He said that he's lost control of Annabelle. Staff listen to him, but don't respect him, and then they go listening to her. Everything he tells 'em to do, Annabelle countermands. But he also said that for the past few days, she's been in the company of a nigger.'

'*What?*' Jimmy roared in fury, wheeling round and grabbing at a chair to prevent himself from falling.

'A nigger called Micah Watkins.'

Jimmy's eyes glared white as he stared in a state of total incomprehension. 'Is that adulterous slut up to her old tricks again? I'll stone her to death, like they used to deal with adulteresses in the old days.'

'Jimmy,' Harlin shouted, 'he's Jonas' brother. She ain't having it off with him. She's the one who told him about what we did to the nigger. Ten bucks says he was the one on the phone. He was the one playing detective.' Jimmy remained silent, shocked. 'To fool you into making a confession,' Harlin added.

The shouting subsided. The room sank into darkness. Jimmy continued to stare, but lost his anger. He looked like a fish gasping for life on a sandy shore. Jimmy blindly felt his way to the table for support and sat down with a bump in one of the armchairs.

Luke opened the mini-bar in the sitting room, and poured each a mineral water. Jimmy gratefully smiled and sipped the drink.

'Jimmy,' Luke said, 'we have to deal with Micah. I think we can assume he hasn't yet been to the police, or else we would have been contacted by the LAPD. I don't know what his gameplan is, but he's a dangerous man, and he has to be seen to. Jimmy, why don't you and Harlin continue your God-given tasks here, and let me deal with the situation?'

Jimmy looked up at Luke and nodded.

Joe Deakin sipped his coffee with a retired life insurance salesman and his wife from San Juan Capistrano. He was telling Joe about the difference between an equity power loan through life insurance and a similar mortgage at considerably higher interest rate through the bank. His eyes caught Jimmy Wilson sitting with a morose Harlin Brown. Odd! These two normally did the rounds of every table in the morning, squeezing shoulders and slapping backs. A revivalist meeting of the early hours. He excused himself and walked over to their table. Jimmy looked up and smiled. Half-heartedly, he said, 'Joseph, good mornin'. How are you?'

Joe sat and the waiter came up to pour him a cup of coffee. 'So what's on the agenda this morning Dr Wilson?' he asked politely.

'Oh, bit o' this, bit o' that. We'll go to Masada and have another good look 'round. Why, Joe, what did you have in mind?'

Joe frowned. This was not a man who lived his life on the rim of a volcano. 'I was thinking that this will be the first morning when you'll truly be looking for the Lord's Testament, guided by the Holy Spirit, after our recent discovery.'

'What?' asked Jimmy, appearing not to understand.

'I thought we were going down again to search the caves of Masada to find what the archaeologists might have missed. It's what we prayed for last night. Another visitation by the Spirit.'

'Oh yes, forgive me.' Understanding dawned on his face. 'Of course. The Testament. Yeah, we'll be looking for that, this morning. That's why we're going to Masada.'

'Are you all right, sir?'

'Of course he's all right,' Harlin snapped. 'Why shouldn't he be?'

'Now Harlin, come on,' Jimmy intervened. 'The last thing I want is tension between you two. We've got enough problems to deal with.'

Joe wondered what problems but decided to let the matter drop for the time being.

Upstairs, eating a chocolate biscuit left over from the previous evening, Luke Carmody missed breakfast in order to hit the phones and track down Micah Watkins. He left Jimmy, Harlin, and the group to clamber onto the air-conditioned buses which would ferry them south from Jerusalem into the Negev desert, and then to the Herodian fortress at Masada.

Daniel and Pazit walked hand in hand, like school-children or young lovers. They skirted a grapefruit grove close to fish ponds which belonged to the next-door *kibbutz*. Their voices were hushed as they laughed at each other's silly remarks.

Pazit stopped in her tracks. Her urgency communicated itself to Dan. He looked at her quizzically. She mouthed, 'Don't say anything. Look over there behind the trees.' A family of voles was leaving the water. A large grey-brown father with a wet and matted coat, a slightly smaller dark brown mother and a dozen babies all followed in a procession one after the other as they struggled up the steep bank of the fish pond onto the raised hillock which divided it from another pond. When they had reached the crest of the low hillock they shook themselves to release the water trapped in their fur. The water droplets flew in spiralling arcs from their bodies, the beads catching the sun, creating a kaleidoscope of spectral colours; it was as though they were one and in accord with the needs of the *kibbutz*, returning water to the land as if they were part of the irrigation system. Dan beamed a smile. He loved being this close to nature. All his life had been lived in cities or buildings. Only rarely did he have the opportunity to enjoy the wonder of God's bounteous earth. He turned to look at Pazit. Her face shone, her skin glowing in the slanting rays of the afternoon sun.

'The *kibbutzniks* shoot them. They eat the fish. I can understand the reason but it's a pity. They're so beautiful,' she said and threaded her fingers through Daniel's.

They walked to the edge of the orchard, he carrying a pannier of grapefruit in his left hand, she carrying the picnic basket in her right.

They skirted the edge of a field and came in sight of the road. As soon as they left the privacy of the field, Daniel took his hand out of Pazit's. They marched on to the track and Dan frowned as he looked onwards. Standing there was a tall, dark figure silhouetted against the setting sun.

'Who's that?' Pazit asked.

'I don't know. Isn't he from your orphanage?'

They walked on. The tall, lean, black figure slowly acquired definitive features, familiar features, as they came nearer to him.

'Good afternoon, your eminence. How pleasant to meet you here,' said Franz Cardinal Kitzinger.

Pazit turned in surprise to Dan. 'Eminence?' But Dan appeared not to be listening to her.

'What are you doing here, Kitzinger? How dare you follow me.'

'Cardinal Rhymer, I'm not following you. I've been sent here by the Holy Father.'

'Why would he send you here?'

'As the representative of the Vatican to take care of arrangements for Bishop Solomonoglou's funeral.'

'And is that all?' asked Daniel.

Kitzinger reacted in surprise. 'Isn't that enough? The bishop is crucified and you ask whether that's the sole reason for my visiting the Holy Land. Eminence, you surprise me. As it happens, that isn't all. I'm also here to visit Father Romain de la Tour.' He looked at Pazit. 'Aren't you going to introduce me to your . . . friend?'

There was more than just a hint of malice and superciliousness in his voice. 'Forgive me. Cardinal Kitzinger, this is Mrs Pazit Fine. She runs the orphanage with Father Francis Gild.'

Like an urbane middle European from the Age of Enlightenment, he stepped forward and held out his hand. 'My dear Mrs Fine, how very nice to meet you.'

Pazit looked at Dan and shook her head quizzically. 'Why didn't you tell me?'

'Please forgive me. It was a sin of omission. I'm afraid that I'm the powerful friend that Francis has in the Vatican. The one that he refused to contact for money. I'm here on a delicate diplomatic mission for his holiness the Pope. To have told you would have been a breach of my diplomatic duty and would have compromised my purpose for being here.'

Kitzinger recoiled, 'Oh, eminence, I hope I haven't said anything untoward. Anything which might have embarrassed you.' But Daniel chose to ignore the sarcasm.

They walked together in angry silence towards the hut. Daniel deposited his grapefruit and excused himself, taking Kitzinger by the arm and marching him out of the door.

'Now, you listen to me you arrogant German—' he left the epithet unfinished. 'How dare you follow me to Israel. Who in God's name gave you permission to track me down when I'm on a mission for his holiness?'

'Cardinal Rhymer, you surprise me. Do you really think you're so central to my sphere of activity that I would traipse over this dusty ground just in search of you? Believe me, I'm here to see Romain de la Tour for discussions on the Dead Sea Scrolls. I just thought to look you up incidentally.'

'But how did you track me here?'

'Eminence, is there something secret about your being here?'

'That's not the issue and you damned well know it.'

'Cardinal Rhymer, I will not be spoken to in this way.' Daniel blew up in anger. 'You arrogant—'

'Please stop using these ridiculous epithets. You've already called me arrogant, and German, as though they were swear-words. I intend to remain civilised even though the behaviour seems to be beyond you.'

Daniel felt deflated. 'I want to know how you traced me here, Cardinal Kitzinger.'

'You told many people that you were going to Israel to lay the groundwork for the Crusade.'

'But nobody knows that I was on this *moshav* except his holiness and me. How did you follow me here?'

'You make it sound so Machiavellian. I have many friends in this country.'

'So you have been spying on me,' said Daniel.

'Spying is such an emotive word. You're a man of great importance in the Catholic hierarchy. Your movements are of interest. Finding out what you're doing is of concern to your brothers. But your concern rather begs the question. If you're here doing nothing wrong, why are you so worried about my enquiries? After all, my staff know where to find me at any given moment.'

Daniel took a deep breath. 'I . . . I'm here to visit my friend Father Gild. We were at seminary together.'

'And while he's away on business, you take his assistant to picnic in the fields? Do you feel that this behaviour is consistent with a prince of the Church?'

Talking with this man was like negotiating a path through rapids from one bank of a river to another.

Daniel retained his composure. 'Mrs Fine is a Jewish lady who works six days a week, morning till night. She had a couple of hours off today and suggested that she show me the orchards. We took a picnic lunch. I owe you no excuses whatsoever.'

'Your eminence,' said Kitzinger, looking around in horror, 'I have to question the propriety of a cardinal, and the holder of the most senior office of the Curia, being alone in a field with a woman.'

Daniel looked at the cardinal in disgust. He represented everything in the Vatican that Daniel detested most—the power, the privilege, the status. He was the antithesis of the Christian that Daniel was desperate to be. Like those early Christians who had suffered unimaginable trials and tribulations for their faith. Faith which was stronger than his. The faith of the mystics. The faith to which he had tried to aspire since being ordained as a priest, the faith which allowed those pure at heart to see visions of Jesus and Mary, the faith which caused stigmata spontaneously to appear in bleeding hands and feet, the faith which produced miracles and moved mountains. He silently prayed to himself, 'Please, dear God, and Your Son, Jesus, give me the faith to believe with all my heart and all my soul and all my might. The faith to be a true Christian and not one dressed in the trappings.'

'Kitzinger, I feel nothing but contempt for you. You should never have been a priest. You should have been a politician or a diplomat. Unctuous and oozing and syco-phantic and kissing small babies when you need to impress, but merciless when you feel threatened. Is there an ounce of God in you, Kitzinger? Has the Lord Jesus laid His blessed hand anywhere within your heart, and shown you the light of faith?'

Franz Cardinal Kitzinger sighed as the diatribe came to an end. He had not realised that he was so hated by the Americans. He knew he was disliked but he thought that their disapproval was the Old versus the New. Now he could see from the venom which had just poured forth that Rhymer, and very possibly His Holiness Pope Innocent himself, hated him with a vengeance normally reserved for arch-enemies.

'Eminence, I won't begin to try to convince you that I am not deeply hurt and offended by your words. I could stand here and argue, indeed defend myself, because you're wrong, very wrong. You know nothing about me, Rhymer. You have no idea how I or my family suffered under the Christ-hating Nazis or of the burning love of Christ which kept me alive when the SS tried to excise the Catholicism from my soul. You know nothing of the fights that I've had with people who have actively worked to dilute or destroy our faith. You may hate me for the trappings with which you see me surrounded but I'm the bulwark against revisionism and people who have tried to divert the faith. There's only one true faith and that's the faith which I have devoted my life to maintaining. Don't you ever consider yourself to be more worthy or more faithful than me. Do you think I don't suffer every time I read of the persecutions and humiliations of God-fearing men and women; of the hideousness of the lives of orphans in India or Africa? Your suffering is felt by every God-fearing Christian.'

They continued their walk in silence. Each man had stated his position. Each retreated to the opposite corner of the ring. As they rounded a bend in the road and came in sight of the fish ponds, Daniel asked, 'So what is it that you want from me, Cardinal Kitzinger?'

'I want nothing from you. I don't want to hold you in my thrall. I'm not in the business of blackmail. I merely want to know that you can be counted on when this obscene idea of the Pope's begins to take shape.'

'Counted on?'

Kitzinger was beginning to lose his patience. 'Don't pretend to be any more obtuse than you really are. You and I are both opposed to this expedition. You've never made any secret of that, despite your closeness to the Pope. We're both frightened of what the Testament could do to our Church.'

Daniel turned and looked at him in anger. 'It's a bit late for that now, isn't it, eminence? The Pope has already announced the Crusade.'

'And the Third Vatican Council. What are your views about that, Cardinal Rhymer?'

Daniel hesitated just long enough for the German to witness Daniel's doubt.

'I thought so,' said the German softly. 'You're as frightened of the Council as I am.'

Daniel defended his friend. 'No I'm not. Look at the wonders that have been introduced since Vatican Two.'

Kitzinger interrupted. 'Only time will tell us whether they were wonders or not. It was a century between the first and second Councils. It should be a further century until the Third Council, not forty years. What's going to happen in the future? A new version of the way we do things every time there's a new pope? It'll be like musical chairs, like the American presidency—unstable and inept, directionless and inconsistent.'

The two men walked on in silence. After they had rounded a corner in a field, Kitzinger continued, 'The Catholic faith cannot endure another shock like Galileo's or Martin Luther's or even Charles Darwin's. When those truths became apparent, the Church had hundreds of millions of faithful throughout the world that would endure with it through thick and thin. But today, Catholicism is hanging by its fingernails. We have a breakaway church in South America, and in Holland.

As if that isn't drastic enough, the Philippines and much of Asia looks as though it will be following its own path within the next few decades. Communism may be dead everywhere except China, Daniel, but apathy, fatalism and a growing sense of irrationality is abroad and spreading like a virus.'

'But that's what Innocent told the press conference just the other week! I thought you were opposed to him', said Daniel.

Kitzinger smiled. 'He's a good and godly man, a man of passion and vigour. What he told the journalists was correct. It's just the method for curing the ills of the world on which we differ. And I know that you, also, disagree with him in regard to the Lord's Testament. Daniel, we're at a crisis point. Soon there will be nothing left of Christ's Church. You and I might even this day be presiding over the end of Catholicism as it has been practised for two thousand years. Why do you think it is that for the last half a century we Catholics have been so cautious in releasing the evidence of the Dead Sea Scrolls? Daniel, you don't like me. You have made no secret of that. My feelings for you are unimportant, but we are both devout Catholics. The faith is intense in both of us. We're custodians of the Church. Let's work together in preventing that godly man, Gabriel Molloy, from making the greatest mistake of his life.'

Daniel Rhymer walked on slowly, in silence.

The buses disappeared down the road which led to the Judean desert and Masada. Joe watched them go and when the last one had rounded a curve and disappeared finally from view, he walked back into the lobby, icy cold after the outdoor heat, and called the lift. He reached the right floor, got out, walked down the corridor to where Luke Carmody's room was situated and knocked. Luke opened the door and looked at Joe with surprise.

'Can I come in?'

Luke hesitated. 'Not right now, I'm kinda busy. I've got some work to do. Maybe we can meet for lunch.' Joe pushed past him. 'Joe, I'm serious. I'm up to my ears in shit, right now.'

'Shit from the church?'

Luke shook his head in embarrassment. 'It's just an expression. I mean, I've got a shit load of work to do.'

'Covering up for your boss?'

Luke looked at him suspiciously. 'Meaning?'

'It's over, Luke. We both know it's over. Jimmy had some kind of phone call this morning. I don't know what it was but it's not going to be all that hard to find out. It has to do with the fact that he beat the shit out of his wife. Half-killed her. And Jonas Watkins? Were you there when he killed him? Cut his dick and his balls off. Were you part of the team?'

Blood drained from Luke's face and he remained speechless. Joe continued, 'It's going to be front page in the *LA Times* next week. I'd say if you were part of it, you'd be looking at life. 'Course if you're the one who points the finger—' Joe shrugged.

'Get out of here!'

Joe smiled. 'Fine.' He started to walk towards the door. He opened the door but hadn't left the room before Luke shouted, 'Wait!' He breathed a sigh of relief, turned and looked questioningly at the young man. 'How can you print that stuff without proof?'

'Who said we ain't got proof?'

'You bastard. You come here pretending you're a friend and you shaft us.'

Joe shrugged. 'Name of the game!'

'Motherfucker!'

'Were you going to tell me something?' asked Joe. 'I was about to go to my room and pack my bags.'

Luke bit his lip. 'Don't go. Just give me a minute to think, for fuck's sake.'

Joe closed the door but didn't move back into the room. He stood in silence. A minute went past, then another minute. An agony of waiting.

'Can you get me out of this? I mean, really get me out of it?' asked Luke.

'No, but if you're the one who gives us the story and if we go to the police with you, you can plea-bargain. It's up to the judge to accept it. If you were just an innocent onlooker, then—'

Luke took out a handkerchief and wiped his lips. He nodded silently.

'How did they do it?' asked Joe.

Luke told him the entire story. Joe stood rooted to the spot for ten minutes as he felt every kick, every blow, every moment of agony and defilement that Annabelle Wilson and Jonas suffered at the hands of the fundamentalist preacher. He walked back into the room and helped himself to a drink from the mini-bar.

She lay in his arms and her fingers curled and uncurled the greying hair on his chest. It hurt but he didn't want her to stop. He pulled her head closer and kissed her. She reached up and licked his earlobe. They kissed. It was a kiss of friendship, rather than passion. All the sexual urgency had disappeared five minutes earlier when he'd exploded inside her and she'd clung to him, pulling him closer and closer to her body, until they were as one.

'I'm phoning Deirdre tonight.'

She tugged his chest hair. He yelped. 'Do you mind not discussing your wife when you're having an adulterous relationship?'

'Sorry! I'm not good at this. It's completely new to me.'

'It's fairly new to me. I'm not in the habit of screwing middle-aged married men, especially ones who aren't Jewish.' He stroked her cheek. 'Why are you phoning her?' she asked.

'I'm telling her I won't be coming back to Australia for some time. I've made a decision. After what Benawie said about the guardians I think you're right. I think we should start to look in Ethiopia. There are almost no Falashas left in Ethiopia. I've checked. Benawie said that just a handful stayed behind. He knows of ten of them. I think it's worth looking for them. It sounds as if they're some sort of guardians or something.'

'But that was years ago, Michael, and they were elderly men who had never looked after themselves in their whole lives,' she said.

'Let's face it,' he said. 'A dozen scholars could spend a dozen years searching the libraries of Rome or Florence or the Bodleian in Oxford. Archaeologists could climb up and down the hills of the Dead Sea and not find anything for another thousand years. This is needle-in-the-haystack time. At least Ethiopia is a haystack that no other archaeologist has ever tried to examine.' She lay curling and uncurling his chest hair.

'Judith, years ago, when I was in Rome, I was friendly with an Ethiopian called Isaac Manitam. He's now the bishop of Ethiopia. I've already phoned him. I didn't tell him why I'm coming to Ethiopia, but he's no fool. He's asked me to come and stay with him.' He breathed deeply before asking. 'How would you like to come?'

Her hand didn't alter its movements. Her body didn't suddenly stiffen. It was as if the words had simply washed over her. 'Are you serious?' she asked.

He nodded. 'You're divorcing Uri. You're already at boiling point with him. At the very worst, we could have a great holiday.'

She laughed. 'You're pragmatic. I'll say that for you.'

'And at best, who knows?' he said.

He felt her body stiffen imperceptibly. 'You'll never leave Deirdre, will you? We'll never marry. She'll never divorce you.'

He sighed but remained silent. An assent to the truth.

He started to speak but she put her fingers to his lips. 'All I know is that I let you go once but I'm not going to let you go again. We're one body. We're one soul. I've lived without you for twenty barren years. Some of them were good. Some of them were empty. Every night I was yearning. When I made love to Uri, I closed my eyes and felt your body and saw your face. I don't give a damn if we have to live together and not be married. I don't give a damn for conventions. I can't live without you. I won't!'

CHAPTER 21

'May I speak with you?' asked Abram, his head bowed deferentially as he approached ibn Saud.

It was the middle of the morning and Eilath was in sight. He had been travelling with the caravan for two days and in that time tangible hostility had grown between himself and the small number of people who travelled behind ibn Saud. Abram couldn't understand why they had begun so warmly towards him, yet, in sight of the end of the journey, they had changed so much. Even the leader of the caravan no longer treated him with the courtesy he once showed.

Ibn Saud looked down at the boy. His face was a mask of displeasure. Children did not speak to a clan leader without the clan leader first indicating he wished to speak. But the boy was a Hebrew.

'Yes?'

'Master, we will soon be in Eilath. I have no way to repay your kindness. I have no money.'

'Fool!' ibn Saud snorted. 'People of the land of Edom do not take money from guests. It is a law.'

Abram bowed his head again in respect and allowed a few camels on the caravan slowly to overtake him. Ibn Saud turned and fixed him with a stare. 'But—'

Abram walked quickly forward until he was close to ibn Saud. 'You owe me your life, for you would surely have died had we not found you. That is a debt which must be repaid.'

Abram's heart dropped. One of the men on the caravan whom he had talked to last night had warned him that this was a custom of the Edomites.

'How may I repay this debt, master?'

'I saved your life, now your life is mine to dispose of as I wish. That is the law.'

'And how will you dispose of my life?' Abram's throat stiffened as he struggled with the words.

Ibn Saud smiled, but remained silent.

It was as Abram feared. He would have to escape unless he was to be sold into slavery. But escape was difficult in Eilath. On either side and behind the port were murderous deserts of sand and rock. To the south was the Sea of Reeds. When he had begun his journey, the port of Eilath was a destination which he longed to see. Now it was to become his prison. John of Syracuse had told him that Eilath was where he could find transport down the Reed Sea until he travelled past the peninsula of Arabia, and arrived at the port of Masawa on the coast of Africa. Then he would go via Asmera to the mountains in which the people of the Agau lived.

But John had not taken into account brigands like ibn Saud. Would he be able to escape from the caravan and ibn Saud's family? Would he be able to negotiate passage on a boat that was sailing south, before he was sold into slavery? If he did escape, where would he go to hide? He had never been to this area before. And without money, how could he survive? The caravan lumbered its way south out of the desert. The sea came into view. The camels growled as they smelt water. Slowly, the collection of buildings stood out from the shore, their form solidifying out of the mirage of the hot air.

After another two hours' travelling, the group stopped at a caravanserai in the northern part of the town of Eilath. Ibn Saud paid for lodging for his people and food and water for the camels. The following day he would go to the markets to sell his balsam, tin, pewter and salt and purchase spices from Arabia and Abyssinia for the return journey to Jerusalem. So sure was he of the impossibility of escaping alive from Eilath that he did not bother to tether Abram by his hands and feet. By nightfall, ibn Saud and four of his wives lay together in a tent outside the courtyard of the caravanserai while the younger members of the caravan and relatives of ibn Saud lay under blankets in the open air. A hot fire crackled, keeping them warm in the freezing night air.

A shape slowly and carefully made its way over to Abram, hidden by the shadows.

'Abram,' a girl's voice whispered. 'I am Avigad. My father is the brother of the chief of our family. For two days I have watched you come from the depths of despair back to strength. You are a nice man. I don't want to see you die as a slave.' At first he was surprised at her ability to speak his language. 'My family lived in Jericho for many years. But when the famine struck, my father begged my uncle to take us in. My father was made a slave. It is very hard for us.'

'Avigad, we cannot talk. We will wake up the men of the tribe. And then we will both be in trouble. Help me to escape,' said Abram.

'Take me with you.'

'What?' he whispered.

'Take me with you and I'll tell you how to escape.'

'But I can't escape into the desert. I nearly died back there and I can't afford to buy passage on a boat.'

'Do you have any skills?'

'I'm a shepherd. I look after sheep.'

'Do you play an instrument? Do you sing? Can you build things? Is there anything you can do well?'

'I am a Hebrew,' Abram laughed.

Avigad moved silently closer to him. He could feel her body through his blanket. He could see her face. She had dark skin and bright eyes and her lips were the full lips of a woman. Yet she was hardly more than a child.

'But you must escape or tomorrow you will begin a living death as a slave,' she said.

'Why is it so important to you that I escape?' asked Abram.

'Take me with you,' she said again. 'I have many skills you can use. And soon I will have breasts that you may kiss.'

Abram was shocked. Edomite women might speak this way but no Hebrew woman ever would. It was unseemly and improper. 'Don't be silly. I can't take you. We're of a different people and I don't know you.'

'Is it because I don't come with a dowry?' she said, discouraged. 'My father is a poor man. Without a dowry, I cannot wed. My uncle and my father hate each other. My uncle should give me a dowry but he will not. He says my father must work without money for ten years before he will give me a dowry. By then I'll be twenty and an old woman. No one will have me. Please, Abram, I have a strong body and I know about what men and women do. I will make you happy. Please, take me.'

'This is wrong.'

'Abram, let me come inside your blanket.'

Abram pulled the blanket tighter around his body. 'Avigad, go away.'

'If you don't take me, I'll scream. Then my father will kill you.'

'Look, I'm not saying I will, but if I do agree to take you, how can we escape? And if we do escape, what will you do? You're a child. You'll be all alone. Why do you want to leave your family?'

Avigad did not answer immediately. A man on the opposite side of the fire coughed and turned over in his sleep. Other people under blankets began to move with the disturbance in the still night air. Abram and Avigad lay stock still, aware of the danger.

She whispered, 'I know a way we can escape. There's a baker's house near the shore of the sea. He has two kilns. One was broken in an earthquake a dozen years ago. After that he built another kiln which he uses. We can hide in the broken kiln while they search for us.'

'Avigad, if I take you with me to get away from here, how will we live?'

'We will steal bread. I know where there is a well for water. If we want fruit, there are date trees all over Eilath. And I know how to live in the desert. You don't.'

'But stealing is a sin. Yahweh tells us that there are ten commandments we must not break. Stealing is one of them.'

'Yahweh?'

'He is my God.'

Abram wanted to tell her about Jesus the Messiah but now wasn't the time.'

'Well Yahweh can provide for you, but if I want to eat, I'm going to steal.'

'But where will you go after we are alone? I must make my way to the mountains of Africa. To the land of Cush.'

'I'll come with you.'

He stifled a laugh as they heard more movements. They were perilously close to being discovered. 'You can't come with me. I'll just leave you here once we're free. You can make your own way.'

'No! I'm coming with you. Agree or I'll scream.'

He couldn't risk calling her bluff. Her scream would mean his death.

'This child, she is your wife?'

'She is my wife'

The captain sneered, one nostril quivering in disgust. His people waited until a girl bled with the moon before marrying her.

'I carry no passengers. Go elsewhere and find a captain foolish enough to take you.' He turned and walked towards the stone jetty where his ship was moored.

It was the second refusal Abram and Avigad had suffered that morning. The fifth since the caravan had left Eilath, her uncle swearing violent oaths against the morning sun. They had hidden in a palm tree.

Already residents were giving them strange looks. And the baker had spotted them twice near the kiln, giving Avigad a second glance, vaguely remembering having seen her before.

Abram ran after the captain. People trading in Judean ports usually had some knowledge of Hebrew. This captain was no exception. 'Master, I'm good with my hands. I can repair sails and do things like that. My wife can cook. I beg you to take us'

'No!'

'But master, we're starving. We have to get to Asmera in the land of the Cushites. If not, we'll die.'

'Then your souls will go to heaven.'

'And you don't care?'

The Egyptian laughed. 'Care? This is a cruel world, hard, not made for children. Did your parents care when they sent you from home to seek your fortune? No! Then why should I care? I have my own problems.'

Abram said, 'Then go in Christ's name.' The moment he mentioned the name of the Saviour, he bit his lip, cursing himself for the stupid lapse.

The captain stopped walking and wheeled around in shock. 'What did you say?' he demanded.

Abram stuttered, 'Nothing. It was an error. Something I picked up. I don't know what it means.'

The Egyptian walked back and gripped Abram roughly by his shoulders. Firmly but gently, he said, 'Boy, tell me what you said. Tell the truth.' There was a look of gentleness buried deep within his suspicious eyes.

'Go in Christ's name,' Abram whispered.

'And do you understand the words you just used?'

'Yes, master.'

'Then you follow the man they call Jesus?'

'Yes, master.'

'And your wife?'

'She's not my wife. I was captured by the caravan which left Eilath three days ago. She is the daughter of a vicious father who beat her. Her father used her body as though she were his wife. She begged me to help her get away from the caravan. We managed to escape by hiding.'

'So she's not a Christian?'

'No, but I am. My father and mother, and my brothers and sisters, were all baptised in the name of the Lord many years ago, although my brothers and sisters are still too young to take Jesus into their hearts. When they are older, like me, they will be told. I come from Galilee.'

The Egyptian stared into the distance. 'Where Our Lord walked and prayed. And where he preached the Sermon on the Mount. Blessed are the—'

'You are a Christian?' gasped Abram.

'I was baptised in the Nile by Bishop Petrasius when I was a boy of twenty.'

Abram looked into the face of the black man and found it had changed. It was no longer hostile and suspicious. It was warm and smiling. It was the first truly compassionate face Abram had seen since leaving his family's home. Even the Jews who had given him shelter along the way had not been as open and warm as the look on this Egyptian's face. Abram dropped the sack he had been carrying all these weeks and threw his arms around the neck of the black man. The captain hugged him back.

'Brother in Christ,' said Abram, fighting back tears.

'Brother in Christ,' said the captain, kissing Abram on the forehead.

Half an hour later, Abram and Avigad were sitting on the deck of the boat under a sailcloth suspended between the prow and the mizzenmast to cast shade onto them and give protection from the intense midday sun. In front of them was a meal of dates, pomegranates, honey, freshly baked bread from the town baker in whose filthy broken kiln they had been hiding for the past four days, as well as dishes of spiced lamb, goat's meat in milk curd and goat's milk.

During the meal, Montemthat told the young couple how he came to be a Christian. 'My people are from the land of Cush. We were conquered in the mists of time by the pharaohs of Egypt, then the Nubians to the north, then the Abyssinians, then the Greeks, then the Romans who still rule our land like they rule the land of Judah.'

'But how did you become a Christian? I didn't think that there were any Christians outside Greece and Rome, and here.'

Montemthat burst out laughing. 'There are many of us up and down the Nile from Buhen in the south to Alexandria on the coast of the great sea.'

'And where . . . what happened . . . what were you before you became a Christian?' asked the young man.

'In the mighty Nile, within the first cataract as it plunges downwards from the mountains of Nubia into the lowlands of Egypt, there is a branch within the river. It's so wide that you can hardly see from one bank to the other. In the river is a large island at a place called Elephantine. In the days before time, an ancient people built a sacred temple there. For longer than people can remember, there have been priests who attended the gods. Ra, Aton, Osiris, Ptha, Sekhmet—all of them. It's interesting that, for hundreds of years, the priests at Elephantine also worshipped the Hebrew god Yahweh.

'Then when the Romans arrived, and after the pharaohs began to lose their power over the people, some of the Egyptians began worshipping new gods. One of them was Jesus. A missionary named Philus of Ephesus converted a few of the monks from Yahweh to Jesus. He told them that the Ark of the Covenant, in which the God Yahweh had placed his holy tablets of stone, was the same in both religions. He said that while the Jews had the wooden ark, the Christians also had an ark. The ark was Mary, the mother of Jesus. She was the ark in which Yahweh had placed the new law, brought by His Son. My father was baptised in the way of John who baptised Jesus. And I was baptised by Bishop Petrasius, who visited the island to instruct the monks. Great, godly man.'

'I'm on a mission for John of Syracuse.'

'I've heard of him,' said Montemthat. 'He is a bishop, a great man, one who follows in the footsteps of the Messiah.'

'That's all I can tell you,' Abram continued. 'Telling you more would imperil my task.' Montemthat smiled. He liked the boy.

'Brother,' said Montemthat, 'keep the details to yourself. But is there anything I can do to assist you in the task? We sail on the afternoon tide and by tomorrow night will be in the land of the Midionites. There we will land and take on a new cargo and maybe some delicacies from Arabia which we cannot purchase in

Eilath. After that, we sail south towards the tip of the peninsula. Where is it that you want to get to?' asked Montemthat.

'I want to get to the port where one sails before reaching the city of Asmera,' answered Abram. 'I believe it's called Masawa.'

Montemthat smiled. 'You're going to the people of the Agau.'

Abram stared in incomprehension. 'How—' But the words failed him.

Montemthat patted the young man on his knee. 'Don't worry. I have no idea why you're going there. Your secret is safe. I know about the Agau because my father told me all about them. When he was a sea captain, he also took missionaries from Eilath to Masawa. Their mission was to convert the Agau, who follow the god of the Hebrews. I assume that's why you're going.'

'Yes,' Abram lied, staring down, unable to look Montemthat in the eyes, 'that's exactly why I'm going.'

'Then I will help you get there, brother Abram. Just like my father before me helped the missionaries, and found grace in the eyes of Jesus.'

In Ben Gurion airport, Joe Deakin found a phone. 'Ben, I've just dictated a story about a bishop who's been crucified—'

'It's just coming in now. Wait a minute.' Joe waited as Ben read the story. The silence was interrupted by a series of expletives as Ben understood the horror of what had happened. When he had finished the incoming flash, he asked, 'Any idea who did this?'

'Yeah. My bet's on the Zion Now! movement. The bishop was kidnapped a couple of days ago.'

'We ran your story.'

'But no ransom note was found and none was delivered. Nobody admitted to it.'

'Then how do you know it was this mob, the Zion . . . whatever it is?'

'Because they're extreme fanatics and they've vowed to stop the Pope's Crusade. My guess is that after they targeted the Church of the Holy Sepulchre they thought to bring pressure on the Pope by kidnapping the bishop.'

'You're crazy. Jews don't go in for this sort of thing. I want as much as you can get. We'll run the story in the early editions and a follow-up and background as soon as you can get it to us. But for fuck's sake, don't drop us in the shit with the B'nai B'rith or the Chief Rabbi. Going up against Jimmy Wilson's bad enough, but going up against a coupla million yiddisher mammas ain't a prospect I relish!'

'Ben, I'm on my way back. I'm at the airport.'

'What?'

'I've got the whole story about Jimmy Wilson from one of his insiders. Game, set and match. I've got the turkey cold.'

'Spill.'

Joe told his editor about Luke's confession.

'Shit! What's happening to this guy, Luke?'

'He's with me. I'm putting him in protection till we can get him a private meeting with the DA.'

'You didn't promise him anything, did you? Money? A new ID?'

'Nothing.'

The crucifixion of Bishop Solomonoglou was front-page news for days in all the morning papers and was the main fare of world radio and television. The Israeli

Prime Minister, interviewed live at his home, promised the nation, the Catholic Church and Christians throughout the world that those who were responsible for this obscenity would be brought to justice. He made veiled references to the act having been perpetrated by well-known fanatics and extremists, but drew just short of openly identifying Rabbi Berg.

By the time he arrived at his office, Prime Minister Moishe Rabbinowitz was ready to step into the cabinet meeting to demand of his Minister for Police the immediate arrest and arraignment of this bastard David Berg, and every mad bastard associated with him. This cancer would be excised from the body of Israeli politics within the hour. Israel did not need its reputation to be tarnished by this moral outrage and Rabbinowitz was determined to make Berg suffer.

He strode down the corridor and as he burst through into the cabinet room, the Minister for Police, the Minister for Religious Affairs and the Attorney-General were already waiting for him. He dispensed with the traditional greetings. 'What the fuck's happening with Berg? Has he been arrested?'

The Minister for Police, Mordecai Thom, cleared his throat. 'David Berg and three of his followers are in Jerusalem Central Police Station.'

'Thank God,' Rabbinowitz sighed and sat down heavily. But his relief was short-lived.

'It's not that simple, Moishe.'

'What do you mean?'

'He walked into the police station and offered his help in bringing to justice the criminals who crucified the bishop. He thinks they might be a breakaway group from the Zion Now! movement.'

'*What?*' Rabbinowitz screamed, grasping the chair to stop himself falling in shock.

'He came in and asked to speak to a police superintendent an hour ago. The superintendent didn't even have time to arrest him. Berg said that he suspected one or two fanatic ex-members of the Zion Now! movement may have been responsible for this obscenity and offered to show us all the documents, membership lists, and make everybody in his group available for us to interview so that we could bring the lunatics to justice. His words, not mine.'

'The arrogant bastard.' The Prime Minister's jaw slackened. 'You've got to be joking. He wants to help us?'

'How can I arrest him?' asked Mordecai. 'At the moment, it's too early to pull any evidence in. We have no direct proof that he was responsible or even involved. We've got to do forensic tests, interview witnesses, the works.'

Something in Rabbinowitz's mind snapped. 'I don't give a fuck about rights and wrongs. I don't care about evidence. I don't care about the law. I want that bastard behind bars. Strung up like he crucified the archbishop. Put him away and find the evidence, but put him away *now*!'

The other ministers in the room turned to the Attorney-General, Gershon Kronowitz. 'Moishe, I know you're furious and disgusted. So is everybody here. And every citizen in Israel. But as the principal law officer in this land, I decide who goes to prison. Until there's sufficient evidence to arrest David Berg on suspicion of murder, kidnapping, or anything else, I refuse to deny him his civil rights.'

It was one irritation too many. The Prime Minister's face flushed red. 'Fuck his civil rights,' he screamed. 'I want David Berg in prison. Israel can't lose its reputation in the world community because of a madman.'

'And Israel can't lose its reputation in the world community as the only country in the Middle East with a record for according civil rights to its citizens. We've already suffered because of what we did to the Palestinians during the *intifada* and that other madman who slaughtered the Muslims in Hebron. It's taken us years to reclaim our reputation. We're not going to lose it because we overreact on a matter like this.'

'Overreact!' yelled the Prime Minister. 'How can you overreact when a man's been crucified? Nobody's been crucified on Israeli soil in a thousand years. It's barbarism. Don't you understand that?'

The other men in the room shrank back from the Prime Minister's fury. The Minister for Religious Affairs said, 'Moishe, please calm down, I'm begging you. Bishop Solomonoglou—and I must remind you that he was my old friend—was not crucified.'

The Prime Minister waved his hand dismissively. 'So he died of natural causes. But he was hung up like a side of beef.'

'I know. It was an outrage. But you can't start throwing around charges of murder against an Israeli citizen when we're talking about lesser crimes like kidnap and manslaughter and unlawful disposal of a dead body.'

The Prime Minister sat down in his chair and took a sip of water. He looked at the three men in the cabinet room, men with whom he had shared a lifetime of political problems. He began to breathe deeply, to calm his emotions and turned to Mordecai Thom. 'So, what are we going to do?' he asked.

'All we can do is to hold him on suspicion of kidnapping. I don't think we can hold him for more than forty-eight hours. During that time, we're going to use everything at our disposal to find proof that he was involved. We're going to pull every single member of the Zion Now! movement, every sympathiser, every relative, in for interview and see what we can get.'

'And if you don't get any evidence?'

'We'll cross that bridge when we get to it.'

The Prime Minister smiled. 'You think he hasn't thought this through? That bastard! You think he isn't laughing at us from the police station? You won't find any evidence. He'll have covered his tracks. That rabbi has driven a wedge between us and the Catholics which will take another two thousand years to heal.'

Jimmy Wilson stormed from the vestibule into the sitting room, then into the bathroom, the bedroom and on to the balcony, watched warily by the manager of the hotel. When he came back, the manager said, 'As I said, Reverend Wilson, Mr Luke Carmody checked out at about midday. I must ask you to leave this room, sir. We've prepared it for another guest.'

'Damn your other guests,' he shouted, storming past the surprised manager.

He threw open the door to Harlin's suite, saw him on the phone and snapped, 'Put that goddamn phone down.'

Harlin said into the receiver, 'I got to go. I'll get back to you in a minute.' He looked at his enraged employer.

'You were right,' Jimmy said, spitting the words. 'Goddamn spineless sonofabitch. What in hell is happenin' here? Why did he just up and leave?'

'That's not the worst of it, Jimmy. That reporter has gone as well. No forwarding address, nothing. I was just checking with the airlines when you came back. They won't disclose any details. Jesus, man, you know what's happening, don't you.'

''Course I know what's happenin'. Christ, I could kill him for this. I could squeeze his—'

'Killing him ain't going to get us anywhere. We're in serious shit here. If Luke's gonna spill his load to that goddamn fuckin' reporter, we're in a shit full of trouble.'

'Get on to the cathedral. I want to know what this Micah Watkins nigger is doin'. I'm goin' to finish him.'

'Jimmy!'

Jimmy turned around and roared, 'I put you in charge of my administration. None of this would have happened if you had kept a tight control. Do I have to do everythin'? Do I have to think for you? Wipe your goddamn ass?'

'Jimmy, I—'

'Not another word, Harlin. I mean it, boy. Not one more word. You get your ass into line. You get on that phone and you start doin' the job I pay you for.'

Back in his own rooms, she was the last person he wanted to see. Only the valium kept him from picking her up physically and throwing her out of his room. She was the very symbol of his anger, the nadir of his loathing, of all that was wrong in his life. Having to act deferentially to stupid old rich women like Mary Beth Yablonsky, just because she was rich, just because she was the widow of some Texas oil guy. And her voice! Kind of mewling and wishy-washy. God! What crap was she going on about?

'My dear Mary Beth, do forgive me. I've had a very strenuous day and I've been communin' with God. Just say that again.'

'I said I took that miraculous document I found in the cave over to this professor in the university here.'

'Yes?'

'Well, I wasn't going to trust that Mr Michael Farber. Not after what he said to you. Heavens, reverend.'

'Good, good. Well, is there anythin' else I can help you with, Mary Beth?'

'The professor I took it to says that Michael Farber ain't all he's cracked up to be. He says he's got crazy ideas. Says he's often on wild goose chases.'

'Right. Right,' responded Jimmy.

'Says that he's flying off to Ethiopia chasing this Testament.' Jimmy nodded. 'But appears that he was right about this Testament I found in the ˙ cave. This Professor Ari somebody says it was from the Book of Malachi. Says Professor Farber was right about that anyway.'

Jimmy nodded vacantly. What was she talking about? She excused herself, realising the man of God was in a state of communing with his Lord. She closed the door quietly. Jimmy stared at the television set. Ethiopia?

CHAPTER 22

The hubbub of conversation slowly subsided as the men gathered realised that His Holiness Pope Innocent was walking towards them. Cardinal Roncello had ensured that the biblical scholars, archaeologists, linguists and religious philosophers who had gathered for the Pope's lesson had been well fed.

Innocent walked to the first man and shook his hand, saying, 'Professor Huentes, how grateful I am that you could come. Dr Velikovski, how very good to see you here.' And he went to each man shaking his hand and calling him by name. He recognised them from the pictures and dossiers that he had received from Dan Rhymer. Each man was touched by the informality and courtesy. The Pope poured himself a cup of coffee and took a plate of sandwiches. The background chatter grew to replace the silence which had greeted the Pope's entrance. After a few moments, he asked everybody to gather around and take their seats. They sat in a semicircle around him, students before their master. 'My dear friends, you have given your time and your services to what may turn out to be the most important and momentous event in the two-thousand-year history of our Catholic Church. Tomorrow when you have all got to know each other better, you will fly to Israel and there you will meet with Father Romain de la Tour and the members of the International Team. You will view their work and agree or disagree with their translations and interpretations and then, each of you being experts in the Holy Land and its early Christian history, or authorities on the early life of the Christian Church, you will determine where is the most likely resting place of the Testament Our Lord Jesus has left. You will also try to predict what Our Lord said in His contemplation.

'I have called this the Ninth Crusade, which indeed it is. The previous Crusades ended in ignominy and caused pain and suffering to millions of people throughout Europe, Asia Minor and the Middle East. This Crusade will be one bound in love, dignity and hope. The entire world, not just the Catholics you represent, prays for your success. If you succeed, you will have been responsible for the greatest gift to mankind, God's word in concrete form. If you do not succeed in ascertaining the final resting place of the Testament, then I beg of you not to view your time as having been wasted or your mission as having been a failure. For who can truly be said to know the mind of God? Maybe if the Almighty had wanted us to find Our Lord's Testament, then He would have made it available before now. Maybe if He wanted to offer us renewed hope, then perhaps all He will show us is this fragment, this tantalising scrap, and let us get on with renewing His Church. But if, as many now believe, we are approaching the coming Apocalypse at the end of the millennium, then this Crusade may succeed in inspiring the flagging spirits of mankind and forcing forever the atheists, the godless, the cynics and the doubting Thomases to accept the eternal majesty of the Father, the Son and the Holy Spirit.'

As each in the gathering made the sign of the Cross, and muttered 'Amen', one of the academics, a Jesuit father from France, interrupted. 'Holy Father, please forgive my question but I have been asked by the other members of this Crusade to ask you a question.' The Pope looked at the young man and smiled. 'We are all concerned about our security following the tragedy that ended the life of Bishop Solomonoglou. While I speak for everyone and assure you of our commitment to this Crusade and its holy work, we must also think of practical issues.'

'Father Bereget, I have already taken steps to ensure the security of you and other members of this team. A private security firm has been hired by the Church in Israel. It contains former members of the Israeli security service, Mossad. Each of you has been assigned a personal security guard. These guardians will ensure your safety. Furthermore I have spoken personally to the Prime Minister of Israel, Mr Rabbinowitz, who has promised me that no effort will be spared in your protection. The internal security agency Shin Bet has also been detailed to assist in your protection. I understand your commitment, father, and the other members of the team. But taking unnecessary risks will not aid the holy mission on which I have sent you.'

He looked at the ten men and saw that his words had relaxed and comforted them. All ten men, as well as the sprinkling of cardinals who had agreed to be present, bowed their heads and mumbled prayers.

Innocent stood, made the sign of the Cross and began a benediction over the heads of his Crusaders.

Harlin Brown's mind was racing from one thought to another. There were so many crocodiles snapping at his heels, he felt he would have to dance over the swamp in order to save himself. One thing he'd learned at Harvard—tackle one problem at a time. Put everything else aside and focus your mind on one big issue. Tackle the hardest issue first. Then, when that was solved, turn to the next problem.

What was the big issue? Luke! And Joe! And Micah! Damn Jimmy! Look at the mess he'd got them into. Foul-mouthed, bigoted, bible-bashing, Southern cretin.

So the task was to concentrate his mind on what to do. He grabbed the phone and dialled through to the church. Within a minute, he was talking to Duane. Harlin had not slept all night and was exhausted, but sleep could come later. He told Duane that Luke and Joe were heading back to the States. Things were going to blow apart. Duane started to go to pieces.

'I don't need your wetass shit now Duane. We gotta think hard. Now you listen to me,' hissed Harlin, 'and you listen good. First, I want you to round up Annabelle and get her up to the church's retreat in Vermont. Even if you have to tie her up and send her there with an armed bodyguard, do it! I want to know everything, and I mean absolutely everything. Fax me a report by tomorrow morning, Israeli time. Second, get control back. Fire half a dozen people on the spot. As soon as I get off the fuckin' phone, march right down there to the secretariat and fire people. Enough so the rest know you're in charge and they'll be running scared for their jobs. The good times are over, Duane, now get your ass in a sling and move it!'

Harlin banged the phone back into its cradle. Who in hell did he know in LA that could track down Micah Watkins? One man! Lieutenant Jose Celebrio.

Annabelle Wilson was sitting beneath the cedar tree fanning herself with a magazine. She knew Duane was walking towards her without even turning to look. The insects which had been a part of the background noise had suddenly fallen quiet. Even the air seemed to be still as though in expectation of momentous events.

'Annabelle, I've got to talk to you.' She didn't turn or even look up. She just continued to stare at the ground, fanning herself slowly to stir the limpid air around her face. 'Annabelle—'

'I heard what you did this morning, Duane. Must have taken real balls to fire six people like that. Good people. People that have worked here for years. Toiled away to make this church a better place for thousands of people.'

'Annabelle, you and I must talk. Now,' he said softly.

'Were you with them that day, Duane? My memory's kind of hazy. I don't recall exactly who was there. I know Jimmy was, and I remember Luke sneerin'. And I'm sure Harlin was there. But I don't remember your face.'

Duane sat down on the circular seat around the base of the tree. They stared into separate parts of the horizon, like hands on a clock-face. 'I have to send you away, Annabelle. I got instructions from Harlin this morning that Jimmy wants you to go to the retreat up in Vermont. You'll like it up there. It's cool at this time of the year.'

'I know what it's like up there. I was the one that chose that piece of ground. So you're sendin' me away, are you? On Harlin's orders. And are Luke and Jimmy all in favour of it?' she said sarcastically. 'Did they take a vote?'

'Luke didn't do any voting.'

'Too shit-scared?'

Duane shook his head. 'He's on his way back to the States with that reporter, Joe what's-his-name.'

It took Annabelle a moment to realise the implications. 'Is he goin'—?'

'I guess.'

'Good. It'll split this place wide open. Let all the festerin' pus come out. But he's still goin' to get his.

They'll still send Luke down for life, no matter if he turns state's evidence.'

Duane bit his lip. 'Were you there, Duane? Were you there when they did it to me?'

Duane didn't answer.

'How could you and Jimmy and Harlin and Luke have done what you did to me? And to Jonas? You're all murderers, beatin' up on women!'

'I didn't touch you, Annabelle. I didn't lay a finger on you or Jonas. I was sick when I saw what Jimmy was doin' to you.'

'Ha!' she sneered.

'I swear to God, Annabelle, I didn't touch you. I was outside throwing up.'

'But you were there. You didn't lift a finger to help me, you sonofabitch.'

'I couldn't. You didn't see the look in Jimmy's eyes. If I had tried to stop him, he would have killed me. He had murder in his eyes, Annabelle, cold murder.'

'You think that makes it all right,' she said softly.

Duane shook his head. 'Every minute, every hour, every day, since what they did to you and Jonas, I've been sick with grief, anger and shame. But I've been too scared to do anything. You think I like myself? You think I feel proud?'

'Then why are you sendin' me away?' Again he lapsed into silence. 'Duane, it's all over. Can't you see that? Don't you realise it's finished. Jimmy's out of control. So's Harlin. Jimmy does things to me I couldn't even talk to you about. I was goin' to leave him and run away with Jonas, but he stopped all that.'

An eternity went by, then he whispered softly, 'You're right, Annabelle. It is all over. I knew that the minute Jimmy killed Jonas. I've just been too scared to move in case they blamed me and the police came after me. With my record, I'd fry.'

Annabelle painfully moved closer to him and put her hand on his knee. Softly she said, 'You used to be kind, compassionate, lovin'. Look what you've become, honey. Scared, withdrawn, angry. They've left you with the shit to do while they're off gallivantin' around creamin' the congregation of a fortune. Ain't that right?'

Duane shrugged.

'We can do somethin',' whispered Annabelle, as though confiding a long-hidden secret. 'We gotta call the police. Somethin's goin' down right now in Israel. I've just been waitin' a few days before I called the police.'

'You call the police and I get busted. My life's over. I'll be jailed as an accessory to murder. Jesus! Do you think I haven't thought about calling in the police every night these past weeks? Putting an end to it.'

'If you're too scared to call in the police, there's somethin' else we can do, Duane honey. We can call in Gerald Curtis.'

Ten minutes later, Duane put down the phone. Annabelle looked at him quizzically. 'Well?' she asked.

Duane smiled and nodded. 'You were right. He was horrified when I told him. Horrified beyond belief. And angry. He was ranting, asking how Jimmy could have done this.'

'What's he going to do?' she asked.

'He's going to phone up a friend that he's got in the LAPD. Get him to come over and take statements. He guarantees that you and I won't be implicated at all in conspiracy. Says that Jimmy will go down for life. So will Harlin. But because I didn't have anything to do with the murder, I'll be a witness for the DA and he can even conceal my identity.'

Annabelle smiled and painfully walked over to where he was sitting. She put her arm around his neck, stroked his hair with her fingers like a mother to a child and said, 'See, I told you.'

It took only forty minutes for the police car to arrive. It screamed to a halt in a cloud of dust in front of the Chrome Cathedral. Annabelle and Duane were standing in the air-conditioned vestibule, waiting in anticipation for their nightmare to be over. Two uniformed officers got out of the front of the car and a tall, heavily built Mexican-looking detective wearing a sharp linen suit slowly opened the door and got out of the rear, staring at the huge building. The three men walked towards the glass doors, which slid open as they came near.

A hot gust of desert wind blew in with them and enshrouded Duane and Annabelle. Duane stepped forward to introduce himself. 'Hi officer, I'm Duane Clarke, this is Mrs Annabelle Wilson.'

'Hear we've got some trouble,' the detective said.

Duane nodded.

'Perhaps we could go somewhere private where we can talk,' said the detective. Duane helped Annabelle walk towards the office to the left of the reception desk in the vestibule. The detective nodded to the two policemen to stay in the lobby. He looked upwards and saw that church staff had come out of their offices to see what was happening. The three sat down.

'I got a call from Mr Gerald Curtis. He tells me you're willing to give evidence against your husband, Reverend Wilson, for first degree murder and other felonies. Also against other officials of the church. Is that right, ma'am?' Annabelle nodded. 'Ma'am, I think this young man better come downtown with me. I can take a full statement there. Tell me, son, have you discussed this matter with anybody else in the church?'

Duane shook his head vigorously. 'No sir. We want this to be as private as possible, until the arrests are made.'

'Good.'

They walked back through the vestibule. Detective Celebrio noticed that the church officials had returned to their offices. He walked outside slowly as Annabelle shuffled towards his car. 'You two boys take Mr Duane Clarke.' He turned around to Annabelle. 'Ma'am, why don't you stay here. You're obviously in no state to do much travelling. We'll take Mr Clarke downtown and you can stop worrying. It's all in hand now.'

Duane walked back and held Annabelle's hand. 'It's over, Annabelle. It can only get better from now on.'

He kissed her tenderly on the cheek. 'Tell them everything, Duane. Everything.'

The three policemen escorted him to the car and Annabelle watched as it drove passed Oscar the gateman who saluted. He was too far away but she knew he would be mouthing the words 'Have a nice day.'

The car was lost in a trail of dust as it disappeared down the long road on the journey out of the desert and towards the city. She turned and as the doors silently slid open, she walked back into the air-conditioned vestibule. She didn't notice, and neither did anyone else in the church, that instead of turning right on the road to Los Angeles or left on the road to San Diego, the police car doubled back on itself and took a side road which led into the vast, arid desert.

The superintendent of police, Meyer Katan, was as close as he had ever been to hitting a prisoner. He had been interrogating Rabbi David Berg almost non-stop for thirty-six hours and each time the grinning buffoon came back to the same answer. 'Superintendent, I was in discussions in the home of two members of the Zion Now! movement during the time that the poor archbishop was kidnapped. You know their names. You know their address. You interviewed people in the house who confirmed the story. I really don't know what more I can tell you.' The rabbi looked at the police superintendent, his grin even more nauseating than normal.

'Now listen to me, you grinning bastard. You think we're stupid? You think we don't know you kidnapped and crucified him? Do you know the damage that you've done to Israel, the worldwide headlines that you've caused? The scandal because of your obscene ideas. You think you can get away with it. We've got one thousand men combing the streets of every town in Israel for evidence.' He stepped closer and thrust his fist menacingly into Berg's face. 'One hair, one fingerprint, one scrap of dead skin which ties you to him and you're gone.'

Rabbi Berg smiled and said, 'Superintendent, during the time that Archbishop Solomonoglou was kidnapped, I was in a home with two colleagues discussing—'

Superintendent Katan spun on his heels and walked out, slamming the door behind him. Neither he nor the chief inspector had succeeded in cracking the facade. Berg was ridiculing the entire police operation. And neither was there any evidence produced so far. Archbishop Solomonoglou's body and the cross had been searched for fingerprints and forensic evidence. All they had found were traces of the skins of oranges. One hundred homes belonging to members of the Zion Now! movement had been raided, hundreds of people taken into custody, premises searched, but not one scrap of evidence had been found. The entire Israeli police department and Shin Bet were at their wits' end and to make matters worse, three fat-cat lawyers representing the Zion Now! movement were right now leaving the Supreme Court with orders for Berg's release due to lack of evidence. Damn the Israeli justice system and its concern for the individual over the good of the nation. Superintendent Katan reached his office and slumped into his chair. He would have to pass the news that he had failed to break Rabbi Berg's story to the Minister for Police.

A small crowd of supporters was gathered outside the Jerusalem police station waiting for the imminent release of David Berg. They were massively outnumbered by journalists and camera crews who had got wind of the Supreme Court's decision. Further away, on the other side of the street and behind barricades, Jews, Christians and Arabs gathered to express their loathing of the man and his deed. The few supporters chanted songs of praise to their leader while the vast majority booed, whistled and jeered. Finally, Rabbi David Berg emerged at the marble steps of the police station. As he stepped towards the microphones, his supporters went wild, cheering and clapping, while, at a distance, demonstrators strained at the barricades which were reinforced by a huge contingent of security police. As he stepped brazenly forward to the bouquet of microphones, the journalists noted how drained and haggard he was. His interrogation during the last day and a half had obviously been intense.

'Let me start off by saying,' he announced, not bothering to answer the shouted questions of reporters, 'that the method of Archbishop Solomonoglou's death is abhorrent to me. It was callous and inhumane but I can only blame the Pope and the College of Cardinals for the events taking place. Their arrogance and insensitivity to the rightful aims and aspirations of the Jewish people has caused this situation to come about. I fear what the future holds for the Christian people in Israel unless the Pope rescinds this obscene idea and sends these crusading scholars back to where they came from. They have no right to be in this country. Israel is not a plaything of the Papists and the Arabs. Unless the people of the world realise that Israel is a strong and independent nation and is the home of the Jews *and the Jews alone* there will be no peace in this land.'

The reporters screamed questions but Rabbi Berg, flanked by his lawyers, turned and walked towards a waiting car.

Cauldrons of soups, stews and lentils were bubbling on the ovens, their steam rising to the low damp ceiling. Four people, their faces red from the heat of the kitchen, moved busily from pot to pot, stirring, adding, sipping and pouring.

Daniel opened the kitchen door, and felt the sudden force of the heat. He stood at the door watching, suddenly immobile, hoping that Pazit would look up and recognise him.

When she did finally glance up, she merely looked at him for a painful moment, then looked down at the pots and pans and continued her work.

'Pazit,' he said from the door, over the noise of bubbling liquids, 'I wonder if you could spare a moment?'

She looked at him again and, after another anxious moment, nodded, gave a few cursory instructions, wiped her hands, and walked to the door.

In silence they left the *chadder ochel* and entered the *moshav*'s central compound. There were no fountains, no seats, no benches where they could sit. 'Can we go for a walk in the orchards? I'd like to see it with you one more time before I leave.' Pazit shrugged her shoulders indifferently. They walked, again in silence, to the edge of the grapefruit trees. Daniel reached up to one of the trees and plucked a fruit. 'One of the things I'll miss most around here is the way in which I can simply reach up and touch God's bounty.' Pazit remained silent. 'Pazit, I don't want to leave here with us as enemies.' Again she shrugged indifferently. 'Will you not speak to me before I leave Israel?'

'What's to say?'

'I didn't lie to you. I couldn't tell you the entire truth. I'm here on a mission for his holiness. To have breached the secrecy of that mission could have imperilled my purpose.'

She laughed, anger hidden by a surface veneer. 'You have very selective reasoning, your eminence.'

'How so?' Daniel said defensively. 'Did I lead you on? Did I tell you anything which was in any way a falsification of my feelings?'

'I'm not angry, just hurt. You stirred up feelings which had been deeply buried for my own protection.'

'Pazit, I'm not the only one with selective reasoning.'

'Meaning?'

'Meaning I know about your weekly visits to Jerusalem. I know that you have a lover up there. Yet you're treating me as though I was responsible for something other than a temporary enjoyment.'

Pazit turned and shook her head. 'You really know nothing, do you Daniel? These weekly visits of mine.' She paused. 'Francis kept pressing me to leave the orphanage and to make a real life for myself. Eventually I started to go to Jerusalem and he assumed that I had a man up there. He even followed me once. Do you want to know what I do? I take myself to a movie. I have dinner in the same restaurant. I stay in a boarding house and I come back the next morning.'

Daniel bit his lip in anger at his accusation. 'I apologise, Pazit. There's much you don't know about me. One thing is that I'm a very weak man, Pazit. There's a part of my being which I've suppressed for most of my life, which rises up like scum to the top of a pot. Unfortunately, I've let it damage you, as well as me. Pazit, you're judging me harshly now. Pray God that some good will come out of our friendship.'

'Good? For whom, Daniel? For you, or for me?'

'For us. If, when I leave here, you can one day think kindly of me, then all may not have been wasted. I revel in our talks, delight in the memory of sharing sunny afternoons with a wonderful person. I'm just sorry that it has ended in acrimony.'

Pazit seemed to relent. 'I enjoyed our time together too. I only wish that it could have been conducted in honesty.' They walked to the end of the orchard. Pazit stopped and asked, 'When you leave here, what will you be doing?'

'During the last few days, I've been speaking to a number of Israelis about the mission which his holiness has sent me on. As a result of those discussions, I will be travelling around the country with a group of scholars. When I get back to Rome, I will be telling the President of the Prefecture for the Economic Affairs of the Holy See to put some urgently needed funds into Francis's bank account. Maybe we can pay you a decent salary, and buy Francis a real car.'

Pazit smiled, for the first time in days. 'I wouldn't say "no" to either of those.'

The conference room of the Dead Sea Hotel was noisy with the laughter and chatter of the small group of men. There was an atmosphere of excitement, of discovery, of men at the beginning of an adventure. It reminded some of the scholars of childhood scout camps or excursions. The feeling of euphoria overcame their normal reserve.

Daniel Rhymer had entered the room unannounced and had absorbed the feeling of ease and comradeship. He was more delighted than he had dared to hope, anticipating that much of his work would involve internecine rivalries. But a feeling of unity, an emotional level above camaraderie seemed to grip all of the Catholic scholars from the moment they had met with the International Team several days earlier and had been privileged to view at first hand the miraculous list.

Daniel sat at the head of the conference table signalling for all of the scholars gathered around the credenza to bring their coffees and plates of sandwiches to the table and to sit attentively.

How to begin? 'Good morning gentlemen'—hardly apt. 'Fellow scholars'—pretentious. He remembered the ease with which Gabriel Molloy dealt with colleagues, and said, 'I don't know how the rest of you feel but I feel that this is one of the most momentous days of my life.' As one, they nodded and gave assent. 'Just to have seen, to have touched such a fragile link with our past is a fulfilment of everything that I've ever hoped or wished.' He should have told them how dubious he felt and how committed he was to the Testament retaining its millennial secrets. But he was here as the Pope's representative and he would play the part.

'Now we have experienced the reality of a list, it's necessary for us to use our combined knowledge to determine where best to search. My own view is that if the list is here, then the Testament cannot be. Were it to have been moved by some early Christian to another place in the vicinity then I doubt he would have left so explicit an instruction. There's a view that it may have been moved to Jerusalem or to other early Christian centres outside of the borders of Roman Judea. But this is an issue on which I'm not qualified to speak. That's why you gentlemen are here. Perhaps now I can ask you whether anybody has formulated a hypothesis.'

Several of the scholars lent forward, eager to contribute their view.

At the end of three hours of intense but good-natured debate, three distinct locations had been determined. One party planned to examine areas within Jerusalem, especially around the current excavations of the Western Wall of the Herodian Temple, where such a document may have been secreted. They would join with archaeologists to search for a geniza where such documents may have been placed. They would beg the keepers of the Muslim mosques to allow infidel Christians for the first time in living memory to join together to see whether the words of a great prophet common to both religions could have been secreted in one of the many unexplored chambers and tunnels below the mosques on the temple mount.

Another group wanted to travel to Egypt to investigate Coptic monasteries and to see whether any of these hid the closely guarded secret. A third group had decided to travel to Antioch in Turkey, the chief town of the Hatay province on the Orontes River. Proponents of the Testament being in Antioch were the most outspoken of the entire scholarly group. It was certain, they said, that the Testament would have been taken to Antioch. It was the earliest of all centres of Christianity after Jerusalem. From AD 40 the followers of Christ were called Christians. Up until AD 55 it was the headquarters of St Paul's missionary journeys. It would be natural, said a German theologian, for a Christian to follow the journey of Paul. And there were many aspects of ancient Antioch which were only recently coming to light. He cited the findings of the celebrated chalice in 1910, believed to have been the cup used at Christ's last supper.

Nobody, not one scholar, mentioned Ethiopia. By the end of the day, even Daniel was beginning to doubt the insights of Professor Farber and why he and his companion were interviewing the Falashas.

'Gentlemen, I think it reasonable to conclude at this stage. We have our missions. We have our purpose for being here. All travel arrangements and letters of introduction will be written to you by the Vatican Secretariat. My purpose for bringing you to the Dead Sea was to inflame your passions, to excite your minds, to wander as we now know our Lord wandered, into the canyons and along the dry river beds and through the massifs where Our Lord walked. Outside, we have a small bus waiting to take us to the area of Masada where Our Lord's Testament was mentioned by this list. When we get there, you will feel, as I have felt in these last few days, the immediacy of the Bible. And now, the physical reality of our Saviour.'

Harlin Brown sat on the beige divan in his hotel suite holding his head, as though it was racked by torment. What was he doing here? Four years of a law degree in Harvard, just so he could wet-nurse a psychotic who had involved him in murder and fraud.

Since that article in the *LA Times*, everything had started to unravel. All his carefully laid plans to replace Gerald Curtis when the old fool retired; to find and appoint younger, more evangelical ministers to train under Jimmy, and eventually take over from him; to spread the church out of the armpit of Southern California, and franchise its operations and methods to the wealthier areas of black and Hispanic America; and who knows, maybe even overseas.

In just a few weeks, he had lost his control over Jimmy, and even over himself. And now he had just defrauded sixty wealthy patrons with some bullshit story about Jimmy in the desert. How long would they believe it? Half of them were sneering as they left the ballroom, mumbling about the way things were. How long could he hold them in Israel before he had to make a refund? Or fight off the law? Jesus! What a fucking mess!

And where was Jimmy? Mumbling up and down the corridors. Phoning the church and appointing some new PR guy, now Luke was gone. PR? That was the last thing that he needed. And making plans with the hotel travel agency to go to Ethiopia. Jesus Christ! Ethiopia! What the fuck was going on? And when Harlin tried to pull him back into line, he had got his head bitten off.

How was he ever going to extricate himself from this situation? Alone in his $500-a-night suite, he slid off the divan to his knees, bent his head, closed his eyes tightly and tried to picture an image of the Almighty who might hear his prayers and offer him advice. He hadn't prayed since he was a child.

The doors leading from LA Customs and into the arrival lounge slid open and the confusion of luggage retrieval gave way to pandemonium as relatives eagerly searched for loved ones who had landed on one of the dozen jumbo jets which had recently arrived. Joe Deakin and Luke Carmody pushed trolleys with their bags.

'Ben? What are you—?'

'Shut up and come with me. You too,' he said to Luke.

The two men pushed their trolleys after the portly figure of Joe's editor and four men, big, strong-looking people, fell in behind them. Luke looked around, 'What's going on?'

'In case you didn't realise it, son, your life is in serious jeopardy. Three of these guys,' Ben said, nodding at the entourage, 'are here to protect your body. That one,' he went on, nodding to a sharply dressed younger man, 'is here to protect your balls. He's a lawyer.'

An hour later they were all ensconced in a large, garish hotel complete with professional tape recording equipment and a video camera and lights.

'Luke, I ought to tell you right from the outset,' said Ben, 'that the *LA Times* will hold out no offers to you other than to present your case accurately and properly to the public. As soon as the interview is over, I'm going to call the DA's office and get a prosecutor down here. How you play it after that is up to you.'

'I want my own lawyer,' Luke said.

'Eventually,' Ben responded. 'Pete Russel here will look after your rights until the DA steps in, then it's over to you.'

Luke eyed the lawyer and then, for over three hours, unburdened himself, telling Joe and Ben every financial manipulation, every act of fraud, every moment of racism and brutality that he had experienced in his three years with Jimmy. He confirmed everything he had told Joe in Israel about Annabelle's beating and Jonas' murder.

Two of the bodyguards were appointed to stay with Luke twenty-four hours a day until he could be handed over to the DA. Joe and Ben headed back to the *LA Times* office. As they pulled away from the Anaheim hotel, Ben said, 'You've done a brilliant job. I take my hat off to you. I thought you were chasing shadows.'

'Thanks boss. So, we going to the DA?'

'Are you off your fucking mind? Luke's going nowhere. I want you to go out and see Annabelle and get her into protection. Meanwhile, I have a phone call to make. A long and deeply satisfying phone call,' said Ben. 'To Israel. As soon as Annabelle is safely tucked away, I want a conversation with the Reverend Dr James Wilson.'

CHAPTER 23

The 737 was two hours from landing in Ethiopia when Judith posed the question that had been plaguing their minds since they began the search. The stewardess had finished clearing their trays of food when Judith asked, 'Suppose we do find it.'

'The chances are one in a million,' Michael said.

'But if we do?'

'It's a Catholic document. I'll take it to Rome and present it to the Pope.'

She smiled. 'It's a Jewish document, Michael. It was written by a rabbi. It's part of the Dead Sea Scrolls collection.'

'It's a work of Christian theology, Judith. You can't escape that.'

She stirred the remnants of a cup of coffee. 'I think we have to do some very serious talking.' Michael nodded and stared out of the window at the ground far below.

Bole Airport was a modern two-storey building, glass-fronted and air-conditioned. It sat incongruously in the middle of verdant fields, an alien form, angular and structured, superimposed upon nature. The only other human artefact was the single black runway pointing into the dense infinity of the jungle. The pilot had warned his passengers that Addis Ababa was built on a high plateau some eight thousand feet above sea level and, contrary to the heat of the lower regions of Ethiopia, was cold, wet and often uncomfortable. As Judith and Michael stepped out onto the concourse, the cold air made their skin prickle. Judith grasped firmly onto Michael's arm as they carried their hand baggage to the doors of the terminal.

Inside the building, Africa had been artificially and garishly recreated to satisfy what the new Ethiopian government, desperate for Western approbation, perceived were the expectations of the tourist trade. Huge murals of grazing antelopes, lions, gazelles and giraffes festooned the walls, fighting for space between massive adverts for accommodation in Addis Ababa, car hire firms, and brands of cigarettes. It was a gaudy blend of the old and the new, the traditional and the modern, and a profound disappointment for Judith. She fancied seeing large black women in colourful tribal costumes, squatting on multi-coloured rugs, selling ornaments of ivory, teak and copper. The world had become unifyingly boring. Michael appeared not to notice his surroundings. She nudged him in the side and motioned to a massive banner strewn across the top of the booths where Customs officials viewed the incoming passengers with suspicion. It said, 'ETHIOPIA—THIRTEEN MONTHS OF SUNSHINE'.

'I don't understand,' said Michael.

'Next time read the information they give you on the plane.'

'Help me.'

'Ethiopia has a calendar with twelve months of thirty days. The last month of the year is a holiday called *Pagume*. It's a six-day-long religious celebration, notable for the gusto of the celebrants. Apparently, everyone spends the whole week pissed out of their skulls.'

'Beats hell out of Lent, Yom Kippur and Ramadan.'

They stood in line as the 127 passengers from the plane waited to be cleared by two desultory Ethiopians, opening passports, looking at visas, asking peremptory questions and sending passengers through to collect their baggage. Judith walked in front of Michael when their turn came. She opened the British passport which she had acquired two days earlier from the Ministry of Foreign Affairs and handed it to the official. He looked at Judith and looked down at her picture. 'How long will you be staying in Ethiopia, Mrs Dawson?'

She smiled. 'About two weeks.'

'And what's the purpose of your visit?'

The official began tapping the details into his computer. He checked her visa details, then stamped and handed the passport back. She thanked him and walked forward as Michael underwent the same procedure. When they were collecting their luggage from the huge carousel, she looked at him and smiled. He wore a look of concern. When they had retrieved their luggage, they walked past three distrusting men in khaki uniforms, each of whom viewed the incoming passengers with suspicion.

Out on the street, they got into a waiting taxi. Michael told the taxi driver to take him to the bishop's palace. 'I felt uncomfortable in there,' he said. 'As though everybody was looking at me with great suspicion.'

Judith smiled. 'You get used to it when you're living in a hostile environment. That's why in Israel, we've made massive efforts to make the airport as friendly as possible. You rarely see guards or security. But it's there!'

They held hands and looked at Addis Ababa as the taxi hurried through. Tall new office blocks and glittering shops shone incongruously beside run-down shanties, the first world investment imperiously conquering the third world heritage of the city. As they drove into the centre of the city, images pressed themselves onto Michael's mind. Tall black Cushite men and women in brilliant multi-coloured robes walked proudly along streets as shorter unkempt men and women in long white linen jackets and jodhpurs scurried in between. In every gutter, on virtually every corner, beggars with huge goitres or lepers dressed in rags held begging bowls, supporting themselves on crutches or sitting immobile, staring into infinity.

The taxi passed a grove of juniper trees and Selassie Cathedral appeared suddenly in front of them. Lying as though dead in the gutter, slowly waving a wooden bowl in lazy circular motions, was a man dressed in the filthiest, fly-blown stained rags that Michael had ever seen on a human being. His scrappy beard covered a mouth devoid of teeth. Michael thought that in his lap he was carrying some dark awful-looking diseased child, but when he stared closer he realised it was the man's scrotum, massive with elephantiasis.

They paid the taxi and walked towards the bishop's palace beside the cathedral. A servant showed Michael and Judith into the bishop's study. The man standing behind the desk was tall, with greying hair. He wore a skull cap and a caftan made of variegated colours. He beamed a smile and his baritone voice boomed, 'Michael Farber!' He opened his arms and walked towards Michael, crushing him in a hug. 'My dear, dear friend. It's been too many years.' They embraced.

'Isaac, I'd like to introduce you to a very dear friend of mine, Judith Abramovitch.'

Judith held out her hand and the bishop grasped it, raised it to his lips and kissed it. She was touched by the European mannerism, strangely in place despite the setting. He led them to the sofa. Michael looked around the study and was entranced by the artefacts. 'I know it's a ridiculous question,' said the bishop, 'but what brings you to Ethiopia?' Michael began to answer but the bishop held up his hands. 'Of course, if it's to do with this latest miraculous find in the desert and you somehow think it has to do with the Falashas.' Michael looked in astonishment. The bishop smiled and said, 'Then keep it completely confidential. I mustn't know.'

Michael was too stunned to react. Even Judith was taken by surprise. The bishop burst out laughing, his baritone changing to a high-pitched, almost girlish giggle. Again, he held up his hands and in a Messianic voice, as though he were preaching, boomed, 'I've been visited by the Holy Spirit and the Holy Spirit said to me that a brilliant archaeologist and biblical scholar called Michael would descend and try to find Christ's Testament among the Falashas.' He giggled again.

'Isaac—' said Michael.

'A simple case of deduction, my dear friend. Nobody visits Ethiopia these days unless it's for a very good reason. We're not exactly on the tourist map. The minute you phoned me, I put two and two together. Michael Farber. Christ's Testament. Has to be the Falashas and this quaint old story about the lost ark. Do you know how many bounty hunters we have here every year? Dozens. All of them land in great secrecy, thinking they've discovered the source of the Ark of the Covenant. They all travel up to Gondar and Lake Tana. They all pay great bribes, vast sums of money to the officials in the Ministry of the Interior to get a permit. And they all go to the monasteries built on islands in the middle of the lake.' There was a malicious twinkle in his eye. 'And the priests love taking their money. Do you know how many Arks of the Covenant we have? Dozens of the damn things. Literally dozens. Every church up there has got a tabot. It's a kind of stone which is said to be a replica of the stones given to Moses.'

Judith said, 'Do we know for sure that the Ark of the Covenant isn't here, your grace?'

'Who knows? Who can be certain of anything? There's one place where the chief priest will not allow anybody to witness his tabot. He claims it's the original ark. Who am I to argue?'

'Well, now you know why we're here, can you help us?' asked Michael.

'What help do you need?'

'Judith and I need to find Falashas. People left over after Operation Moses.'

The bishop shrugged. 'There are a few Falashas still in this country. Not many. Some married out. Some refused to go. Do you have a particular Falasha in mind?'

Judith stood and walked towards the fireplace, where the bishop was standing. She picked up a carved wooden statute of a replica of Solomon and Sheba. 'We think that there was a small group of elders who were kept apart from the rest of the Falashas. We don't know much about them. All we know is that they were called the Guardians. Quite why we haven't yet discovered.'

The bishop nodded his head. 'And you think that these Guardians may hold the key?' She nodded. 'Why on earth do you believe that Christ's Testament might have found its way to Ethiopia?' Michael explained his theory about the early Christian who may have travelled to Alexandria and then to the holy city of Elephantine before struggling up to the source of the Nile and leaving the holy document with the Guardians. 'A very fanciful notion, if I may say, Michael.'

'Right now, Isaac, there are scholars scouring the world. There are some who are re-looking at ancient documents in Rome. Others who are travelling to Alexandria, to Ephesus. There are even people who have gone to Afghanistan, where they believe Christ ended his life. And that's apart from the dozens of groups who are scouring the Dead Sea area. There's a worldwide search on. It's pure luck as to who finds what.'

The bishop rang a bell and within a second a servant opened the door. The bishop ordered coffee and refreshments for his guests. 'Michael, one of my duties is to protect the souls of people unfortunate enough to be incarcerated by the regime. I have priests who regularly visit the jails in Addis Ababa, in Gondar and in other provincial capitals. It's a chief form of friction between myself and the government. They seem to think that I'm one of the informants for Amnesty International. Total nonsense of course,' he said, suppressing a smile. 'However, over the past few weeks, one of my priests has been helping an elderly Falasha in a prison in Gondar. The regime up there thought he was a subversive. They found him one day, wandering around the town and he couldn't prove his identity, so they locked him up. He kept saying that he wanted to go to Jerusalem. It wasn't a very clever thing to say. I have no idea but it's possible that this man may provide a link to these Guardians of yours.'

'Your grace, can we visit this man?'

'I can see no reason why not.' Michael and Judith smiled at each other.

An hour later, they were ensconced in a bedroom freshening up for dinner. Sitting at his desk, Bishop Manitam picked up the phone. The voice that answered it spoke Hebrew. Eventually Cardinal Rhymer came to the phone.

'My dear Isaac, how good to speak to you again.'

'And to you, Daniel.'

'Are they there?'

'Yes.' And he related the conversation.

'I see,' said Daniel. 'And you'll let me know what happens between them and this elderly Jewish gentleman?'

'Of course.'

'God be with you, Isaac.'

'And with you, your eminence.'

'Bit liberal of him to let us sleep together,' said Judith.

Michael kissed her on the forehead. 'He's one of those people who doesn't ask questions about that sort of thing. He probably finds it easier.'

'He's being very hospitable,' she said. 'Though I didn't enjoy the meal much.'

'I guess you get used to antelope eventually.'

She reached over and turned on the light, intending to read, her nerves still tingling from their lovemaking. Michael was annoyed. He wanted to fall asleep. It had been a long day. 'It would be too much to hope that this old Falasha was a Guardian, wouldn't it?'

Judith nodded. 'Yeah. But you never know your luck in a big city.'

He started to drift but Judith realised she had re-read the same paragraph three times. 'Michael . . .'

A sleepy voice mumbled, 'Um?'

'In Israel I told you I wasn't going to let you go again. I was sort of staking my claim on you. But I don't want you to be influenced just because I'm leaving Uri. I was going to leave him anyway, regardless of whether you and I—'

'Ah huh.'

She dug him in the ribs. 'For God's sake, wake up. This is important.'

He turned around. 'Can't we talk in the morning?' he said stretching.

'No, I want to talk now. I don't want you to leave Deirdre just for me. I want you to leave her because she's no longer right for you. You have to think about your son.'

Michael folded his hands behind his head and nestled in the pillow. 'Do you seriously think I haven't spent every waking moment when I'm with you thinking of the effect of what I'm doing? It makes no difference to Christopher whether I'm around or not. He has no emotions. No conscious understanding, not even of where he is. As for Deirdre, she's never done a single deliberate thing to harm me in all her life, Judith. I once loved her very deeply. But the woman who once loved me is now devoted—body, mind and soul—to a shell of a human being. I'm excluded, Judith. I guess my decision is only partly due to you. I was immersing myself twenty-four hours a day in my work and religion as a way of escaping the horror of what my home life had become. I didn't think for one moment—not for one solitary second—that something beautiful could ever happen in my life again. And you have.'

Judith closed her book and put her arm around his head, drawing him close to her breast. She stroked his face, allowing him to fall asleep in her protective embrace.

The city of Gondar in the foothills of the high Semien mountains is surrounded by huge dark craggy peaks. Vast volcanic teeth jutting into a cold blue sky. On the DC–3, Michael read about the foundation of the city in the middle 1600s by Ethiopian emperors who roamed the country trailing retinues of as many as 50000 people. The description of the emperors' courts was of a medieval progression, a massive, seemingly endless orgy of eating and battle.

As their plane landed on the plateau, many miles from Gondar, Michael looked out of the window to try to define some remnants of the medieval architecture. But all he saw was row upon row of corrugated army barracks, aging tanks and a few helicopters. A bus carried Michael and Judith from the airport to the walls of Fasilades' Castle in Gondar. The city was frenetic, a smaller version of Addis Ababa, with architecture dating back hundreds of years. Old buses, trucks and jeeps belonging to the United Nations and World Vision relief agencies, as well as 1950s American rust buckets, belched foul brown smoke into the air as they sped through the squares and up the narrow twisting road-ways. And through the melee of vehicles, as though the twentieth century had failed in its attempt to impinge upon their lifestyle, trotted horses, oxen and donkeys pulling traps and carts; some carrying ragged passengers, others mounds of colourful fruits, vegetables or spices.

They walked to the outskirts of the town centre, directed by locals to the prison. The commandant was at first hesitant about admitting them, despite Bishop Manitam's letter of introduction. He phoned a senior officer in Bahar Dar and after conferring, put the phone down and said to Michael, 'I'll get the prisoner for you.'

As he assigned a prison guard to bring the old Falasha Jew, Judith reached over, grasped Michael's hands, and whispered, 'Don't build up your hopes.' He nodded. The man was tall, lean and wearing rags which must once have been white, but were now stained by foul-smelling excrement and signs that he had suffered many beatings over a prolonged period of time. Brown dried blood had congealed on the back, sides and buttocks of his jodhpurs. His skin was broken by weeping sores and wounds which refused to heal in the pestilential cells from which he had come. Michael and Judith intro-duced themselves. The prison commandant translated but the man held up his hand. 'My name is Wossen. I speak English.'

'I'll leave you alone. Are you prepared to pay this man's fine?'

Michael nodded. The prison commandant shrugged indifferently. He left saying, 'I'll go and draw up the release papers.'

When they were alone, Wossen looked at Michael and Judith in suspicion. He had so rarely seen white people and now they had dropped out of nowhere and paid the fine imposed for being a vagrant, allowing his release.

'Why are you doing this?' he asked in faltering English.

Judith answered, 'We're here to help you and your people.'

'My people are all gone,' said Wossen smiling.

'We're from Israel,' she continued. 'I live in Jerusalem.'

The old man's eyes seemed to spark with an inner glow. Michael nodded enthusiastically. 'We're here to help you.'

'You're here to take me to Jerusalem?'

'If that is your wish, then yes.'

The old man swallowed and Judith realised that he was about to cry. She walked over and put her arm around him, leading him to a chair. He sat. He looked around to see if anybody would object to his sitting in the presence of white people. 'Why did you not go to Israel when the others left?'

'I was married to an Amharic woman. We had children. When my people all left, her people treated her very badly. They spat at her. She became an outcast. She told me to go. The village elder forced me out. I have no home. I wander the streets, like a beggar. When they found me they realised I was from the Agau, a Jew, a Falasha. I am arrested. I am held here. No one knows.'

His voice cracked with age and isolation. Judith reached over and held his hand. The old man's eyes began to brim with tears. It was the first true human contact he had enjoyed in years. 'We will care for you.'

They took two rooms in the Hotel Selassie off one of the main squares of Gondar. 'Why is everything called Selassie?' asked Judith. 'I thought after they got rid of the emperor they would have changed all the names.'

Michael shook his head. 'Selassie means trinity. It has nothing to do with the name of the emperor. This is an intensely religious country. There is an old saying that the key to Ethiopia opens the door to the church.'

Michael helped Wossen remove his clothes and was disgusted by the smell of his weeping sores. Judith knocked timorously on the door to the old man's room and handed Michael the liniments and medicines she had brought from a nearby pharmacy as well as new clean clothes.

Michael helped Wossen bathe, sponging the sores on his back delicately and allowing him the dignity of washing his own face and chest and legs. Michael dried his back carefully with a towel and applied the medicine. When the old man was dressed and clean, Judith appeared in his room with a plate full of dates, entsete, bread and chicken stew. Wossen eyed it greedily and tore the bread and scooped the stew into his mouth. They watched him with the pleasure of parents. When he had finished, he sat back and nodded in appreciation. 'You are my friends,' he said.

Judith told him again why they had travelled to Ethiopia and about their need to find the Guardians. He nodded as he listened. 'There is such a man. He was not known to my tribe. When all my people left, he and others stayed behind. When my wife told me to go, I wandered. I found him and the others. They spoke

Ge'ez. They spoke Hebrew. They were very . . .' He searched for the word and played a charade with his hands. Michael interpreted, 'Secretive?' Wossen nodded enthusiastically. 'Yes, yes. They told me to go. That was two years ago. I haven't heard of them since.'

'Can you take us to them?' Judith asked casually, not wanting to show enthusiasm.

'Am I to go with you to Jerusalem?' asked Wossen.

'Yes. As we return, you will return with us. This I promise you,' Michael said.

'I will take you,' said Wossen.

Binyussef the Guardian descended from the mountain onto the plain which led down to the reed banks of Lake Tana. On his way down, he skirted the fields of Amba Giorgis. He walked slowly for the last mile as he approached his village. These days he had to be cautious. When his people lived there, he occupied a house of prestige on the periphery of the village. He lived with other Guardians. Although they rarely talked to the people of the tribe, they were treated with a wary regard, a muted respect. Nobody knew what they did or why they were withdrawn. It was a secret known only to tribal leaders.

Since his people had left, his life had become very different. Most of his possessions had been stolen. Except the books. As he walked into his village, he glanced surreptitiously left and right in case he would be accosted by one of the soldiers, but no one saw him. It was the end of the day and people were busy preparing food or returning from the fields. He walked to his hut and kissed the doorpost with his hand as he entered. He didn't know why he did it, but it made him feel comfortable.

Binyussef sat down and began to pray, rocking forwards and back with a gentle motion, intoning words under his breath that his heart sang. He was happy again. He looked around the room. So little left. He stood and gathered the ancient prayer books which were all that remained of his previous life. His link with his people. There were no more than a handful now, but they were precious. He opened the *sefer kodesh*, and touched the pages. He didn't read but looked at the beauty of the script, the delicate brush strokes of the proud ancients who had written the book. He traced the outline of the letters from the serifs to the bold downstrokes, kissing his finger each time he finished a word. Binyussef closed the book and opened another, placing it on his lap as he would nurse a baby. This book he read aloud, singing the archaic rhythmic incantations. And the third and fourth and fifth books until he had touched each page, each book. His children.

Outside the door, it was now dark. Safe. He picked up his children and carried them under his cloak to the edge of Lake Tana. A half a mile away. The ground was once marshy but now the reeds were dry. He placed the books delicately down on the ground, stroking them again to feel their proud strength, their ethereal beauty, as though their inner majesty surged into his body and gave him strength. Out of the folds of his robe, he took a box of matches. He gathered dry reeds which had fallen and made them into a pile. He lit the reeds which flared instantly, crackling and spitting. Sparks flew up into the sky, smoke-like incense, curled upwards to form a tracery. He placed the first book on top of the pyre, its pages open to the heat. He began to cry. To shut out the noise of the fire, and the pain his children would feel, Binyussef sang an age-old Hebrew melody. He began softly, but as the crackling grew louder, as the fire took hold of the pages, and the old, dry parchment burst into flame, he sang louder and louder until his voice was like a wail in the black night sky.

When the first book was ablaze, he placed the second book, then the third, and the fourth until all the books were aflame in the conflagration. It was a holocaust for his eyes alone, a sacrifice, a final ritual burnt offering. It was his way of severing himself forever from his land, a rite of passage into the new world of Israel. He would leave nothing behind which could be found and abused by the Godless ones. Only the objects of veneration high above in the closed, dark cave.

The countryside through which they drove was a patchwork of verdant greens and startling yellows. Brilliant yellows. In fact, though he was concentrating on the eccentric tracks which led south-eastwards from Gondar up into the stark highlands, Michael felt as though he was part of a living kaleidoscope. As the murderous ravines became more savage, the colours in the atmosphere of the higher realms took on a new intensity. Yellows, reds, mauves, whites and oranges stood out starkly against the cloudless indigo sky.

In the back of the jeep sat Wossen, looking bemused, a biblical figure transported by the magic of the twentieth century. In the front of the jeep, Judith stared at the vastness of the countryside. Range after range of limitless mountains stretched seething with life into the far horizon. Huge scars carved by untold aeons of tectonic movement and erosion had created sheer-sided depths of sunless valleys. She was breathless in awe of the majesty of the Ethiopian highlands. She compared it to the minuscule sliver of land called Israel, which was her home, a tiny crescent hanging by its fingernails to vast arid and lifeless deserts. Michael glanced at her and recognised that this wasn't a time for conversation.

They had driven in the early hours of the morning from Gondar along the road which led towards Debre Tabor, a one time centre of Falasha culture, now a small town taken over by Amharic people, eager to claim the deserted huts and buildings left when the Falashas had decamped en-masse to travel to Israel. Towards the end of the journey, Wossen tapped Michael on the shoulder and pointed to a path which led right off the main track towards Lake Tana. It was a huge emerald blue lake which caught the melting snow of the surrounding highlands before thundering over a series of cataracts and becoming the Blue Nile, the source of Egypt's fertility.

Automatically, Michael checked in his wing mirror before turning and realised how meaningless the gesture was. They hadn't seen another vehicle in the past hour. The main track became little more than a pot-holed path, snaking its way around juniper and eucalypt trees. There were numerous clearings, inside each a collection of huts surrounded by teff and entsete plantations. The huts were conical with figurines and shapes constructed on the highest point of the roof. Magic symbolism to ward off evil spirits or incantations by the owners to pray for fortune.

Before arriving at Lake Tana, Wossen said, 'We must stop here.' They pulled the jeep over into a small beaten clearing where papyrus boats had been placed in preparation for the day's fishing. They locked the jeep and walked parallel with the lake, though some distance from its shore, through a path beaten into the wilderness. As they turned a corner, they saw higher up from the path a large, almost regal house. It was built in a stature of greater importance than any other house in the district, larger, more imposing, of greater solidity. The remnants of a fire could be both seen and smelt close to the lake shore.

In the doorway sat an old man. He looked at them impassively. The closer they walked, the more he appeared to be asleep, sitting like Mahatma Ghandi crosslegged in the porch of his house, staring into infinity. A feeling of trepidation came over the three, as though to disturb him would be a sin. He was a short man, bald, wearing a sweat-stained white cotton shirt and the traditional jodhpurs of Ethiopian men.

Judith walked over to where the old man sat and whispered, 'Are you well?' He did not respond. In Hebrew, she said, '*Ata beseder?*'

Her words appeared to stir him from his trance. Slowly his eyes began to re-focus on the present. He looked at the woman, seeing her for the first time. '*Medebert lashon kodesh?*' he asked in a bemused tone. Wossen tapped Michael on the shoulder, wondering what was being said. Michael whispered, 'He's asking whether she speaks the holy language. He means Hebrew.'

'Master,' said Judith in Hebrew. 'I speak our language. I am from Jerusalem. I am sent here to help you by other people of the Agau, who are now living good lives among their own people.'

The old man nodded. He asked, 'Who are these?' Judith explained. 'I have made the decision to travel to Jerusalem to join my people. You are here to take me?'

'Yes, Master,' said Judith. 'we will take you. But first, may we enter your home? We have travelled far to find you. We are tired.' She helped the old man up and they entered his house. He felt strangely uncomfortable as the others walked in. Judith introduced them. Wossen bowed low deferentially. The old man allowed them to sit on wooden stools and gave them a yellow stew from a large pot. They ate the stew with wooden spoons. It was a bland concoction of stringy vegetables. It was all Michael could do not to grimace at the texture.

'I am Binyussef. In Hebrew, this means son of Joseph. I didn't travel with my people when they left to go to Jerusalem. I chose to remain but I am now ready to go. Last night, I burnt my books. I will leave nothing behind for the barbarians. We will travel.'

'Master,' said Michael. 'We bring you greetings from the leader of the people of the Agau, Benawie.' Binyussef nodded in appreciation and smiled.

'Benawie is a great leader. I had few friends amongst my people, the Agau. He visited us from time to time.'

'Us?' asked Judith.

Binyussef nodded. 'They are all dead now. The last few years have been bad for us. All my friends who lived in this house have died. Some walked into Debre Tabor and never returned. Others died of old age or loneliness. I was younger than most. Younger and fitter. I've survived but now I'm lonely. Now I want to rejoin my people.'

'Master,' said Judith. 'We cannot return to Israel immediately, though I swear to you we will go shortly. Benawie sent us here on a mission. A mission to find some people who are very important to the people of the Agau.'

The old man remained silent. Michael gently continued the conversation. 'These people, Binyussef, hold the key to many great secrets. Secrets of the people of the Agau, the people who are cruelly called Falashas by the Ethiopians, but who are not outcasts. They are members of the family of Jews.'

The old man nodded. 'And who are these people you seek?'

'We seek the Guardians,' said Judith.

There was no immediate reaction. No sudden intake of breath, as though he was stunned. The old man merely remained silent and became withdrawn. He nodded towards Wossen and said, 'This man must go. I remember him from two years ago. He came to see me and I sent him away then. He must not be in this house.'

Michael turned around and told Wossen in English what Binyussef had said. He asked him to go down to the shores of the lake until the business was concluded. Subserviently, Wossen agreed, bowed deferentially to the old man and walked out of the door.

'I do not know who these Guardians are. Your presence here is of no value,' said Binyussef.

'Then we have wasted our time,' said Michael. 'Because Benawie told us that although he didn't know what the Guardians guarded, he did know with absolute certainty that they were the people in whom the future of his people rested.'

Binyussef smiled. 'The future of the people of the Agau rests with Jerusalem. We have no future here.'

'But your traditions?' said Judith.

The old man nodded. 'Our traditions remain in these mountains.'

'Binyussef,' said Michael. 'We know you are a Guardian. We know that you guard the secrets of the Ark of the Covenant and the great treasures of the Temple of Solomon. We know these things.' It was a risk. A wild card to play. Michael awaited a reaction. Judith remained silent.

Binyussef took a deep breath and stood. He walked over to the back wall of the large central living area of his house. There stood a bookshelf, a makeshift construction of twisted planks and logs. It was empty. Binyussef touched the depleted shelves with his fingertips. Above them was a symbol. A painted Hebrew letter. He reached up and touched it and then kissed his finger. Judith stared at him intently, not understanding the symbolism of the gesture. But Michael knew instinctively. Binyussef turned around and said to the two younger people, 'Children, last night I burned my books. I was saying goodbye to this land. I was about to walk towards Lake Tana, and then north to Gondar. From there, I hoped to be taken to Addis Ababa and somehow to travel to Jerusalem.' Michael was impelled to ask a question but instinct told him to remain silent. Judith reached over and held Michael's hand. They stared intently at the old man. 'For thousands of years, since the time of King Josiah, there have been Guardians who have protected the greatest secret of the people of the Agau. To be chosen as a Guardian was never an honour or even a duty, like a circumcision, for nobody knew. A boy was born and grew into his youth and then suddenly men would appear from the edge of the village where the people were forbidden to go. Beyond even to the house where the women went when they were unclean every month. Beyond, into the very jungle, which hid us. And when one of their number died, these men would seek out a young boy and they would take him from his parents, and they would never see him again. Every day, certain women from the village would leave food at our door. Our work from morning till evening was to pray . . .' He looked cautiously at them.

'And to guard the treasures belonging to your people,' finished Michael.

The old man nodded. 'I am revealing to you a secret which has not been told for two thousand years. I am the last of the Guardians. Beyond me there is nobody. Men have died for revealing the secret. But if I don't reveal it, the secret will be gone for all time. That was why I was going to Jerusalem. To ask permission of my people to reveal the secret to them. So that some could return and be Guardians.'

Judith shook her head. 'Why didn't you reveal the secret when your people left?'

The old man smiled. 'Because we thought that many would return. Jerusalem isn't clean. The Temple has been destroyed. The Temple of Solomon was made foul and corrupt by King Josiah's father and grandfather, and it was destroyed by barbarians from the north. The second Temple was destroyed by the Romans. My people wait for the third Temple to be built.'

'There is a third Temple, Binyussef,' said Judith. 'It's the state of Israel. The Jewish people have come back. Israel is the rebuilt Temple.'

The old man shook his head. 'No, my daughter. The Temple is covered with a mosque where people pray to Allah. We know this from the Muslims who live in Ethiopia.'

'Then when you go to Israel, you will disclose the location of the Temple treasures?' said Michael.

The old man nodded. 'I will tell the leaders. Then they must decide. For with me dies the secret.'

There was a long silence in the dark and smoky room. Michael asked, 'Amongst the treasures of the Temple, Binyussef, we think there's another treasure. A treasure which doesn't belong to the Temple. It's a treasure of the Christians. Do you know anything of this treasure?' The old man shrugged. Michael continued. 'We think it's a scroll. We think it was placed with the Guardians or with the people of the Agau in the first century after the death of the Christian founder, Jesus. It may be in a clay pot. Do you know if this is amongst your treasury?'

Binyussef searched his memory. 'I am Guardian to many treasures. Not the Ark of the Covenant. This was lost. Many people have come here to search amongst the monasteries for the Ark of the Covenant, but it was destroyed. The treasures we have are the treasures of the Levites and the Cohanim, the symbols of power of the tribes of Israel.'

'But the Testament of Jesus?' asked Michael, his voice cracking with anxiety.

'Things of Jesus are not treasures for us.'

'Then you don't have it?' said Judith.

'We have a clay pot which we do not revere. Legend tells of a boy who came to the people of the Agau and gave us pointers and other holy objects from the Temple. This boy asked us to look after this jar for him and we have done it for many years. I don't know what it contains.'

Michael swallowed. 'Binyussef, this is not of the Jews or even of the people of the Agau. This belongs to the Christian people. This isn't part of your treasury. I beg of you to take me to this place and to retrieve this document. Let all the other treasures stay until the people of the Agau decide. But this one thing must return with me. I'm begging of you.'

'I don't know you. I don't know this child either,' he said pointing to Judith. 'You could be an agent of the devil. You could be from the government of Ethiopia trying to trick me. How do I know you are who you say you are?' Michael began to recite the book of Genesis in Hebrew. When he had finished the first twenty verses, Judith continued for another five. Binyussef nodded. 'You are who you say you are. You are Jews. You are familiar as I am with the holy books. But even so, I don't know I can trust you. How do I know that if I reveal the place where the Guardians have guarded for these thousands of years, that you will not use it for your own purposes? These things have great value.'

'Binyussef, there is no way that we can convince you other than for you to look into our hearts. We don't come with promises of riches. We come with a plea. We're begging you to let this one treasure return to the bosom of the Christian people,' said Michael.

'But you are Jews. What is this document to you? It means nothing to us.'

'I am no longer a Jew. I became a Christian twenty years ago. I decided to forsake my religion to follow the Messiah called Jesus.'

A leaden silence descended on the room. The old man nodded in sorrow and understanding. 'Many of our people converted to follow Christ and to follow the Allah of the Muslims. It was an easy way out for them, a weakness. They married women of the Amharic tribe. They followed another God.'

In his defence, Judith held Michael's hand and said, 'Binyussef, Michael's conversion wasn't weakness. In fact, it took great strength and courage. He went against the wishes of his father and mother and of people who loved him, to follow a God in whom we did not believe. For his sake, not mine, he's seeking the Testament of his Messiah.'

Binyussef suddenly realised that Michael and Judith loved each other with an intensity which had been denied him all his life. He felt a pang of jealousy. His middle life had been hollow and difficult, living in isolation from women. He had dreamed many dreams of the comfort of a woman. He looked at Michael, then at Judith. Slowly he said, 'I will take you there. But you must swear to me that you will reveal the location of the cave to no one.'

Immediately, Michael said, 'I swear.'

But Judith said, 'I'm sorry, Binyussef. I can't make that promise. These holy objects are of greater value to me and the Jewish people than any other things. They're the lifeblood of my religion. I can't make this promise.'

Michael bit his tongue in anguish. He could see his future slipping away by her damnable honesty and integrity. Binyussef walked slowly back to the table and sat down. He stared ahead of him, through the open door, through the jungle, into the blue glimpses of Lake Tana a hundred feet below them. Judith held out her hand and squeezed Binyussef's arm. At any other time of his life, he would have been shocked by the touch of a woman but this woman was both motherly and daughterly at the same time. He felt her innate goodness, her honesty, her morality.

'Will you at least promise not to reveal the location until I am back in Jerusalem and have spoken with my people . . . or until I am dead?'

'Yes, this I swear,' said Judith.

'Then I will take you to the place of the cave.'

Before they left, Michael went down to speak to Wossen. 'Can you wait in the house? We must go on a journey. We will return for you.' He gave him some money. 'Don't worry, Wossen. You'll be perfectly safe.'

Wossen nodded. 'I await your return. You are my friend.'

CHAPTER 24

The ass lumbered towards them, its head shrouded in a cloud of flies, its tail flicking from side to side in a vain effort to scare them away. Every few moments its body twitched like a demented soul, shifting the cargo within the panniers on its side. The more it twitched the more flies seemed to rise from its flesh to surround it.

The noise of the quayside, the shouts and gesticulations, the languages which Abram and Avigad didn't understand, all combined in a melee of confusion. Montemthat shook his head and laughed. 'Do you expect me to buy that bundle of rags and bones?' he said to the merchant trying to sell him the donkey. 'It won't live to leave this port, let alone struggle up the mountains to the high country.'

'What!' cried the elderly merchant. 'This is a newborn animal. Not a year old. As strong as a bull, as surefooted as a goat, and it will live as long as an elephant. How dare you say this?'

'Old fool,' sneered Montemthat. 'I've been buying asses for twenty years and I've never seen one that looked this sick. It should be put down before it spreads its disease. You want twenty. I'll give you five.'

The old man hawked and spat on the ground. 'Five? How dare you insult me? Five! He's worth fifteen, if he's worth one. I'll not take less than fifteen.'

'You'll take ten and like it.'

'Twelve.'

'Eleven.'

The two men spat on their hands and clasped on the deal. Montemthat took out eleven coins from his purse and paid the old man, who walked off in the direction of the ass, mumbling, 'My children will starve and people like you will laugh over their graves.' He was still mumbling when he removed the panniers, hoisted them onto his own shoulders and shuffled off in the direction of the town, groaning under their weight.

Montemthat led the ass and the two young people around the portside market, buying goatskins of wine, milk, cheeses, fruits, flour, yeasts to make their bread rise overnight, and salt. Never once did he look to Abram for payment. Yet at each stall, Abram kept on asking Montemthat why he was paying so much from his own pocket. At the stall where an old man was selling bunches of a strange yellow plant, like giant hands, which he called 'banan', Montemthat turned to Abram and said, 'Brother, stop feeling guilty. What I do for you today, you will do for an apostle when you are my age. My reward will come in Heaven.'

Abram was so taken aback he could hardly speak. Montemthat had called him an apostle, likening him to Paul, Matthew, Mark, Luke, and the blessed John. He had never begun to consider himself in the same ranks as the Apostles. Yet, what was the difference? They were the men just three generations earlier, when Abram's great grandfather had been alive, who had spread the word of the Lord. Now he, Abram, was spreading the word. Well, taking it to a safer place.

When he had purchased enough food and drink to last them the journey to the people of the Agau, they began the long walk south. The coastal plain was lush and filled with date palms and wild lemon, lime and orange trees. Every bend in the road brought new adventure. Travelling away from the port, they met small families on foot, or large groups with pack animals and camels walking towards the coast. Always suspicious, Montemthat guided his tiny group away from the road so that he did not pass too close to them. By the end of the day, they were all exhausted from the long walk and eager to make camp. Montemthat led the ass off the rocky path to an area where the palm trees seemed to grow more thickly. He took out a huge iron knife, almost as long as his arm, which he wore concealed in his robes, and hacked away at the vegetation to expose a path.

After a long walk, Montemthat stopped and held up his hand. He sniffed the air and climbed to the top of a nearby rock. 'There,' he said, pointing in a direction deeper into the bush to a clearing in which a deep blue waterhole rested in the setting sun. It was surrounded by trees and bushes bearing fruits and berries. Montemthat tethered the ass to a tree and Avigad slumped down to rest.

'Montemthat, Avigad, come here,' Abram said.

Both walked over. Abram kneeled on the yielding loamy soil; Montemthat kneeled with him, the big Egyptian still towering over the younger man. Avigad shook her head. 'Don't ask me to pray. I won't join you in your ritual. I pray to Astarte. She is my protector.'

'Many weeks ago,' he told her, 'I was sent by a wise man on a mission. My mother was terrified. Although she is a Christian, she doesn't have my faith or the faith of my father. My mother thought it would be the last time she would ever see me. When I set out on the journey, I was full of hope and enthusiasm. Yet when I was journeying by the western shore of the Sea of Salt, my faith wavered. I doubted Christ. I felt He was abandoning me. Yet—'

'Yet, we came along and saved you,' she said.

Abram nodded and smiled. 'But who brought you to me? If your journey had been halted, Avigad, say when your animal wandered off with its load of balsam, I would not have been found. I would be dead. If you had made better speed, you would have been in Eilath by the time I fell down in the sand and I would have died. Don't you see, Avigad? There has to be a Christ, a Messiah. Life could not have cast its bones without a ruling hand. Without Him, I would now be dead.'

Avigad shook her head. 'So?'

'So He has brought us together for a purpose.'

'What purpose is that?' she asked.

'He wants us, Montemthat and me, to baptise you and to make you into a Christian. To follow our ways. To renounce forever the pagan idols which you follow and to follow in the footsteps of the Son of God.' Avigad shrugged. Abram continued. 'For you, there will be eternal life. An end to evil, to sinning and to doubt. For you, there will be peace forever more.'

'You're going to convert me. Baptise me. Does it hurt?'

'No, it doesn't hurt,' said Montemthat.

The ceremony took five minutes. Afterwards, they all hugged. 'Welcome, Avigad. You are now a sister,' said Montemthat.

Abram heard the music floating on the wind long before the others were awake. At first, he thought he was still in a dream, because the harmony was so angelic and ethereal. But lying there, he soon realised that the freezing air of the early morning had caused a covering of white mist to descend on his blankets. He remembered that he was high in the mountains of Abyssinia and the music was a part of the strangeness of his surroundings.

He stood silently so as not to disturb the other two who lay huddled around the cold dead embers of the fire and made his way to the edge of the clearing. Only the ass moved. It brayed as it felt a disturbance in the still, early morning air. Abram had drawn his blanket close around his body. The air last night had been colder than anything he had ever known, and this morning the sun had not yet risen to warm them. As he stood, listening to the rhythmical sound of his water bouncing off thick fleshy leaves and dripping to the ground, he heard a dog bark in the far distance. Its bark was immediately followed by the noise of a flute or some instrument played in the mouth, which wafted through the canopy of trees with their large waxen leaves in the deep, impenetrable bush. His water finished, he stood stock still to listen. As though interrupted by rocks or some other object, the music seemed to fade in and out, carried like a spirit on the gentle breath of the dawn.

And above the flute, Abram heard the sound of voices singing together in prayer. They rose and fell on the wind. He strained to listen. It was a different type of sound from the voices he had heard lower down on the coast before they began to ascend to the top of the plateau in the Semien range of mountains. These were gentle prayers to the worship of His Father Yahweh. The music from far below him, music on the shores of Africa, was discordant and threatening. The voices of the highlands sang in harmony, though a harmony unlike anything he had heard.

As he stood listening, Montemthat appeared beside him. 'Three or four leagues, no more,' he said.

Abram turned. Montemthat explained, 'The holy city of Axum is just above that range. The music is the sound of the priests.'

By mid-morning, they had climbed the rest of the foothills and had reached the high plateau. It was a vast expanse, bigger than any valley or plain that Abram had ever seen. From his vantage point on top of a hill on the edge of the plateau, he looked far into the smoky distance. The entire plateau was divided as far as his eyes could see into clumps of jungle separated by vast grassy plains. And in the plains were collections of huts built in a circular fashion around the edge of empty space. Abram's young eyes could detect five villages in the distance but could not peer any further through the mist. Yet by the shape of the far distant mountains, Abram knew that the plateau went on and on, perhaps even to the edge of the world.

'Where is Axum?' he asked Montemthat. The tall Egyptian nodded to the south-west. Through the nearby jungle, Abram could just make out a large clearing with buildings of a different from the wattle, daub and reed huts that lay on the plateau floor. The buildings of Axum in the far distance were substantial, permanent, much like the buildings of the cities of Judea.

When the sun began to descend to the top of the range of mountains far in the west, at the very edge of the plateau, the three trudged wearily to the outskirts of the city of Axum. The buildings began to appear out of the surrounding jungle and a man appeared walking confidently towards them on the path. He wore a headdress made of feathers embedded in the skull of an animal. In his hand, he carried a spear far taller than himself. He had massive shoulders and well-defined muscles. Abram had seen similar men in the Roman fair at Caesarea. The man was a warrior and only Montemthat showed no fear at his appearance. He stopped and held out his spear at arm's length. He said words that nobody understood. Montemthat shook his head and replied in his own language, which Abram believed was Egyptian. The warrior shook his head. Montemthat then spoke in one of the Arabian languages. The warrior again shook his head. Abram greeted him in Hebrew. The warrior nodded and said, 'You speak the language of the ancients.' Only Avigad found him difficult to understand, as her knowledge of Hebrew was rudimentary.

Montemthat said, 'We are friends. We are here to see your elders. We carry no weapons. We mean no harm.'

'We have known of your arrival for four days. Why are you approaching the holy city of Axum?'

'We wish to speak to your elders. We have a gift,' said Abram.

'Give me your gift,' said the warrior.

'It is a gift of no value,' said Montemthat smiling.

'Then it is not a fitting gift,' replied the warrior.

'The gift has value to those who follow the one true God.'

The warrior smiled. 'The name of the one true God?'

'His name,' said Abram, 'shall not be spoken except by the High priest in Jerusalem.'

'And the name that shall not be spoken contains how many letters?'

'Four,' said Abram, '*Yud, hey, vav, hey.*'

The warrior nodded. 'We call this Yahweh.'

'We call this Yahweh,' said Abram.

The warrior turned and said, 'Follow me.' He led them into the city. They entered by the main path, which led to a square. Clustered around the square were tall buildings made of stone. Stairs on the outside of the buildings led to rooftops. In the centre of the square was a collection of single upright stones which Abram saw had been carved. One of the stones was so tall it eclipsed the rooftops of all the buildings in the city. Its needle-like point almost touched the clouds.

On the outside of all of the stones were markings. The tops of the smaller stones had been hollowed and inside were pools of blood with flies buzzing madly around. Behind the vertical stones was a large flat stone, supported on each corner by four pillars. The flat stone was also covered in blood and behind it were containers into which the remnants of the blood of whatever animal had been sacrificed still dripped slowly. And in the very centre of the open square were the remains of a huge fire where embers still glowed red hot. The warrior led them around the periphery of the open area to the largest of all the stone buildings. It was bigger than any synagogue which Abram had been into and rivalled in its size the buildings of the Romans. Even Avigad, wise and well-travelled as she was, was overawed by the size of the building. Montemthat did not display any emotions but walked majestically behind the warrior. They entered the building and the heat of the late afternoon sun disappeared as they stood inside the cool entryway. Abram adjusted his eyes to the dark enclosure, lit only by a vivid shaft of light from a window high on the upper level. In the dim recesses of the building, the shapes of people slowly emerged out of the gloom. Avigad moved and stood close to Abram as she looked around the room. By the time their eyes were accustomed to the gloom, an old man stood and walked over to them. The warrior spoke to him in the language which he had first used. The old man nodded and the warrior turned, departing without glancing again at the three of them.

'I am Gedaliah. I am the High priest of Axum. You have a gift for me?'

Montemthat stepped forward, his large frame dominating the slightly built old priest. He bowed reverentially. 'Holy one, we have been travelling many days. These young people have come from the land of Judea. I myself am a man of Egypt and have escorted them to your holy city. Before we discuss our business, may we sit and refresh ourselves?'

The old priest was visibly shaken. 'I apologise. It is so rare to see strangers in Axum that I forgot our ancient laws of hospitality. Please forgive an old man. Go, sit and refresh yourself.'

As the sun rose on the following day, Montemthat and Abram spoke about the nature of the gift. 'They're expecting an object for a gift. When you tell them that your gift is the word of the Lord Jesus, they will be disappointed. We must repay their hospitality by preaching the word. Are you prepared?'

'I have a gift,' said Abram.

'What?' asked Montemthat.

'Holy objects,' Abram replied.

'Holy?'

'From the Temples of Solomon and Herod.'

Montemthat shrugged. The Temple held no significance for him. 'Why are these holy?'

'They're not holy,' said Abram. 'What is holy is the scroll inside one of the jars.' Montemthat willed him to continue. 'John of Syracuse told me that Our Lord had written His Testament and vision of the future and had deposited it with the Essenes in the Judean desert at a place called Masada.'

'I know this Masada. People say it is a cursed place, a fortress. They say that it will be where the final war occurs between the Israelites and the Romans.'

Abram nodded. 'But many years ago, when the Essene community was abandoned, when Jerusalem was destroyed, the priests hid the sacred writings in caves near Masada. One which they hid was a Testament written by Our Lord, Jesus Himself.'

Abram picked up his bag and reached inside it. He withdraw a jar and held it reverentially in his hands. 'In this jar is the very scroll that Our Lord Jesus wrote in His own hand.'

Montemthat reached out to touch it. Abram placed it in his hands. The Egyptian raised the clay pot to his lips and kissed it. He examined it, first reading the leaden wax seal and then the fading inscription in ink on the jar's outer surface. 'And why have you come here?'

'To give it to the people of the Agau for safe-keeping.'

'But these are Jews.'

'Yes, I know,' said Abram. 'But some are converting to our way and John of Syracuse believes that there is no place in the world safe from the Romans other than this land.'

After a moment, Montemthat said, 'You were right to keep the truth from me. Only now do you trust me. Come, brother, before we go to face the Jews, let us pray.'

After breakfast, Abram and Montemthat were led into a meeting hall. Behind Gedaliah were a dozen other old men sitting crosslegged in a semicircle on the floor, some on rugs, some on straw and some on the bare earth. Avigad had been taken by the women of the city and was learning how to wash herself ritually and what prayers to say after a long journey.

Gedaliah bade them welcome. 'Was our hospitality good?'

'Yes, holy one.' Abram nodded. 'It was very good. We have slept and eaten and we thank you.'

'And your gift?'

'Holy one, we have the gift of silver bells, a silver pointer and something else. The bells and the pointer are from the Temple of King Solomon of blessed memory.'

The moment he said the name of the ancient king, the entire group reacted in shock. Abram stared around the semicircle of priests to see why their reaction was so unexpected.

'King Solomon?' said Gedaliah. The boy nodded. 'Abram, are you aware of the part King Solomon played in the history of the people of the Agau?'

Abram looked at Montemthat, who also registered surprise. 'No, holy one, I'm not.' The old man smiled.

'Many hundreds of years ago, in the time of our father Moses and when the Bible was first written, after the children of Israel had escaped from the land of the pharaohs and were led into the Promised Land, there arose a great king.' He spoke as though he were intoning an ancient benediction. 'This king was Solomon and he was wise beyond his years and rich beyond wealth and wanted for nothing. The Queen of Sheba, whose people were the people of the land of Cush, heard about Solomon and travelled to see him with a mighty following. She carried with her precious jewels, gold, myrrh, frankincense and other aromatic gums and spices of priceless value. She travelled by ship from the city of Ophir to the port of Eilath, where she took her caravan of camels, servants and dancing girls up into the Holy City of Jerusalem. In that high and mighty city, she was overwhelmed by the richness and power of King Solomon and she fell in love with him. The result of their union was King Menelik, of blessed memory, who brought the law of Moses to the people of the Agau. Many years later, Menelik returned to Jerusalem to see his father but Solomon refused to acknowledge him as his heir and from that time on the people of the land of Israel were no longer the Chosen People. Thereafter, Solomon forfeited his right to be called the leader of the Chosen People. He had seduced our queen and forfeited his right to be beloved in the eyes of Yahweh. The people of the Agau then became the Chosen People.'

Abram sat listening in amazement. The story told to him by Gedaliah was at odds with the stories he had learned from the Bible told to him by his father. He knew of Solomon and Sheba from the book written about the Kings of Israel but he had never heard of this Menelik. And now he was told that the Jews were not the Chosen People!

'Then you do not revere Solomon?' he asked.

'We revere his greatness and we revere the Temple that he built and the objects therein, but we do not revere him for what he did to our queen, nor the manner in which he refused to recognise Menelik as his rightful heir.'

'Then these gifts are of no value to you,' said Abram, dejectedly.

The old man smiled and shook his head. 'These gifts are of great value. For they are part of the story of Moses and the Law as given to the Jews for its permanent resting place in the Temple.'

A murmur of noise rose in the background as the priests whispered excitedly to each other. Gedaliah said, 'Let me see these objects from the Temple of Solomon.'

Abram stood and reached into the bag which he had brought with him. He handed the objects over to the old man, who examined them in the dusty light of the meeting hall. He tinkled the bell and ran his finger lovingly along the fine edges of the pointer, tracing the central finger of the tiny, jewel-encrusted hand. He turned and called over one of his subordinates, who took the objects and handed them around the semicircle. Gedaliah nodded in appreciation. 'How are we to believe that these are from the Temple of Solomon?'

'I took them from caves in Masada where they had been hidden by a group of ancients called the Essenes.'

The old man shook his head. 'I don't know these people.'

'They were not of the priestly Cohanim and of the Levites but lived like hermits in the desert praying to Yahweh for their salvation.'

The old priest nodded. The story sounded believable. 'And how did these ancients come by objects from the Temple which was destroyed by King Nebuchadnezzar?'

'I don't know,' said the boy. Gedaliah was pleased by his honesty. One of the priests in the background stood up and walked forward to squat just behind Gedaliah. He whispered into the ear of the high priest, who nodded.

'My brother Radai is knowledgeable of ancient Hebrew writings. He tells me that the writing on these objects is very old. He says they're real. Abram, you have brought a gift of great value, for which I thank you.'

There was a murmur in the background as each of the priests affirmed his appreciation.

'What will you do with these objects from the Temple?' asked Abram.

'They will be taken to a special place by one of the guards.'

'And where is this place?' Montemthat asked.

'It's high in the mountains. Only we know where it is. It is protected night and day by our guards. No one is allowed near.'

'And what,' continued Montemthat, 'is in this secret place, if I may ask?'

Gedaliah turned to the other priests, some of whom nodded. 'We have the Torah, the Holy Law of the Prophet Moses and we have other precious works brought to us from the Temple many years past in the time of King Josaiah.'

'What other precious things?' asked Montemthat.

'Things which must not be spoken of,' said the old priest, shaking his head.

'Do you guard the Ark of the Covenant?' Abram asked.

The old man reacted in shock for the second time since he and Abram had been speaking. 'Why do you think this?' he asked.

'You said that you guard the precious works from the Temple. King Josaiah was the man who cleansed the Temple of the idols and other objects of abomination put there by his father, Amon, and his father's father, Manasseh. Since the time of King Josaiah, the Ark of the Covenant has been lost to the people of Israel.'

There was a murmur of anger and amazement in the room. One of the priests said something in Ge'ez which Abram did not understand. Gedaliah translated, 'My brother says "These things are hidden knowledge. How do you know them?"'

'Holy one,' Abram answered, 'to me they are not hidden. I have known these things and been taught them since I was a boy.'

'Truly, your people teach you much secret wisdom. But in answer to your question, have you ever heard of a holy temple built by the Jews on the island of Elephantine in the middle of the River Nile at the first cataract before it descends into the sea?'

'I know of this island,' Montemthat interrupted. 'It was where I was baptised in the name of the prophet Jesus.'

Gedaliah held up a skeletal hand to stop Montemthat talking. 'What is this word, baptised?'

Montemthat explained the way of immersing unclean people into water to cleanse their souls. The old man nodded in interest. 'So you know of this island? Then you would know that the temple housed the Ark of the Covenant when Josaiah ordered the Levites to remove it from Jerusalem.'

'Why would he do that?' asked Abram.

'Because of his fear that the people of the north, the Babylonians, under their king, Nebuchadnezzer, would soon march on Jerusalem and steal the ark containing the tablets of the Lord on which the Law was written.'

'So the ark is in the temple on Elephantine?'

'No,' said Montemthat. 'There is no longer a temple. It is now a place of worship of the Egyptian Gods.'

'Then where is the ark?' asked Abram.

Gedaliah smiled. 'Safely guarded by my people in a place where no one shall find it. Although we are craftsmen with stone, we decided many years ago not to build a temple to house the ark. For that temple could be discovered as was the Temple of Solomon, and destroyed. Rather it is hidden and guarded by us. It is brought out and carried here to be worshipped once a year by our people, who gather in the Great Square of Axum.'

Abram nodded and cleared his throat. He asked, 'Holy one, would you also guard something else for me?'

'What is it?' Gedaliah asked in surprise.

Abram reached in and pulled out the jar containing the scroll of Jesus' Testament. 'It is something which I took from the same cave where I found these holy objects.'

The old priest held out his hand. He examined it. 'What is it?' he asked ingenuously.

'It contains the Testament of one of the Essenes, a man called Jesus.'

'Is this the same Jesus, the prophet, in whose name you were baptised?' the old man asked Montemthat, who nodded and said, 'Jesus is a very great prophet of the Jewish people. His words will live forever.'

'He is a prophet as Isaiah and Jeremiah are prophets?'

'He is as great as these.'

The old man nodded gravely. 'Is he as great as Moses, the lawgiver?'

'He is as great as Moses.'

'If he is so great, why have we heard nothing of him?'

'Jesus has only just died. Not one hundred years past.'

The old man looked deeply into Montemthat's eyes and then looked at Abram. Montemthat sat still, not daring to interrupt. 'And these are his prophecies?' said Gedaliah, holding up the jar.

'I don't know, holy one. This is His Testament. It was sealed in the jar by the great seal of the Essenes. It is only to be opened on the Day of Judgement.'

The other priests, who had sat silently during this exchange, began to talk between themselves. Radai, who was still sitting behind Gedaliah, asked, 'If it cannot be opened until the Day of Judgement, how are we to know its truth? How are we to obey its orders and prophecies? What value is a sealed Testament?'

'I don't know,' said Abram in despair.

Montemthat intervened. 'Holy one, the disciples of the prophet Jesus are in the land of Judea and are spreading throughout the world. Soon they will come to you. That, I promise. But because Judea is straining under the iron foot of the Romans, those who follow the teachings of the prophet Jesus have asked this boy to bring His Testament here for safe keeping. He has no idea what is in this Testament. Neither do I. But we trust in those who follow Jesus and we trust in the teachings of Jesus. We only ask that you place this Testament in your secret place to be guarded against its theft and desecration.'

Gedaliah turned to his colleagues, who slowly began to nod in agreement. 'You ask for little. Yet it means much to you. We will guard this pot with our lives and look forward to reading the teachings of the Prophet Jesus. In the meantime, tonight we will feast and sacrifice lamb, and over the feast, you Abram and you Montemthat will tell us of the teachings of this prophet Jesus, so that we may be prepared when one of His followers comes to us with His words.'

Montemthat stood at the edge of the city, looking down a path as it disappeared north-east, deep into the grass plateau and then into the jungles beyond. To his left was another path which led to the western rim of the plateau and disappeared over the top to meander its way down towards the Nile River, which ultimately led to Alexandria and the Mediterranean coast. He looked at Abram. 'What will you do with the other testaments?' asked Montemthat, indicating the sack containing the scrolls of Abimelech the Good and many others.

Abram shrugged, 'I'll bury them in a high place along the way for all eternity where only the Lord God will see.'

Montemthat nodded, and asked, 'Are you sure you will not come with me?'

Abram smiled and touched his friend's arm. 'These last four or five days have given me a chance to think clearly for the first time in my life. I have never been so at ease as when I was telling the priests and people of Axum about the wondrous words of Jesus Christ, Our Lord. I know my mission in life. It is to spread the word.' He smiled at his friend Montemthat and his 'wife', Avigad. 'You know, Montemthat, many days ago, you called me an apostle. Your words were prophetic, because it is my intention to devote my life to being one of the apostles of Our Lord.'

'And you still intend to go to Rome, despite the dangers of that city?' Abram nodded. 'Then, God go with you, brother,' he said, and threw his arms around the younger man. They hugged and Abram felt his resolve flow out of his body but he knew that his path was ordained.

He turned to Avigad and said, 'You must return to my land and live with my family. They will welcome you as a daughter. Tell them what has happened to me and where I have gone. Tell them that I shall return in a year, or maybe two, and begin my work as an apostle in the birthplace of the Lord. But now you must travel with Montemthat and he will look after you.'

Montemthat nodded. Avigad looked at her young 'husband' and tears welled up in her eyes. 'Oh, Abram, I will miss you so.'

He threw his arms around her and kissed her gently on the neck. 'Go,' he said, 'before my strength fails me.'

Avigad and Montemthat drew away from him and walked down their path towards the north-east and the Red Sea. Abram picked up his bag. It was full of food and drink supplied to him by the people of the Agau. They had been generous and loving brothers and, although he had only told them about Christ and had not baptised them, when an apostle arrived, they would be prepared.

With heavy footsteps, he walked along the path. After ten minutes, like Lot's wife, he turned to see if he could catch sight of his two friends in the distance. Through the tall grass, he saw the black muscular frame of his brother Montemthat striding purposefully towards the coast. Out of the corner of his eye, he caught a movement behind him, close to the trees.

Abram's heart leapt for joy but he dared not show emotion. It would be wrong for her to come with him.

It was too dangerous. 'Please don't be angry, Abram. You spoke to everyone about the way of Christ, even me. Surely I should arrive in Rome as your first convert.'

The simple and inescapable logic made him beam a smile. They walked towards the west, he in front, she, at her insistence, behind.

CHAPTER 25

Jimmy Wilson sat mumbling, while the stewardess buckled his seatbelt in preparation for landing in Ethiopia. He had been babbling constant prayers throughout the flight, the mantra of a desperate man. That son of Satan, that reporter. It was him who started it all, him who had unpicked the finely woven tapestry which was his church, his life. And that phone call from Ben somebody. 'I've interviewed Luke, and he's spilled the beans . . . He's holed up where you'll never find him. Annabelle too . . . I'm giving you the right of reply before calling in the DA.' Right of reply! Hah! Who in fuck did he think he was dealin' with? Some black, some Mex? He was talkin' to the Reverend Jimmy Wilson, a man who had led prayer meetin's all over America! Threatenin' Jimmy with the DA! Makin' him sound like some two-bit dumbass hillbilly!

Harlin had panicked, gone right over the fuckin' top, shat himself. The yellow-backed, spineless useless Harvard asshole. Who needed him? Jimmy had to get the Testament. That was it. Only way out. Once he had got that Testament then everythin' would be all right. No grand jury, no DA, no judge in a black coat sentencin' him. He would be untouchable. He would be the apostle on earth of Christ Jesus. Dear sweet Jesus, God Almighty. Had to get the Testament. Had to get the Testament!

Jimmy Wilson spent the day in his hotel room in Addis Ababa throwing around money as if it were confetti. First the concierge, then the hotel manager, then the manager's cousin, who worked in the Ministry of

Defence, and finally the cousin's employer, who was a close friend of a senior official in the Ministry of the Interior.

'For a price, Dr Wilson, I can organise permission for you to go anywhere.'

'I want to follow a Professor Farber. I know he landed here a couple of days ago. I want to know where he's gone and how he's got there. And I want to know within the next twenty-four hours.'

The Ethiopian official nodded as he accepted the handful of American dollars. He smiled and said, 'This will not be a problem, Dr Wilson. Not a problem at all.'

The DC–3 took two hours from Addis Ababa to be gliding low over the foothills of Mt Gebo on its approach to Gondar. The pilot was aiming to fly in between the two peaks on his way to the 7000-foot high tablelands of northern Ethiopia. The plane flew higher and higher until it was level with the crests of the distant ranges.

The plane skirted the city and landed on the tarmac runway of the airport. It was nothing more than a grey scar on the flat landscape of the plateau. Beside the runway were four or five other propeller-driven planes and two military helicopters, green and grey giant grasshoppers prepared to pounce on any intruders.

Jimmy Wilson shook hands with the bemused pilot, blessed him, and carried his luggage into the tin shed which served as the arrivals hall. There were three un-manned desks, a broken chair, a settee which had lost all its stuffing, black bakelite telephones and torn posters on the walls displaying 1950s turboprop passenger planes.

Jimmy walked out of the tin shed into the hot and dusty Azzezo airport concourse. There he saw an

Ethiopian dressed in a crisp military uniform, weighted down by epaulettes and insignia, leaning against the bonnet of a jeep. He was grinning at Jimmy. Behind him, there was a collection of military barracks, a township with no office towers against the skyline, no restaurants, no hotels, none of the trappings of Western civilisation. Merely a soldier's encampment.

'You must be Jimmy Wilson,' said the Ethiopian.

'What if I am?' said Jimmy suspiciously.

'Please, don't be aggressive. I'm here to be of assistance to important visitors. I am Colonel Shala Wagshun. I'm the military commander for the Gondar region. Also in charge of public relations,' he said with a broad self-deprecating grin.

Half an hour later, Jimmy was seated in the back of Colonel Wagshun's jeep being driven around the city of Gondar. 'Colonel,' said Jimmy. 'I have to get to the Lake Tana area.'

'Why, my friend?'

'Well, colonel, a friend of mine came over here just recently,' said Jimmy. 'Name of Michael Farber. A white man. I'd like to get in touch with him.'

'What part of Lake Tana do you want to see?'

'Well, it's not actually Lake Tana but it's the place that my friend is goin' to,' said Jimmy.

'And where is that?'

Jimmy shrugged. 'I'm afraid I don't know. All I know is that he's goin' to go somewhere down in that area.'

The colonel looked questioningly at him. 'My friend, Lake Tana is one of Ethiopia's largest lakes. It's nearly one hundred kilometres long. Naturally, it's heavily populated with hundreds of villages dotted around its shore. And worse, there are many islands within the lake which are inhabited by monks in their churches. Have you any idea what part of Lake Tana your friend is going to?'

Jimmy said, 'I'm afraid I don't know. I made no arrangements. I'll just have to follow him and see where he goes.'

The colonel remained silent. His jeep bounced over the rutted tarmac road. The streets were crowded with people who walked aimlessly from place to place. There were few cars in the streets but hundreds of bicycles and carts pulled by donkeys or buffalo. In the centre of the city they saw dozens of shops, each of them small and dusty in their outer appearance. Large signs, pock-marked with holes from where retreating militias and guerilla armies had thrown rocks and shot bullets, carried the names of distant places in three languages. The signs pointed to Axum, Debre Tabor, Addis Ababa and Metema. The colonel explained that Metema was out of bounds, a settlement on the disputed border with the Sudan. They passed the remains of magnificent stone palaces looking like the Crusader fortresses of Israel or the castles of England and France. They stood proud and timeless against the deep blue sky and the murderous sun, sentinels of Ethiopia's long and turbulent history. It was once a prosperous country in the Byzantine Empire, but the prosperity had long since vanished, the bare stone walls the only reminders.

Everywhere, churches appeared on street corners or encased like precious stone jewels in luscious tropical gardens. And between the architectural wonders dating back hundreds of years sat ramshackle cockroach-infested wooden shacks which, unlike the stone edifices, had suffered the degradation of the climate, a tropical garden during the dry months but a monsoonal broth in the winter. Along the pavement walked Ethiopian Coptic priests, bedecked in robes decorated with bright red and gold symbols, looking like actors in an Elizabethan drama. Villagers were in tow, following like sheep, and the priests seemed to be conducting lessons in living Christianity as they walked from home to home or church to church. Shop windows were covered in dust, demanding faith and trust from residents to look inside. They passed the window of a butcher shop and saw carcasses of grey meat hanging with blowflies crawling into and over them. Jimmy felt like a god, descending on the slime-living denizens of the underworld. On the sides of the streets in deep pitted gutters were dozens of bare carts covered with produce from which men and women were selling home-made goods. In between the carts, on the ground, women were hunched in front of straw mats on which were laid out a few meagre goods that they were trying to sell. Bolts of cloth and flax, jewellery, clay pots, copperware and leather.

'It's possible I may be able to help you find this friend of yours,' said the colonel. 'But it will involve a great deal of work on the part of my staff and unfortunately I am restricted in what I can pay them for their time.'

Jimmy smiled, suddenly lucid, at ease in a medium with which he was familiar. 'I'd defray all your expenses, and much, much more.'

An hour later, Jimmy was sitting in the bar of a two-star hotel, waiting for the colonel to come back from making a telephone call.

'Good news,' Colonel Wagshun said, 'not only have I traced your friend and found out in which direction he was heading, but I have also arranged from a very good friend of mine for you to hire a vehicle and camping equipment at very modest rates. Unfortunately there are no hotels from here onwards, especially around Lake Tana, and you will need to sleep the night under God's canopy.'

It took an hour before the colonel arrived to pick him up from the hotel in his hired Toyota Landcruiser.

Attached to the back was a small canvas-covered trailer. Seated in the front of the cabin was Colonel Wagshun and an Ethiopian wearing a sergeant's uniform. The colonel smiled reassuringly. 'This is Sergeant Didasa of the Oromo people. He will protect us from lions and hyenas and other creatures on the way.' The sergeant sat staring rigidly ahead, ramrod stiff and unsmiling on the front seat, looking through the windshield, an automaton whose thought processes were at the behest of his colonel.

As they drove away from the outskirts of Gondar city, towards Amber Giorgis and Lake Tana, bush encroached more heavily on to the roadway until it became a two-lane track which seemed to have been scored by some gigantic fingernail through the undergrowth. Although the limit of the jungle was below the level of the plateau, the trees in the area were lush and plentiful. Often on the journey the road passed through villages. In the fields were men and women cutting down the palm leaves.

Their jeep emerged into a clearing, a collection of a dozen conical-roofed huts made of wattle and mud daub. In the road, lazily moving out of the path of the Landcruiser, were desultory men and women, the men in traditional white jodhpurs, jackets and *shamma*, the women in variegated robes which fell shapelessly from neck to ground. Colonel Wagshun smiled. 'Were you not a minister of the church, I would suggest you go inside,' he said, pointing to the biggest of the buildings on the roadside.

'What goes on?' asked Jimmy.

'It's called a *tedj bet*. It's a tavern, a roadside inn, a—' the colonel laughed again, 'and a brothel. You see, Dr Wilson, in Ethiopia we have a very broad-minded approach to relationships between men and women.'

'Colonel,' Jimmy sneered, 'in my country, these places would be condemned by God-fearin' men as dens of iniquity. But we're not in my country. We're in yours. And the Lord Jesus reminded us of different customs of different peoples when He said, "Render unto Caesar that which is Caesar's". He also warned us about pre-judgin' when He said, "Let he who is without sin cast the first stone"'.

'And are you able to cast the first stone?' asked the colonel.

'Would that I was not a sinner, colonel,' Jimmy said, 'but we're all sinners in God's eyes.'

'That's why we abandoned God in favour of Marx. He's far less demanding.' The colonel burst out laughing again.

They passed through a village and re-entered the bush, intersected with fields of dura, the mottled heads of the plant above the green and yellow stalks waving in the breeze. In a further field, a tall, thin Ethiopian farmer, sweat glistening on his skin, was striking the backs of two oxen pulling a wooden plough through the rocky earth. They sped past village after village, each with no more than thirty or forty huts. The huts were round and made of the ubiquitous *musa ensete* plant stalks and leaves, the thatched roofs like the conical hats of witches in medieval Europe.

In every village was a stone building, with a crucifix on its roof. 'You got a lot of Christian buildings around here, colonel,' said Jimmy.

'Yes, we have been a Christian nation since the fourth century after the death of Jesus. Christianity is still very much a part of our way of life despite our adoption of Communism when we overthrew Haile Selassie.'

'I thought you had a lot of Jews up here?' Jimmy asked.

'No,' said the colonel. 'Not any more. At one time, the Falashas were all over this area. But since the Zionist State was formed, we have sent them on their way and now there are none left.'

'None!' exclaimed Jimmy.

The colonel shrugged his shoulders. 'Maybe some, who knows. But most have gone. It's a good thing. They brought the evil eye.'

'What?'

'Yes!' said the colonel. 'They were stonemasons and blacksmiths and craftsmen. They brought the evil eye. They had the power at night to change into hyenas and to stalk Christian villages. It's a well-known fact.'

They drove on south. The sun began to settle behind the mountains of the west of the country.

Finally, they stopped and made camp. Before they went to sleep, the colonel warned, 'Oh, and by the way, if you hear screaming in the night, don't worry. It'll only be the monkeys'. He laughed. Jimmy began to feel irritated at his constant giggle. People laughing at him infuriated Jimmy. His daddy used to laugh at him. He'd worked his butt off so people didn't laugh at him.

As the fire crackled and the smoke and sparks disappeared upwards into the canopy of the trees high above their heads, Jimmy finished off the last of his *musa ensete*. He lay back and stared up into the blackness through the canopy of the trees. The sergeant was sitting outside of the light of the fire at a respectful distance, quietly eating by himself. He hadn't spoken a word or looked at them since Gondar. Colonel Wagshun stood up and threw another log on to the fire, which blazed in an angry crackle of smoke, sparks and hissing gas. 'This man is a good friend of yours?' asked the colonel.

'What man's that?' said Jimmy.

'The man you are following, Farber.'

'Yeah, he's a real close friend.'

'I see,' said the Ethiopian, sitting down and picking up a mug of coffee, considering. Finally, he continued, 'I know the reason you want to see him. He instigated the release of an old man in prison in Gondar, a Falasha.'

'I thought you said there were no Falashas left,' snapped Jimmy.

'I said there might be one or two. He obviously is one of the few. The fact is that they are heading towards the Lake Tana area where the Falashas used to live. You are also going in search of something. What is it that you are looking for, Dr Wilson?'

'I'm here to find the Ark of the Covenant.'

The colonel slowly nodded. 'That's exactly what they told my men when they arrived in Gondar. Interesting. I didn't believe their story either.'

When Jimmy opened his eyes, the first thing he saw was a flight of pink flamingos rising into the blush of dawn. The vivid blue sky was obliterated by their dusty pink bodies and wide brocaded wings, wheeling and arcing over the still water and the green umbrella of trees.

The flap of his tent was open and it took him several moments before he realised where he was. The jungle was wild, untamed. Noises of screaming, chattering, laughing, hissing and roaring were carried like a hideous symphony on the wind. Its alienness frightened him. He coughed, shook his head to clear the remnants of his dream-filled night and crawled through the flap. In the clearing, the burnt embers of the previous night's fire had been reactivated, and a new fire was crackling underneath cooking utensils. A delicious smell of freshly roasted coffee and some form of oats or pulse cereal gently bubbling on a tripod greeted him as he stood and stretched his back. Sitting close to the fire and drinking coffee, lost in thought, was Colonel Wagshun. The air was cold and clear, a result of the high altitude. Jimmy noticed Sergeant Didasa through the clearing in the trees and behind him was Lake Tana, a majestic sweep of dark blue water whose mirror-like surface reflected the white clouds and the occasional small flock of flamingos and herons which had risen later than the main body of birds.

'Good morning,' Colonel Wagshun smiled. 'I hope you slept well.'

'Mornin', colonel,' said Jimmy, full of bonhomie and early morning joviality. 'Didn't realise that we were so close to the lake. It's no more than twenty yards down there,' he said, pointing through the trees.

The colonel replied, 'We were actually travelling beside the lake for about half an hour before we camped. It's deceptive, you know. There's no really clear shore to Lake Tana. We are on what are called the Dembea Plains. They're alluvial soils. They wash down from the mountains around here and so the shores of the lake are always getting shallower and shallower with silt. Very fertile. So the new soil allows fast-growing trees to spring up.'

Jimmy walked over and accepted a cup of coffee. It was bitter and acrid. 'Incredible wildlife you got here, colonel. I was woken by some pink birds, flamingos I think. The noise of their wings was quite overpowerin'.'

'They're one of the wonders of the world, the pink flamingos of this area. Perhaps you would like some breakfast,' he said, pointing at the pot.

'Maybe afterwards, thanks. Tell me, colonel, why is Sergeant Didasa with us?'

'He is our watchman. If there is the slightest disturbance at night, he is instantly awake. Nothing can get past Sergeant Didasa.'

Jimmy poured himself some more coffee.

'Colonel, I'm goin' to lay it on the line. You're a man I can trust. You've got the same love of money as I've got.' The colonel looked at him impassively. 'What I told you last night—about my search for the Ark of the Covenant—it ain't true.' The colonel nodded. 'Truth is, colonel, I'm here chasin' this professor because he's lookin' for Christ's Testament. He thinks it might have been brought here.'

The colonel sipped his coffee. 'Why does he think that, Dr Wilson?'

'I don't know, sir. I ain't asked him. I've only met him once but I'm trustin' his instincts. Truth is, colonel, I have to find that Testament. It ain't the money. I need it and I need it bad. If you help me, you can have ten per cent of what I reap from this. Swiss bank account, house in America. You name it, you got it. That's how big this thing is.'

'Why do you think Professor Farber is on the right trail?'

Jimmy shrugged. 'I've communed with the Lord and Jesus Christ Himself told me that His Testament lies yonder.' Jimmy nodded towards the mountains. 'Somewhere out there.'

The colonel remained silent. Jimmy looked at Sergeant Didasa. He continued to stare past Jimmy, past the clearing, into the denseness of the jungle.

Their Landcruiser slipped from side to side on the track as it climbed to the top of the hillock. They had left the road because Colonel Wagshun's radio reception was interrupted by the high range of mountains to the east. When the Landcruiser finally breasted the hill, below them they could see much of the broad expanse of Lake

Tana and its surrounds. The colonel stopped the car and applied the safety brake. He took out his radio, turned the dial and pressed the button on the receiver.

'Bahir Dar, Bahir Dar, are you receiving? Over.'

There was a hiss of atmospherics and at last, a thin incoming voice said, 'Bahir Dar receiving. Over.'

'This is Colonel Wagshun. We are interested in the movements of a Rover jeep containing two Caucasians, one male, one female, and an elderly Falasha Jew. They were last seen twenty kilometres south-west of Gondar travelling on the eastern bank of Lake Tana towards the Gojan Massif. Have they passed you yet?'

'Colonel, we have been getting reports of this vehicle. They have permission to be in the area from the Ministry of the Interior in Addis.'

'Yes, yes, I know,' Colonel Wagshun snapped back irritably. 'They're not illegals. I'm merely asking whether you have seen them? Over.'

'Sir, they were last seen heading towards the village of Enda Bagona and told our patrol that they were heading towards Ambober. We saw no reason to stop them.'

'Damn!' said the colonel. 'They're travelling all over the place.'

'Colonel, a message came in for you from Addis. Two officials from the Ministry of Internal Security are flying to Gondar to talk with you. Over.'

The colonel stiffened and replaced the receiver. 'We have problems.'

Jimmy looked at him in surprise. 'What problems, colonel?'

'You said to me that they were heading towards Lake Tana. But they're now heading north towards Ambober. They appear to be following a most unusual path, all over the mountainsides. Why is this? Why did you make me come this way?'

'I had no idea where they were headin', colonel, or what they're up to now. All I knew was that they had come towards Lake Tana. I don't know what their destination is.'

The colonel sighed in annoyance. 'Well, they have indeed come here. But now they have headed north. Do you want us to follow them?'

Jimmy nodded and stared through the windscreen.

Avi Simons felt utter contempt for David Berg. No, more than contempt! A hatred. That a man who professed the Jewish religion had committed such acts of bestiality. Avi couldn't equate Berg with being a rabbi. A madman, a maniac, a fascist. Anything, but not a rabbi.

Simons had been out of prison for two days and, since arriving home, had been a prisoner in his own house, too scared to walk into the streets in case people recognised him, pointed and said, 'That's the man who crucified the archbishop.'

Avi had sent his wife and daughters to stay with his mother at Netanya. At any moment, he knew he would be re-arrested. He and the others had only been released on a technicality. It wouldn't take them long to find the evidence. They must have found something by now. Oh God, why had he gone along with it? Why hadn't he just said no?

The doorbell rang. It resounded through the empty house like a klaxon. Avi jumped out of his chair in fright. His heart pounding, he looked through the drawn curtains of the house. In the dark outside, he could see only a single figure standing at the door. Sweating in guilt, he opened the door. The man standing there was tall, muscular. His dress said nothing about who he was or what he might want.

'Avi?'

'Who are you?'

'I'm a friend. I have something to tell you.'

'What kind of a friend? Who are you?'

'Avi, let me come in.'

'Not until you tell me who you are.'

'Please, let me in. This is for your own good.'

Avi opened the door and the man walked past. He followed him into the living room. The man turned around and pointed a Colt .357 at his chest. Avi opened his mouth in fear and surprise.

'Sorry,' said the man, and put a bullet straight into Avi's heart. His body was propelled backwards and crashed onto a coffee table, then slid dead onto the floor. The man took a prayer book out of his pocket. He opened it to re-read the inscription which he had read a dozen times while sitting in the car before entering. 'Property of Rabbi David Berg.' He threw the prayer book on Avi's dead body and walked out the door, leaving the smell of cordite and death behind him.

When he was in his car, he stabbed a series of numbers into his mobile phone. It was answered immediately.

'Superintendent Katan's office.'

'I want to speak to Meyer. Tell him it's David.'

'David?'

'Just tell him I want to talk to him.'

'David?'

'Meyer, how are you?'

'Good.

'I've done it.'

He heard the Superintendent of Police sigh. It had been a hard decision but one that was necessary. 'Thank you.'

'Don't mention it. Do you want me to pick up our friend?'

'No, that's something I want to do personally. Let's see the bastard talk his way out of this one.'

Pope Innocent walked from his private apartment into the small receiving chamber adjacent to the magnificent frescoed audience room. As he was only meeting one other person, he had instructed that Cardinal Kitzinger be escorted to the smaller room. It was less intimidating, less formal. Kitzinger had only just arrived back in Rome after representing the papacy at the funeral of Archbishop Hiram Solomonoglou, and had demanded an immediate audience. It was an audience that Gabriel Molloy was not looking forward to. He already knew of the cardinal's attitude from the terse notes that he had received. They had been courteous and respectful but devoid of warmth and covering a layer of contempt and anger. Gabriel knew that this coming meeting would be a clash of personalities, an ideological conflict between the Old World and the New. It was a meeting that he could certainly do without. The pressures on him at the moment were unbelievable. But Kitzinger had insisted.

He entered the room and smiled openly. 'Your eminence, how good to see you. I'm so pleased that you've arrived back safely from the Holy Land.'

'Holy Father,' said Kitzinger walking over and grasping the Pope's hand, bowing and kissing his ring.

'Coffee?' asked the Pope.

'No thank you. I think it best if I come straight to the point.' The Pope nodded. 'Holy Father, as you know I have just returned from burying a dear servant of the Vatican, Archbishop Solomonoglou. He died of natural causes, but his death was hastened by this cruel and evil kidnap.'

'A terrible—'

Kitzinger put his hand up to stop the Pope from speaking. It was the action of the teacher towards the pupil, the confident to the unsure, the old against the new. But because Kitzinger had the floor, Gabriel Molloy deferred. 'Your holiness, the killing is merely a symptom of the malaise which has come about as a result of your massive indiscretion in calling a Crusade.' Gabriel felt his hackles beginning to rise but remained silent. 'You did not seek the advice of the Curia for this Crusade. You did not ask us about calling the Third Vatican Council. You have made pre-emptive decisions which affect the very nature of the Church as though it was yours to do with as you wish.'

'May I remind you, your eminence, that I am the Pope, elected by a majority of cardinals.'

'Don't dare lecture me on your ascendancy to the papacy. You were a compromise candidate. Don't be arrogant enough to think that you have carried the important members of the Curia with you. You may have been elected by cardinals whose realms lay outside of Europe and whose people are crying out for change, but the vast body of Catholics, those represented by the cardinals of Europe, did not vote for you.'

Gabriel rose to stand shoulder to shoulder with the German prelate. 'If there was one ounce of faith within your body, Kitzinger, you would accept that my election was ordained by God Himself, whose spirit descended upon the conclave and who guided the minds of your peers.' He thrust his finger at Kitzinger's chest. 'Your peers, cardinal, those men who are equal in rank and status with you.'

'Men who come from Africa and Asia! What do they know about the spirit of Christianity? Oh, I know they're faithful and I know that most of them are God-fearing but they know nothing of tradition. They're parvenus. They don't have two thousand years of history to guide them in their decision-making.'

Gabriel could hardly control his anger. He felt his heart beating and his face flushing in fury. 'Those are your brothers, Kitzinger,' he shouted. 'They are men who were guided by God. Are you saying that God only comes to Europeans?'

'That's not what I'm saying, but I am saying that only Europeans can appreciate the effect of decisions judged in millennia. These people who voted for you are like children. Faithful, articulate, loving and devoted, but they're the children of our faith. We are the dogmatists. We are the men who hold the future of our faith intact.'

Gabriel was lost for words. The awful, extraordinary outburst had robbed him of his calmness. All he felt was disgust and a profound sense of disdain, as though talking to Kitzinger was sullying his inner peace. 'Get out, Kitzinger. Get out right now before I have you removed by the Swiss Guards. You're a disgrace, a despicable man. I ban you from my apartments. I ban you from talking to me and I swear by Holy God and His Son Jesus Christ, that if ever . . . ever! . . . I hear you talk in this way again, I will excommunicate you.'

Kitzinger stood his ground. It was a scene which had not been played out in the Vatican apartments since the days of the Medici popes. Both men tall, brilliant, at opposite sides of the spectrum, staring in hatred at each other.

Kitzinger snapped in fury. 'Will banning me bring back Hiram Solomonoglou?' Gabriel remained silent. 'You can be as self-righteous as you want but you'll never undo the damage that your New World impetuousness has brought about. No matter what you do to me, you cannot undo the hatred for the Catholic Church which you have caused. By your single-minded arrogance and quest for self-gratification, you have succeeded in turning a momentous discovery into a poisonous dagger which will strike at the heart of every Catholic.'

Gabby's body ached. He just wanted to be removed from this hideous room. To be out again in the fields or working with the poor and the powerless and the diseased, bringing peace and hope to those who needed it. He didn't want to be a man of supreme power, engaged in damaging discussions with arrogant German theologians. But the papacy was his for the rest of his life and, until the day he died, he would meet its demands to the very best of his poor abilities.

'Kitzinger, I reject your accusations. You are a mean and low-spirited man. Contemptuous and arrogant of those around you. Incapable of seeing good in the motives of others. You have no history of pastoral care. You should leave the Vatican and go to where people are suffering, get your hands dirty by wiping the sweat from people's brows or the blood from their wounds. You should help carry the dead in from the streets of Calcutta or help the blacks of Africa in their struggles. Kitzinger, you should learn the true nature of Christianity. The meaning that was practised by Our Lord.'

'My family is the Church. The very Church that you're trying to take away from me by your mania to modernise. To strip us of our institutions. To pull the carpet from under our feet in the vain hope of discovering some new and improved solution to our problems. But you're like every anarchist, Molloy. Destroy! And after destruction, you give no thought to who has to rebuild. What you're destroying can never be rebuilt.'

'I'm not an anarchist, Kitzinger,' the Pope whispered. 'You've accused me of the crime of being true to my religion, when all I am is a simple priest trying to bring Christ's living testimony to Christians and open up a window onto the fustian language and traditions of the Church. To bring it closer to God-fearing men and women. To get rid of the claptrap and verbiage and to get closer to the message of Christ.'

'And to get rid of the works of the Apostles, of Matthew, Mark, Luke and John, and to drive St Peter off his throne. The chair given to him by Christ.'

Kitzinger slowly turned without kissing the Pope's ring and walked out of the audience chamber. Pope Innocent was left alone.

CHAPTER 26

The jeep drew to a halt at the top of the rise. Michael Farber opened the door and stepped out on to the track. He looked around at the scenery, the vast blue waters of Lake Tana reflecting the deep blue sky and the majestic mountains which rose all around them. Michael slammed the door in irritation. It was their fifth, no!, their sixth stop that day. He stretched his back and felt the sweat which made his shirt stick to his skin. He looked through the windscreen at Binyussef, who stared through the dusty glass as if in a daze, looking neither right nor left. Michael was becoming increasingly irritated with the Ethiopian's inscrutable smile, as though he were a Buddhist monk, possessed of knowledge but refusing to divulge it to the uninitiated.

For two days, they had been travelling from north to south, east to west along the northern reaches of Lake Tana, from its sweeping shore, up into the highlands around the city of Lalibela. They had skirted the northern reaches of the city of Gondar and approached the lofty rocky summit of Mt Hoharwa. But at each stopping point, a dozen times a day, Binyussef shook his head with infuriating consistency, smiled apologetically and said, 'I'm sorry. I don't recognise this place.'

Michael went behind a bush and relieved himself. He heard the car door slam, turned and saw that Judith had got out to stretch her back. Despite the heat, she was less affected than him. He finished, walked over to her and said, 'I get the distinct impression we're being led up the garden path. I can't understand why. At first he seemed keen to assist us. What in the name of sweet Jesus is going on?'

'My impression is that he was so happy to find people who were not out to abuse him that he loosened his tongue. He told us things that he's obviously come to regret. I think that now we're back in his region, he's reinvested himself with the title of Guardian,' said Judith.

'Then how are we to discover where Christ's Testament could be hidden?' he demanded, the frustration leaching into his tone. 'There are so many thousands of caves, so many twists and turns in this convoluted landscape that without him we don't stand a chance.' So far to come, so much time expended, for so little result.

When they returned to the jeep, Binyussef had already got out. Judith laid out a rug and began to set out the plastic plates and prepared a mid-afternoon snack.

Michael lay back looking up at the velvet blue sky. Strange insects flitted above his head. He looked at the olive green in the canopy of trees.

'This is a waste of time,' he said. 'He isn't going to show us where the cave is. I don't blame him really. I suppose he was overcome with relief at seeing us but the last couple of days travelling must have given him second thoughts. Let's face it. We're asking him to tell us the most closely guarded secret his people have held.'

Judith lay down and stroked his forehead. Binyussef looked on, not understanding their English.

'Of course, if he had taken us to where it was stored, we'd still have a major problem,' said Judith.

Michael looked at her. 'Getting it back?'

'No,' she said. 'Where we'd take it. The unresolved problem between you and me. Michael, this is a treasure of the world, not of the Christians. This is part of the Dead Sea Scrolls heritage.'

'Judith, for God's sake, let's not start this again. You know in your heart this document belongs to Rome.'

'I don't know that Michael. I don't know any such thing. Rome was where Peter and Paul ended their days. But it was purely artificial. It could just as easily have been Athens. The centre of the church was Jerusalem. If it hadn't been for Paul, that's where the centre of Catholicism would be today.'

'But look at the reality,' he said angrily. 'Look at today. Deal in facts for God's sake.'

Binyussef wondered why they were arguing. In his house, the young man and woman had been so close, such lovers, but in the last two days, a coldness had come between them. He felt responsible for the coldness. Every time they drew close to where the cave was, Binyussef held back, not wanting to show them, wanting to retain the secret. He looked at them with sadness in his eyes.

'Bugger the reality, Michael. Christ was a Jewish prophet. The document belongs to Israel.'

'And bugger yourself. He renounced Judaism for the new way. The new way! That document goes to Rome.'

'And would you put Christ's Testament on public show, like we've done with the Dead Sea Scrolls?' she demanded. 'Would you build a special museum so that people from all the world, from every faith, can gaze at His words?' Michael didn't answer but continued to stare up at the sky. 'How would you and your Catholic friends exhibit them, Michael? Would they rest eternally in the Sistine Chapel on a marble pedestal? How would you deal with something as immeasurably valuable as this document?' Still, he didn't answer. He remembered his conversation with Ari Wallenstein. What should be done if the Testament were to be found. Ari's perspective was that of a Jew. Michael now represented the interests of the Catholic Church. Thank God it wasn't his decision. All he would do was to hand it over to the

Catholic hierarchy for safekeeping. After that, it was up to the priests, and the doctors of law.

'I will reveal the place,' said Binyussef suddenly. 'Then my people will say whether to transport the Temple objects to Israel. If they say yes, you will return for them. If they say no, will you keep the secret until I am dead?'

They made camp and spent the night. Nobody spoke very much. They were too overawed by the prospects of the morning.

The flamingos, rising out of the water of the lake, woke them and they broke camp and set off along the beaten track into the highlands of the Semien Mountains. The old man sat back in comfort in the deep cushioned seats of the jeep. The last time he had walked up this trail it had taken him half a day to climb. Then he had been viewed with suspicion and hostility by the soldiers from Addis Ababa and the strangers who were relocated into his village. Then he had been alone.

They passed through the *teff* fields and through the dry scrub and dead grasses which, along with acacia and tamarind trees and bushes, were the only things capable of clinging on to the sides of the hills.

He looked back through the rear window of the jeep and saw the mosaic pattern of fields of oats, maize and barley growing in the lower regions. The jeep continued to climb up the steep foothills of Mt Hoharwa until the track faded into the surrounding country. The jeep slipped and strained against the increasingly large rocks until Michael heaved it to the side, turned and said, 'How much further? From here, we can go only by foot.'

'It is a climb,' Binyussef replied. 'It is not far, but steep.'

Michael jumped out of the jeep and surveyed the land. It was arid and the vegetation was much more sparse. He was overcome by a sense of almost incalculable excitement as though at any moment he could reach out and touch the majesty of his Lord, his Christ. He fell on his knees and began to pray. It was an intensity of prayer and feeling which he hadn't experienced for years, not since he had first converted. That initial blush had fulfilled his entire heart and soul. He had been transported into a higher plane of existence by the fervour of his Christ, but the years had dulled the joy and only now, in the highlands of Ethiopia, an armlength from his Messiah's very words, he was revisited with the joy and with the intensity of that initial pleasure.

Judith walked slowly over to him and put her arm around him. 'Michael,' she said softly. 'Do you want to stay here while I go and get it?'

He looked at her. 'No!' he said, his voice breaking with emotion. 'No. I must go.'

She helped him to his feet and they walked up the narrow pathway, climbing steeply. The old man had more strength than they'd expected. Judith was fit from her years of military service and found the climb relatively easy going. Michael, who had tried to remain fit, found it harder, puffing and panting, but there was a feeling of magnetism which impelled him upwards, each foot impatiently covering more and more ground until he climbed higher and higher after the others towards the zenith of his life.

They rounded a corner. The track had disappeared long ago. There was no sign of humanity or that any person had ever been in this area. They didn't even stop for a rest or refreshment, the spirit had captured them and was pulling them upwards.

They rounded a bend in front of them and, just below the crest of the mountain, hidden by the overhang of a steep rock ledge, they saw a massive boulder. It had rolled and fused with the mountainside. Michael looked around but could see no cave, no temple, no structure which could house their quarry. Judith kept her eyes firmly on Binyussef. All three continued to pant from the exertion.

Binyussef turned and pointed his skeletal hand at the boulder. 'What?' said Michael.

'This is what you seek,' said Binyussef. 'Apart from the Guardians, you are the first people in three thousand years to have seen this cave. In the days of the high priests of the city of Axum, before it became Christian, this cave was known. Then it was many days' journey by the Guardians. When Axum was taken by the Christians, the people of the Agau moved south to Lake Tana and its surroundings. Then we were a mighty people. We were half of the population of Abyssinia. Today, we are few.'

But Michael wasn't listening. He was staring at the cave mouth, covered by the huge boulder. He was within a heartbeat of touching the words of his holy Christ. His heart was pounding, not from the exertion of the long climb, but from the proximity to God. In this high place, in this desolate land, in this alien environment, Michael was about to touch the mystery on which his life had revolved. There were no words he could say. His heart was too full of fear and longing. Judith moved forward but Binyussef held up his hand to stop her and she shrank back out of reverence for his age-old calling. Binyussef turned and walked towards the boulder. He was almost dwarfed by it. It stood half as high again as he did and as they walked closer they could see that it had been supported on two runnels, tree trunks which had met to form a 'V' so that the boulder could run down them like some huge, slow-moving train and fuse itself forever against the cave mouth.

'How are we going to roll that back?' asked Michael.

Judith shook her head. Michael looked around for some implement, some mechanical device. But he soon realised how silly the idea was that in this desolate place, dozens of miles from civilisation, at the top of a mountain in the midst of nowhere, he should find a device belonging to the twentieth century. Binyussef walked over and smiled proudly. 'Come here,' he said.

They trooped over and looked at the face of the rock which was parallel to the cave mouth.

'Good God,' Michael exclaimed. Through the centre of the huge boulder, a small cavity had been carved out. Looking deeper into the depression, they could see that the cavity was a hollow conduit, which tunnelled right through the rock to emerge as a tiny gleam of light on the other side.

'That must be all of eight or nine feet long,' said Judith. 'Right through the heart of the rock. What an incredible feat of engineering. It must have been done millennia ago.'

'But what's it for?' asked Michael.

Binyussef stood back proudly as the white people admired the abilities and sophistication of his ancestors. He walked over to the edge of the plateau and pushed away a small rock. It was hiding a depression in the ground where, neatly coiled, were two ancient block and tackle pulleys and lengths of stout rope. At closer inspection, the rope turned out to be heavily matted intertwined lengths of flax.

'Sorry,' said Michael in growing frustration, 'but I'm still at a loss. What do we do with this?'

'Pity you didn't serve time in the Israeli army, Michael. It's really very simple,' said Judith. She picked up one of the heavy blocks and tackle, and carried it over to a jutting rock pinnacle at the edge of the clearing. Binyussef nodded keenly. He reached into the small depression and picked up the second, which he placed halfway between the edge of the clearing and the cave mouth.

'It's a simple double-pulley system. You should have studied Archimedes instead of Augustine when you converted. Two pulleys together can move a weight like that boulder as easily as rolling an egg. You thread the ropes through the pulleys, through the hole that they dug out of the centre of the rock, and pull on the end of the remaining rope.'

Judith carried the rope to the boulder and threaded one end through until Binyussef was able to pull it through on the opposite side of the boulder. Within minutes, they had threaded the rope correctly through the two pulleys, joined the pulleys together, and taken up the slack. They began to pull on the rope.

Michael took one end of the rope tied around the pinnacle on the edge of the clearing and pulled until he had taken up all the slack. Binyussef took the other rope, tied through the boulder. Binyussef nodded and, together, the two men pulled.

Immediately, the ropes strained against each other. As they pulled together harder, Michael saw that the rock strained and began to roll back up the two tree-trunk railings on the ground. When there was a small gap between the cave mouth and the boulder, Binyussef trapped his rope in between the pulley and the other rope, and said, 'Enough. We only need to open it a small distance.'

Both of them complained, but Binyussef held up his hand. 'I am here to take the jar of the man Jesus. I will allow you to take some other things out so you may see them in the light, but they must go back. You made me a promise. When I am dead, or if my people say they may be taken to Israel, then you can see everything. Until then, I am the Guardian. I am the Law.'

They walked over to the boulder and Judith checked its distance from the cave mouth. 'That's enough. That'll get us in,' she said.

'That's not wide enough, we can't get in there,' said Michael. 'We'll have to open it more. Go back to the pulleys.'

'Stop!' said Judith urgently. Binyussef looked in wonder. 'I won't let you. We can't transgress on Binyussef's good faith. The gap's big enough. Go back to those pulleys and he'll lose all trust in us.'

'But we've found the location of the cave.'

'Thanks to Binyussef.' She turned on him angrily. 'We play this game according to his rules, Michael. Understand?'

Michael wondered whether to argue with her. But her look was one of insistence. She sought to reassure him.

'I can get in. Don't worry,' said Judith. 'I can slip in quite easily. Give me the flashlight.'

'No,' said Binyussef. 'I must say prayers.'

They waited several minutes while Binyussef mumbled age-old prayers to Yahweh. Neither wanted to interrupt his devotions. He turned to them and nodded. 'I will be first,' he said. Judith gave him the flashlight and he knelt down on the ground where the gap was widest and eased his head, then his shoulders and the rest of his body, into the cave. When his feet had disappeared inside, Judith followed. Michael put his mouth to the cave's entrance. 'What's in there? What can you see?' he asked like an impatient child.

An agonising minute later, her muffled voice said, 'It's like the Holy of Holies. It's full of wonders. I can't see too clearly but the light of the torch is revealing objects like candelabra and sentinels and huge golden eagles that probably stood in front of the Holy Ark, and breastplates of the Torahs. Oh Michael, I wish you could come in here.' He could hear the emotion in her voice, as though she were fighting back tears.

Michael shouted, 'Is it there? Can you see it?' There were long moments before she answered. It was an agony. 'Yes, Michael, it's here. I'm holding it in my hands.'

Michael bit his lip to stop himself from crying out. He mumbled a prayer of thanksgiving to God.

The first to come out was Binyussef. He emerged arms first, then his head and then his body. In his hands were breastplates and gold and ivory ornaments of extraordinary beauty and antiquity. As he stood, he clutched them to his chest as though they were of his body. But Michael wasn't looking. He was waiting for Judith to emerge. She came out and stood, but her hands contained nothing. She looked at Michael and smiled. He looked questioningly at her and reverentially she took from the inside of her shirt a small, faded dun-coloured jar, fastened around its lip with a fraying, dull, decayed strand of cord, the ends of which were joined beneath a small thick disc of lead.

Michael reached out with his two hands open. Judith placed the jar containing the Testament of Jesus Christ into his hands.

The radio-telephone crackled, the signal thin and asthmatic. Colonel Wagshun pulled it from its cradle. He listened, then responded gruffly. 'Where?' He nodded. 'How long ago?' He paused. 'Have they moved or are they still there?' He replaced the receiver.

Jimmy, eyes drawn and vacant, had spent the hours since morning mumbling. He turned and looked at the colonel distantly. 'What's going on?' he asked.

'It seems our friends have been sighted setting up camp for the night north of Lake Tana, about two kilometres out of the village of Giorgis.' Jimmy nodded as though the information was of no interest. 'Aren't you pleased?' asked the colonel. Jimmy shrugged his shoulders. 'You surprise me, Dr Wilson. This is the news you came to hear. We've finally caught up with your friends.'

'Colonel, I—' He sank back into the seat and became the sort of man who was a derelict, mumbling and shuffling along the pavements of Addis Ababa.

'Aren't you going to tell me what you want to do?'

Jimmy shook his head. Sharply, the colonel said, 'For God's sake, man, pull yourself together.'

'I'm a sinner,' Jimmy whispered. 'I sinned once in America when I . . . when I—'

'I don't want to know about your past, Dr Wilson,' Colonel Wagshun said without interest. 'All I want is instructions.' Jimmy remained silent. 'Do you want me to organise for the permanent departure of these three people? It will cost a great deal if you do, a great deal.'

Talk of money made Jimmy pay attention. He turned around and said, 'I've already paid you a fortune, Wagshun, and I've offered you ten per cent of my income from the Testament. It's more than a man like you could earn in a thousand years. You can't get blood out of a stone. As to these people, I don't know.'

'I fail to understand you, Wilson. You're nearing the end of the road, yet you're unwilling to tread the final step which leads to success.'

Jimmy stared down at his hands as the Landcruiser bumped over the potholes on the road towards Gondar. The colonel allowed several minutes to pass by before saying, 'They're camped by the lake. Nobody will know if their bodies go missing. In this part of the world they can disappear without a trace. It happens every day. Nature and politics are both killers.'

Jimmy looked at him contemptuously. 'How much?'

Colonel Wagshun smiled. 'Good! I see you're taking that final step. The cost is fifty thousand dollars.'

'Fifty thousand!' Jimmy exclaimed.

'Each!'

'You have to be kiddin'.'

'Do it yourself.'

'Don't I even get group rates?'

The colonel laughed. 'If you want a discount, there's an easier way than me soiling my hands. They're travelling with an old Falasha. The Amharic people hate the Falashas. They're a very superstitious community. Let's just say that the right word to the elder of the nearby village and our friends won't escape the district alive.'

'So long as these natives don't harm the Testament.'

The colonel nodded. 'Special offer, Dr Wilson. Three for the price of one.'

Several moments went past until Jimmy nodded. 'Why so much?' he asked.

The colonel laughed. 'I have pressing needs.'

They were like children receiving birthday presents. They were laughing and joking and every few minutes they looked at the jar, fearful of opening it and exposing it to the pollution of the twentieth century. Michael couldn't resist touching the jar as though an organic electricity flowed from it into his body.

'It's the word of God. It's God's gift to mankind. I just can't believe it. Dear God Almighty, I can't believe it.'

Judith, though excited, said, 'Who can say? The Jew in me says this is a wonderful document. But it's only the writings of the prophets. Yet I'm experiencing such a strong feeling that I'm in the presence of something intensely spiritual. How does it make you feel?'

Michael thought for a moment. 'It makes me feel as if I'm in the presence of God Himself. I just can't frame the words that express the feelings.'

They put the jar back into the pannier. Binyussef looked at them both. He didn't understand the English they were using but he knew the look of ecstasy.

They had camped beside Lake Tana before making the journey back south towards Addis Ababa. Binyussef gathered reeds, bark and stalks to make a crackling fire. They were camped on a rock a dozen feet above the shore, to protect themselves from crocodiles.

Michael unpacked some provisions and made a meal of beans, tinned meat and breads which they ate with relish. It had been a long, hard day, a day which had ended in the most satisfying exhaustion that Judith and Michael had ever known. After the meal, they lay back on their rugs, staring up at the countless stars. It was a vast, moonless canopy but the stars were so clear and plentiful that they illuminated the ghostly outlines of the far-off mountains.

'I think we have to talk,' Judith said.

'Yes. What are we going to do now?'

She sighed. 'You know it has to go back to Israel, Michael. It belongs to the Jewish people as much as the Christians. If it goes to Rome, we'll be dispossessed. Rome will take ownership.'

'But Jews will have access to it. A special museum will be built around it, like the museum that was built for the Dead Sea Scrolls. The whole world will know where to find it. It'll be the most visited, the most looked-at document on earth.'

'But Michael, darling, it's part of the Dead Sea Scrolls. Please understand from my point of view. Jesus wrote it while he was at Qumran. It has to return to be part of our heritage.'

'But it's the word of Christ, Judith.'

'No, Michael. It's the word of Jeshua the Nazarene, a simple, wonderful, brilliant Judean mystic.'

'But how do you know what He said until we've read the Testament? It's the word of God,' said Michael. 'I'm telling you.' There was desperation in his voice. 'You must believe me.'

She reached over and held his hand. 'No, I don't believe you. I love you, Michael. I love you more than anything. I've loved you since we were first together as students. I'd do anything for you, but not this! This scroll is from the Dead Sea. End of story. You know I can't let you take it to Rome.'

He lay back and breathed deeply. Visions went through his mind of using force, seducing her, of threats, and of pleas. But in the end it was his will against hers; hers against his. In the end, there would be no resolution. In the end it would be like it was twenty years ago, where he would follow his conscience and lose, for the second time, the only woman he had ever truly loved.

'I think we should put it back,' he said softly.

She turned and looked at him, frowning. He continued. 'If you and I are quarrelling, imagine what's going to happen when the Catholics and the Protestants and the Jews all get hold of it.'

'Put it back?'

He nodded. 'We've had it for less than a couple of hours and already we're at each other's throats. I think it has to be returned to the cave and you and I have to go and talk to the Vatican and the Chief Rabbi of Israel and Ari. We have to tell them we've found it somewhere in Ethiopia, but we're unwilling to tell anybody where it is until written agreements have been signed for its disposition. To everybody's satisfaction. Force them into a peaceful accord. No agreement, no Testament.'

Judith thought about it for a while and finally agreed. They sat up and looked at Binyussef, crosslegged, his silhouette highlighted by the reed fire. They told him their decision and he nodded. 'I will keep this thing with me. I will stay here as the Guardian. You go home and do what you have to do and when you're ready, return to me.'

His words were so simple, so elegantly beautiful, that Judith began to cry. Michael put his arm around her and said, 'How does it feel to go back empty-handed?'

She put her hand on his. 'I'm not going back empty-handed, Michael. I have knowledge. And I have you.'

He nodded. 'And your husband?'

She shrugged indifferently. Michael thought about Deirdre. Then about Christopher. He breathed deeply, lay back on the rock and let his thoughts fly upwards into the cold night air.

As daylight crept above the glistening peaks of Lake Tana's mountaintops, Binyussef said his final goodbye to Michael and Judith. He promised them that he would be all right, that he would look after himself.

They drove him to the house where he had lived all his adult life. Wossen came to the door as the three approached. He bowed low in deference to the holy and spiritual man who walked between the white man and the white woman.

'Wossen,' said Michael. 'We have brought Binyussef back. We must return to where we came from. There are many things that we must do. We must go to Jerusalem to talk to your people. Then we must go to

Rome to talk with the Pope and tell him certain things. Then we must talk to leaders of other Christian churches. It may take many weeks for us to talk to these people. But Judith and I cannot take you and Binyussef back with us yet. The world must decide what is to be done. We will return as soon as is possible and we will bring the love and hope of the people of the world.'

Wossen nodded. 'I will look after Binyussef,' he said. 'Now I am strong and free.'

They embraced and said goodbye. Michael and Judith walked back down the path towards their jeep. Wossen felt strangely ill-at-ease alone with this mystical and holy man, unsure of what to do or what to say. The old man looked up at Wossen, smiled, and nodded. He stood and out of the folds of his dirty shirt he took a strange ancient jar. He walked over to the empty book shelves against the wall of his home and placed the jar on its side on the top shelf. Binyussef stood looking at the jar for many moments, then he touched it with his hand, reached up and touched the Hebrew writing above the bookshelf and kissed his hand. He turned and sat at the table, staring out of the door towards the lake.

Sergeant Didasa lowered his binoculars as he saw the jeep driving off. He would wait until night.

Jimmy woke up with a start, trying to define meaning from the voices outside. Sergeant Didasa had returned and was speaking in Amharic to Colonel Wagshun. Jimmy had spent the night in restless prayer, praying that the sergeant would have tracked down Michael Farber. Praying that today he would get his hands on the Testament. That his troubles would be over.

When the sergeant had finished, Colonel Wagshun looked at Jimmy and shook his head sadly. All his hopes, all his aspirations, his way out of the nightmare that surrounded him, suddenly disappeared. Jimmy bowed his head, cupped his hands over his face and started to cry. Colonel Wagshun felt his lips curling in disgust.

Isaac Manitam was on his knees in Selassie Cathedral in Addis Ababa when a servant touched him gently on the shoulder. He looked up from his trance, and the man whispered, 'There's a man here who wishes to speak to you urgently. I think you'd better come.'

They walked the short distance from the cathedral to the bishop's residence in silence. In his study was a tall, elegantly dressed Ethiopian army colonel with sparkling epaulettes and gold braids across his uniform. 'I am Colonel Wagshun. Do I have the honour of addressing Bishop Manitam?'

'You do.'

'Your grace, you and I have never met but I realise that you consider us enemies. You think I persecute your priests. I think they meddle in the affairs of the State. However, for the time being we must put our differences to one side for I have in my possession something which transcends all of our petty squabbles and I need your assistance to save my life. A fair trade, I think.'

'I'd hardly call the systematic torture of hundreds of innocent people petty, colonel.'

Colonel Wagshun waved the comment aside. 'Before I tell you what it is I have in my possession, let me tell the terms and conditions. I require a Vatican passport, diplomatic immunity, the robes of a Catholic priest and for you to escort me out of the country tomorrow.'

Isaac Manitam laughed aloud. 'Where on earth do you think I can get a diplomatic passport from? And as for you masquerading as a priest . . .'

'Bishop, before you reply with objections, why not have a look at this.'

Colonel Wagshun reached into his briefcase and withdrew a faded dun-coloured jar. Isaac Manitam knew instantly what it was. He reached out to touch it but with a thin smile, the colonel replaced it in his briefcase, saying, 'I believe we have to conclude an agreement before I hand this over to you.'

Isaac Manitam looked him in the eyes and nodded. 'I must make a phone call first to a certain friend in Israel. I believe everything else will be simple.'

Half an hour later, Isaac re-entered the study where the colonel was waiting patiently. 'I have spoken to his eminence, Cardinal Rhymer, the Secretary of State for the Vatican. He tells me to issue you with a letter of authority from my episcopate which is as good as a diplomatic passport. I assume you will not be wanting for money?'

The colonel laughed. 'Be assured that I have adequate means outside Ethiopia.'

'Then you will have everything else you require, colonel. May I at least hold the Testament until you give it to me properly tomorrow?'

The colonel shrugged indifferently and handed over the jar.

Christ's Testament! Isaac held the jar lovingly in his hands. The seal was still intact. He gently forced it open and removed the Testament. It was the word of God; he was the first Christian in two thousand years to have received it into his hands.

It had been passed down to him from the innocent waters of Lake Tana, source of the River Nile, the mother of Egypt. Isaac had seen the lake in his mind as his priests had tried to discover where Michael and his companion were travelling. He had seen it glisten in the sunshine, gleaming with scintillas as its waters lapped against its gentle shore. And in his mind's eye he had followed its cold, blue waters as they cascaded from the high mountains, down the Ethiopian plateau into the Sudan, then northwards through the ancient land of Egypt until reaching the Mediterranean. The very waters in which the infant Moses had been set adrift in the papyrus raft, to grow as a son of Pharaoh before leading the children of Israel in the greatest exodus of all time, into the Promised Land. And as the water travelled from the land of the heathen into the land of the one true God, Moses himself had climbed high up to the summit of Mount Sinai and had been made custodian of the word of God. And Moses gave the word of God to the children of Israel. But it had been too holy to be seen by any but the priests, and so Moses had instructed Bezalel son of Uri, son of Hur, of the tribe of Judah, to build an ark to surround the sacred words of God and the words of God were hidden from the people forever. Only the high priests were ever permitted to see the word of God.

And Isaac was a high priest who held the word of God. And for the second time in the history of humanity, the source of the Nile had delivered another Testament, a new Testament, into the hands of a sinful world.

CHAPTER 27

The young man's weather-burned skin was partially hidden by the white linen cloak he wore over his head. Beside him, not behind him as was the custom of the people of Nubia, walked a tall and confident young woman. They had been travelling for so long now that they had lost the excitement which they first felt in seeing different lands. Wherever they travelled, they were greeted and made welcome, either by the Jews or, when they found a community, by the Christians.

Abram and Avigad had been journeying for two years since leaving the people of the Agau. It was in the city of Ephesus that Abram made his first true convert to Christianity. Montemthat told him that Avigad was his first convert to the faith, but in his heart, Abram knew that Christ wanted him to convert the unbelievers. By the time he baptised Avigad, she was already a believer. How could he admit to the high priests in Rome that his success as a proselytiser had amounted to converting the one and only convert who had become his wife? The woman whom he converted in Ephesus was a prostitute.

Abram had been walking back to the inn late one night after attending a service amongst the small Christian community, when he had taken the wrong turning, left instead of right. He should have walked up the hill to where Avigad eagerly awaited his return. But instead Abram turned left into the street of the prostitutes and was greeted by the sight of women wearing red veils. He turned and walked away quickly but the whores cackled in laughter behind his back. It made him angry. Anger was not an emotion he had yet managed to control. It would take him years to subdue his anger with a world which rejected the Messiah and to give himself over only to the love of Christ. Remembering the suffering of Christ and the ridicule He had endured at the hands of the Romans and the Jews, Abram turned in love and walked back into their midst. They numbered twenty. They were fat and greasy and smelled strongly of perfumes and looked as though they had been well used by men. One came over to him. The pustules on her face were open and weeping, making Abram grimace and avert his eyes. She ignored his disdain. It happened all the time. She said, 'Open my legs with a coin.'

He shook his head and made a sign of the Cross, saying, 'Woman, do you not know that your body is the Temple of God and that you sin against God when you perform these acts?'

The cackling of the women grew to a howl of laughter. Their derision stung him. One picked up some mud from the ground and threw it at him. It hit his cloak, staining it black where the mud adhered. Abram brushed it off, without anger. After all, it was the way in which Romans chose their senators. Those vying for elective office wore white tunics, *candida*. The candidate with the cleanest tunic was the least hated by the public and became a senator. And had not the Messiah, Jesus Christ, said, 'Turn the other cheek,' and so he continued to brush it away and said, 'Woman, you will never touch my spirit with what you throw at me. My body is merely a vessel of the Lord.'

One woman sneered, walked up to him and spat. 'You Christians! Tight with your money. Tight with your backsides. What's the matter? Scared to have fun?'

He was being taunted and he mumbled the words of Christ to himself, but he couldn't bring his heart to condemn these women. For they were the broken and used pots of society. Were it not for the insatiable lusts of men, these women would be good and dutiful wives and daughters. 'God bless you,' he said to the woman who had thrown the mud. 'I will pray for you tonight that your soul may be redeemed.'

He turned and walked back to where he had taken the wrong path. As he retreated their laughter grew. He felt them sneering. One threw a stone and it hit him in the small of his back, but he continued to walk, ignoring them and praying for their salvation, for their enlightenment. He walked up the hill, past the Office of the *Satrap* where the business of the port was conducted, and heard laughter coming from the inn. He turned to enter the inn and go up to his room when he heard a scuffling behind him. He turned quickly, afraid it might be robbers. A shadow flitted past his eye and hid in the doorway of a building.

'Who's there?' he said nervously. There was no reply. 'I have no money. I have no purse. You rob me at your cost.' The shadow within the doorway moved. A woman dressed in a red scarf emerged. He recognised her as one of the harlots from the road of the prostitutes. 'Who are you?' he asked.

She stared at him. In the road where she worked, she was the one with authority and power. But away from her road, she felt timid, an outcast from society. She didn't answer. 'Daughter, what is your name?' asked Abram. Still she didn't answer. 'Why are you following me?'

'Who is God?' she asked, her voice timorous.

'God is the one true divine overlord, the creator of the world, the blessed spirit,' he answered simply.

There was a silence between them as she absorbed his answer. 'Who is Christ?' she asked.

'Christ is His Son. Yahweh sent His only begotten Son Jesus to be the Christ on earth. To be the redeemer of all mankind so that our sins fall upon His shoulders and we are cleansed.'

'Am I cleansed of sins?'

'Daughter, in the land where the Son of God preached love and forgiveness, the land where He was crucified by the Romans for your sins, He loved and lived with sinners and prostitutes.'

She cackled, 'Not much of a God, to live with whores.'

'No, daughter. For it is sinners who make up the world. We are all of us sinners, and the Christ died to cleanse us of our sins.'

'So I am cleansed?'

'So long as you sin no more, and accept Jesus into your heart. So long as you allow your sins to be washed away by the immaculate water of the baptism.'

The whore stood and thought for a moment. 'And if I sin tomorrow, letting men have their way of me, can I be cleansed then?'

'Yes. Jesus Christ loves you and will forgive you anything until you let Him into your heart. But once you have accepted Him as God on earth, then you must sin no more, for once you do, you reject Him and the Kingdom of Heaven.'

'If I accept Him, will I be safe forever?'

'If you are baptised in His way, then, yes, you are safe forever and your soul will be purified and your heart will be open to goodness and light.'

The woman nodded, repeating his words slowly to herself. Abram stood there. The moment turned into a minute. As he waited for her reaction, he knew that, were he to speak, were he to move towards her, then, like a terrified quarry, she would bolt from his grasp. He was the hunter. His weapons were the words of Christ. The woman nodded. 'Thank you,' she said, turned and began to walk down the hill.

'Daughter, go with Christ. You have begun the path to redemption by opening your heart to questions.'

She stopped in her path. Abram's heart beat wildly. She was going to turn and come back to him. He prayed silently to himself. The woman turned and looked at him. She smiled, turned back and walked away from him towards the street of the prostitutes. Abram stood rooted to the spot for ten minutes, incapable of moving. It was the greatest moment of his young life, greater even than touching the words that the Lord Jesus had written and that he had given over to the people of the Agau. For a soul had been placed in his hands and he could feel how close he was to redeeming it forever from purgatory into the blessed light of Christ.

The following night, he was returning to his lodgings when the woman again appeared out of the shadow of the doorway. She stood looking at him. He tried to define the thoughts going through her head, but her face was a mask of uncertainty. Abram smiled at her and said, 'Will you be my guest? My wife has prepared a meal. Will you join us?'

The woman shrank back as though he had abused her. 'I cannot go inside,' she said incredulously. 'I will not be allowed. I wear the red scarf of a prostitute.'

'You are with me.'

'I cannot shame you. You will be dishonoured.'

'My honour is with Christ in Heaven, and with you as my guest; not with these men in the inn. Not with the people on this earth below Heaven.'

The prostitute cast her eyes downwards, nodded and followed him. During supper he told her about the wonders of Christ, the miracles He had performed and the message which He had died in order to spread. By the end of evening, he had laid his hand upon her head and converted her to the way of Christ. She refused to go back to her house but said that she would sleep on the floor at the foot of their bed, in order to follow Abram and Avigad, if necessary as their servant, so that she could learn more about Christ.

Abram's heart was filled to overflowing with a love of life. Within the year, he had become a man in the eyes of his wife, a missionary in the eyes of the Christians they had met along the way, and a direct link to Christ for Diana, the first of many people he would convert to the way of the Messiah. A month later, they left the city and journeyed from Ephesus back towards Rhodes, landing on the Lycaonian Coast at Tarsus to visit the birthplace of Saul, and then to Derbe, Lystra and Iconium. All along the way they met communities of Jews and worshippers of pagan gods and the three spoke to them gently and reassuringly about the mission of Jesus Christ on earth. The urgency that Abram felt for reaching Rome disappeared in the joy of converting souls to eternal life.

A year and a half later, after following much of the route written about by the blessed Paul, the three finally arrived in Rome. Avigad had seen many large and magnificent cities—Corinthus, Nicopolis, Neapolis and Alba—but she had never seen a city as large and magnificent as Rome. It was sumptuous, the stuff of which dreams are made; it was as she imagined the buildings of Heaven. Rome's palaces, circuses, public squares and temples burned white in the glaring sun, the marble of the buildings pure and unsullied against the bright blue sky. And the people in the streets . . . thousands upon thousands of them. More people than she had ever seen in her life. People going everywhere in all directions at once, a confusion of humanity, noisy, bustling, shouting, laughing, talking in strange and unpleasant tongues and wearing clothes which Abram told her were from different parts of the Roman world. It was a monstrous nightmare, a hellish concoction of strange sounds and sights. Yet the purity, the symmetry of the buildings took her breath away, overshadowed her experiences of the desert and the cities of the east, and made her feel as though she were a child again.

Abram and Diana walked along the Via Pontifex towards the Circus of Mars and, as they walked, Avigad shrank away from its overpowering size. She looked up and as though touching the clouds above, rows of columns, one upon another, stood like sentinels against her. On top of the hundreds of huge marble columns were winged figures, standing in a multitude of different poses—some were holding horns, others harps, others appeared to be waving. It was as though, above the heads of the populace, the gods were living a separate existence. And as if the presence of statues on pillars was not intimidating enough, on the apex of the buildings, caught in mid-action, were friezes of men riding chariots, slaves set in the silent obedience of stone, women throwing garlands at their heroes. Avigad's mouth drooped in shock as she walked past one building, then another, shaking her head in speechless amazement.

Abram put his arm around her, understanding immediately how she felt. He whispered in her ear, 'All this is nothing compared to the Kingdom of Heaven.' She turned and smiled, and held his hand. Diana, her best friend and companion, walked around and put another arm around Avigad's shoulders, and reassured her, 'In my life as a harlot I was visited by many Romans. They told me of the Circus of Mars and the

Colosseum and the House of the Senate. I never thought I would see it. Yet, seeing it now, it's not so grand as they made out. For when one walks in the path of the Lord, one sees great buildings in one's mind's eye.'

They settled into an inn close to the Circus Maximus, just a short walk from the River Tiber, and began to put out enquiries for the local Christian community. From travellers they had met along the road and from what they had been told by Bishop Polycarp of Smyrna, Abram knew that the persecutions begun in the reign of the hated Emperor Nero had now come to an end and that the Christians, while ridiculed by the Romans, were tolerated. Trajan and Hadrian had been reasonable in their dealings. The publican told him that there was a local meeting of Christians in a room adjacent to the public baths and directed them, warning them that the Christians were up to no good and to be careful of their ceremonies, which he said confidently were naked orgies in which the blood of children was drunk and women were forced to perform bestial rights with the church leaders. Abram thanked his host and assured him that the tales he had heard were untrue.

'Friend,' said the innkeeper, 'you'd better know that in the early years the Christians were accused and punished by the emperors for all the disasters which occurred. Even disasters for which they were clearly not responsible. Same thing could happen again, if we get more emperors like we used to have.'

'What types of things were they accused of?' asked Abram, as he and the two women prepared to leave the premises.

'Barbarian invasions, plagues, floods and earthquakes, increased prices of wheat. The first Christians were blamed for the fire that destroyed much of Rome in the reign of Nero,' the innkeeper said, laughing.

'How were they punished?' asked Avigad. She had a fairly good idea, but wanted to know whether the rumours were correct.

'They were part of our sports. They were covered with animal skins, smeared with blood, and chased around the arena of the Circus Maximus and other arenas by dogs and lions. They were torn to pieces. He laughed out loud as Avigad and Diana recoiled in horror. As if prearranged, a huge roar rose from the Circus Maximus, the crowd enjoying some spectacle. Abram prayed it was the spectacle of chariot races, rather than sport with live quarry.

When dusk fell and the streetlights of Rome were lit by the lamplighter, Abram blessed Avigad and Diana and walked off in the direction that he had been advised. When he arrived at the large house, close to the Temple of Claudius, the room was full of thirty or more men and women, who sat peacefully drinking wine and talking. On the wall was a cloth banner with a drawing of two fish, both of which had been caught in the mouth on either arm of an anchor. Below was the word 'ICHTHYS', which Abram recognised as the Greek word for fish, the symbol for Christians throughout the world, an acronym for 'Jesus Christ, Son of God, Man'. On the left hand side of the sign were the conjoined Greek letters CHI RHO, another symbol which told Abram that he was with Christians. As he entered the room, the low level of conversation came to a halt. People stared at the stranger. He lifted his right hand and made the sign of the Cross and smiled. Nobody smiled back. A slight, balding man on the far side of the room stood and walked over to him. In silence, the assembly parted to allow him through. 'I am Theodorus.'

'I am Abram.'

'Where are you from?'

'I am from Judea.'

There was a mumble of inaudible conversation. 'Many men say they have come here from Judea. Most are Jews.'

'I am a Christian. I am here with my wife Avigad, a convert from the Edomites. We travel with a friend, a convert from the city of Ephesus.'

'Why have you come, Abram?'

'I have come to seek the Bishop of Rome, one known as Pope Hyginus. The one who is the father of the Christians. I have come because I wish him to appoint me to be an apostle of Christ.'

The room fell into silence. Theodorus glanced round. The suspicion was self-evident. 'We need no apostles.'

'Then I have wasted my journey.'

'Yes, you have,' said Theodorus.

Abram looked and felt dejected. 'May I sit and pray?'

'To what God do you pray?'

'I pray to the one true Christ.'

'And what food and drink is there in the one true Christ?'

'The bread of his body and the wine of his blood,' Abram replied. He felt the tension in the room begin to ease, except for the suspicion of Theodorus.

'That's something you could have learned from anyone. The Emperor Hadrian has been taught all about our beliefs by the blessed Pope Hyginus. We make no secret of our beliefs and yet we're still persecuted.'

'But I understood the persecutions were at an end.'

Theodorus smiled ruefully, and nodded to an old white-haired woman sitting in the corner. 'Ask Claudia over there. Her beautiful daughter Drusilla was raped and murdered by men who persecuted us.'

'Theodorus,' Abram sighed, 'in my journeys I have seen many good and many hideous things. Men rape

561

and murder followers of all religions. Was she persecuted and murdered because she was a Christian, or because she was a young woman? Was it lust or was it because she was a follower?'

Theodorus remained silent but Abram knew from the tenor of the room that he was gaining respect. At last Theodorus said, 'For one so young, you speak wisely. Are you really a Christian, deep down in your heart, or are you here to betray us?'

'Like Judas betrayed Our Lord? Like Thomas doubted Him? Like Peter denied him three times? Theodorus, we are brothers in Christ. I have travelled this world to be blessed by Pope Hyginus and to be made into an apostle. Already I have converted harlots, sailors on ships who have carried us from port to port, Jews in synagogues, and Phoenician traders. I have spread His word as far as I am able but I lack the authority and I am here to learn and to be sent out as a missionary.'

Theodorus slowly held out his hand. People in the room smiled. Abram grasped his hand and the two men hugged. 'Welcome, brother,' said Theodorus. 'Stay with us.'

Abram sat and Theodorus continued the lesson. When he had finished, they drank wine, ate bread and chatted about the way in which Christianity was spreading so fast among the poor of Rome.

Theodorus told him, 'Christians are allowed to worship, but not freely. We are heavily taxed by the Emperor Hadrian.' Abram realised that there was much work to be done.

The next day, Abram brought Avigad and Diana to meet Theodorus, a butcher in the Via Palatine. He liked them both, especially Diana, who showed him a new way of cutting up a side of lamb, to be more economical. 'Where did you learn these skills?' he asked her.

Her hands bloody, she turned to him and smiled. 'My father was a seller of meat in Ephesus before the trouble with the Romans. He was killed. I used to watch him cut the meat. Every day, he would show me something new. Although I was forced to become a harlot, I have not forgotten the skills.'

Theodorus smiled. Avigad and Abram held hands in the shop. She whispered, 'Do you think we could have introduced a man and a woman and produced a marriage?'

The thought had not occurred to Abram. It was too domestic for his mind. That night, Theodorus took Abram deep into the catacombs below Rome, catacombs where Christians met and were buried in a manner which fitted their religion. The catacombs which were used as burial chambers of the Christians lay deeply within one of the limestone hills beneath Rome. The path was lit by torches but was treacherous, with rocks strewn around the floor of the cavern. From deep within the echoing chamber, Abram heard the communion of prayer. As they walked, he saw the light of the underground chamber lit by one hundred flares. The ceiling was supported by massive pillars and platforms. He marvelled at the size and complexity of the construction.

Men and women were on their knees chanting a hymn and praying. Before them, the Bishop of Rome, Hyginus sat and prayed. Abram knelt within the catacombs, surrounded by Christians, and joined in their prayers. He prayed for many things that day. He prayed for himself, that he would shortly be appointed an apostle by Pope Hyginus and sent throughout the world to spread the word of Christ. He prayed for his parents and his brothers and sisters, imagining their distress at not knowing whether he was alive or dead. One day, maybe this year, maybe next, he would return to Judea like John of Syracuse had returned, and bless them. He prayed for Christians throughout the world, for an end to their suffering and persecution and an acceptance by Romans and Greeks, Jews and idolaters of the divinity of Jesus the Messiah. And he prayed for success in his mission to convert the pagans to the one true way.

Deep in prayer, unaware of what was occurring around him, Abram felt a hand touch his shoulder. He looked up and saw the old smiling face of Pope Hyginus. Abram looked at the controversial priest, a man hated by those who wished to develop the faith in ways which the blessed saints would not approve. Like a rock, he stood against the tide of gnosticism and false worship, and preached orthodoxy and tradition.

But despite the controversy which surrounded his episcopate, Hyginus was known far and wide as a man who fought evil wherever it appeared. It was why Abram had come to talk with him, to be taught by him and to be appointed as one of his missionaries.

Pope Hyginus reached down and encouraged the young man to stand. They embraced deep below ground, in the dark and smoke-filled atmosphere, beneath the frantic streets of the city of Rome, hugging each other in a loving kiss, young boy and old man, as the Christians looked on in approval.

Abram was at last complete.

They walked painfully over the track which led to the top of the hill. She had looked at him closely as they neared the end of the journey, concerned that his emotion would affect his thoughts. She looked at him and thought how much he had changed in the last five years, taller, stronger, yet worn by the length of their journeys and the difficulties of the paths they had trod. She thought back to the ridicule he had suffered at the hands of the Jews, at the anger and beatings from the Greeks and Romans, to the imprisonment he had suffered in Antioch and the way she had been raped by evil men in Athens. It had been a long and difficult journey back but, despite all the trials, she revered every moment she spent with her husband.

She thought back in silence to the two children that had been born to them but that had died before celebrating their first birthdays, to the number of times that she had been light with child and had miscarried due to the strain of their work. Among her own people she would have been called barren and become an outcast, yet every loss made Abram hold her closer and love her more. They had spoken often of Montemthat, wondering where the huge Egyptian was, whether he was plying the sea in trade, or whether he himself was now working for their Saviour.

They climbed to the crest of the hill and Abram looked down at the sweep of the valley and the cluster of houses which filled the valley floor. It was larger than it had been when he had left. More houses had been built further up the hill, more fields, he could see, were under cultivation. Without speaking, he pointed to a house in the distance, a house surrounded by fields, heavy with crops. Avigad peered at it closely. In the distance, she could see three men working in the fields. Two were digging and one was sowing.

'To every thing there is a season and a time to every purpose under heaven,' he told her.

They walked hand in hand down the path towards the centre of the village but turned off to a smaller path which led to his former home. Smoke was coming from a brick chimney. As they walked through the fields which he remembered as his inheritance, the men stopped working and looked up. They stared at the bedraggled man and woman, their clothes identifying them as travellers, that they were poor, that they had journeyed for many leagues without rest. The custom would have been to offer them shelter without thought of reward, but these days the Romans were everywhere. The older of the men walked over to the couple and greeted them.

'I am Ezekiel. What do you wish from us?'

The couple remained silent. The man licked his lips. Ezekiel looked at his beard. It was matted and in its depths he saw vegetation. They had slept rough for many nights.

'Ezekiel?' said the man, his voice hoarse. He put his hand up to touch Ezekiel's cheek. Ezekiel stood still, not fending off the approach. The older man stroked his cheek. 'When I was last here, you were the height of my waist. You have grown, Ezekiel. You are a man.'

Ezekiel shook his head in wonder. 'Who are you? I don't know you.'

'Yes you do. You know me well. But you do not know my wife. This is Avigad of the desert people.'

The man smiled and Ezekiel's eyes widened. 'Abram?' he asked tentatively. Abram nodded. 'Abram!'

Abram opened his arms and the brothers embraced for the first time in five years. They walked towards the house as Ezekiel called his other brothers. They were much younger children when Abram had taken his journey. He did not recognise them at all. Before they entered the house, Ezekiel stopped Abram and said in a low voice. 'You should know that our father has died. He died two years ago. He was working in the fields clearing stones and the strain was too great. He didn't suffer. He died almost straight away.'

Abram nodded. He would feel the grief later. 'And mother?'

Ezekiel smiled. 'Mother is mother.'

They entered the house. Sarah turned around in surprise. The meal wasn't yet ready. She looked at the stranger and his wife. Her eyes narrowed. Five years ago, a stranger had entered her house, a stranger who smelt of the fields, an unkempt traveller, a stranger who had taken her son away. Tears flooded into her eyes as she ran to embrace the son who had returned.

A huge security guard stood outside Ben Brady's office on the fourteenth floor of the *LA Times* building. Like Cerberus, he refused admission to anybody whose name wasn't contained in a list given to him every morning by Ben. Inside Ben's office was a stenographer, the paper's lawyer, Ben, Joe Deakin and Luke Carmody. The latest man to arrive, admitted by the security guard after close scrutiny of his identification, was a lawyer whom Luke had selected from a list suggested by the lawyer representing the paper. Luke's lawyer, Donald Leigh, tried to take control from the earliest moment.

'I've only had an hour or so to discuss this whole matter with my client, and I have to tell you that I'm not in the least bit happy with your treatment. Firstly, you've offered him no financial security whatsoever for his future. Secondly, you've held him incommunicado for the past four days, denying his constitutional rights—'

Ben looked at him with a menacing grimace. 'Sit down, shut up, and don't say a word. Tomorrow morning Jimmy Wilson arrives back in LAX. Tomorrow afternoon your client gets handed over to the DA. Tomorrow evening, the *LA Times* runs the biggest goddamn story since Pearl Harbor. Now, you've got two options. One is for me to lock you in an office until tomorrow night if you keep talking. The other is to sit down, listen to what's going on and start working for your client when we hand him over to the DA.'

Furious, Donald Leigh turned to Luke and said, 'You and me ought to go into another office and have a very serious talk. If you want me to represent you—'

'I know what I'm doing,' said Luke. 'When the shit hits the fan tomorrow and I get arrested by the DA, that's when I need you. Until then, I'm not interested in wheeling and dealing. I just want to get this behind me. It's my decision. I've done wrong and it's my way of making amends.'

Knowing he was beaten, the lawyer nodded and poured himself a cup of coffee.

Ben and Joe went back to arguing about the headline. 'You've got to have "madman" in the headline or else you're going to lose the thrust. For God's sake, Ben, this guy is a killer.'

Ben shook his head vigorously. 'We go with this headline,' he said, stabbing at the mock-up of the page: 'TOP CHURCH MAN IN MURDER FRAUD SCAM'.

Joe stood and paced the floor like a panther. 'We've got to call him "nuts" or "crazed" or "insane" or something. You have to strike right at the core with the fact that this guy is a madman.'

'No,' said the newspaper's lawyer. 'Do that and the judges will come down on you like a shitful of bricks.'

'I'm not interested in his constitutional rights,' shouted Joe. 'I'm interested in nailing this bastard.'

'That's for the courts to do,' said the lawyer. 'You're a reporter. Your job is to report facts. Not opinion.'

'Okay,' shouted Ben over the argument. 'What if we say "TOP CHURCH MAN THOUGHT INSANE AFTER MURDER FRAUD ALLEGATION"?'

The lawyer stood and came face to face with Ben. 'Ben, for Christ's sake,' he shouted. 'The guy can be off his fuckin' tree but say that before his trial and he could spend the rest of his life in some insane asylum. Don't you understand yet? We have to paint this guy as evil. Not as mad. We can't let the public have any sympathy for the son of a bitch.'

The phone interrupted the animosity in the room. Ben grabbed it. 'Yeah, send her up.'

He looked at Luke. 'It's Annabelle. She's on her way up.'

After she had passed through the three levels of security, Annabelle walked into the room. All the men stood. She still retained marks from the beating she had suffered at her husband's hands all those weeks ago. She eyed Luke coldly. Though the men in the room didn't associate him directly with the beatings and murders, she knew that he had been one of those who had caused her untold grief. No matter about his last minute confession, she couldn't ever forgive him for what he'd done to her. She ignored him as he smiled ingratiatingly.

'Annabelle,' said Ben, walking over and kissing her on the cheek. 'How are you finding the accommodation?'

'It's lovely, thank you. It's exactly what I wanted. It's quiet and peaceful. I'm really grateful.'

Joe pulled out a chair for Annabelle. 'The reason we've asked you to come, is to photograph you as part of the story that's running tomorrow. And to show you what we're writing so you can give final verification.' She nodded. 'We've handpicked a photographer. He won't say a word about who you are. Nobody will know until the story breaks tomorrow. That I swear.'

She looked at Ben. Over the past few days, she had grown to like and admire him for his honesty and integrity. 'Duane?' she asked.

Joe shook his head. 'Lieutenant Celebrio has sworn a deposition that he and the two officers were in another place 120 miles away from the cathedral. They have witnesses to prove it. There's no record at all of Duane's arrest or disappearance. The police have interviewed Gerald Curtis but . . .' Ben shook his head.

Annabelle nodded. 'Another lamb to the slaughter.'

Luke looked down at his feet in shame.

The 747 shuddered to a halt at LA International Airport. The air bridge swung to join the terminal to the plane. The first to exit was a man wearing the black suit, black shirt and white collar of a Christian minister. He was prepared. His PR man had called him in Addis Ababa and told him that everyone would be there. Everyone. It would be like a Roman circus where the Christians fed the lions of the media.

He walked down the airless corridor, feeling the heat of the noonday sun on the smoked glass. He was quickly escorted through Immigration and Customs because the Reverend Dr Jimmy Wilson would not be exiting through the normal channels but would be shown into a media room at LAX which was bursting at the seams with men, women and equipment, awaiting his arrival.

At the door was Gerald Curtis, wearing his blue vicuña suit, the trademark of the wealthy man. Gerald's eyes were glazed in excitement. He did not even say hello. 'Have you got it? Let me see it,' he rasped. 'The shit's hit the fan. They're onto us. We have to get you outta here.'

Jimmy held up his hand. 'Wait and see.'

'Jimmy, I—' but Jimmy silenced him. He burst through the doors into the air-conditioned room and felt the heat of the lights as they turned on to illuminate his arrival. He was flooded by a wash of luminescence. A spectral shadow danced a jig on the rear wall as he walked towards the long table covered with green baize on which was a bouquet of microphones. He sat down and the audience fell into silence.

'Ladies and gentlemen, firstly I want to thank you all for comin'. Secondly, I have asked you here because, like Paul the Apostle in the days of the Lord, I want you to be my messengers. I want you ladies and gentlemen of the world's press to carry for me a message into the darkest corners of the world. A message which will bring light and hope and peace. Because this is a message from God Himself.'

He stretched out his arms in the air. 'God spoke to me in the mountains of Ethiopia. The very Lord Jesus Christ whom we all worship came down to me as I was about to touch His Testament and bring it back to you. That's right, ladies and gentlemen, I have found the last will and Testament of Jesus Christ.'

There were audible gasps in the audience.

'I had gone there with one of the old Black Jews called the Falashas,' Jimmy continued. 'This man had shown me where Christ's Testament has lain buried for two thousand years. I walked into a cave alone, my friends.' His voice began to tremble and rise to a crescendo. 'I was frightened and overcome by the awe and the solemnity of the occasion. And there before me on a marble altar, white and pure like the driven snow, lay a brown folded piece of parchment. It was covered with biblical writin' and letters and I peered down and started to read it and, as if by magic, the words changed into English, and I could read every word. And I read the words that Christ Himself had written, just before the pain of His crucifixion two thousand years ago, and what I read filled me with hope and with joy because these were the very words of God Himself, written through His Son Jesus Christ Our Lord. And when I had read Christ's words, I leaned down but before I could pick it up, there was a wind which blew up inside the cave itself and this wind forced me back and I stood with my back against the wall of the cave and my eyes were tight closed with fear, and a voice of beauty and joy said to me, "Jimmy open your eyes". And I opened my eyes and there was the Lord Himself, Jesus Christ, standin' before me, floatin' on a cloud, dressed in white and He said to me, "Jimmy, don't take my Testament, for the sceptics and the atheists will deny it like Peter denied me three times. But these are my words. Remember them. And go and preach them in the marketplaces of the world." And the Lord whispered His words into my ear so that none other could hear and when I had learned the words, the Lord said to me, "You are my representative on earth. Through you I have come again."'

Perspiration was running down his forehead. A fleck of saliva appeared at the corner of his mouth. Gerald Curtis shrank against the wall in horror. He turned and looked at the audience of journalists. Some were smiling openly. Some buried their heads so they didn't laugh out loud. Gerald knew it was the end. Jimmy would be crucified by the media for this wanton act of sacrilege. He turned and looked at Jimmy, who stood and shouted out, 'I am the resurrection and the life. I am the way. Follow me and you will have everlasting life.'

Four policemen walked into the back of the hall. Beside them was the Los Angeles DA, the city editor of the *LA Times* and Joe Deakin, one of his reporters. Two of the officers walked over to Gerald Curtis, who blanched as they cautioned him and led him towards the door.

As they walked Jimmy to the door of the media room, he passed a knot of people. He stared at them vacantly, lost in his mind, his thoughts racing from one spectral image to another. He didn't see their faces. He didn't recognise them. He didn't know them. But they knew him. Joe reached over and held Annabelle's hand, but even she was distracted from the drama. Her deep thoughts were on the future of the church and what she would do with it, now it was cleansed. She looked at Micah, a man of goodness and decency, and wondered whether perhaps he could be persuaded to train for the priesthood.

Only Ben frowned, showing no signs of satisfaction or relief that the nightmare was at an end. He shook his head. The Jimmy who had committed all the acts of evil was nowhere to be found. The man who was being hauled into a waiting police car was a shell who would spend the rest of his life institutionalised. Justice? It was all too late.

CHAPTER 28

In the third year of the pontificate of Innocent, Bishop of Rome, Vicar of Jesus Christ, Servant of the Servants of God.

Swathed in the luminescent white and gold vestments of Supreme Pontiff, Innocent was dwarfed as he stood before the Wailing Wall of the Temple of Herod. The monolithic blocks eclipsed even the most devout celebrant, as they had done for two thousand years. Yet Innocent's imposing figure was the focus of everyone's attention. There was little colour in the rest of the vast assembly of worshippers. His bishops and cardinals were dressed in reds and blacks, but the entire Jewish community of celebrants wore dull hues of grey and blue. Only the rabbis carrying the Scrolls of the Law wore the white *tallit* prayer-shawls, giving some colour to their worship.

Pope Innocent stood at the base of the Wailing Wall and looked upwards towards the sky. The towering structure of vast lifeless stone blocks with tufts of living grasses between the cracks overpowered him. It was as though the majesty of the ancients still held sway over the insignificant people who today represented their thoughts and genius.

Innocent's body was tired but his mind was electrified. He reached out and touched the sacred stones of the Temple of Herod and felt a union between his papacy and the agony of those who had suffered in the name of all religions.

He had begun the day, the first of his official visit to Israel, by praying at the altar of the Church of the Holy Sepulchre, kneeling before the stone which had supported the mortal body of his eternal Messiah.

Then he had joined with his Muslim brothers and prayed to Allah at the Mosques of Omar and Al Aksa. And as the sun was beginning to set over the golden roofs of Jerusalem, he had walked through the gate of the Temple Mount, followed by dozens of security men and his entourage of bishops and cardinals, nuns and priests to be met at the Israeli section of the Old City by Prime Minister Moishe Rabbinowitz and his entire Cabinet. Pope Innocent greeted the Prime Minister with a kiss and the two men, followed by their acolytes, walked down towards the Wailing Wall where the Pope joined in *ma'ariv* prayers.

Innocent said a blessing in Hebrew, taught to him by the local bishop, and he could see the delight on the faces on the crowds of orthodox Jews as they listened to his appalling accent. The Chief Rabbi of Jerusalem nodded with approval and satisfaction. The fifteen-minute service was followed by a noisy *kiddush*, where hundreds of people drank glasses of wine and nibbled herring and chopped egg canapes.

Innocent had been moved to tears by his experience of kneeling before the tomb of his Christ in the Sepulchre; he had been rendered speechless by the fervour and passion of the prayers of the Muslims in their mosques; but the geniality and good humour of the elderly Jews following their prayers at the Wailing Wall was the perfect end to a day of a completion in his life. He slept well that night.

The following morning, he dressed in the clothes of a simple priest and escaped out of the back door of the King David Hotel in order to fulfil an obligation he had committed himself to eighteen months earlier.

He and his bodyguards drove out of Jerusalem and down the long winding escarpment which led towards the plains on which the city of Tel Aviv had been built by the early Zionists. At the bottom of Jerusalem's hill, the driver turned right into a side road which led ultimately to a series of collective farms. The Israeli bodyguard told him they were called *moshavs*. As the car drove into Father Francis Gild's orphanage, the father and a dozen of his children were standing at the gate, eagerly awaiting him. Innocent had insisted that the visit was to be unreported and of a strictly private nature. The car stopped and Innocent got out. He was surprised how Francis had aged in the twenty years since they had last seen each other, and he wondered whether the cares of his own high office had inflicted the same damage. Francis was barely able to suppress an enormous grin on his face.

'Holy Father,' he said, walking over to kiss his ring.

'Don't be ridiculous, Francis,' said Innocent, and grabbed the man by his shoulders, hugging him like a bear.

The children, who had been sworn to secrecy about the visit, were astonished that the Pope himself was just an ordinary human being dressed in ordinary priest's clothes. Innocent walked over to the children and headed for the littlest boy, picking him up and kissing him gently on the cheek. He gathered the others around his legs and said, 'So, before I talk to Father Gild, are you going to show me your *chaddar ochel*?'

They laughed with delight at his accent, and all barriers between mortals and Pope having been demolished, they pulled and tugged him into the dining room. There, he saw a woman aged in her late forties or early fifties, smiling at him. Francis introduced the Pope to Pazit Fine. The room was laid out for a banquet and the little boys ran up to Innocent with trays of food and sandwiches. Having finished breakfast an hour earlier, he was anything but hungry, but so as not to disappoint them, he tucked into the food. He invited his body-guards over. They had started to relax by the time they entered the dining room. Innocent and Francis spoke for five animated minutes, catching up as best they could on old times.

It was Francis who broke the mood first. 'I suppose you want to see Daniel?' Innocent nodded. 'He's in one of the children's classrooms teaching. He spends much of his time there.' Innocent appeared hurt by his old friend's indifference to the visit. Francis hastily explained, 'He didn't want the very little children to be too disrupted by all the excitement.'

As he and Francis walked out of the *chaddar ochel*, Francis gripped the Pope's arm. 'Gabby, he's very different from the man—'

'Yes, I know. I've read your letters a dozen times each.'

'His following is enormous. Christians come from all over Israel. Gabby, the beauty of his messages is quite beyond anything I've ever heard before. It's like listening to Aquinas or St Francis.'

Innocent nodded. They walked behind the *chaddar ochel* into a dormitory area and then entered a classroom. Gabriel Molloy was so shocked by Daniel's appearance that he was overcome. He looked even thinner. His hair was wilder and less kempt than it had been in Rome, and the clothes he wore were those of the simple parish priest, slightly crumpled as though time spent on the artifice of dressing was time away from the importance of his mission. But these were nothing but the outward symbols. It was the look in his eyes which made Pope Innocent wonder whether he was looking at the same man who had resigned a year and a half earlier as his Secretary of State. Daniel looked up from where he was sitting, surrounded by a dozen adoring children to whom he was talking, and smiled as the two men walked in.

Children turned round expectantly, but Daniel hushed them, stroking their heads, and whispering to them like a mother calming her children. Daniel smiled as he looked at Gabriel Molloy. Gabriel felt a glow of warmth in the room.

Daniel stood and walked slowly towards the two men. He held out his arms towards his lifelong friend and, as he drew closer, he hugged the Pope, kissing him on both cheeks.

Into his ear, he whispered, 'May the Lord God Our Father grant you peace and everlasting joy. May you find in your time with us the inner peace and tranquillity for which you have been searching all your life.'

Again he kissed him on both cheeks and on the forehead and walked beside him towards the door. Daniel smelled of the fields. In Rome, he had always smelled of after-shave. Innocent wanted to respond, to give some greeting, some words of understanding, but his mind was reeling from the look he had seen in Daniel's eyes. When he thought about it, there was nothing he needed to say.

'You've eaten?' asked Daniel. The Pope merely nodded. 'And your journey to Israel has fulfilled your expectations?' Again, he merely nodded. 'Come, we will walk through the fields and talk as brothers talk.'

Francis left them to wander from the dusty buildings into the fields. As she always did whenever he walked alone, Pazit Fine followed Daniel a dozen steps behind. The two Israeli security guards, members of Shin Bet, began to walk in the direction that the Pope had taken but Francis restrained them. 'Please leave them alone. I promise you they will come to no harm.'

'Sorry, father.'

'Well at least stay some distance away from them so you can't be noticed. They have much to talk about.'